JIM BUTCHER

THE DRESDEN FILES

DEATH MASKS

www.orbitbooks.net

ORBIT

First published in Great Britain in 2005 by Orbit
This paperback edition published in 2011 by Orbit
Reprinted 2012 (twice), 2013

A CIP catalogue record for this book
is available from the British Library.

ISBN 978-0-356-50031-7

Typeset in Janson Text by Palimpsest Book Production Limited,
Falkirk, Stirlingshire
Printed and bound by CPI Group (UK) Ltd, Croydon, CR0 4YY

Papers used by Orbit are from well-managed forests
and other responsible sources.

MIX
Paper from
responsible sources
FSC® C104740

Orbit
An imprint of
Little, Brown Book Group
100 Victoria Embankment
London EC4Y 0DY

An Hachette UK Company
www.hachette.co.uk

www.orbitbooks.net

EATH MASKS

A nsation pulsed against my palm, and the hairs along m e up straight.

I'm good,' I muttered. I picked up the Shroud and tu go.

an stood behind me, dressed in black fatigue pants, a h ket, and battered combat boots. Her peroxide-blonde ha ut very short, but it did nothing to detract from the ap her features. She was elegantly pretty and pleasant to lo

n she had pointed at my nose wasn't pretty, though. It gly old .38 revolver, a cheap Saturday-night special.

reful not to move. Even a cheap gun can kill you, and I I could raise a shield in time to do me any good. She'd ta off guard. I'd never heard her coming, never sensed h nce.

n, I'm good,' the woman echoed, her accent high British, a of amusement in her voice. 'Put the package down.'

By Jim Butcher

The Dresden Files

Storm Front
Fool Moon
Grave Peril
Summer Knight
Death Masks
Blood Rites
Dead Beat
Proven Guilty
White Night
Small Favour
Turn Coat
Changes
Ghost Story
Cold Days

Side Jobs: Stories from the Dresden Files

The Codex Alera

Furies of Calderon
Academ's Fury
Cursor's Fury
Captain's Fury
Princeps' Fury
First Lord's Fury

In memory of
Plumicon and Ersha,
fallen heroes

1

Some things just aren't meant to go together. Things like oil and water. Orange juice and toothpaste.

Wizards and television.

Spotlights glared into my eyes. The heat of them threatened to make me sweat streaks through the pancake makeup some harried stagehand had slapped on me a few minutes before. Lights on top of cameras started winking on, the talk-show theme song began to play, and the studio audience began to chant, 'Lah-REE, Lah-REE, Lah-REE!'

Larry Fowler, a short man in an immaculate suit, appeared from the doors at the rear of the studio and began walking to the stage, flashing his porcelain smile and shaking the hands of a dozen people seated at the ends of their rows as he passed them. The audience whistled and cheered as he did. The noise made me flinch in my seat up on the stage, and I felt a trickle of sweat slide down over my ribs, beneath my white dress shirt and my jacket. I briefly considered running away screaming.

It isn't like I have stage fright or anything, see. Because I don't. It was just really hot up there. I licked my lips and checked all the fire exits, just to be safe. No telling when you might need to make a speedy exit. The lights and noise made it a little difficult to keep up my concentration, and I felt the spell I'd woven around me wobble. I closed my eyes for a second, until I had stabilized it again.

In the chair beside me sat a dumpy, balding man in his late forties, dressed in a suit that looked a lot better than mine. Mortimer Lindquist waited calmly, a polite smile on his face, but muttered out of the corner of his mouth, 'You okay?'

'I've been in house fires I liked better than this.'

'You asked for this meeting, not me,' Mortimer said. He frowned as Fowler lingered over shaking a young woman's hand. 'Showboat.'

'Think this will take long?' I asked Morty.

He glanced beside him at an empty chair, and at another beside me. 'Two mystery guests. I guess this one could go for a while. They shoot extra material and edit it down to the best parts.'

I sighed. I'd been on *The Larry Fowler Show* just after I'd gone into business as an investigator, and it had been a mistake. I'd had to fight my way uphill against the tide of infamy I'd received from association with the show. 'What did you find out?' I asked.

Mort flicked a nervous glance at me and said, 'Not much.'

'Come on, Mort.'

He opened his mouth to answer, then glanced up as Larry Fowler trotted up the stairs and onto the stage. 'Not now. Wait for a commercial break.'

Larry Fowler pranced up to us and pumped my hand, then Mort's with equally exaggerated enthusiasm. 'Welcome to the show,' he said into a handheld microphone, then turned to face the nearest camera. 'Our topic for today is "Witchcraft and Wizardry – Phony or Fabulous?" With us in order to share their views are local medium and psychic counselor Mortimer Lindquist.'

The crowd applauded politely.

'And beside him, Harry Dresden, Chicago's only professional wizard.'

There was a round of snickering laughter to go with the applause this time. I couldn't say I was shocked. People don't believe in the supernatural these days. Supernatural things are scary. It's much more comfortable to rest secure in the knowledge that no one can reach out with magic and quietly kill you, that vampires exist only in movies, and that demons are mere psychological dysfunctions.

Completely inaccurate but much more comfortable.

Despite the relative levels of denial, my face heated up. I hate it when people laugh at me. An old, quiet hurt mixed in with my nervousness and I struggled to maintain the suppression spell.

Yeah, I said spell. See, I really am a wizard. I do magic. I've run into vampires and demons and a lot of things in between, and I've got the scars to show for it. The problem was that technology doesn't seem to enjoy coexisting with magic. When I'm around, computers crash, lightbulbs burn out, and car alarms start screaming in warbling, drunken voices for no good reason. I'd worked out a spell to suppress the magic I carried with me, at least temporarily, so that I might at least have a chance to keep from blowing out the studio lights and cameras, or setting off the fire alarms.

It was delicate stuff by its very nature, and extremely difficult for me to hold in place. So far so good, but I saw the nearest cameraman wince and jerk his headset away from his ear. Whining feedback sounded tinnily from the headset.

I closed my eyes and reined in my discomfort and embarrassment, focusing on the spell. The feedback died away.

'Well, then,' Larry said, after half a minute of happy talk. 'Morty, you've been a guest on the show several times now. Would you care to tell us a little bit about what you do?'

Mortimer widened his eyes and whispered, 'I see dead people.'

The audience laughed.

'But seriously. Mostly I conduct séances, Larry,' Mortimer said. 'I do what I can to help those who have lost a loved one or who need to contact them in the beyond in order to resolve issues left undone back here on earth. I also offer a predictions service in order to help clients make decisions on upcoming issues, and to try to warn them against possible danger.'

'Really,' Larry said. 'Could you give us a demonstration?'

Mortimer closed his eyes and rested the fingertips of his right hand on the spot between his eyes. Then in a hollow voice he said, 'The spirits tell me . . . that two more guests will soon arrive.'

The audience laughed, and Mortimer nodded at them with an easy grin. He knew how to play a crowd.

Larry gave Mortimer a tolerant smile. 'And why are you here today?'

'Larry, I just want to try to raise public awareness about the realm of the psychic and paranormal. Nearly eighty percent of a recent survey of American adults stated that they believed in the existence of the spirits of the dead, in ghosts. I just want to help people understand that they do exist, and that there are other people out there who have had strange and inexplicable encounters with them.'

'Thank you, Morty. And Harry – may I call you Harry?'

'Sure. It's your nickel,' I responded.

Larry's smile got a shade brittle. 'Can you tell us a little bit about what you do?'

'I'm a wizard,' I said. 'I find lost articles, investigate paranormal occurrences, and train people who find themselves struggling with a sudden development of their own abilities.'

'Isn't it true that you also consult for the Special Investigations department at Chicago PD?'

'Occasionally,' I said. I wanted to avoid talking about SI if I could. The last thing CPD would want was to be advertised on *The Larry Fowler Show*. 'Many police departments across the country employ such consultants when all other leads have failed.'

'And why are you here today?'

'Because I'm broke and your producer is paying double my standard fee.'

The crowd laughed again, more warmly. Larry Fowler's eyes flashed with an impatient look behind his glasses, and his smile turned into a gnashing of teeth. 'No, really, Harry. Why?'

'For the same reasons as Mort – uh, as Morty here,' I answered. Which was true. I'd come here to meet Mort and get some information from him. He'd come here to meet me, because he refused to be seen near me on the street. I guess you could say I don't have the safest reputation in the world.

'And you claim to be able to do magic,' Larry said.

'Yeah.'

'Could you show us?' Larry prompted.

'I could, Larry, but I don't think it's practical.'

Larry nodded, and gave the audience a wise look. 'And why is that?'

'Because it would probably wreck your studio equipment.'

'Of course,' Larry said. He winked at the audience. 'Well, we wouldn't want that, would we?'

There was more laughter and a few catcalls from the crowd. Passages from *Carrie* and *Firestarter* sprang to mind, but I restrained myself and maintained the suppression spell. Master of self-discipline, that's me. But I gave the fire door beside the stage another longing look.

Larry carried on the talk part of the talk show, discussing crystals and ESP and tarot cards. Mort did most of the talking. I chimed in with monosyllables from time to time.

After several minutes of this, Larry said, 'We'll be right back after these announcements.' Stagehands held up signs that read APPLAUSE, and cameras panned and zoomed over the audience as they whistled and hooted.

Larry gave me an annoyed look and strode offstage. In the wings, he started tearing into a makeup girl about his hair.

I leaned over to Mort and said, 'Okay. What did you find out?'

The dumpy ectomancer shook his head. 'Nothing concrete. I'm still getting back into the swing of things in contacting the dead.'

'Even so, you've got more contacts in this area than I do,' I said. 'My sources don't keep close track of who has or hasn't died lately, so I'll take whatever I can get. Is she at least alive?'

He nodded. 'She's alive. That much I know. She's in Peru.'

'Peru?' It came as a vast relief to hear that she wasn't dead, but what the hell was Susan doing in Peru? 'That's Red Court territory.'

'Some,' Mort agreed. 'Though most of them are in Brazil and the Yucatán. I tried to find out exactly where she was, but I was blocked.'

'By who?'

Mort shrugged. 'No way for me to tell. I'm sorry.'

I shook my head. 'No, it's okay. Thanks, Mort.'

I settled back in my seat, mulling over the news.

Susan Rodriguez was a reporter for a regional yellow paper called the *Midwestern Arcane*. She'd grown interested in me just after I opened up my practice, hounding me relentlessly to find out more about all the things that go bump in the night. We'd gotten involved, and on our first date she wound up lying naked on the ground in a thunderstorm while lightning cooked a toad-like demon to gooey bits. After that, she parlayed a couple of encounters with things from my cases into a widespread syndicated column.

A couple of years later, she wound up following me into a nest of vampires holding a big to-do, despite all my warnings to the contrary. A noble of the Red Court of Vampires had grabbed her and begun the transformation from mortal to vampire on her. It was payback for something I'd done. The vampire noble in question thought that her standing in the Red Court made her untouchable, that I wouldn't want to start trouble with the entire

Court. She told me that if I fought to take Susan back, I would be starting a worldwide war between the White Council of wizards and the vampires' Red Court.

Which I did.

The vampires hadn't forgiven me for taking Susan back from them, probably because a bunch of them, including one of their nobility, had been incinerated in the process. That's why Mort didn't want to be seen with me. He wasn't involved in the war, and he intended to keep it that way.

In any case, Susan hadn't gone all the way through her transformation, but the vamps had given her their blood thirst, and if she ever gave in to it, she'd become one of the Red Court. I asked her to marry me, promising her that I'd find a way to restore her humanity. She turned me down and left town, trying to sort things out on her own, I guess. I still kept trying to find a way to remove her affliction, but I'd received only a card and a postcard or three from her since she'd left.

Two weeks ago, her editor had called to say that the columns she usually sent in for the *Arcane* were late, and asked if I knew how to get in touch with her. I didn't, but I started looking. I got zip, and went to Mort Lindquist to see if his contacts in the spirit world would pay off better than mine.

I hadn't gotten much, but at least she was alive. Muscles in my back unclenched a little.

I looked up to see Larry come back onstage to his theme music. Speakers squealed and squelched when he started to talk, and I realized I'd let my control slip again. The suppression spell was a hell of a lot harder than I thought it would be, and getting harder by the minute. I tried to focus, and the speakers quieted to the occasional fitful pop.

'Welcome back to the show,' Larry told a camera. 'Today we are speaking with practitioners of the paranormal, who are here to share their views with the studio audience and our viewers at home. In order to explore these issues further, I have asked a couple of experts with opposing viewpoints to join us today, and here they are.'

The audience applauded as a pair of men emerged from either side of the stage.

The first man sat down in the chair by Morty. He was a little over average height and thin, his skin burned into tanned leather by the sun. He might have been anywhere between forty and sixty. His hair was greying and neatly cut, and he wore a black suit with a white clerical collar sharing space with a rosary and crucifix at his throat. He smiled and nodded to Mort and me and shook hands with Larry.

Larry said, 'Allow me to introduce Father Vincent, who has come all the way from the Vatican to be with us today. He is a leading scholar and researcher within the Catholic Church on the subject of witchcraft and magic, both historically and from a psychological perspective. Father, welcome to the show.'

Vincent's voice was a little rough, but he spoke English with the kind of cultured accent that seemed to indicate an expensive education. 'Thank you, Larry. I'm very pleased to be here.'

I looked from Father Vincent to the second man, who had settled in the chair beside me, just as Larry said, 'And from the University of Brazil at Rio de Janeiro, please welcome Dr Paolo Ortega, world-renowned researcher and debunker of the supernatural.'

Larry started saying something else, but I didn't hear him. I just stared at the man beside me as recognition dawned. He was of average height and slightly heavy build, with broad shoulders and a deep chest. He was dark-complected, his black hair neatly brushed, his grey-and-silver suit stylish and tasteful.

And he was a duke of the Red Court – an ancient and deadly vampire, smiling at me from less than an arm's length away. My heart rate went from sixty to a hundred and fifty million, fear sending silver lightning racing down my limbs.

Emotions have power. They fuel a lot of my magic. The fear hit me, and the pressure on the suppression spell redoubled. There was a flash of light and a puff of smoke from the nearest camera, and the operator staggered back from it, tearing off his headphones with one of the curses they have to edit out of daytime TV. Smoke began to rise steadily from the camera, along with the smell of burning rubber, and the studio monitors shrieked with feedback.

'Well,' Ortega said, under his breath. 'Nice to see you again, Mister Dresden.'

I swallowed and fumbled at my pocket, where I had a couple of wizard gadgets I used for self-defense. Ortega put his hand on my arm. It didn't look as if he was exerting himself, but his fingers closed on my wrist like manacles, hard enough to send flashes of pain up through my elbow and shoulder. I looked around, but everyone was staring at the malfunctioning camera.

'Relax,' Ortega said, his accent thick and vaguely Latinate. 'I'm not going to kill you on television, wizard. I'm here to talk to you.'

'Get off me,' I said. My voice was thin, shaky. Goddamned stage fright.

He released me, and I jerked my arm away. The crew rolled

the smoking camera back, and a director type with a set of headphones made a rolling motion with the fingers of one hand. Larry nodded to him, and turned to Ortega.

'Sorry about that. We'll edit that part out later.'

'It's no trouble,' Ortega assured him.

Larry paused for a moment, and then said, 'Dr Ortega, welcome to the show. You have a reputation as one of the premier analysts of paranormal phenomena in the world. You have proven that a wide variety of so-called supernatural occurrences were actually clever hoaxes. Can you tell us a little about that?'

'Certainly. I have investigated these events for a number of years, and I have yet to find one that cannot be adequately explained. Alleged alien crop circles proved to be nothing more than a favorite pastime of a small group of British farmers, for example. Other odd events are certainly unusual, but by no means supernatural. Even here in Chicago, you had a rain of toads in one of your local parks witnessed by dozens if not hundreds of people. And it turned out, later, that a freak windstorm had scooped them up from elsewhere and deposited them here.'

Larry nodded, his expression serious. 'Then you don't believe in these events.'

Ortega gave Larry a patronizing smile. 'I would love to believe that such things are true, Larry. There is little enough magic in the world. But I am afraid that even though we each have a part of us that wishes to believe in wondrous beings and fantastic powers, the fact of the matter is that it is simple, primitive superstition.'

'Then in your opinion, practitioners of the supernatural—'

'Frauds,' Ortega said with certainty. 'With no offense meant to your guests, of course. All of these so-called mediums, presuming they aren't self-deluded, are simply skilled actors who have acquired a fundamental grasp of human psychology and know how to exploit it. They are easily able to deceive the gullible into believing that they can contact the dead or read thoughts or that they are in fact supernatural beings. Why, with a few minutes' effort and the right setting, I am certain that I could convince anyone in this room that I was a vampire myself.'

People laughed again. I scowled at Ortega, frustration growing once more, putting more pressure on the suppression spell. The air around me started to feel warmer.

A second cameraman yelped and jerked off his squealing earphones, while his camera started spinning about slowly on its stand, winding power cables around the steel frame it rested on.

The on-air lights went out. Larry stepped to the edge of the stage, yelling at the poor cameraman. The apologetic-looking director appeared from the wings, and Larry turned his attention to him. The man bore the scolding with a kind of oxenlike patience, and then examined the camera. He muttered something into his headset, and he and the shaken cameraman began to wheel the dead camera away.

Larry folded his arms impatiently, then turned to the guests and said, 'I'm sorry. Give us a couple of minutes to get a spare camera in. It won't take long.'

'No problem, Larry,' Ortega assured him. 'We can just chat for a moment.'

Larry peered at me. 'Are you all right, Mister Dresden?' he

asked. 'You look a little pale. Could you use a drink or something?'

'I know I could,' Ortega said, his eyes on me.

'I'll have someone bring them out,' Larry said, and strode offstage toward his hairstylist.

Mort had engaged Father Vincent in quiet conversation, his back very firmly turned toward me. I turned back to Ortega, warily, my back stiff, and fought down the anger and fear. Usually being scared out of my mind is kind of useful. Magic comes from emotions, and terror is handy fuel. But this wasn't the place to start calling up gales of wind or flashes of fire. There were too many people around, and it would be too easy to get someone hurt, even killed.

Besides which, Ortega was right. This wasn't the place to fight. If he was here, he wanted to talk. Otherwise, he would have simply jumped me in the parking garage.

'Okay,' I said, finally. 'What do you want to say?'

He leaned a little closer so that he wouldn't have to raise his voice. I cringed inwardly, but I didn't flinch away. 'I've come to Chicago to kill you, Mister Dresden. But I have a proposal for you that I want you to hear, first.'

'You really need to work on your opening technique,' I said. 'I read a book about negotiations. I could loan it to you.'

He gave me a humorless smile. 'The war, Dresden. The war between your people and mine is too costly, for both of us.'

'War's a pretty stupid option to take, generally speaking,' I said. 'I never wanted it.'

'But you began it,' Ortega said. 'You began it over a point of principle.'

'I began it over a human life.'

'And how many more would you save by ending it now?' Ortega asked. 'Not merely wizards suffer from this. Our attention to the war leaves us less able to control the wilder elements of our own Court. We frown upon reckless killings, but wounded or leaderless members of our Courts often kill when they do not truly need to. Ending the war now would save hundreds, perhaps thousands of lives.'

'So would killing every vampire on the planet. What's your point?'

Ortega smiled, showing teeth. Just regular teeth, no long canines or anything. The vampires of the Red Court look human – right up until they turn into something out of a nightmare. 'The point, Dresden, is that the war is unprofitable, undesirable. You are the symbolic cause of it to my people, and the point of contention between us and your own White Council. Once you are slain, the Council will accept peace overtures, as will the Court.'

'So you're asking me to lay down and die? That's not much of an offer. You really need to read that book.'

'I'm making you an offer. Face me in single combat, Dresden.'

I didn't quite laugh at him. 'Why the hell should I do that?'

His eyes were expressionless. 'Because if you do it would mean that the warriors I have brought to town with me will not be forced to target your friends and allies. That the mortal assassins we have retained will not need to receive their final confirmations to kill a number of clients who have hired you in the past five years. I'm sure I need not mention names.'

Fear and anger had been about to settle down, but they came

surging back again. 'There's no reason for that,' I said. 'If your war is with me, keep it with me.'

'Gladly,' Ortega said. 'I do not approve of such tactics. Face me under the dueling laws in the Accords.'

'And after I kill you, what?' I said. I didn't know if I could kill him, but there was no reason to let him think I wasn't confident about it. 'The next hotshot Red Duke does the same thing?'

'Defeat me, and the Court has agreed that this city will become neutral territory. That those living in it, including yourself and your friends and associates, will be free of the threat of attack so long as they are in it.'

I stared hard at him for a moment. 'Chicago-blanca, eh?'

He quirked a puzzled eyebrow at me.

'Never mind. After your time.' I looked away from him, and licked sweat from my upper lip. A stagehand came by with a couple of bottled waters, and passed them to Ortega and to me. I took a drink. The pressure of the spell made flickering colored dots float across my vision.

'You're stupid to fight me,' I said. 'Even if you kill me, my death curse would fall on you.'

He shrugged. 'I am not as important as the whole of the Court. I will take that risk.'

Hell's bells. Dedicated, honorable, courageous, self-sacrificial loonies are absolutely the worst people in the world to go up against. I tried one last dodge, hoping it might pay off. 'I'd have to have it in writing. The Council gets a copy too. I want this all recognized, official under the Accords.'

'That done, you will agree to the duel?'

I took a deep breath. The last thing I wanted to do was square off against another supernatural nasty. Vampires scared me. They were strong and way too fast, and had an enormous yuck factor. Their saliva was an addictive narcotic, and I'd been exposed to it enough to make me twitch once in a while, wondering what it would be like to get another hit.

I barely went outside after dark these days, specifically because I didn't want to encounter any more vampires. A duel would mean a fair fight, and I hate fair fights. In the words of a murderous Faerie Queen, they're too easy to lose.

Of course, if I didn't agree to Ortega's offer, I'd be fighting him anyway, probably at a time and place of his choosing – and I had the feeling that Ortega wasn't going to show the arrogance and overconfidence I'd seen in other vampires. Something about him said that so long as I wasn't breathing, he wouldn't care much how it happened. Not only that, but I believed that he would start in on the people I cared about if he couldn't have me.

I mean, come on. It was clichéd villainy at its worst.

And an undeniably effective lever.

I'd like to say that I carefully weighed all the factors, reasoned my way to a levelheaded conclusion, and made a rational decision to take a calculated risk, but I didn't. The truth is, I thought of Ortega and company doing harm to some of the people I cared about, and suddenly felt angry enough to start in on him right there. I faced him, eyes narrowed, and didn't bother to hold the anger in check. The suppression spell began to crack, and I didn't bother to keep it going. The spell shattered, and the build-up of wild energy rushed silently and invisibly over the studio.

There was a cough of static from the speakers on the stage before they died with loud pops. The floodlights overhead suddenly burst with flashes of brilliance and clouds of sparks that fell down over everyone on the stage. One of the two surviving cameras exploded into fire, bluish flames rising up from out of the casing, and heavy power outlets along the walls started spitting orange and green sparks. Larry Fowler yelped and leapt up into the air, batting at his belt before pitching a smoldering cell phone to the floor. The lights died, and people started screaming in startled panic.

Ortega, lit only by the falling sparks, looked grim and somehow eager, shadows dancing over his features, his eyes huge and dark.

'Fine,' I said. 'Get it to me in writing and you've got a deal.'

The emergency lights came up, fire alarms started whooping, and people started stumbling toward exits. Ortega smiled, all teeth, and glided off the stage, vanishing into the wings.

I stood up, shaking a little. A piece of something had apparently fallen and hit Mort's head. There was a small gash on his scalp, already brimming with blood, and he wobbled precariously when he tried to stand. I helped him up, and so did Father Vincent on the other side of him. We lugged the little ectomancer toward the fire doors.

We got Mort down some stairs and outside the building. Chicago PD was on the scene already, blue and white lights flashing. Fire crews and an ambulance or three were just then rolling up on the street. We settled Mort down among a row of people with minor injuries, and stood back. We were both panting a little as the emergency medtechs started triage on the wounded.

'Actually, Mister Dresden,' Father Vincent said, 'I must confess something to you.'

'Heh,' I said. 'Don't think I missed the irony on that one, padre.'

Vincent's leathery mouth creased into a strained smile. 'I did not really come to Chicago merely to appear on the show.'

'No?' I said.

'No. I really came here to—'

'To talk to me,' I interjected.

He lifted his eyebrows. 'How did you know?'

I sighed, and got my car keys out of my pocket. 'It's just been that kind of day.'

2

I started walking for my car, and beckoned Father Vincent to follow. He did, and I walked fast enough to make him work to keep up with me. 'You must understand,' he said, 'that I must insist upon strict confidentiality if I am to divulge details of my problem to you.'

I frowned at him and said, 'You think I'm a crackpot at best, or a charlatan at worst. So why would you want me to take your case?'

Not that I would turn him down. I wanted to take his case. Well, more accurately, I wanted to take his money. I wasn't in the bad fiscal shape of the year before, but that meant only that I had to fend the creditors off with a baseball bat rather than a cattle prod.

'I am told you are the best investigator in the city for it,' Father Vincent said.

I arched an eyebrow at him. 'You've got something supernatural going on?'

He rolled his eyes. 'No, naturally not. I am not naive, Mister

Dresden. But I am told that you know more about the occult community than any private investigator in the city.'

'Oh,' I said. 'That.'

I thought about it for a minute, and figured it was probably true. The occult community he had in mind was the usual New Age, crystal-gazing, tarot-turning, palm-reading crowd you see in any large city. Most of them were harmless, and many had at least a little ability at magic. Add in a dash of feng-shui artists, season liberally with Wiccans of a variety of flavors and sincerities, blend in a few modestly gifted practitioners who liked mixing religion with their magic, some followers of voodoo, a few Santerians and a sprinkling of Satanists, all garnished with a crowd of young people who liked to wear a lot of black, and you get what most folks think of as the 'occult community.'

Of course, hiding in there you found the occasional sorcerer, necromancer, monster, or demon. The real players, the nasty ones, regarded that crowd the same way a ten-year-old would a gingerbread amusement park. My mental early-warning system set off an imaginary klaxon.

'Who referred you to me, padre?'

'Oh, a local priest,' Vincent said. He took a small notebook from his pocket, opened it, and read, 'Father Forthill, of Saint Mary of the Angels.'

I blinked. Father Forthill didn't see eye-to-eye with me on the whole religion thing, but he was a decent guy. A little stuffy, maybe, but I liked him – and I owed him for favors past. 'You should have said that in the first place.'

'You'll take the case?' Father Vincent asked, as we headed into the parking garage.

'I want to hear the details first, but if Forthill thinks I can help, I will.' I added, hastily, 'My standard fees apply.'

'Naturally,' Father Vincent said. He toyed with the crucifix at his throat. 'May I assume that you will spare me the magician rigmarole?'

'Wizard,' I said.

'There's a difference?'

'Magicians do stage magic. Wizards do real magic.'

He sighed. 'I don't need an entertainer, Mister Dresden. Just an investigator.'

'And I don't need you to believe me, padre. Just to pay me. We'll get along fine.'

He gave me an uncertain look and said, 'Ah.'

We reached my car, a battered old Volkswagen Bug named the Blue Beetle. It has what some people would call 'character' and what I would call lots of mismatched replacement parts. The original car may have been blue, but now it had pieces of green, white, and red VWs grafted onto it in place of the originals as they got damaged in one way or another. The hood had to be held down with a piece of hanger wire to keep it from flipping up when the car jounced, and the front bumper was still smashed out of shape from last summer's attempt at vehicular monster-slaughter. Maybe if Vincent's job paid well, I'd be able to get it fixed.

Father Vincent blinked at the Beetle and asked, 'What happened?'

'I hit trees.'

'You drove your car into a tree?'

'No. Trees, plural. And then a Dumpster.' I glanced at him self-consciously and added, 'They were little trees.'

His uncertain look deepened to actual worry. 'Ah.'

I unlocked my door. Not that I was worried about anyone stealing my car. I once had a car thief offer to get me something better for a sweetheart rate. 'I guess you want to give me the details somewhere a little more private?'

Father Vincent nodded. 'Yes, of course. If you could take me to my hotel, I have some photographs and—'

I heard the scuff of shoes on concrete in time for me to catch the gunman in my peripheral vision as he rose from between a pair of parked cars one row over. Dim lights gleamed on the gun, and I threw myself across the hood of the Beetle, away from him. I crashed into Father Vincent, who let out a squeak of startled surprise, and the pair of us tumbled to the ground as the man started shooting.

The gun didn't split the air with thunder when it fired. Typically, guns do that. They're a hell of a lot louder than anything most folks run into on a day-to-day basis. This gun didn't roar, or bark, or even bang. It made a kind of loud noise. Maybe as loud as someone slamming an unabridged dictionary down on a table. The gunman was using a silencer.

One shot hit my car and caromed off the curve of the hood. Another went by my head as I struggled with Father Vincent, and a third shattered the safety glass of a ritzy sports car parked beside me.

'What's happening?' Father Vincent stammered.

'Shut up,' I snarled. The gunman was moving, his feet scuffing on the concrete as he skirted around my car. I reached around the Beetle's headlight and fumbled at the wire holding the hood down while the man came closer. It gave way and the hood wobbled up as I reached into the storage compartment.

I looked up in time to see a man, medium height and build, mid thirties, dark pants and jacket, lift a small-caliber pistol, its end heavy with a manufactured silencer. He fired, but he hadn't taken time to aim at me. He wasn't twenty feet away, but he missed.

I drew the shotgun out of the car's trunk and flicked off the safety as I chambered a round. The gunman's eyes widened and he turned to run. He shot at me again on the way, shattering one of the Beetle's headlights, and he kept shooting toward me as he skittered back the way he came.

I jerked back behind the car and kept my head down, trying to count his shots. He got to eleven or twelve and the gun went silent. I stood up, the shotgun already at my shoulder, and sighted down the barrel. The gunman ducked behind a concrete column and kept running.

'Dammit,' I hissed. 'Get in the car.'

'But—' Father Vincent stammered.

'Get in the car!' I shouted. I got up, twisted the hanger wire on the hood back into place, and got in. Vincent got in the passenger side and I shoved the shotgun at him. 'Hold this.'

He fumbled with it, his eyes wide, as I brought the Beetle to life with a roar. Well. Not really a roar. A Volkswagen Bug doesn't roar. But it sort of growled, and I mashed it into gear before the priest had managed to completely shut the door.

I headed for the parking garage's exit, whipping around the ramps and turns.

'What are you doing?' Father Vincent demanded.

'He's an outfit hitter,' I spat. 'They'll have the exit covered.'

We screeched around the final corner and toward the parking garage's exit. I heard someone yelling in a breathless voice, and a couple of large and unfriendly-looking men in a car parked across the street were just getting out. One of them held a shotgun, and the other had a heavy-duty semiautomatic, maybe a Desert Eagle.

I didn't recognize the thug with the shotgun, but Thug Number Three was an enormous man with reddish hair, no neck, and a cheap suit – Cujo Hendricks, right hand enforcer to the crime lord of Chicago, Gentleman Johnny Marcone.

I had to bounce the Beetle up onto the sidewalk at the parking-garage exit to get around the security bar, and I mowed down some landscaped bushes on the way. I jounced over the curb and into the street, hauling the wheel to the right, and mashed the accelerator to the floor.

I glanced back and saw the original gunman standing at a fire-exit door, pointing the silenced pistol at us. He snapped off several more shots, though I only heard the last few, as the silencer started to give out. He didn't have a prayer of a clean shot, but he got lucky and my back window shattered inward. I gulped and took the first corner against the light, nearly colliding with a U-Haul moving truck, and kept accelerating away.

A couple of blocks later, my heart slowed down enough that I could think. I slowed the car down to something approaching the speed limit, thanked my lucky stars the suppression spell had fallen apart in the studio and not in the car, and rolled down my window. I stuck my head out for a second to see if Hendricks and his goons were following us, but I didn't see anyone coming along behind us, and took it on faith.

I pulled my head in and found the barrel of the shotgun pointed at my chin, while Father Vincent, his face pale, muttered to himself under his breath in Italian.

'Hey!' I said, and pushed the gun's barrel away. 'Careful with that thing. You wanna kill me?' I reached down and flicked the safety on. 'Put it down. A patrolman sees that and we're in trouble.'

Father Vincent gulped, and tried to lower the gun below the level of the dash. 'This weapon is illegal?'

'Illegal is such a strong word,' I muttered.

'Oh, my,' Father Vincent said with a gulp. 'Those men,' he said. 'They tried to kill you.'

'That's what hitters for the outfit do,' I agreed.

'How do you know who they are?'

'First guy had a silenced weapon. A good silencer, metal and glass, not a cheapo plastic bottle.' I checked out the window again. 'He was using a small-caliber weapon, too, and he was trying to get real close before he started shooting.'

'Why does that matter?'

It looked clear. My hands trembled and felt a little weak. 'Because it means he was using light ammunition. Subsonic. If the bullet breaks the sound barrier, it sort of defeats the point of a silenced weapon. When he saw I was armed, he ran. Covered himself doing it, and went for help. He's a pro.'

'Oh, my,' Father Vincent said again. He looked a little pale.

'Plus I recognized one of the men waiting at the exit.'

'Someone was at the exit?' Father Vincent said.

'Yeah. Some of Marcone's rent-a-thugs.' I glanced back at the shattered window and sighed. 'Dammit. So where are we going?'

Father Vincent gave me directions in a numb voice, and I concentrated on driving, trying to ignore the quivering in my stomach and the continued trembling of my hands. Getting shot at is not something I handle very well.

Hendricks. Why the hell was Marcone sending goons after me? Marcone was the lord of the mean streets of Second City, but generally he didn't like to use that kind of violence. He thought it was bad for business. I had believed Marcone and I had an understanding – or at least an agreement to stay out of each other's way. So why would he make a move like this?

Maybe I had already stepped over a line somewhere, that I didn't know existed.

I glanced at the shaken Father Vincent.

He hadn't told me yet what he wanted, but whatever it was, it was important enough to covertly drag one of the Vatican's staff all the way to Chicago. Maybe it was important enough to kill a nosy wizard over, too.

Hoo-boy.

It was turning into one hell of a day.

3

Father Vincent directed me to a motel a little ways north of O'Hare. It was a national chain, cheap but clean, with rows of doors facing the parking lot. I drove around to the back of the motel, away from the street, frowning. It didn't look like the kind of place someone like Vincent would stay in. The priest left my car almost before I'd set the parking brake, hurried to the nearest door, and ducked inside as quickly as he could open the lock.

I followed him. Vincent shut the door behind us, locked it, and then fiddled with the blinds until they closed. He nodded at the room's little table and said, 'Please, sit down.'

I did, and stretched out my legs. Father Vincent pulled open a drawer on the plain dresser, and drew out a file folder, held closed with a wide rubber band. He sat down across from me, took off the rubber band, and said, 'The Church is interested in recovering some stolen property.'

I shrugged and said, 'Sounds like a job for the police.'

'An investigation is under way and I am giving your police

department my full cooperation. But . . . How to phrase this politely.' He frowned. 'History is an able teacher.'

'You don't trust the police,' I said. 'Gotcha.'

He grimaced. 'It is only that there have been a number of associations between Chicago police and various underworld figures in the past.'

'That's mostly movies now, padre. You may not have heard, but the whole Al Capone thing has been over for a while.'

'Perhaps,' he said. 'Perhaps not. I simply seek to do everything within my power to recover the stolen article. That includes involving an independent and discreet investigator.'

Aha. So he didn't trust the police and wanted me to work for him on the sly. That's why we were meeting at a cheap motel rather than wherever he was really staying. 'What do you want me to find for you?'

'A relic,' he said.

'A what?'

'An artifact, Mister Dresden. An antique possessed by the Church for several centuries.'

'Oh, that,' I said.

'Yes. The article is fragile and of great age, and we believe that it is not being adequately preserved. It is imperative that we recover it as quickly as possible.'

'What happened to it?'

'It was stolen three days ago.'

'From?'

'The Cathedral of Saint John the Baptist in northern Italy.'

'Long ways off.'

'We believe that the artifact was brought here, to Chicago, to be sold.'

'Why?'

He took an eight-by-ten glossy black and white from the folder and passed it to me. It featured a fairly messy corpse lying on cobblestones. Blood had run into the spaces between the stones, as well as pooling a little on the ground around the body. I think it had been a man, but it was hard to tell for certain. Whoever it was had been slashed to almost literal ribbons across the face and neck – sharp, neat, straight cuts. Professional knife work. Yuck.

'This man is Gaston LaRouche. He is the ringleader of a group of organized thieves who call themselves the Churchmice. They specialize in robbing sanctuaries and cathedrals. He was found dead the morning after the robbery near a small airfield. His briefcase contained several falsified pieces of American identification and plane tickets that would carry him here.'

'But no whatsit.'

'Ah. Exactly.' Father Vincent removed another pair of photos. These were also black and white, but they looked rougher, as if they had been magnified several times. Both were of women of average height and build, dark hair, dark sunglasses.

'Surveillance photos?' I asked.

He nodded. 'Interpol. Anna Valmont and Francisca Garcia. We believe they helped LaRouche with the theft, then murdered him and left the country. Interpol received a tip that Valmont had been seen at the airport here.'

'Do you know who the buyer is?'

Vincent shook his head. 'No. But this is the case. I want you to find the remaining Churchmice and recover the artifact.'

I frowned, looking at the photos. 'Yeah. That's what they want you to do too.'

Vincent blinked at me. 'What do you mean?'

I shook my head impatiently. 'Someone. Look at this photo. LaRouche wasn't murdered there.'

Vincent frowned. 'Why would you say that?'

'Not enough blood. I've seen men who were torn up and bled out. There's a hell of a lot more blood.' I paused and then said, 'Pardon my French.'

Father Vincent crossed himself. 'Why would his body be found there?'

I shrugged. 'A professional did him. Look at the cuts. They're methodical. He was probably unconscious or drugged, because you can't hold a man still very easily when you're taking a knife to his face.'

Father Vincent pressed one hand to his stomach. 'Oh.'

'So you've got a corpse found out in the middle of a street somewhere, basically wearing a sign around his neck that says, "The goods are in Chicago." Either someone was incredibly stupid, or someone was trying to lead you here. It's a professional killing. Someone meant his corpse to be a clue.'

'But who would do such a thing?'

I shrugged. 'Probably a good thing to find out. Do you have any better pictures of these two women?'

He shook his head. 'No. And they've never been arrested. No criminal record.'

'They're good at what they do then.' I took the photos. There were little dossiers paper-clipped to the back of the pictures, listing known aliases, locations, but nothing terribly useful. 'This one isn't going to be quick.'

'Worthwhile goals rarely are. What do you need from me, Mister Dresden?'

'A retainer,' I said. 'A thousand will do. And I need a description of this artifact, the more detailed the better.'

Father Vincent gave me a matter-of-fact nod, and drew a plain steel money clip from his pocket. He counted off ten portraits of Ben Franklin, and passed them to me. 'The artifact is an oblong length of linen cloth, fourteen feet, three inches long by three feet, seven inches wide made of a handwoven three-to-one herringbone twill. There are a number of patches and stains on the cloth, and—'

I held up my hand, frowning. 'Wait a minute. Where did you say this thing was stolen from?'

'The Cathedral of Saint John the Baptist,' Father Vincent said.

'In northern Italy,' I said.

He nodded.

'In Turin, to be exact,' I said.

He nodded again, his expression reserved.

'Someone stole the freaking *Shroud of Turin*?' I demanded.

'Yes.'

I settled back into the chair, looking down at the photos again. This changed things. This changed things a lot.

The Shroud. Supposedly the burial cloth used by Joseph of Arimathea to wrap the body of Christ after the Crucifixion. Capital Cs. The cloth supposedly wrapped around Christ when he was resurrected, with his image, his blood, imprinted upon it.

'Wow,' I said.

'What do you know about the Shroud, Mister Dresden?'

'Not much. Christ's burial cloth. They did a bunch of tests in the seventies, and no one was able to conclusively disprove it. It almost got burned a few years back when the cathedral caught fire. There are stories that it has healing powers, or that a couple of angels still attend it. A bunch of others I can't remember right now.'

Father Vincent rested his hands on the table and leaned toward me. 'Mister Dresden. The Shroud is perhaps the single most vital artifact of the Church. It is a powerful symbol of the faith, and one in which many people believe. It is also politically significant. It is absolutely vital to Rome that it be restored to the Church's custody as expediently as possible.'

I stared at him for a second, and tried to pick out my words carefully. 'Are you going to be insulted if I suggest that it's very possible that the Shroud is, uh . . . *significant*, magically speaking?'

Vincent pressed his lips together. 'I have no illusions about it, Mister Dresden. It is a piece of cloth, not a magic carpet. Its value derives solely from its historical and symbolic significance.'

'Uh-huh,' I said. Hell's bells, that's where plenty of magical power came from. The Shroud was old, and regarded as special, and people believed in it. That could be enough to give it a kind of power, all by itself.

'Some people might believe otherwise,' I said.

'Of course,' he agreed. 'That is why your knowledge of the local occult may prove invaluable.'

I nodded, thinking. This could be something completely mundane. Someone could have stolen a moldy old piece of cloth to sell it to a crackpot who believed it was a magic bedsheet. It could be that the Shroud was nothing more than a symbol, an antique, a historical Pop-Tart – nifty, but ultimately not very significant.

Of course, there was also the possibility that the Shroud was genuine. That it actually *had* been in contact with the Son of

God when he had been brought back from the dead. I pushed that thought aside.

Regardless of why or how, if the Shroud *was* something special, magically speaking, then it could mean a whole new – and nastier – ball game. Of all the various weird, dark, or wicked powers who might abscond with the Shroud, I couldn't think of any who would do anything cheerful with it. All sorts of supernatural interests might be at play.

Even discounting that possibility, mortal pursuit of the Shroud seemed to be deadly enough. John Marcone might already be involved, as well as the Chicago police – probably Interpol and the FBI, too. Even sans supernatural powers, when it came to finding people the cops were damned good at what they did. Odds were good that they'd locate the thieves and haul in the Shroud within a few days.

I looked from the photos to the cash, and thought about how many of my bills I could pay off with a nice, fat fee courtesy of Father Vincent. If I got lucky, maybe I wouldn't have to put myself in harm's way to do it.

Sure.

I believed that.

I put the money in my pocket. Then I picked up the photos too. 'How can I get in touch with you?'

Father Vincent wrote a phone number on the motel's stationery and passed it to me. 'Here. It's my answering service while I'm in town.'

'All right. I can't promise you anything concrete, but I'll see what I can do.'

Father Vincent stood up and said, 'Thank you, Mister Dresden. Father Forthill spoke most highly of you, you know.'

'He's a sport,' I agreed, rising.

'If you will excuse me, I have appointments to keep.'

'I'll bet. Here's my card, if you need to get in touch.'

I gave him a business card, shook hands, and left. At the Beetle, I stopped to open the trunk and put the shotgun back in it, after taking the shell from the chamber and making sure the safety was on. Then I pulled out a length of wood a little longer than my forearm, carved over with runes and sigils that helped me focus my magic a lot more precisely. I tossed my suit jacket in over the gun, and dug out a silver bracelet dangling a dozen tiny, medieval-style shields from my pocket. I fastened that to my left arm, slipped a silver ring onto my right hand, then took my blasting rod and set it beside me on the car seat as I got in.

Between the new case, the outfit hitter, and Duke Ortega's challenge, I wanted to make damn sure that I wasn't going to get caught with my eldritch britches down again.

I took the Beetle home, to my apartment. I rent the basement apartment of a huge, creaking old boardinghouse. By the time I got back, it was after midnight and the late-February air was speckled with occasional flakes of wet snow that wouldn't last once they hit the ground. The adrenaline rush of *The Larry Fowler Show* and then the hired-goon attack had faded, and left me aching, tired, and worried. I got out of the car, determined to head for bed, then get up early and start to work on Vincent's case.

A sudden sensation of cold, rippling energy and a pair of muffled thumps from the stairs leading down to my apartment changed my mind.

I drew out my blasting rod and readied the shield bracelet on my left wrist, but before I could step over to the stairs, a pair of figures flew up them and landed heavily on the half-frozen ground beside the gravel parking lot. They struggled, rolling, until one of the shadowy figures got a leg underneath the form on top of it, and pushed.

The second figure flew twenty feet through the air, landed on the gravel with a thump and a cough of expelled air, then got up and sprinted away.

Shield readied, I stepped forward before the remaining intruder could rise. I forced an effort of will through the blasting rod, setting the runes along its length alight with scarlet. Fire coalesced at the tip of the rod, bright as a road flare, but I held the strike as I stepped forward, shoving the tip of the blasting rod down at the intruder. 'Make a move and I'll fry you.'

Red light fell over a woman.

She was dressed in jeans, a black leather jacket, a white T-shirt, and gloves. She had her long, midnight hair tied back in a tail. Dark, oblique eyes smoldered up at me from beneath long lashes. Her beautiful face held an expression of wary amusement.

My heart thudded in sudden pain and excitement.

'Well,' Susan said, looking from the sizzling blasting rod up to my face. 'I've heard of running into an old flame, but this is ridiculous.'

4

Susan.

My brain locked up for a good ten seconds as I stared down at my former lover. I could smell the scent of her hair, the subtle perfume she wore, mixing with the new-leather scent of her jacket and another, new smell – new soap, maybe. Her dark eyes regarded me, uncertain and nervous. She had a small cut on the side of her mouth, beading with drops of blood that looked black in the red light of the blasting rod's fire.

'Harry,' Susan said, her voice quiet and steady. 'Harry. You're scaring me.'

I shook myself out of my surprise and lowered the blasting rod, stepping over to her. 'Stars and stones, Susan. Are you all right?'

I offered her my hand and she took it, rising easily to her feet. Her fingers were feverishly warm, and wisps of winter steam curled from her skin. 'Bruises,' she said. 'I'll be fine.'

'Who was that?'

Susan glanced the way her attacker had run and shook her head. 'Red Court. I couldn't see his face.'

I blinked at her. 'You ran off a vampire? By yourself?'

She flashed me a smile that mixed weariness with a sense of pleasure. She still hadn't taken her hand from mine. 'I've been working out.'

I looked around a bit more, and tried to reach out with my senses, to detect any trace of the unsettling energy that hovered around the Reds. Nothing. 'Gone now,' I reported. 'But we shouldn't hang around out here.'

'Inside then?'

I started to agree, and then paused. A horrible suspicion hit me. I let go of her hand and took a step back.

A line appeared between her eyebrows. 'Harry?'

'It's been a rough year,' I said. 'I want to talk, but I'm not inviting you in.'

Susan's expression flickered with comprehension and pain. She folded her arms over her stomach and nodded. 'No. I understand. And you're right to be careful.'

I took another step back and started walking toward my reinforced-steel door. She walked a few feet away, and at my side, where I could see her. I went down the stairs and unlocked the door. Then I pushed out an effort of will to temporarily disable the protective spells laid over my house that amounted to the magical equivalent of a land mine and burglar alarm all in one.

I went in, glanced at the candleholder on the wall by the door, and muttered, '*Flickum bicus.*' I felt a tiny surge of energy flowing out of me, and the candle danced to life, lighting my apartment in dim, soft orange.

My place is basically a cave with two chambers. The larger one was my living area. Bookshelves lined most of the walls, and where they didn't I had hung a couple of tapestries and an original *Star Wars* movie poster. I'd scattered rugs all over my floor. I had laid down everything from handmade Navajo rugs to a black area rug with Elvis's face, fully two feet across, dominating the piece. Like the Beetle, I figured some people would call my ragtag assembly of floor coverings eclectic. I just thought of them as something to walk on besides freezing-cold stone floor.

My furniture is much the same. I got most of it secondhand. None of it matches, but it's all comfortable to sprawl on, and my lights are dim enough to let me ignore it. A small alcove held a sink, an icebox, and a pantry for food. A fireplace rested against one wall, the wood all burned down to black and grey, but I knew it would still be glowing under the ash. A door led to my tiny bedroom and the apartment's three-quarters bath. The whole place may have been ragged, but it was very tidy and clean.

I turned to face Susan, and didn't put down my blasting rod. Supernatural creatures cannot lightly step across the threshold of a home unless one of the rightful residents invites them in. Plenty of nasties can put on a false face, and it wasn't inconceivable that one of them had decided to try to get close to me by pretending to be Susan.

A supernatural being would have a hell of a time getting over a threshold without being invited in. If that was some kind of shapeshifter rather than Susan or, God help me, if Susan had gone all the way over to the vampires, she wouldn't be able to enter. If it was the real Susan, she'd be fine. Or at least, the threshold wouldn't hurt her. Getting paranoid suspicion from her ex-boyfriend might do its own kind of damage.

On the other hand, there was a war on, and Susan probably

wouldn't be happy to hear I'd gotten myself killed. Better safe than exsanguinated.

Susan didn't pause at the door. She stepped inside, turned around to close and lock it, and asked, 'Good enough?'

It was. Relief, coupled with a sudden explosion of naked emotion, roared through me. It was like waking up after days of anguish to find that the pain was gone. Where there had been only hurt, there was suddenly nothing, and other feelings rushed in to fill the sudden void. Excitement, for one, that quivering teenage nervousness that accompanies expectation. A surge of warm emotion, joy and happiness rolled together with a chittering glee.

And in the shadows of those, a few things darker but no less vibrant. Sheer, sensual pleasure in the scent of her, in looking at her face, her dark hair again. I needed to feel her skin under my hands, to feel her pressed to me.

It was more than mere need – it was hunger. Now that she was standing there in front of me, I needed her, all of her, as much as I needed food or water or air, and possibly more. I wanted to tell her, to let her know what it meant to me that she was there. But I'd never been very good at expressing myself verbally.

By the time Susan turned around again, I was already pressed up against her. She let out a quiet gasp of surprise, but I leaned gently into her, pressing her shoulders to the door.

I lowered my mouth to hers, and her lips were soft, sweet, fever-hot. She went rigid for a second, then let out a low sound and wound her arms around my neck and shoulders, kissing me back. I could feel her, the slender, too-warm strength and softness of her body. My hunger deepened, and so did the kiss, my tongue touching hers, lightly teasing. She responded as ardently as I did, her lips almost desperate, low whimpers vibrating through her mouth and into mine. I started to feel a little dizzy and disoriented, and though some part of me warned against it, I only pressed harder against her.

I slid one hand over her hip, beneath the jacket, and slipped up under the T-shirt she wore to curl around the naked sweetness of her waist. I pulled her hard against me, and she responded, her breath hot and quick, lifting one leg to press against mine, winding around my calf a little, pulling me nearer. I lowered my mouth to her throat, tongue tasting her skin, and she arched against me, baring more of her skin. I drew a line of kisses up to her ear, gently biting, sending quivering shock waves through her as she shook against me, her throat letting out quiet sounds of deepening need. I found her eager lips again, and her fingers tightened in my hair, drawing me hard against her.

My dizziness grew. Some kind of coherent thought did a quick flyby of my forebrain. I struggled to take notice of it, but the kiss made it impossible. Lust and need murdered my reason.

A sudden, shrieking hiss startled me, and I jerked back from Susan, looking wildly around.

Mister, my bobtailed, battle-scarred tomcat, had leapt up onto the stones before the fireplace, his luminous green eyes wide and fixed on Susan. Mister weighs about thirty pounds, and thirty pounds of cat can make an absolutely impossible amount of noise.

Susan shuddered and pressed her palm against my chest, turning her face away from me. She pushed, something gentle rather than insistent. My lips burned to touch hers again, but I closed my eyes and took slow, shuddering breaths. Then I backed away from her. I had meant to go stir up the fire – not *that* fire, the literal one – but the room tilted wildly and it was all I could do to stumble into an easy chair.

Mister leapt up into my lap, more daintily than he had any right to be able to do, and rubbed his face against my chest, rumbling out a purr. I fumbled up one hand to pet him, and after a couple of minutes the room stopped spinning.

'What the hell just happened?' I muttered.

Susan emerged from the shadows and crossed the candlelit room to take up the fireplace poker. She stirred through the ashes until she found some glowing orange-red, and then began adding wood to the fire from the old iron hod beside the fireplace. 'I could feel you,' she said, after a minute. 'I could feel you going under. It . . .' She shivered. 'It felt nice.'

Boy, did it. And I bet it would feel even nicer if all those clothes hadn't been in the way. Aloud, all I said was, 'Under?'

She looked over her shoulder at me, her expression hard to read. 'The venom,' she said quietly. 'They call it their Kiss.'

'I guess I can't blame them. It sounds a lot more romantic than "narcotic drool."' Some parts of me lobbied for a cessation of meaningless chat and an immediate resumption of any line of thought that would lead to discarded clothing upon the floor. I ignored them. 'I remember. When . . . when we kissed before you left. I thought I'd imagined it.'

Susan shook her head, and sat down on the stones before the fireplace, her back straight, her hands folded sedately in her lap. The fire began to grow, catching onto the new wood, and though the light of it curled around her with golden fingers, it left her face veiled in shadow. 'No. What Bianca did to me has changed me already, in some ways. Physically. I'm stronger now. My senses are sharper. And there's . . .' She faltered.

'The Kiss,' I mumbled. My lips didn't find the word to their liking. They liked the real thing a lot better. I ignored them, too.

'Yes,' she said. 'Not like one of them can do. Less. But still there.'

I mopped at my face with my hand. 'You know what I need?' Either a naked, writhing, eager Susan or else a liquid-nitrogen shower. 'A beer. You want one?'

'Pass,' she said. 'I don't think lowering my inhibitions would be healthy right now.'

I nodded, got up, and went to my icebox. It's an actual icebox, the kind that runs on honest-to-goodness ice rather than Freon. I got out a dark brown bottle of Mac's home-brewed ale and opened it, taking a long drink. Mac would be horrified that I drank his beer cold, since he prided himself on an old-world brew, but I always kept a couple in there, for when I wanted it cold. What can I say. I'm an unlettered, barbaric American wizard. I drank off maybe half of it and put the cold bottle against my forehead afterward.

'Well,' I said. 'I guess you didn't come over to, uh . . .'

'Tear your clothes off and use you shamelessly?' Susan suggested. Her voice sounded calm again, but I could sense the underlying tone of her own hunger. I wasn't sure whether I should be unsettled by it or encouraged. 'No, Harry. It isn't . . . that isn't something I can afford to do with you. No matter how much either of us wants it.'

'Why not?' I asked. I knew why not already, but the words jumped from my brain to my mouth before I could stop them. I peered suspiciously at the beer.

'I don't want to lose control,' Susan said. 'Not ever. Not with anyone. But especially not with you.' There was a silence in which only the fire made any noise. 'Harry, it would kill me to hurt you.'

More to the point, I thought, *it would probably kill me too. Think about her instead of yourself, Harry. Get a grip. It's just a kiss. Let it go.*

I drank the rest of my beer, which wasn't anywhere near as nice as other things I'd done with my mouth that night. I checked the fridge and asked Susan, 'Coke?'

She nodded, looking around. Her gaze hesitated on the fireplace mantel, where I kept the card and three postcards I'd received from her, along with the little grey jewelry box that held the dinky little ring she'd turned down. 'Is someone else living here now?'

'No.' I got out a couple of cans, and took one over to her. She took it from me without touching my fingers. 'Why do you ask?'

'The place looks so nice,' she said. 'And your clothes smell like fabric softener. You've never used fabric softener in your life.'

'Oh. That.' You can't tell people about it when faeries are doing your housework, or they get ticked off and leave. 'I sort of have a cleaning service.'

'I hear you've been too busy to clean up,' Susan said.

'Just making a living.'

Susan smiled. 'I heard you saved the world from some kind of doom. Is it true?'

I fiddled with my drink. 'Sort of.'

Susan laughed. 'How do you sort of save the world?'

'I only saved it in a Greenpeace kind of way. If I'd blown it, there might have been a historically bad storm, but I don't think anyone would have noticed the real damage for thirty or forty years – climate change takes time.'

'Sounds scary,' Susan said.

I shrugged. 'Mostly I was just trying to save my own ass. The world was a twofer. Maybe I'm getting cynical. I suspect the only thing I accomplished was to keep the faeries from screwing up the place so that we could screw it up ourselves.'

I sat down on the chair again, and we opened the Cokes and drank in silence for a bit. My heart eventually stopped pounding quite so loudly.

'I miss you,' I said finally. 'So does your editor. She called me a couple of weeks ago. Said your articles had quit coming in.'

Susan nodded. 'That's one reason I'm here. I owe her more than a letter or a phone call.'

'You're quitting?' I asked.

She nodded.

'You find something else?'

'Sort of,' she said. She brushed her hair back from her face with one hand. 'I can't tell you everything right now.'

I frowned. For as long as I'd known her, Susan had been driven by a passion for discovering the truth and sharing it with other people. Her work at the *Arcane* had arisen from her stubborn refusal to deny things she saw as the truth, even if they had seemed insane. She was one of the rare people who stopped and thought about things, even weird and supernatural things, instead of dismissing them out of hand. That's how she'd begun work at the *Arcane*. That was how she had originally met me.

'Are you all right?' I asked. 'Are you in trouble?'

'Relatively speaking, no,' she said. 'But you are. That's why I'm here, Harry.'

'What do you mean?'

'I came to warn you. The Red Court—'

'Sent Paolo Ortega to call me out. I know.'

She sighed. 'But you don't know what you're getting into. Harry, Ortega is one of the most dangerous nobles of their Court. He's a warlord. He's killed half a dozen of the White Council's Wardens in South America since the war started, and he's the one who planned and executed the attack on Archangel last year.'

I sat straight up at that, the blood draining from my face. 'How do you know about that?'

'I'm an investigative reporter, Harry. I investigated.'

I toyed with the Coke can, frowning down at it. 'All the same. He came here asking for a duel. A fair fight. If he's serious, I'll take him on.'

'There's more that you need to know,' Susan said.

'Like what?'

'Ortega's opinion on the war is not the popular one within the Red Court. A few of the upper crust of the vampires support his way of thinking. But most of them like the idea of a lot of constant bloodshed. They also like the idea of a war to wipe out the White Council. They figure that if they get rid of the wizards once and for all, they won't have to worry about keeping a low profile in the future.'

'What's that got to do with anything?'

'Think about it,' Susan said. 'Harry, the White Council is fighting this war reluctantly. If they had a decent excuse, they'd end it. That's Ortega's whole plan. He fights you, kills you, and then the White Council sues for peace. They'll pay some kind of concession that doesn't involve the death of one of their members, and that will be that. War over.'

I blinked. 'How did you find out—'

'Hello, Earth to Harry. I told you, I investigated.'

I frowned until the lines between my eyebrows ached. 'Right, right. Well, as plans go, I guess it sounds good,' I said. 'Except for that middle part where I die.'

She gave me a small smile. 'Much of the rest of the Red Court would rather you kept on breathing. As long as you're alive, they have a reason to keep the war going.'

'Swell,' I said.

'They'll try to interfere with any duel. I just thought you should know.'

I nodded. 'Thanks,' I said. 'I'll—'

Just then, someone knocked firmly at my door. Susan stiffened and rose, poker in hand. I got up a lot more slowly, opened a drawer in the night table beside the chair, and drew out the gun I kept at home, a great big old Dirty Harry Callahan number that weighed about seventy-five thousand pounds. I also took out a length of silk rope about a yard long, and draped it over my neck so that I could get it off in a hurry if need be.

I took the gun in both hands, pointed it at the floor, drew back the hammer, and asked the door, 'Who is it?'

There was a moment's silence and then a calm, male voice asked, 'Is Susan Rodriguez there?'

I glanced at Susan. She straightened more, her eyes flashing with anger, but she put the poker back in its stand beside the fireplace. Then she motioned to me and said, 'Put it away. I know him.'

I uncocked the revolver, but I didn't put it away as Susan crossed to the door and opened it.

The most bland-looking human being I had ever seen stood on the other side. He was maybe five nine, maybe one seventy-five. He had hair of medium brown, and eyes of the same ambiguous shade. He wore jeans, a medium-weight brown jacket, and worn tennis shoes. His face was unmemorable, neither appealing nor ugly. He didn't look particularly strong, or craven, or smart, or particularly anything else.

'What are you doing here?' he asked Susan without preamble. His voice was like the rest of him – about as exciting as a W-2.

Susan said, 'I told you I was going to talk to him.'

'You could have used the phone,' the man pointed out. 'There's no point to this.'

'Hi,' I said in a loud voice, and stepped up to my door. I towered over Blandman. And I had a great big gun in my hand, even if I did keep it pointed down at the floor. 'I'm Harry Dresden.'

He looked me up and down and then looked at Susan.

Susan sighed. 'Harry, this is Martin.'

'Hi, Martin,' I said. I switched my sidearm to my other hand and thrust mine at him. 'Nice to meet you.'

Martin regarded my hand and then said, 'I don't shake hands.' That was evidently all the verbal interaction I merited, because he looked back at Susan and said, 'We have to be up early.'

We? *We?*

I looked at Susan, who flushed with embarrassment. She glared at Martin and then said to me, 'I need to go, Harry. I wish I could have stayed longer.'

'Wait,' I said.

'I wish I could,' she said. 'I'll try to call you before we go.'

There was that *we* again. 'Go? Susan—'

'I'm sorry.' She stood up on tiptoe and kissed my cheek, her too-warm lips soft. Then she left, brushing past Martin just hard enough to jostle him into taking a little step to keep his balance.

Martin nodded to me and walked out too. After a minute I followed them, long enough to see them getting into a cab on the street outside.

We.

'Hell's bells,' I muttered, and stalked back inside my house. I slammed the door behind me, lit a candle, stomped into my little bathroom, and turned on the shower. The water was only a couple degrees short of becoming sleet, but I stripped and got in anyway, simmering with several varieties of frustration.

We.

We, we, we. Which implied she and someone else together. Someone who was not me. Was she? Susan, with the Pedantic Avenger there? That didn't track. I mean, hell's bells, the guy was just so dull. Boring. Blasé.

And maybe stable.

Face it, Harry. Interesting you might be. Exciting you might be. Stable you ain't.

I pushed my head under the freezing water and left it there. Susan hadn't said they were together. Neither had he. I mean, that wouldn't be why she had broken off the kiss. She had a really good reason to do that, after all.

But then again, it wasn't like we were together. She'd been gone for better than a year.

A lot can change in a year.

Her mouth hadn't. Or her hands. Or the curve of her body.

Or the smoldering sensuality of her eyes. Or the soft sounds she made as she arched against me, her body begging me to—

I looked down at myself, sighed, and turned the water to its coldest setting.

I came out of the shower shriveled and turning blue, dried off, and got into bed.

I had just managed to get the covers warm so that I could stop shivering when my phone rang.

I swore sulfurously, got out of bed into the freezing air, snatched up the phone, and growled, 'What.' Then, on the off chance it was Susan, I forced some calm into my voice and said, 'I mean, hello?'

'Sorry to wake you, Harry,' said Karrin Murphy, the head of Chicago PD's Special Investigations division. SI routinely handled any crime that fell between the cracks of the other departments, as well as being handed the really smelly cases no one else wanted. As a result, they wound up looking into all kinds of things that weren't easily explained. Their job was to make sure that things were taken care of, and that everything typed up neatly into the final report.

Murphy called me in as a consultant from time to time, when she had something weird that she didn't know how to handle. We'd been working together for a while, and Murphy had gotten to where she and SI could handle your average, everyday supernatural riffraff. But from time to time, she ran into something that stumped her. My phone number is on her quick dial.

'Murph,' I said. 'What's up?'

'Unofficial business,' she said. 'I'd like your take on something.'

'Unofficial means not paid, I guess,' I said.

'You up for any pro bono work?' She paused and then said, 'This could be important to me.'

What the hell. My night had pretty much been shot anyway. 'Where do you want me?'

'Cook County Morgue,' Murphy said. 'I want to show you a corpse.'

5

They don't make morgues with windows. In fact, if the geography allows for it, they hardly ever make morgues above the ground. I guess it's partly because it must be easier to refrigerate a bunch of coffin-sized chambers in a room insulated by the earth. But that can't be all there is to it. Under the earth means a lot more than relative altitude. It's where dead things fit. Graves are under the earth. So are Hell, Gehenna, Hades, and a dozen other reported afterlives.

Maybe it says something about people. Maybe for us, under the earth is a subtle and profound statement. Maybe ground level provides us with a kind of symbolic boundary marker, an artificial construct that helps us remember that we are alive. Maybe it helps us push death's shadow back from our lives.

I live in a basement apartment and like it. What does that say about me?

Probably that I overanalyze things.

'You look pensive,' Murphy said. We walked down an empty hospital corridor toward the Cook County Morgue. We'd had to go the long way around so that I could avoid any areas with important medical equipment. My leather duster whispered around my legs as I walked. My blasting rod thumped against my leg rhythmically, where I'd tied it to the inside of the duster. I'd traded in my slacks for blue jeans and my dress shoes for hiking boots.

Murphy didn't look like a monster-hunting Valkyrie. Murphy looked like someone's kid sister. She was five nothing, a hundred and nothing, and was built like an athlete, all springy muscle. Her blonde hair hung down over her blue eyes, and was cut close in back. She wore nicer clothes than usual – a maroon blouse with a grey pantsuit – and she had on more makeup than was her habit. She looked every inch the professional businesswoman.

That said, Murphy was a monster-hunting Valkyrie. She was the only person I'd ever heard of who had killed one with a chainsaw.

'I said you look pensive, Harry,' she repeated, a little louder.

I shook my head and told Murphy, 'I don't like hospitals.'

She nodded. 'Morgues spook me. Morgues and dogs.'

'Dogs?' I asked.

'Not like beagles or cocker spaniels or anything. Just big dogs.'

I nodded. 'I like dogs. They give Mister something to snack on.'

Murphy gave me a smile. 'I've seen you spooked. It doesn't make you look like that.'

'What do I look like?' I asked.

Murphy pursed her lips, as though considering her words. 'You look worried. And frustrated. And guilty. You know, romance things.'

I gave her a wry glance, and then nodded. 'Susan's in town.'

Murphy whistled. 'Wow. She's . . . okay?'

'Yeah. As much as she can be.'

'Then why do you look like you just swallowed something that was still wriggling?'

I shrugged. 'She's in town to quit her job. And she was with someone.'

'A *guy*?' Murphy asked.

'Yeah.'

She frowned. 'With him, or *with* him?'

I shook my head. 'Just with him, I think. I don't know.'

'She's quitting her job?'

'Guess so. We're going to talk, I think.'

'She said so?'

'Said she'd get in touch and we'd talk.'

Murphy's eyes narrowed, and she said, 'Ah. One of those.'

'Eh?' I said, and eyed her.

She lifted her hands, palms out. 'None of my business.'

'Hell's bells, Murph.'

She sighed and didn't look up at me, and didn't speak for a few steps. Finally she said, 'You don't set up a guy for a good talk, Harry.'

I stared at her profile, and then scowled down at my feet for a while. No one said anything.

We got to the morgue. Murphy pushed a button on the wall and said, 'It's Murphy,' at a speaker next to the door. A second later, the door buzzed and clicked. I swung open the door and held it for Murphy. She gave me an even look before she went through. Murphy does not respond well to chivalry.

The morgue was like others I'd seen, cold, clean, and brightly lit with fluorescent lights. Metal refrigerator doors lined one wall. An occupied autopsy table sat in the middle of the room, and a white sheet covered its subject. A rolling medical cart sat next to the autopsy table, another by a cheap office-furniture desk.

Polka music, heavy on accordion and clarinet, *oompahed* cheerfully through the room from a little stereo on the desk. At the desk sat a small man with a wild shock of black hair. He was dressed in medical scrubs and green bunny slippers, complete with floppy ears. He had a pen clenched in one hand, and scribbled furiously at a stack of forms.

When we came in, he held up a hand toward us, and finished his scribbling with a flourish, before hopping up with a broad smile. 'Karrin!' he said. 'Wow, you're looking nice tonight. What's the occasion?'

'Municipal brass are tromping around,' Murphy said. 'So we're all supposed to wear our Sunday clothes and smile a lot.'

'Bastards,' the little guy said cheerfully. He shot me a glance. 'You aren't supposed to be spending money on psychic consultants, either, I bet. You must be Harry Dresden.'

'That's what it says on my underwear,' I agreed.

He grinned. 'Great coat, love it.'

'Harry,' Murphy said, 'this is Waldo Butters. Assistant medical examiner.'

Butters shook my hand, then turned to walk to the autopsy table. He snapped on some rubber gloves and a surgical mask. 'Pleased to meet you, Mister Dresden,' he said over his shoulder. 'Seems like every time you're working with SI my job gets really interesting.'

Murphy chucked me on the arm with one fist, and followed Butters. I followed her.

'Masks on that tray to your left. Stay a couple of feet back from the table, and for God's sake, don't throw up on my floor.' We put on masks and Butters threw back the sheet.

I'd seen corpses before. Hell's bells, I'd created some. I'd seen what was left of people who had been burned alive, savaged to death by animals, and who had died when their hearts exploded out of their chests, courtesy of black magic.

But I hadn't ever seen anything quite like this. I shoved the thought to the back of my head, and tried to focus purely upon taking in details. It wouldn't do to think too much, looking at this. Thinking too much would lead me to messing up Butters's floor.

The victim had been a man, maybe a little over six feet tall, thin build. His chest looked like twenty pounds of raw hamburger. Fine grid marks stretched vertically from his collarbones to his belly, and horizontally across the width of his body. The cuts were spaced maybe a sixteenth of an inch apart, and the grid pattern slashed into the flesh looked nearly flawless. The cuts were deep ones, and I had the unsettling impression that I could have brushed my hand across the surface of that ruined body and sent chunks of flesh pattering to the floor. The Y-incision of the autopsy had been closed, at least. Its lines marred the precision of the grid of incisions.

The next thing I noticed were the corpse's arms. Or rather, the missing bits of them. His left arm had been hacked off two or three inches above the wrist. The flesh around it gaped, and a shard of black-crusted bone poked out from it. His right arm had been severed just beneath the elbow, with similar hideous results.

My belly twitched and I felt myself taking one of those

prevomit breaths. I closed my eyes for a second and forced the impending reaction down. *Don't think, Harry. Look. See what there is to see. That isn't a man anymore. It's just a shell. Throwing up won't bring him back.*

I opened my eyes again, tore my gaze from his mutilated chest and hands, and forced myself to study the corpse's features.

I couldn't.

His head had been hacked off, too.

I stared at the ragged stump of his neck. The head just wasn't there. Even though that's where heads *go*. Ditto his hands. A man should have a head. Should have hands. They shouldn't simply be *gone*.

The impression it left on me was unsettling – simply and profoundly wrong. Inside me, some little voice started screaming and running away. I stared down at the corpse, my stomach threatening insurrection again. I stared at his missing head, but aloud all I said was, 'Gee. Wonder what killed him.'

'What *didn't* kill him,' Butters said. 'I can tell you this much. It wasn't blood loss.'

I frowned at Butters. 'What do you mean?'

Butters lifted one of the corpse's arms and pointed down at dark mottling in the dead grey flesh, just where the corpse's back met the table. 'See that?' he asked. 'Lividity. If this guy had bled out, from his wrists or his neck either one, I don't think there'd be enough blood left in the body to show this much. His heart would have just kept on pumping it out of his body until he died.'

I grunted. 'If not one of the wounds, then what was it?'

'My guess?' Butters said. 'Plague.'

I blinked and looked at him.

'Plague,' he said again. 'Or more accurately plagues. His insides looked like models for a textbook on infection. Not all the tests have come back yet, but so far every one I've done has returned positive. Everything from bubonic plague to strep throat. And there are symptoms I've found in him that don't match any disease I've ever heard of.'

'You're telling me he died of disease?' I asked.

'Diseases. Plural. And get this. I think one of them was smallpox.'

'I thought smallpox was extinct,' Murphy said.

'Pretty much. They have some in vaults, probably some in some bioweapon research facilities, but that's it.'

I stared at Butters for a second. 'And we're standing here next to his plague-ridden body why?'

'Relax,' Butters said. 'The really nasty stuff wasn't airborne. I disinfected the corpse pretty well. Wear your mask and don't touch it, you should be fine.'

'What about the smallpox?' I said.

Butters's voice turned wry. 'You're vaccinated.'

'This is dangerous, though, isn't it? Having the body out like this?'

'Yeah,' Butters said, his voice frank. 'But County is full, and the only thing that's going to happen if I report an occurrence of free-range smallpox is another evaluation.'

Murphy shot me a warning look and stepped a very little bit between me and Butters. 'You got a time of death?'

Butters shrugged. 'Maybe forty-eight hours ago, tops. All of those diseases seemed to sprout up at exactly the same time. I make cause of death as either shock or a massive failure and necrosis of several major organs, plus tissue damage from an outrageously high fever. It's anyone's guess as to which one gets the blue ribbon. Lungs, kidneys, heart, liver, spleen—'

'We get the point,' Murphy said.

'Let me finish. It's like every disease the guy had ever had contact with all got together and planned when to hit him. It just isn't possible. He probably had more germs in him than blood cells.'

I frowned. 'And then someone Ginsued him after he died?'

Butters nodded. 'Partly. Though the cuts on his chest weren't postmortem. They had filled with blood. Tortured before he died, maybe.'

'Ugh,' I said. 'Why?'

Murphy regarded the corpse without any emotion showing in her cool blue eyes. 'Whoever cut him up must have taken the arms and hands to make it hard to identify him after he died. That's the only logical reason I can think of.'

'Same here,' said Butters.

I frowned down at the table. 'Why prevent identification of the corpse if it had died of disease?' Butters began to lower the arm slowly and I saw something as he did. 'Wait, hold it.'

He looked up at me. I pressed closer to the table and had Butters lift the arm again. I had almost missed it against the rotted tone of the dead man's flesh – a tattoo, maybe an inch square, located on the inside of the corpse's biceps. It wasn't fancy. Faded green ink in the shape of a symbolic open eye, not too different from the CBS network logo.

'See there?' I asked. Murphy and Butters peered at the tattoo.

'Do you recognize it, Harry?' Murphy asked.

I shook my head. 'Almost looks old Egyptian, but with fewer lines. Hey, Butters, do you have a piece of paper?'

'Better,' Butters said. He got an old instant camera off the bottom tray of one of the medical carts, and snapped several shots of the tattoo. He passed one of them over to Murphy, who waved it around a little while the image developed. I got another.

'Okay,' I said, thinking out loud. 'Guy dies of a zillion diseases he somehow contracted all at once. How long do you think it took?'

Butters shrugged. 'No idea. I mean, the odds against him getting all of those at once like that are beyond astronomical.'

'Days?' I asked.

'If I had to guess,' Butters said, 'I'd say more like hours. Maybe less.'

'Okay,' I said. 'And during those hours, someone uses a knife on him and turns his chest into tuna cubes. Then when they're done, they take his hands and his head and dump the body. Where was it found?'

'Under an overpass on the expressway,' Murphy said. 'Like this, naked.'

I shook my head. 'SI got handed this one?'

Murphy's face flickered with annoyance. 'Yeah. Homicide dumped it on us to take some high-profile case all the municipal folk are hot about.'

I took a step back from the corpse, frowning, putting things together. I figured odds were pretty good that there weren't all that many people running around the world torturing victims by carving their skin into graph paper before murdering them. At least I hoped there weren't all that many.

Murphy peered at me, her expression serious. 'What. Harry, do you know something?'

I glanced from Murphy to Butters and then back again.

Butters raised both his hands and headed for the doors, stripping his gloves and dumping them in a container splattered with red biohazard signs. 'You guys stay here and Mulder it out. I have to go down the hall anyway. Back in five minutes.'

I watched him go and said, after the door swung shut, 'Bunny slippers and polka music.'

'Don't knock it,' Murphy said. 'He's good at his job. Maybe too good.'

'What's that mean?'

She walked away from the autopsy table, and I followed her. Murphy said, 'Butters was the one who handled the bodies after the fire at the Velvet Room.'

The one I'd started. 'Oh?'

'Mmm-hmm. His original report stated that some of the remains recovered from the scene were humanoid, but definitely not human.'

'Yeah,' I said. 'Red vampires.'

Murphy nodded. 'But you can't just stick that in a report without people getting their panties in a bunch. Butters wound up doing a three-month stint at a mental hospital for observation. When he came out, they tried to fire him, but his lawyer convinced them that they couldn't. So instead he lost all his seniority and got stuck on the night shift. But he knows there's weirdness out there. He calls me when he gets some of it.'

'Seems nice enough. Except for the polka.'

Murphy smiled again and said, 'What do you know?'

'Nothing I can tell you,' I said. 'I agreed to keep the information confidential.'

Murphy peered up at me for a moment. Once upon a time, that comment might have sent her into a fit of stubborn confrontation. But I guess times had changed. 'All right,' she said. 'Are you holding back anything that might get someone hurt?'

I shook my head. 'It's too early to tell.'

Murphy nodded, her lips pressed together. She appeared to weigh things for a moment before saying, 'You know what you're doing.'

'Thanks.'

She shrugged. 'I expect you to tell me if it turns into something I should know.'

'Okay,' I said, staring at her profile. Murphy had done something I knew she didn't do very often. She'd extended her trust. I'd expected her to threaten and demand. I could have handled that. This was almost worse. Guilt gnawed on my insides. I'd agreed not to divulge anything, but I hated doing that to Murphy. She'd gone out on a limb for me too many times.

But what if I didn't tell her anything? What if I just pointed her toward information she'd find sooner or later in any case?

'Look, Murph. I specifically agreed to confidentiality for this client. But . . . if I were going to talk to you, I'd tell you to check out the murder of a Frenchman named LaRouche with Interpol.'

Murphy blinked and then looked up at me. 'Interpol?'

I nodded. 'If I were going to talk.'

'Right,' she said. 'If you'd said anything. You tight-lipped bastard.'

One corner of my mouth tugged up into a grin. 'Meanwhile, I'll see if I can't find out anything about that tattoo.'

She nodded. 'You figure we're dealing with another sorcerer type?'

I shrugged. 'Maybe. But if you give someone a disease with

magic, it's usually so that you make it look like they *haven't* been murdered. Natural causes. This kind of mishmash . . . I don't know. Maybe it's something a demon would do.'

'A real demon? Like *Exorcist* demon?'

I shook my head. 'Those are the Fallen. The former angels. Not the same thing.'

'Why not?'

'Demons are just intelligent beings from somewhere in the Nevernever. Mostly they don't care about the mortal world, if they notice it at all. The ones who do are usually the hungry types, or the mean types that someone calls up to do thug work. Like that thing Leonid Kravos had called up.'

Murphy shivered. 'I remember. And the Fallen?'

'They're very interested in our world. But they aren't free to act, like demons are.'

'Why not?'

I shrugged. 'Depends on who you talk to. I've heard everything from advanced magical resonance theory to "because God said so." One of the Fallen couldn't do this unless it had permission to.'

'Right. And how many people would give permission to be infected and then tortured to death,' Murphy said.

'Yeah, exactly.'

She shook her head. 'Going to be a busy week. Half a dozen professional hitters for the outfit are in town. The county morgue is doing double business. City Hall is telling us to bend over backward for some bigwig from Europe or somewhere. And now some kind of plague monster is leaving unidentifiable, mutilated corpses on the side of the road.'

'That's why they pay you the big bucks, Murph.'

Murphy snorted. Butters came back in, and I made my goodbyes. My eyes were getting heavy and I had aches in places where I hadn't known I had places. Sleep sounded like a great idea, and with so many things going on, the smart option was to get lots of rest in order to be as capably paranoid as possible.

I walked the long route back out of the hospital, but found a hall blocked by a patient on some kind of life-support machinery being moved on a gurney from one room to another. I wound up heading out through the empty cafeteria, into an alley not far from the emergency room exit.

A cold chill started at the base of my spine and slithered up over my neck. I stopped and looked around me, reaching for my blasting rod. I extended my magical senses as best I could, tasting the air to see what had given me the shivers.

I found nothing, and the eerie sensation eased away. I started down the alley, toward a parking garage half a block from the hospital, and tried to look in every direction at once as I went. I passed a little old homeless man, hobbling along heavily on a thick wooden cane. A while farther on, I passed a tall young black man, dressed in an old overcoat and tattered and too-small suit, clutching an open bottle of vodka in one heavy-knuckled hand. He glowered at me, and I moved on past him. Chicago nightlife.

I kept on moving toward my car, and heard footsteps growing closer, behind me. I told myself not to be too jumpy. Maybe it was just some other frightened, endangered, paranoid, sleep-deprived consultant who had been called to the morgue in the middle of the night.

Okay. Maybe not.

The steady tread of the footsteps behind me shifted, becoming louder and unsteady. I spun to face the person following me, raising the blasting rod in my right hand as I did.

I turned around in time to see a bear, a freaking grizzly bear, fall to all four feet and charge. I had already begun preparing a magical strike with the rod, and the tip burst into incandescent light. Shadows fell harshly back from the scarlet fire of the rod, and I saw the details of the thing coming at me.

It wasn't a bear. Not unless a bear can have six legs and a pair of curling ram's horns wrapping around the sides of its head. Not unless bears can somehow get an extra pair of eyes, right over the first set, one pair glowing with faint orange light and one with green. Not unless bears have started getting luminous tattoos of swirling runes on their foreheads and started sprouting twin rows of serrated, slime-coated teeth.

It came charging toward me, several hundred pounds of angry-looking monster, and I did the only thing any reasonable wizard could have done.

I turned around and ran like hell.

6

I'd learned something in several years of professional wizarding. Never walk into a fight when the bad guys are the ones who set it up. Wizards can call down lightning from the heavens, rip apart the earth beneath their enemy's feet, blow them into a neighboring time zone with gale-force winds, and a million other things even less pleasant – but not if we don't plan things out in advance.

And we're not all that much tougher than regular folks. I mean, if some nasty creature tears my head off my shoulders, I'll die. I might be able to lay out some serious magical pounding when I need to, but I'd made the mistake of tangling with a few things that had prepared to go up against me, and it hadn't been pretty.

This bear-thing, whatever the hell it was, had followed me. Hence, it had probably picked its time and place. I could have stood and blasted away at it, but in the close quarters of the alley, if it was able to shrug off my blasts, it would tear me apart before I could try Plan B. So I ran.

One other thing I'd learned. Wheezy wizards aren't all that

good at running. That's why I'd been practicing. I took off at a dead sprint and fairly flew down the alley, my duster flapping behind me.

The bear-thing snarled as it came after me, and I could hear it slowly gaining ground. The mouth of the alley loomed into sight and I ran as hard as I could for it. Once I was in the open with room to dodge and put obstacles between me and the creature, I might be able to take a shot at it.

The creature evidently realized that, because it let out a vicious, spitting growl and then leapt. I heard it gather itself for the leap, and turned my head enough to see it out of the corner of my eye. It flew at my back. I threw myself down, sliding and rolling over the asphalt. The creature soared over me, to land at the mouth of the alley, a good twenty feet ahead. I skidded to a stop and went running back down the alley, a growing sense of fear and desperation giving my feet a set of chicken-yellow wings.

I ran for maybe ten seconds, gritting my teeth as the creature took up the pursuit again. I couldn't keep up a full sprint forever. Unless I thought of something else, I was going to have to turn and take my chances.

I all but flattened the tall young black man I'd seen earlier when I leapt over a moldering pile of cardboard boxes. He let out a startled noise, and I answered it with a low curse. 'Come on!' I said, grabbing his arm. 'Move, move, move!'

He looked past me and his eyes widened. I looked back and saw the four glowing eyes of the bear-creature coming at us. I hauled him into motion, and he picked up speed and started running with me.

We ran for a few seconds more before the little old derelict

I'd seen earlier came limping along on his cane. He looked up, and the dim light from the distant street glinted on a pair of spectacles.

'Augh,' I shouted. I shoved my running partner past me, toward the old man, and snarled, 'Get him out of here. Both of you run!'

I whirled to face the bear-creature, and swept my blasting rod to point right at it. I ran some force of will down into the energy channels in the rod and with a snarled, '*Fuego!*' sent a lance of raw fire whipping through the air.

The blast slammed into the bear-creature's chest, and it hunched its shoulders, turning its head to one side. Its forward charge faltered, and it slid to a stop, crashing against a weathered old metal trash can.

'What do you know,' I muttered. 'It worked.' I stepped forward and unleashed another blast at the creature, hoping to either melt it to bits or drive it away. The bear-thing snarled and turned a hateful, murderous gaze at me with its four eyes.

The soulgaze began almost instantly.

When a wizard looks into someone's eyes, he sees more than just what color they are. Eyes are windows to the soul. When I make eye contact for too long, or too intently, I get to peek in through the windows. You can't hide what you are from a wizard's soulgaze. And he can't hide from you. You both see each other for what you are, within, and it's with a clarity so intense that it burns itself into your head.

Looking on someone's soul is something you never forget.

No matter how badly you might want to.

I felt a whirling, gyrating sensation and fell forward, into the bear-thing's eyes. The glowing sigil on its forehead became a blaze of silver light the size of a stadium scoreboard set against a roundish cliffside of dark green and black marble. I expected to see something hideous, but I guess you can't judge a monster by the slime on its scales. What I saw instead was a man of lean middle years dressed in rags. His hair was long and straight, wispy grey that fell down to his chest. He stood in a posture of agony, his wiry body stretched out in an arch, with his hands held up and apart, his legs stretched out. I followed the lines of his arms back and up and saw why he stood that way.

He'd been crucified.

The man's back rested against the cliff, the great glowing sigil stretching out above him. His arms were pulled back at an agonizing angle, and were sunk to the elbow in the green-black marble of the cliff. His knees were bent, his feet sunk into the stone as well. He hung there, the pressure of all his weight on his shoulders and legs. It must have been agonizing.

The crucified man laughed at me, his eyes glowing a shade of sickly green, and screamed, 'As if it will help you! Nothing! You're nothing!'

Pain laced his voice, making it shrill. Agony contorted the lines of his body, veins standing out sharply against straining muscle.

'Stars and stones,' I whispered. Creatures like this bear-thing did not have souls to gaze upon. That meant that regardless of appearances to the contrary, this thing was a mortal. It – no, *he* – was a human being. 'What the hell is this?'

The man screamed again, this time all rage and anguish, void of words. I lifted a hand and stepped forward, my first instinct to help him.

Before I got close, the ground began to shake. The cliff face rumbled and slits of seething orange light appeared, and then widened, until I faced the second set of eyes, eyes the size of subway tunnels, opening on the great marble cliff. I stumbled several steps back, and that cliff face proved to be exactly that – a face, cold and beautiful and harsh around that fiery gaze.

The quaking in the earth increased, and a voice louder than a Metallica concert spoke, the raw sense of the words, the vicious anger and hate behind them hitting me far more heavily than mere volume.

GET OUT.

The sheer force of presence behind that voice seized me and threw me violently back, away from the tortured man at the cliff-side and out of the soulgaze. The mental connection snapped like dry spaghetti, and the same force that had thrown my mind away from the soulgaze sent my physical body flying back through the air. I hit an old cardboard box filled with empty bottles and heard glass shattering beneath me. The heavy leather duster held, and no broken shards buried themselves in my back.

For a second or two, I just lay on my back, stunned. My thoughts were a hectic whirlpool I couldn't calm or control. I stared up at the city's light pollution against the low clouds, until some tiny voice in me started screaming that I was in danger. I shoved myself to my knees, just as the bear-creature smacked a trash can aside with one of its paws and started toward me.

My head was still ringing with the after-effects of the soul-gaze and the psychic assault that had broken the connection. I lifted my blasting rod, summoned up every bit of will I could scrape together out of the confusion, and spat a word that sent another lance of flame toward the bear-creature.

This time the blast didn't even slow it down. The set of

orange eyes flared with a sudden luminance, and my fire splashed against an unseen barrier, dispersing around the creature in sheets of scarlet. It let out a screaming roar and lumbered toward me.

I tried to get up, stumbled, and fell at the feet of the little old homeless guy, who leaned on his cane and stared at the creature. I had a dim impression of his features – Asian, a short white beard around his chin, heavy white eyebrows, and corrective glasses that made his eyes look the size of an owl's.

'Run, dammit!' I shouted at him. I tried to lead by example, but my balance was still whirling and I couldn't get off the ground.

The old man did not turn to run. He took off his glasses and pushed them at me. 'Hold, please.'

Then he took a deliberate step forward with his cane, placing himself between me and the bear-creature.

The creature hurled itself at him with a bellow, rearing up on its hindmost legs. It plunged down at the white-haired man, jaws gaping, and I couldn't do anything but watch it happen.

The little man took two steps to one side, pirouetting like a dancer. The end of his wooden cane lashed out and struck the creature's jaws with a crunching impact. Bits of broken yellow teeth flew from the creature's mouth. The little man continued his turn and evaded its claws by maybe an inch. He wound up behind the creature, and it turned to follow him, huge jaws snapping in rage.

The man darted back, staying just ahead of the thing's jaws, and in a blur of sudden light on metal he drew from his cane a long blade, the classic single-edged, chisel-pointed katana. The steel flashed at the creature's eyes, but it ducked low enough that the scything blade only whipped the top couple of inches from one of its ears.

The creature screamed, entirely out of proportion with the injury, a yowl that almost sounded human. It lurched back, shaking its head, a fine spray of blood sprinkling from its wounded ear.

At this point, I noticed three things.

One. The creature was paying me no attention whatsoever. Yippee ki yay. My head still spun wildly, and if it had come for me, I didn't think I could have done anything about it.

Two. The old man's sword was not reflecting light. It was emitting it. The water-patterned steel of the blade glowed with a steady silver flame that slowly grew brighter.

Three. I could feel the humming power of the sword, even from several yards away. It throbbed with a steady, deep strength, as quiet and unshakable as the earth itself.

In my entire life, I'd seen only one sword imbued with that much power.

But I knew that there were a couple more.

'Oi!' shouted the little old man, his English heavily accented. 'Ursiel! Let him go! You have no power here!'

The bear-creature – Ursiel, I presumed – focused its four-eyed gaze on the little man and did something unsettling. It spoke. Its voice came out quiet, smooth, melodious, words somehow slithering out through the bear's jaws and throat. 'Shiro. Look at yourself, little fool. You are an old man. You were at the peak of your strength when last we met. You cannot defeat me now.'

Shiro narrowed his eyes, his sword gripped in one hand, the length of wooden sheath held in the other. 'Did you come here to talk?'

Ursiel's head tilted to one side, and then the smooth voice murmured, 'No. Indeed I did not.'

It whirled, whipping its head toward me, and lunged. As it did, there was a rustle of cloth and then an old overcoat spun through the air, spreading like a fisherman's net. It fell over Ursiel's face, and the demon drew up short with a frustrated howl. It reached up and tore the coat from its head.

While it did, the tall young black man stepped between Ursiel and me. As I watched, he drew a long, heavy saber from the scabbard at his hip. The sword hummed with the same power as Shiro's, though in a slight variation, a different note within the same chord. Silver light flared from the blade's steel, and behind the demon, Shiro's blade answered it with more of its own radiance. The young man looked back at me, and I caught a glimpse of dark, intense eyes before he faced the demon, and said in a rumbling basso, words flavored with a thick Russian accent, 'Ursiel. Let him go. You have no power here.'

Ursiel hissed, the orange eyes blazing brighter by the moment. 'Sanya. Traitor. Do you really think any of us fears even one of the Three, in your pathetic hands? So be it. I will take you all.'

Sanya spread his empty hand to one side of his body in mocking invitation, and said nothing.

Ursiel roared and flew at Sanya. The big man extended the saber, and the weapon took Ursiel high on one shoulder, plunging through muscle and sinew. Sanya braced himself as the demon's body hit him, and though the impact drove his feet back across six inches of concrete, he held it up and away from me.

Shiro let out a ringing cry I wouldn't have believed a little old man could make, and Ursiel screamed, thrashing and flailing. Sanya shouted something in what sounded like Russian, and drove forward with both hands on the hilt of the impaling saber, overbearing Ursiel and sending the demon sprawling onto his back. Sanya followed, staying close, and I saw him throw his weight onto the demon as he twisted the hilt of the saber thrust through it.

He'd been too aggressive. Ursiel's paw hit him squarely upon one shoulder, and I heard the snap of breaking bone. The blow threw the young man away from the demon, and he rolled across the ground and into a wall, an explosive breath of pain forced from him as he hit.

Ursiel recovered its feet, tore the saber from its shoulder with a jerk of its jaws, and went after Sanya, but the white-haired old man menaced its flank, forcing it away from the wounded man and, incidentally, from me. For a few seconds, the old man and the demon circled each other. Then the demon lashed out at Shiro, a flurry of slashes with its claws.

The old man ducked them, retreating, his sword flickering and cutting. Twice, he left cuts on the demon's paws, but though it screamed in rage, it only seemed to grow less intimidated, more angry. The old man's breathing grew visibly labored.

'Age,' Ursiel's voice purred amidst its attack. 'Death comes, old man. Its hand is on your heart now. And your life has been spent in vain.'

'Let him go!' spat the old man between breaths.

Ursiel laughed again and the green pair of eyes glowed brighter. Another voice, this one not at all beautiful, the words twisted and snarling, said, 'Stupid preacher. Time to die like the Egyptian did.'

Shiro's expression changed, from stolid, controlled ferocity to something much sadder, much more resolved. He faced the demon for a moment, panting, and then nodded. 'So be it.'

The demon drove forward, and the old man gave ground,

slowly forced into a corner of the alley. He seemed to be doing pretty well, until one close swipe of the demon's claws caught the glowing silver blade near its hilt, and sent it spinning away. The old man gasped and pressed back against the corner, panting, holding his right hand against the left side of his chest.

'So it ends, Knight,' purred the smooth, demon-voice of Ursiel.

'*Hai*,' the old man agreed quietly. He looked up above him, at a fire escape platform ten feet off the ground.

A shadowed figure dropped over the rail of the platform, steel rasping as it did. There was a low thrum of power, a flash of silver, and the hiss of a blade cutting the air. The shadowy figure landed in a crouch beside the creature.

The demon Ursiel jerked once, body stiffening. There was a thump.

Then its body toppled slowly over to one side, leaving its monstrous head lying on the alley floor. The light died from its four eyes.

The third Knight rose away from the demon's corpse. Tall and broad-shouldered, his close-cut hair dark and feathered with silver, Michael Carpenter snapped the blade of his broad sword, *Amoracchius*, to one side, cleaning droplets of blood from it. He put it back into its sheath, staring down at the fallen demon, and shook his head.

Shiro straightened, his breathing quick but controlled, and went to Michael's side. He gripped the larger man's shoulder and said, 'It had to be done.'

Michael nodded. The smaller Knight recovered the second sword, cleaned the blade, and returned it to its wooden sheath.

Not far from me, the third Knight, the young Russian, pushed himself up from the ground. One of his arms dangled uselessly, but he offered the other to me. I took his hand and rose on wobbly legs.

'You are well?' he asked, his voice quiet.

'Peachy,' I responded, wobbling. He arched an eyebrow at me, then shrugged and went to recover his blade from the alley floor.

The after-effects of the soulgaze had finally begun to fade, and the simple shock and confusion began to give way to a redundant terror. I hadn't been careful enough. One of the bad guys had caught me off guard, and without intervention I would have been killed to death. It wouldn't have been anything quick and painless, either. Without Michael and his two companions, the demon Ursiel would have torn me limb from literal limb, and I wouldn't have been able to do a damned thing about it.

I had never encountered a psychic presence of such raw magnitude as upon the great stone cliff face. Not up close and personal like that, anyway. The first shot I'd taken at him had surprised and annoyed him, but he had been ready for the second blast and swatted aside my magical fire like an insect. Whatever Ursiel had been, he had been operating on a completely different order of magnitude than a mere punk of a mortal wizard like me. My psychic defenses aren't bad, but they had been crushed like a beer can under a bulldozer. That, more than anything, scared the snot out of me. I had tried my psychic strength against more than a few bad guys, and I had never felt so badly outclassed. Oh, I knew there were things out there stronger than me, sure.

But none of them had ever jumped me in a dark alley.

I shook, and found a wall to lean on until my head cleared

a little, and then walked stiffly over to Michael. Bits of broken glass fell from folds in my duster.

Michael glanced up as I came over to him. 'Harry,' he said.

'It isn't that I'm not glad to see you,' I said. 'But you couldn't have jumped down and beheaded the monster about two minutes sooner?'

Michael was usually pretty good about taking a joke. This time he didn't even smile. 'No. I'm sorry.'

I frowned at him. 'How did you find me? How did you know?'

'Good advice.'

Which could have been anything from spotting my car nearby to being told by an angelic chorus. The Knights of the Cross always seemed to turn up in bad places when they were badly needed. Sometimes coincidence seemed to go to incredible lengths to see to it that they were in the right place at the right time. I didn't think I wanted to know. I nodded at the demon's fallen body and said, 'What the hell was that thing?'

'He wasn't a thing, Harry,' Michael said. He continued staring down at the remains of the demon, and just about then they started shimmering. It only took a few seconds for the demon to dissolve into the form of the man I'd seen in the soulgaze – thin, grey-haired, dressed in rags. Except that in the soulgaze, his head hadn't been lying three feet away like that. I didn't think a severed head should have held an expression, but it did, one of absolute terror, his mouth locked open in a silent scream. The sigil I'd seen on the cliff face stood out on his forehead like a fresh scab, dark and ugly.

There was a glitter of orange-red light, the sigil vanished, and something clinked on the asphalt. A silver coin a little smaller than a quarter rolled away from the man's head, bounced against my foot, and then settled onto the ground. A second later, the body let out a hissing, sighing sound, and began to run with streaks of green-black goo. The body just deflated in on itself, noxious fumes and a spreading puddle of disgusting slime the only things remaining.

'That's it,' I said, staring down and trying to keep myself from visibly trembling. 'The weirdness has just gone off the end of my meter. I'm going home and going to bed.' I bent to recover the coin before the slime engulfed it.

The old man snapped his cane at my wrist, growling, 'No.'

It stung. I jerked my hand back, shaking my fingers, and scowled at him. 'Stars and stones, Michael, who *is* this guy?'

Michael drew a square of white cloth from his pocket and unfolded it. 'Shiro Yoshimo. He was my teacher when I became a Knight of the Cross.'

The old man grunted at me. I nodded at the wounded man and asked, 'How about him?'

The tall black man glanced up at me as the old Knight began examining his arm. He looked me up and down without any sign of approval, glowered, and said, 'Sanya.'

'The newest of our Order,' Michael added. He shook out the cloth, revealing two pairs of crosses embroidered in silver thread upon it. Michael knelt down and picked up the coin through the cloth, turned it over, then folded the cloth completely around the silver.

I frowned down at the coin as he did. One side bore some ancient portrait, maybe of a man's profile. The opposite side had some other design that was hidden under a stain in the shape of a rune – the one I'd seen on the demon Ursiel's forehead.

'What's that?' I asked.

'Shiro was protecting you,' Michael said, rather than answering the question. Michael looked over at Shiro, who stood with the towering Sanya, and asked, 'How is he?'

'Broken arm,' the old man reported. 'We should get off the street.'

'Agreed,' rumbled Sanya. The older Knight fashioned a makeshift sling from the shredded overcoat, and the tall young man slipped his arm into it without a sound of complaint.

'You'd better come with us, Harry,' Michael said. 'Father Forthill can get you a cot.'

'Whoa, whoa,' I said. 'You never answered my question. *What* was *that*?'

Michael frowned at me and said, 'It's a long story, and there's little time.'

I folded my arms. 'Make time. I'm not going anywhere until I know what the hell is going on here.'

The little old Knight snorted and said, 'Hell. That is what is going on.' He opened his hand to me and said, 'Please give them back.'

I stared at him for a second, until I remembered his spectacles. I handed them to him, and he put them on, making his eyes goggle out hugely again.

'Wait a minute,' I said to Michael. 'This thing was one of the Fallen?'

Michael nodded, and a chill went through me.

'That's impossible,' I said. 'The Fallen can't do . . . things like *that*.' I gestured at the puddle of slime. 'They aren't allowed.'

'Some are,' Michael said, his voice quiet. 'Please believe me. You are in great danger. I know what you've been hired to find, and so do they.'

Shiro stalked down to the end of the alley and swept his gaze around. 'Oi. Michael, we must go.'

'If he will not come, he will not come,' Sanya said. He glared at me, then followed Shiro.

'Michael,' I began.

'Listen to me,' Michael said. He held up the folded white cloth. 'There are more where this one came from, Harry. Twenty-nine of them. And we think they're after you.'

7

I followed Michael's white pickup truck in the Blue Beetle to Saint Mary of the Angels Cathedral. It's a big, big church, a city landmark. If there's anything you like in the way of gothic architecture, you can find it somewhere on Saint Mary's. We parked near the back of the cathedral, and went to the delivery entrance, a plain oak door framed by lovingly tended rose vines.

Michael knocked at the door, and I heard the sound of multiple bolts being undone before the door opened.

Father Anthony Forthill opened the door. He was in his late fifties, balding, and carried a comfortable weight of years. He wore black slacks and a black shirt, the stark white square of his clerical collar sharply delineated. He was taller than Shiro, but a lot shorter than everyone else there, and beneath his glasses his eyes looked strained.

'Success?' he asked Michael.

'In part,' Michael responded. He held up the folded cloth and said, 'Put this in the cask, please. And we'll need to splint an arm.'

Forthill winced, and accepted the folded cloth with the kind of ginger reverence paid only to explosives and samples of lethal viruses. 'Right away. Good evening, Mister Dresden. Come in, all of you.'

'Father,' I answered. 'You look like my day so far.'

Forthill tried to smile at me, then padded away down a long hallway. Michael led us deeper into the church, up a flight of stairs to a storage room whose boxes had been stacked to the ceiling to make room for a number of folding cots, blocking the view of any windows. A mismatched pair of old lamps lit the room in soft gold.

'I'll get food, something to drink,' Michael said quietly. He headed back out of the room. 'And I need to call Charity. Sanya, you'd better sit down until we can see to your arm.'

'I'll be fine,' Sanya said. 'I will help with food.'

Shiro snorted and said, 'Sit, boy.' He headed for the door, catching up to Michael, and said, 'Call your wife. I will do the rest.' The two left together, their voices lowering to bare murmurs as they entered the hall.

Sanya glowered at the door for a moment and then settled down on one of the bunks. He looked around at the room for a moment, and then said, 'You use the forces of magic, I take it.'

I folded my arms and leaned against the wall. 'What gave it away?'

He bared his teeth, white against his dark skin. 'How long have you been a Wiccan?'

'A what?'

'A pagan. A witch.'

'I'm not a witch,' I said, glancing out the door. 'I'm a wizard.'

Sanya frowned. 'What is the difference?'

'Wizard has a Z.'

He looked at me blankly.

'No one appreciates me,' I muttered. 'Wicca is a religion. It's a little more fluid than most, but it's still a religion.'

'And?'

'And I'm not really big on religion. I do magic, sure, but it's like . . . being a mechanic. Or an engineer. There are forces that behave a certain way. If you know what you're doing, you can get them to work for you, and you don't really need a god or a goddess or a whatever to get involved.'

Sanya's expression became surprised. 'You are not a religious man, then.'

'I wouldn't burden any decent system of faith by participating in it.'

The tall Russian regarded me for a moment and then nodded slowly. 'I feel the same way.'

I felt my eyebrow arch, Spock-like. 'That's a joke, right?'

He shook his head. 'It is not. I have been an atheist since childhood.'

'You've got to be kidding me. You're a Knight of the Cross.'

'*Da*,' he said.

'So if you're not religious, you risk your life to help other people because . . . ?'

'Because it must be done,' he answered without hesitation. 'For the good of the people, some must place themselves in harm's way. Some must pledge their courage and their lives to protect the community.'

'Just a minute,' I said. 'You became a Knight of the Cross because you were a *communist*?'

Sanya's face twisted with revulsion. 'Certainly not. Trotsky. Very different.'

I stopped myself from bursting out in laughter. But it was a near thing. 'How did you get your sword?'

He moved his good hand to rest on the hilt of the blade, where it lay beside him on the cot. '*Esperacchius*. Michael gave it to me.'

'Since when has Michael gone running off to Russia?'

'Not that Michael,' Sanya said. He pointed a finger up. 'That Michael.'

I stared at him for a minute and then said, 'So. You get handed a holy sword by an archangel, told to go fight the forces of evil, and you somehow remain an atheist. Is that what you're saying?'

Sanya's scowl returned.

'Doesn't that strike you as monumentally stupid?'

His glare darkened for maybe a minute before he took a deep breath and nodded. 'Perhaps some could argue that I am agnostic.'

'*Agnostic?*'

'One who does not commit himself to the certain belief in a divine power,' he said.

'I know what it means,' I said. 'What shocks me is that you think it applies to you. You've *met* more than one divine power. Hell, one of them broke your arm not half an hour ago.'

'Many things can break an arm. You yourself said that you do not need a god or goddess to define your beliefs about the supernatural.'

'Yeah, but I'm not agnostic. Just nonpartisan. Theological Switzerland, that's me.'

Sanya said, 'Semantics. I do not understand your point.'

I took a deep breath, still holding back the threat of giggles, and said, 'Sanya. My point is that you have got to be more than a little thick to stand where you are, having seen what you've seen, and claim that you aren't sure whether or not there's a God.'

He lifted his chin and said, 'Not necessarily. It is possible that I am mad, and all of this is a hallucination.'

That's when I started laughing. I just couldn't help it. I was too tired and too stressed to do anything else. I laughed and enjoyed it thoroughly while Sanya sat on his cot and scowled at me, careful not to move his wounded arm.

Shiro appeared at the door, bearing a platter of sandwiches and deli vegetables. He blinked through his owlish glasses at Sanya and then at me. He said something to Sanya in what I took to be Russian. The younger Knight transferred his scowl to Shiro, but nodded his head in a gesture deep enough to be part bow, before he rose, claimed two sandwiches in one large hand, and walked out.

Shiro waited until Sanya was gone before he set the platter down on a card table. My stomach went berserk at the sight of the sandwiches. Heavy exertion coupled with insane fear does that to me. Shiro gestured at the plate and pulled up a couple of folding chairs. I sat down, nabbed a sandwich of my own, and started eating. Turkey and cheese. Heaven.

The old Knight took a sandwich of his own, and ate with what appeared to be a similar appetite. We munched for a while in contented silence before he said, 'Sanya told you about his beliefs.'

I felt the corners of my mouth start to twinge as another smile threatened. 'Yeah.'

Shiro let out a pleased snort. 'Sanya is a good man.'

'I just don't get why he'd be recruited as a Knight of the Cross.'

Shiro looked at me over the glasses, chewing. After a while, he said, 'Man sees faces. Sees skin. Flags. Membership lists. Files.' He took another large bite, ate it, and said, 'God sees hearts.'

'If you say so,' I said.

He didn't answer. Right about the time I finished my sandwich, Shiro said, 'You are looking for the Shroud.'

'That's confidential,' I said.

'If you say so,' he said, using my own inflection on the words. The wrinkles at the corners of his eyes deepened. 'Why?'

'Why what?'

'Why are you looking for it?' he asked, chewing.

'If I am – and I'm not saying that I am – I'm doing it because I've been hired to look for it.'

'Your job,' he said.

'Yeah.'

'You do it for money,' he said.

'Yeah.'

'Hmph,' he said, and pushed his glasses up with his pinky. 'Do you love money then, Mister Dresden?'

I picked up a napkin from one side of the platter, and wiped my mouth. 'I used to think I loved it. But now I realize that it's just dependency.'

Shiro let out an explosive bark of laughter, and rose, chortling. 'Sandwich okay?'

'Super.'

Michael came in a few minutes later, his face troubled. There wasn't a clock in the room, but it had to have been well after midnight. I supposed if I had called Charity Carpenter that late, I'd be troubled after the conversation, too. She was ferocious where her husband's safety was concerned – especially when she heard that I was around. Okay, admittedly Michael had gotten pretty thoroughly battered whenever he came along on a case with me, but all the same I didn't think it was fair of her. It wasn't like I did it on purpose.

'Charity wasn't happy?' I asked.

Michael shook his head. 'She's worried. Is there a sandwich left?'

There were a couple. Michael took one and I took a second one, just to keep him company. While we ate, Shiro got out his sword and a cleaning kit, and started wiping down the blade with a soft cloth and some kind of oil.

'Harry,' Michael said finally. 'I have to ask you for something. It's very difficult. And it's something that under normal circumstances I wouldn't even consider doing.'

'Name it,' I said between chews. At the time, I meant it literally. Michael had risked his life for me more than once. His family had been endangered the last time around, and I knew him well enough to know that he wouldn't ask something unreasonable. 'Just name it. I owe you.'

Michael nodded. Then looked at me steadily and said, 'Get out of this business, Harry. Get out of town for a few days. Or stay home. But get out of it, please.'

I blinked at him. 'You mean, you don't want my help?'

'I want your safety,' Michael said. 'You are in great danger.'

'You're kidding me,' I said. 'Michael, I know how to handle myself. You should know that by now.'

'Handle yourself,' Michael said. 'Like you did tonight? Harry, if we hadn't been there—'

'What?' I snapped. 'I'd have been dead. It isn't like it isn't going to happen sooner or later. There are enough bad guys after me that one of them is eventually going to get lucky. So what else is new.'

'You don't understand,' Michael said.

'I understand all right,' I said. 'One more wacky B-horror-movie reject tried to kill me. It's happened before. It'll probably happen again.'

Shiro said, without looking up from his sword, 'Ursiel did not come to kill you, Mister Dresden.'

I considered that in another pregnant silence. The lamps buzzed a little. Shiro's cleaning cloth whispered over the steel of his sword.

I watched Michael's face and asked, 'Why was he there then? I'd have put down money that it was a demon, but it was just a shapechange. There was a mortal inside it. Who was he?'

Michael's gaze never wavered. 'His name was Rasmussen. Ursiel took him in eighteen forty-nine, on his way to California.'

'I saw him, Michael. I looked in his eyes.'

Michael winced. 'I didn't know that.'

'He was a prisoner in his own soul, Michael. Something was holding him. Something big. Ursiel, I guess. He's one of the Fallen, isn't he?'

Michael nodded.

'How the hell does that happen? I thought the Fallen aren't allowed to take away free will.'

'They aren't,' Michael said. 'But they are allowed to tempt. And the Denarians have more to offer than most.'

'Denarians?' I asked.

'The Order of the Blackened Denarius,' Michael said. 'They see an opportunity in this matter. A chance to do great harm.'

'Silver coins.' I took a deep breath. 'Like the one you wrapped up in blessed cloth. Thirty pieces of silver, eh?'

He nodded. 'Whoever touches the coins is tainted by the Fallen within. Tempted. Given power. The Fallen leads the mortal deeper and deeper into its influence. Never forcing them. Just offering. Until eventually they have surrendered enough of themselves and—'

'The thing gets control of them,' I finished.

Michael nodded. 'Like Rasmussen. We try to help them. Sometimes the person realizes what is happening. Wants to escape their influence. When we face them, we try to wear the demon down. Give the person taken the chance to escape.'

'That's why you kept talking to it. Until its voice changed. But Rasmussen didn't want to be free, did he?'

Michael shook his head.

'Believe it or not, Michael, I've been tempted once or twice. I can handle it.'

'No,' Michael said. 'You can't. Against the Denarians, few mortals can. The Fallen know our weaknesses. Our flaws. How to undermine. Even warned and aware of them, they have destroyed men and women for thousands of years.'

'I said I'll be fine,' I growled.

Shiro grunted. 'Pride before fall.'

I gave him a sour glance.

Michael leaned forward and said, 'Harry, please. I know that your life has not been an easy one. You're a good man. But you are as vulnerable as anyone. These enemies don't want you dead.' He looked down at his hands. 'They want *you*.'

Which scared me. Really scared me. Maybe because it seemed to disturb Michael so much, and very little disturbs him. Maybe because I had seen Rasmussen, and would always be able to see him there, trapped, wildly laughing.

Or maybe it was because part of me wondered if it would be so impossible to find a way to use the power the coin obviously offered. If it had made some random schmuck on the way to pan for gold into a killing machine that it took all three Knights of the Cross to handle, what could someone like me do with it?

Beat the living snot out of Duke Paolo Ortega. That's for sure.

I blinked, refocusing my eyes. Michael watched me, his expression pained, and I knew that he'd guessed at my thoughts. I closed my eyes, shame making my stomach uneasy.

'You're in danger, Harry,' Michael said. 'Leave the case alone.'

'If I was in so much danger,' I responded, 'why did Father Vincent come and hire me?'

'Forthill asked him not to,' Michael said. 'Father Vincent . . . disagrees with Forthill on how supernatural matters are to be handled.'

I stood up and said, 'Michael, I'm tired. I'm really damned tired.'

'Harry,' Michael chided me.

'Darned,' I mumbled. 'Darned tired. Darn me unto heck.' I headed for the door and said, 'I'm heading home to get some sleep. I'll think about it.'

Michael stood up, and Shiro with him, both of them facing me. 'Harry,' Michael said. 'You are my friend. You've saved my life. I've named a child for you. But stay out of this business. For my sake, if not for your own.'

'And if I don't?' I asked.

'Then I'll have to protect you from yourself. In the name of God, Harry, please don't push this.'

I turned and left without saying good-bye.

In this corner, one missing Shroud, one impossibly and thoroughly dead corpse, one dedicated and deadly vampire warlord, three holy knights, twenty-nine fallen angels, and a partridge in a pear tree.

And in the opposite corner, one tired, bruised, underpaid professional wizard, threatened by his allies and about to get dumped by his would-be girlfriend for John Q. Humdrum.

Oh, yeah.

Definitely bedtime.

8

I fumed and brooded all the way back to my apartment, the Beetle's engine sputtering nervously the whole time. Mister was sitting at the top of the steps, and let out a plaintive meow as I shut and locked up my car. Though I kept my blasting rod and shield bracelet ready in case any vanilla goons were waiting around with more silenced guns, I was fairly confident no preternasties were hanging around in ambush. Mister tended to make lots of noise and then leave whenever supernatural danger was around.

Which just goes to show that my cat has considerably more sense than me.

Mister slammed his shoulder against my legs, and didn't quite manage to trip me into falling down the stairs. I didn't waste any time getting inside and locked up behind me.

I lit a candle, got out some cat food and fresh water for Mister's bowls, and spent a couple of minutes pacing back and forth. I glanced at my bed and wrote it off as a useless idea. I was too worked up to sleep, even tired as I was. I was already chin deep in alligators and sinking fast.

'Right, then, Harry,' I mumbled. 'Might as well do some work.'

I grabbed a heavy, warm robe off its hook, shoved aside one of my rugs, and opened the trapdoor leading down to the subbasement. A folding ladder-staircase led down to the damp stone chamber beneath, where I kept my lab, and I padded down it, my robe's hem dragging against the wooden steps.

I started lighting candles. My lab, barring a brief bout of insanity, generally reflects the state of my own mind – cluttered, messy, unorganized, but basically functional. The room isn't large. Three worktables line three of the walls in a U shape, and a fourth table runs down the center of the U, leaving a narrow walkway around it. Wire utility shelves line the walls above the tables. Piled on the shelves and tables are a vast array of magical ingredients, plus that sort of miscellaneous domestic clutter that in households of more substance always winds up in a big drawer in the kitchen. Books, notebooks, journals, and papers line the shelves, together with containers and boxes and pouches full of all sorts of herbs, roots, and magical ingredients, from a bottle of snake hisses to a vial of milk-thistle extract.

At the far end of the room there was a patch of floor kept completely clear of all clutter. A copper ring set into the stone of the floor, my summoning circle, resided there. Experience had shown me that you never can tell when you might need a ritual circle to defend yourself from magical attack, or for its other most obvious use – keeping a denizen of the Nevernever a temporary prisoner.

One of the shelves had less on it than the others. At either end rested a candleholder, long since over-run with many colors of melted wax until they were nothing but mounds, like a honeybee Vesuvius. Books, mostly paperback romances, and various small and feminine articles took up the rest of the shelf, but for where a bleached human skull sat in the middle. I picked up a pencil and rapped it against the shelf. 'Bob. Bob, wake up. Work to be done.'

Twin points of orange and gold light kindled in the shadows of the skull's eye sockets, and grew brighter as I went about the room lighting half a dozen candles and a kerosene lamp. The skull rattled a little, and then said, 'It's only a few hours from dawn, and you're just starting up? What gives?'

I started getting out beakers and vials and a small alcohol burner. 'More trouble,' I said. 'It's been one hell of a day.' I told Bob the Skull about the television studio, the vampire's challenge, the hit man, the missing Shroud, and the plague-filled corpse.

'Wow. You don't do things halfway, do you, Harry?'

'Advise now; critique later. I'm going to look into things and whip up a potion or two, and you're going to help.'

'Right,' Bob said. 'Where do you want to start?'

'With Ortega. Where is my copy of the Accords?'

'Cardboard box.' Bob said. 'Third shelf, on the bottom row, behind the pickling jars.'

I found the box and pawed through it until I had found a vellum scroll tied shut with a white ribbon. I opened it and peered down at the handwritten calligraphy. It started off with the word *Insomuch*, and the syntax got more opaque from there.

'I can't make heads or tails of this,' I said. 'Where's the section about duels?'

'Fifth paragraph from the end. You want the Cliff's Notes version?'

I rolled the scroll shut again. 'Hit me.'

'It's based on Code Duello,' Bob said. 'Well, technically it's based on much older rules that eventually inspired the Code Duello, but that's just chickens and eggs. Ortega is the challenger, and you're the challenged.'

'I know that. I get to pick the weapons and the ground, right?'

'Wrong,' Bob said. 'You pick the weapons, but he gets to choose the time and location.'

'Damn,' I muttered. 'I was going to take high noon out in a park somewhere. But I guess I can just say that we'll duel with magic.'

'If it's one of the available choices. It almost always is.'

'Who decides?'

'The vampires and the Council will pick from a list of neutral emissaries. The emissary decides.'

I nodded. 'So if I don't have it as an option I'm screwed, right? I mean, magic, wizard, kind of my bag.'

Bob said. 'Yeah, but be careful. It's got to be a weapon that he can use. If you pick one he can't, he can refuse it, and force you to take your second choice.'

'Meaning what?'

'Meaning that regardless of what happens, if he doesn't want to fight you in magic, he won't have to. Ortega didn't get to be a warlord without thinking things through, Harry. Odds are that he has a good idea what you can do and has planned accordingly. What do you know about him?'

'Not much. Presumably he's tough.'

Bob's eyelights stared at me for a minute. 'Well, Napoléon, I'm sure he'll never overcome that kind of tactical genius.'

I flicked my pencil at the skull in annoyance. It bounced off a nose hole. 'Get to the point.'

'The point is that you'd be better off taking something you can predict.'

'I'm better off not fighting to begin with,' I said. 'Do I need to get a second?'

'You both do,' Bob said. 'The seconds will work out the terms of the duel. His should be getting in touch with yours at some point.'

'Uh. I don't have one.'

Bob's skull turned a bit on its shelf and banged its forehead gently into the brick wall a few times. 'Then get one, dolt. Obviously.'

I got another pencil and a pad of yellow lined paper and wrote *To do* across the top, and *Ask Michael about duel* underneath it. 'Okay. And I want you to find out whatever you can about Ortega before dawn.'

'Check,' Bob said. 'I have your permission to come out?'

'Not yet. There's more.'

Bob's eyelights rolled. 'Of course there's more. *My* job sucks.'

I got out a jug of distilled water and a can of Coke. I opened the can, took a sip, and said, 'That corpse Murphy showed me. Plague curse?'

'Probably,' Bob agreed. 'But if it was really that many diseases, it was a big one.'

'How big?'

'Bigger than that spell the Shadowman was using to tear hearts out a few years ago.'

I whistled. 'And he was running it off of thunderstorms and ceremonial rites, too. What would it take to power a curse that strong?'

'Curses aren't really my thing,' Bob hedged. 'But a lot. Like maybe tapping into a sorcerous ley line, or a human sacrifice.'

I sipped more Coke, and shook my head. 'Someone is playing some serious hardball then.'

Bob mused, 'Maybe the Wardens used it to get nasty on a Red Court agent.'

'They wouldn't,' I said. 'They wouldn't use magic like that. Even if technically it was the diseases that killed the guy, it's too damn close to breaking the First Law.'

'Who else would have that kind of power?' Bob asked me.

I turned to a fresh page and sketched out a rough version of the tattoo on the corpse. I held it up to show it to Bob. 'Someone who didn't like this, maybe.'

'Eye of Thoth,' Bob supplied. 'That the tattoo on the corpse?'

'Yeah. Was this guy in someone's secret club?'

'Maybe. The eye is a pretty popular occult symbol though, so you can't rule out the possibility that he was an independent.'

'Okay,' I said. 'So who uses it?'

'Plenty of groups. Brotherhoods connected to the White Council, historic societies, a couple of fringe groups of occult scholars, personality cults, television psychics, comic book heroes—'

'I get the point,' I said. I turned to a fresh page and from razor-sharp memory sketched out the symbol I'd seen on the demon Ursiel's forehead. 'Do you recognize this?'

Bob's eyelights widened. 'Are you insane? Harry, tear that paper up. Burn it.'

I frowned. 'Bob, wait a minute—'

'Do it now!'

The skull's voice was frightened, and I get nervous when Bob gets frightened. Not much can scare Bob out of his usual wiseass-commentator state of mind. I tore up the paper. 'I guess you recognize it.'

'Yeah. And I'm not having anything to do with that bunch.'

'I didn't hear that, Bob. I need information on them. They're in town, they've taken a shot at me, and I'm betting they're after the Shroud.'

'Let them have it,' Bob said. 'Seriously. You've got no idea the kind of power this group has.'

'Fallen, I know,' I said. 'Order of the Blackened Denarius. But they have to play by the rules, right?'

'Harry, it isn't just the Fallen. The people they've taken are nearly as bad. They're assassins, poisoners, warriors, sorcerers—'

'Sorcerers?'

'The coins make them effectively immortal. Some of the Order have had a thousand years to practice, and maybe more. That much time, even modest talents can grow teeth. Never mind everything experience would have taught them, everything they could have found to make themselves stronger over the years. Even without infernal superpowers, they'd be badass.'

I frowned, and tore the bits of paper into smaller bits. 'Badass enough to manage that curse?'

'There's no question that they'd have the skill. Maybe enough that they wouldn't need as big a power source.'

'Great,' I said, and rubbed at my eyes. 'All right, then. Big-leaguers all around. I want you to track down the Shroud.'

'No can do,' Bob said.

'Give me a break. How many pieces of two-thousand-year-old linen are in town?'

'That's not the point, Harry. The Shroud is . . .' Bob seemed to struggle to find words. 'It doesn't exist on the same wavelength as me. It's out of my jurisdiction.'

'What are you talking about?'

'I'm a spirit of intellect, Harry. Of reason, logic. The Shroud isn't about logic. It's an artifact of faith.'

'What?' I demanded. 'That doesn't make any sense.'

'You don't know everything, Harry,' Bob said. 'You don't even know a lot. I can't touch this. I can't come anywhere near it. And if I even try, I'll be crossing boundaries I shouldn't. I'm not going up against angels, Dresden, Fallen, or otherwise.'

I sighed, and lifted my hands. 'Fine, fine. Is there someone I can talk to?'

Bob was quiet for a moment before he said, 'Maybe. Ulsharavas.'

'Ulsha-who?'

'Ulsharavas. She's an ally of the *loa*, an oracle spirit. There's details about halfway through your copy of *Dumont's Guide to Divinationators*.'

'How are her prices?'

'Reasonable,' Bob said. 'You've got everything you need for the calling. She isn't usually malicious.'

'Isn't usually?'

'The *loa* are basically good guys, but they all have their darker aspects, too. Ulsharavas is a pretty gentle guide, but she's been harsh before. Don't let your guard down.'

'I won't,' I said, and frowned. 'One more thing. Swing by Marcone's place and see if there's anything interesting there. You don't have to go all David Niven; just take a look around.'

'You think Marcone's involved in this one?'

'His thugs already took a poke at me. I might as well find

out whatever I can. I give you permission to leave in pursuit of that information, Bob. Get back before dawn. Oh, do we still have that recipe for the antivenom to vampire spit?'

A cloud of orange lights flowed out of the skull, across the table, and then up the stairs. Bob's voice, oddly modulated, floated back to me. 'Red notebook. Don't forget to light the wardflame while I'm gone.'

'Yeah, yeah,' I muttered. I gave Bob a minute to clear my wards, then got down a three-candle holder with green, yellow, and red candles on it. I lit the green one and set the candle-holder aside. I got out *Dumont's Guide* and read over the entry for Ulsharavas. It looked pretty simple, though you couldn't be too careful whenever you called something in from the Nevernever.

I took a couple of minutes to gather what I'd need. The oracle spirit couldn't put together a body for herself, not even a nebulous cloud of light, like Bob could. She required a homunculus to manifest in the mortal world. Dumont recommended a newly dead corpse, but as the only one I was likely to find was my own, I needed a substitute. I found it in another box and plopped it down in the center of my summoning circle.

I added a cup of whiskey and a freshly opened tin of Prince Albert's chewing tobacco to the circle, the required down payment to convince Ulsharavas to show up. It was the last of my whiskey and the last of the tins of tobacco, so I added *Get more scotch and Prince Albert in a can* to my to-do list, and stuck it in my pocket.

I spent a couple of minutes sweeping the floor around the circle, so that I wouldn't kick a stray hair or bit of paper across the circle and flub it up. After a brief deliberation I chalked down another circle outside the copper one. Then I took a moment to go over the guide a last time, and to clear my head of distractions.

I took a deep breath and gathered in my strength. Then I focused, reached down, and touched the copper circle, willing a tiny jolt of power into it. The summoning circle closed. I felt it as a tingling prickle on the back of my neck and a faint warmth on the skin of my face. I repeated the process with the chalk circle, adding a second layer, and then knelt down by the circle, lifting both hands palms-up.

'Ulsharavas,' I murmured, willing energy into the words. My voice shook oddly, skittering around tones in what seemed a random fashion. 'Ulsharavas. Ulsharavas. One lost in ignorance seeks you. One darkened by the lack of knowledge seeks your light. Come, guardian of memory, sentinel of the yet to come. Accept this offering and join me here.'

At the conclusion of the ritual words, I released the power I'd been holding, sending it coursing from me into the circle, and through it to seek out the oracle spirit in the Nevernever.

The response came immediately. A sudden swirl of light appeared within the copper circle, and briefly made the barrier around it visible as a curved plane of blue sparkles. The light drizzled down over the homunculus, and a moment later it twitched, then sat up.

'Welcome, oracle,' I said. 'Bob the Skull thought you might be of some help.'

The homunculus sat up and stretched out pudgy arms. Then it blinked, looked at its arms, and rose to stare down at itself. It looked up at me with one eyebrow raised, and asked, in a tiny voice, 'A Cabbage Patch doll? You expect me to help you while wearing *this*?'

It was a cute doll. Blonde ringlets fell to her plush shoulders, and she wore a pink-and-blue calico dress, complete with matching ribbons and little black shoes. 'Uh, yeah. Sorry,' I said. 'I didn't have anything else with two arms and two legs, and I'm pressed for time.'

Ulsharavas the Cabbage Patch doll sighed and sat down in the circle, legs straight out like a teddy bear's. She struggled to pick up the comparatively large cup of whiskey, and drank it down. It looked like she was taking a pull from a rain barrel, but she downed the whiskey in one shot. I don't know where it went, given that the doll didn't actually have a mouth or a stomach, but none of it spilled onto the floor. That done, she thrust a tiny fist into the tobacco and stuffed a wad of it into her mouth.

'So,' she said, between chews. 'You want to know about the Shroud, and the people who stole it.'

I lifted my eyebrows. 'Uh. Yeah, actually. You're pretty good.'

'There are two problems.'

I frowned. 'Okay. What are they?'

Ulsharavas peered at me and said, 'First. I don't work for *bokkor*.'

'I'm not a *bokkor*,' I protested.

'You aren't a *boungun*. You aren't a *mambo*. That makes you a sorcerer.'

'Wizard,' I said. 'I'm with the White Council.'

The doll tilted her head. 'You're stained,' she said. 'I can feel black magic on you.'

'It's a long story,' I said. 'But mostly it isn't mine.'

'Some of it is.'

I frowned at the doll and then nodded. 'Yeah. I've made a bad call or two.'

'But honest,' Ulsharavas noted. 'Well enough. Second is my price.'

'What did you have in mind?'

The doll spat to one side, flecks of tobacco landing on the floor. 'An honest answer to one question. Answer me and I will tell you what you seek.'

'Yeah, right,' I said. 'You could just ask me for my Name. I've heard that one before.'

'I didn't say you'd have to answer in full,' the doll said. 'I certainly do not wish to threaten you. But what you would answer, you must answer honestly.'

I thought about it for a minute before I said, 'All right. Done.'

Ulsharavas scooped up more tobacco and started chomping. 'Answer only this. Why do you do what you do?'

I blinked at her. 'You mean tonight?'

'I mean always,' she answered. 'Why are you a wizard? Why do you present yourself openly? Why do you help other mortals as you do?'

'Uh,' I said. I stood up and paced over to my table. 'What else would I do?'

'Precisely,' the doll said, and spat. 'You could be doing many other things. You could be seeking a purpose in life in other careers. You could be sequestered and studying. You could be using your skills for material gain and living in wealth. Even in your profession as an investigator, you could do more to avoid confrontation than you do. But instead you consign yourself to a poor home, a dingy office, and the danger of facing all manner of mortal and supernatural foe. Why?'

I leaned back against my table, folded my arms, and frowned at the doll. 'What the hell kind of question is that?'

'An important one,' she said. 'And one that you agreed to answer honestly.'

'Well,' I said. 'I guess I wanted to do something to help people. Something I was good at.'

'Is that why?' she asked.

I chewed over the thought for a moment. Why *had* I started doing this stuff? I mean, it seemed like every few months I was running up against situations that had the potential to horribly kill me. Most wizards never had the kind of problems I did. They stayed at home, minded their own business, and generally speaking went on about their lives. They did not challenge other supernatural forces. They didn't declare themselves to the public at large. They didn't get into trouble for sticking their noses in other people's business, whether or not they'd been paid to do so. They didn't start wars, get challenged to duels with vampire patriots, or get the windows shot out of their cars.

So why did I do it? Was it some kind of masochistic death wish? Maybe a psychological dysfunction of some sort?

Why?

'I don't know,' I said, finally. 'I guess I never thought about it all that much.'

The doll watched me with unnerving intensity for a full minute before nodding. 'Don't you think you should?'

I scowled down at my shoes, and didn't answer.

Ulsharavas took one last fistful of tobacco, and sat back down in her original position, settling her calico dress primly about her. 'The Shroud and the thieves you seek have rented a small vessel docked in the harbor. It is a pleasure craft called the *Etranger*.'

I nodded and exhaled through my nose. 'All right then. Thank you for your help.'

She lifted a tiny hand. 'One thing more, wizard. You must know why the Knights of the White God wish you to stay away from the Shroud.'

I arched an eyebrow. 'Why?'

'They received part of a prophecy. A prophecy that told them that should you seek the Shroud, you will most assuredly perish.'

'Only part of a prophecy?' I asked.

'Yes. Their Adversary concealed some of it from them.'

I shook my head. 'Why are you telling me this?'

'Because,' Ulsharavas said. 'You must hear the second half of the prophecy in order to restore the balance.'

'Uh. Okay.'

The doll nodded and fixed me with that unsettling, unblinking stare. 'Should you seek the Shroud, Harry Dresden, you will most assuredly perish.'

'All right,' I said. 'So what happens if I don't?'

The doll lay down on her back, and wisps of light began flowing back out of her, back from whence Ulsharavas had come. Her voice came to me quietly, as if from a great distance. 'If you do not, they all die. And this city with them.'

9

I hate cryptic warnings. I know, the whole cryptic-remark concept is part and parcel of the wizard gig, but it doesn't suit my style. I mean, what *good* is a warning like that? All three Knights and the population of Chicago would die if I didn't get involved – and my number would be up if I did. That sounded like the worst kind of self-fulfilling crap.

There's a case to be made for prophecy; don't get me wrong. Mortals, even wizards, all exist at a finite point in the flow of time. Or, to make it simple, if time is a river, then you and I are like pebbles in it. We exist in one spot at a time, occasionally jostled back and forth by the currents. Spirits don't always have the same kind of existence. Some of them are more like a long thread than a stone – their presence tenuous, but rippling upstream and down as a part of their existence, experiencing more of the stream than the pebble.

That's how oracle spirits know about the future and the past. They're living in them both at the same time they're delivering mysterious messages to you. That's why they only give brief warnings, or mysterious dreams or prophetic knock-knock jokes, or however they drop their clues. If they tell you too much, it will change the future that they're experiencing, so they have to give out the advice with a light touch.

I know. It makes my head hurt too.

I don't put much stock in prophecy. As extensive and aware as these spirits might be, they aren't all-knowing. And as nutty as people are, I don't buy that any spirit is going to be able to keep an absolute lock on every possible temporal outcome.

Maybe-genuine prophecies aside, I could hardly drop the case now. In the first place, I'd been paid up front, and I didn't have the kind of financial breathing space I would need to be able to turn down the money and pay my bills at the same time.

In the second place, the risk of imminent death just didn't hit me the same way it used to. It wasn't that it didn't scare me. It did, in that kind of horrible, uncertain way that left me with nothing to focus my fears upon. But I've beaten risks before. I could do it again.

You want to know another reason I didn't back off? I don't like getting pushed around. I don't like threats. As well-intentioned and polite and caring as Michael's threat had been, it still made me want to punch someone in the nose. The oracle's prophecy had been another threat, of sorts, and I don't let spirits from the Nevernever determine what I'm going to do, either.

Finally, if the prophecy was right, Michael and his brother Knights could be in danger, and they had saved my skinny wizard's ass not long ago. I could help them. They might be heaven-on-wheels when it came to taking on bad guys in a fight, but they weren't investigators. They couldn't run these thieves down the way I could. It was just a question of making them see reason.

Once I'd convinced them that the prophecy they'd received wasn't wholly correct, everything would be fine.

Yeah, right.

I shoved those thoughts aside, and checked the clock. I wanted to move on Ulsharavas's tip as soon as possible, but I was beat and likely to make mistakes. With all the bad guys running around town, there was no sense in going out there into the dark, exhausted and unprepared. I'd wait for the potions to be ready and Bob to come back from his mission, at least. Sunlight would cut down on the risk as well, since Red Court vampires got incinerated by it – and I doubted these Denarian fruitcakes would get along with it either.

Thus prioritized, I checked my notes, and started putting together a couple of potions that would offer me a few hours of protection from the narcotic venom of the Red Court. The potions were simple ones. Brewing any kind of potion required a base liquid, and then several other ingredients meant to bind the magic put into the potion to the desired effect. One ingredient was linked to each of the five senses, then one to the mind and one to the spirit.

In this case, I wanted something that would offset the venomous saliva of the Red Court vampires, a narcotic that rendered those exposed to it passively euphoric. I needed a potion that would ruin the pleasurable sensations of the poison.

I used stale coffee as my base ingredient. To that I added hairs from a skunk, for scent. A small square of sandpaper for touch. I tossed in a small photo of Meat Loaf, cut from a magazine, for sight. A rooster's crow I'd stored in a small quartz crystal went in for hearing, and a powdered aspirin for taste. I cut the surgeon general's warning label from a pack of cigarettes and chopped it fine to add in for the mind, and then lit a stick of the incense I sometimes used while meditating and wafted some of the smoke into the two bottles for the spirit. Once the potions were bubbling over a burner, I drew in my wearied will and released power into the mixes, suffusing them with energy. They fizzed and frothed with gratifying enthusiasm.

I let them simmer for a while, then took them from the fire and emptied them into a pair of small sports-drink bottles. After that, I slumped on a stool and waited for Bob to come home.

I must have nodded off, because when my phone rang, I jerked myself up straight and nearly fell off my stool. I clambered up the ladder and picked up the phone.

'Dresden.'

'Hoss,' said a weather-beaten voice on the other end. Ebenezar McCoy, a sometime teacher of mine, sounded businesslike. 'Did I wake you up?'

'No, sir,' I said. 'I was up anyway. Working on a case.'

'You sound tired as a coal-mine mule.'

'Been up all night.'

'Uh-huh,' Ebenezar said. 'Hoss, I just called to let you know not to worry about this duel nonsense. We're going to slap it down.'

By 'we,' Ebenezar meant the Senior Council members. Seven of the most experienced wizards on the White Council held positions of particular authority, especially during times of crisis, when quick decisions were needed. Ebenezar had turned down his chance at a seat on the Senior Council for nearly fifty years. He took it only recently to block a potentially fatal political attack directed against yours truly by some of the more conservative (read, fanatic) members of the White Council.

'Slap it down? No, don't do that.'

'What?' Ebenezar said. 'You *want* to fight this duel? Did you fall and hit your head, boy?'

I rubbed at my eyes. 'Tell me about it. I'll work out something to give me a shot at winning.'

'Sounds like your wagon's already pretty full to be letting this vampire push you.'

'He knew where to push,' I said. 'Ortega brought a bunch of goons into town. Vampires and straight hit men, too. He says that if I don't face him he's going to have a bunch of people I know killed.'

Ebenezar spat something in what I presumed was Gaelic. 'You'd better tell me what happened, then.'

I told Ebenezar all about my encounter with Ortega. 'Oh, and a contact of mine says that the Red Court is divided over the issue. There are lots of them who don't want the war to end.'

'Of course they don't,' Ebenezar said. 'That fool of a Merlin won't let us take the offensive. He thinks his fancy wards will make them give up.'

'How are they working out?' I asked.

'Well enough for now,' Ebenezar admitted. 'One major attack has been pushed back by the wards. No more Council members have been killed in attacks on their homes, though the Red Court's allies are putting pressure on ours, and a few Wardens have died on intelligence-gathering missions. But it isn't going to last. You can't win a war sitting behind a wall and hoping the enemy decides to leave.'

'What do you think we should do?'

'Officially,' Ebenezar said, 'we follow the Merlin's lead. More than anything, now, we need to stay together.'

'What about unofficially?'

'Think about it,' Ebenezar snorted. 'If we just sit here, the vampires are going to take apart or drive away our allies and then we'll have to take them all on alone. Look, Hoss. Are you sure about this duel?'

'Hell no,' I said. 'I just didn't see much choice. I'll figure out something. If I win, it might be worth it to the Council. Neutral territory for meeting and negotiating could come in handy.'

Ebenezar sighed. 'Aye. The Merlin will think the same thing.' He was quiet for a moment before he said, 'Not much like the days on the farm, is it, Hoss?'

'Not much,' I agreed.

'Do you remember that telescope we set up in the loft?'

Ebenezar had taught me what I knew of astronomy, on long, dark summer evenings in the Ozark hills, hay doors to the barn's loft open, stars overhead shining in the country darkness by the millions. 'I remember. That asteroid we discovered that turned out to be an old Russian satellite.'

'Asteroid Dresden was a better name than Kosmos Five.' He chuckled and added, as an afterthought, 'Do you remember whatever happened to that telescope and such? I kept meaning to ask you but I never got around to it.'

'We packed it in that steamer trunk in the horse stall.'

'With the observation logs?'

'Yeah,' I said.

'Oh, that's right,' Ebenezar said. 'Obliged.'

'Sure.'

'Hoss, we'll agree to the duel if that's what you want. But be careful.'

'I don't plan to roll over and die,' I said. 'But if something should happen to me . . .' I coughed. 'Well, if it does, there are some papers in my lab. You'll know how to find them. Some people I'd like to make sure are protected.'

'Of course,' Ebenezar said. 'But I'm likely to carry on cranky if I have to drive all the way up to Chicago twice in as many years.'

'Hate for that to happen.'

'Luck, Hoss.'

'Thanks.'

I hung up the phone, rubbed tiredly at my eyes, and stomped back down to the lab. Ebenezar hadn't come out and said it, but the offer had been there, behind the old man's talk of days gone by. He'd been offering me sanctuary at his farm. It wasn't that I didn't like Chicago, but the offer was a tempting one. After a couple of rough years slugging it out with various bad guys, a quiet year or two on the farm near Hog Hollow, Missouri, sounded tempting.

Of course, the safety offered in that image was an illusion. Ebenezar's place was going to be as well protected as any wizard's on earth, and the old man himself could be a terrible foe. But the Red Court of vampires had a big network supporting it and they didn't generally bother to play fair. They'd destroyed a wizard stronghold the previous summer, and if they'd cracked that place they could do it to Ebenezar's Ozark hideaway too. If I went there and they found out about it, it would make the old man's farm too tempting a target to pass by.

Ebenezar knew that as well as I did, but he and I shared a common trait – he doesn't like bullies either. He'd be glad to have me and he'd fight to the death against the Reds if they came. But I didn't want to draw that kind of thing down on him.

I was grateful for the old man's support, but I owed him more than that.

Besides, I was almost as well protected here in Chicago. My own wards, defensive screens of magic to protect my apartment, had kept me safe and alive for a couple of years, and the presence of a large mortal population kept the vampires from trying anything completely overt. Wizards and vampires notwithstanding, everyone in the supernatural community knew damned well that plain old vanilla mortals were one of the most dangerous forces on the planet, and went out of their way not to become too noticeable to the population at large.

The population at large, meanwhile, did everything it possibly could to keep from noticing the supernatural, so that worked out. The vampires had taken a poke or two at me since the war began, but it hadn't been anything I couldn't handle, and they didn't want to risk being any more obvious.

Thus, Ortega and his challenge.

So how the hell was I supposed to fight a duel with him without using magic?

My bed called to me, but that thought was enough to keep me from answering. I paced around my lab for a while, trying to think of some kind of weapon that would give me the most advantage. Ortega was stronger, faster, more experienced, and more resistant to injury than me. How the hell was I supposed to pick a weapon to go up against that? I supposed if the duel could be worked into some kind of pizza-eating contest I might have a shot, but somehow I didn't think that the Pizza Spress Hungry Man Special was on the list of approved weaponry.

I checked the clock and frowned. Dawn was only minutes away, and Bob wasn't back yet. Bob was a spirit being, a spirit of intellect from one of the more surreal corners of the Nevernever. He wasn't evil as much as he was magnificently innocent of any kind of morality, but as a spirit, daylight was a threat to him as surely as it was to the vampires of the Red Court. If he got caught out in it, it could kill him.

Dawn was about two minutes off before Bob returned, flowing down the ladder and toward the skull.

Something was wrong.

Bob's manifestation of a candle flame-colored cloud of swirling lights bobbed drunkenly left and right on its way back to the shelf with the skull. Purple globs of glowing plasm dribbled from the cloud in a steady trail, striking the floor, where they winked out into blobs of transparent goo. The cloud flowed into the skull, and after a moment, faint violet flames appeared in the skull's empty eye sockets.

'Ow,' Bob said, his voice tired.

'Hell's bells,' I muttered. 'Bob, you all right?'

'No.'

Bob? Monosyllabic? Crap. 'Is there anything I can do to help?'

'No,' Bob said, faintly. 'Rest.'

'But—'

'Report,' Bob said. 'Have to.'

Right. He'd been sent out on a mission and he was feeling pressured to finish it. 'What happened?'

'Wards,' Bob said. 'Marcone's.'

I felt my mouth fall open. 'What?'

'Wards,' Bob repeated.

I sat down on my stool. 'How the hell did Marcone get wards?'

Bob's tone became a shade contemptuous. 'Magic?'

The insult relieved me a little. If he was able to be a wiseass he'd probably be okay. 'Could you tell who did the wards?'

'No. Too good.'

Damn. A spell had to get up pretty early in the morning to get around Bob. Maybe he'd been hurt worse than I thought. 'What about Ortega?'

'Rothchild,' Bob said. 'Half a dozen vamps with him. Maybe a dozen mortals.'

Bob's eyelights flickered and guttered. I couldn't risk losing Bob by pushing him too hard – and spirit or not, he wasn't immortal. He wasn't afraid of bullets or knives, but there were things that could kill him. 'Good enough for now,' I said. 'Tell me the rest later. Get some sleep.'

Bob's eyelights flickered out without another word.

I frowned at the skull for a while and then shook my head. I collected my potion bottles, cleaned up the work area, and turned to leave and let Bob get some rest.

I was leaning over the wardflames to blow them out when the green candle hissed and shrank to a pinpoint of light. The yellow candle beside it flared up without warning, brighter than an incandescent lightbulb.

My heart started pounding and nervous fear danced over the back of my neck.

Something was approaching my apartment. That's what it meant when the flame spread from the green to the yellow candle. Warning spells I had threaded out to a couple of blocks from my house had sensed the approach of supernatural hostility.

The yellow candle dimmed, and the red candle exploded into a flame the size of my head.

Stars and stones. The intruder that had triggered the warning system the wardflames were linked to was getting closer; and it was something big. Or else a lot of somethings. They were heading in fast to set off the red candle so quickly, only a few dozen yards from my house.

I dashed up the ladder from the lab and got ready to fight.

10

I got up the ladder in time to hear a car door shut outside my apartment. I'd lost my .357 during a battle between the Faerie Courts hosted on clouds over Lake Michigan the previous midsummer, so I'd moved my .44 from the office to home. It hung on a gun belt on a peg beside the door, just over a wire basket I'd attached to the wall. Holy water, a couple cloves of garlic, vials of salt, and iron filings filled the basket, intended to be door prizes for anything that showed up in an attempt to suck my blood, carry me off to faerieland, or sell me stale cookies.

The door itself was reinforced steel, and could stand up to punishment better than the wall around it. I'd had a demon come a-knocking before, and I didn't want an encore performance. I couldn't afford new furniture, even secondhand.

I belted on the gun, shook out my shield bracelet, and took up my staff and blasting rod. Anything that came through my door would have to contend with my threshold, the aura of protective energy around any home. Most supernatural things didn't do so well with thresholds. After that, they'd have to force their way past my wards – barriers of geometrically aligned energy that would block out physical or magical intrusion, turning that energy back upon its source. A small, gentle push at my wards would result in a similar push against whatever was trying to get in. A swift or heavy push would result in more energy feeding back onto the attacker. Within the wards were sigils of fire and ice, which were designed to deliver bursts of destructive energy about as powerful as your average land mine.

It was a solid and layered defense. With luck, it should be enough to stop a considerable amount of threat from even reaching my door.

And since I'm such a lucky guy, I took a deep breath, pointed my blasting rod at the door, and waited.

It didn't take long. I expected flashes of magical discharge, demon howls, maybe some kind of pyrotechnics as evil magic clashed against my own defensive spells. Instead I got seven polite knocks.

I peered at the door suspiciously and then asked, 'Who's there?'

A low, rough man's voice growled, 'The Archive.'

What the hell. 'The Archive who?'

Evidently the speaker didn't have a sense of humor. 'The Archive,' the voice repeated firmly. 'The Archive has been appointed emissary in this dispute, and is here to speak to Wizard Dresden about the duel.'

I frowned at the door. I vaguely remembered mention of an Archive of some sort during the last White Council meeting I'd attended, as a neutral party. At the time, I'd assumed it had been some sort of arcane library. I'd had other things on my mind at the time, and I hadn't been listening too closely. 'How do I know who you are?'

There was a rasp of paper on stone, and an envelope slid under my door, one corner poking out. 'Documentation, Wizard Dresden,' the voice replied. 'And a pledge to abide by the laws of hospitality during this visit.'

Some of the tension left my shoulders, and I lowered the gun. That was one good thing about dealing with the supernatural community. If something gave you its word, you could trust it. Within reason.

Then again, maybe that was just me. Of all the things I'd encountered, I'd been more of a weasel about keeping my word than any of them. Maybe that's why I was leery about trusting someone else.

I picked up the envelope and unfolded a sheet of plain paper certifying that its bearer had been approved by the White Council to act as emissary in the matter of the duel. I passed my hand over it and muttered a quick charm with the last password I'd gotten from the Wardens, and in response a brief glowing pentacle appeared centered on the paper like a bioluminescent watermark. It was legit.

I folded the paper closed again, but I didn't set my rod and staff aside just yet. I undid the dead bolt, muttered my wards back, and opened the door enough to see outside.

A man stood on my doorstep. He was nearly as tall as me but looked a lot more solid, with shoulders wide enough to make the loose black jacket he wore fit tightly on his upper arms. He wore a navy blue shirt and stood so that I could see the wrinkles caused by the straps of a shoulder rig. A black ball cap reined in dark golden hair that might have fallen to his shoulders. He hadn't shaved in a few days, and had a short white scar below his mouth that highlighted the cleft in his chin. His eyes were grey-blue and empty of any expression in a way I had seldom seen. Not like he was hiding what he felt. More like there was simply nothing there.

'Dresden?' he asked.

'Yeah.' I eyed him up and down. 'You don't look very Archive-esque.'

He lifted his eyebrows, a mildly interested expression. 'I'm Kincaid. You're wearing a gun.'

'Only when company comes over.'

'I haven't seen any of the Council's people carrying a gun. Good for you.' He turned and waved his hand. 'This shouldn't take long.'

I glanced past him. 'What do you mean?'

A second later, a little girl started down my stairs, one hand carefully on the guide rail. She was adorable, maybe seven years old, her blonde hair still baby-fine and straight, clipped neatly at her shoulders and held back with a hairband. She wore a plain little corduroy dress with a white blouse and shiny black shoes, and her coat was a puffy down-filled jacket that seemed like a bit of overkill for the weather.

I looked from the kid to Kincaid and said, 'You can't be bringing a child into this.'

'Sure I can,' Kincaid said.

'What, couldn't you find a baby-sitter?'

The child stopped a couple of steps up so that her face was even with my own and said, her voice serious and marked with a faint British accent, 'He *is* my baby-sitter.'

I felt my eyebrows shoot up.

'Or more accurately my driver,' she said. 'Are you going to let us in? I prefer not to remain outdoors.'

I stared at the kid for a second. 'Aren't you a little short for a librarian?'

'I am not a librarian,' the child said. 'I am the Archive.'

'Hang on a minute,' I said. 'What do you—'

'I am the Archive,' the child said, her voice steady and assured. 'I assume that your wards detected my presence. They seemed functional.'

'*You?*' I said. 'You've got to be kidding.' I extended my senses gingerly toward her. The air around her fairly hummed with power, different from what I would expect around another wizard, but strong all the same, a quiet and dangerous buzz like that around high-tension power lines.

I had to suppress a sudden rush of apprehension from showing on my face. The girl had power. She had a hell of a lot of power. Enough to make me wonder if my wards would be enough to stop her if she decided to come through them. Enough to make me think of little Billy Mumy as the omnipotent brat on that old episode of *The Twilight Zone*.

She regarded me with implacable blue eyes I suddenly did not want to take the chance of looking into. 'I can explain it to you, wizard,' she said. 'But not out here. I have neither an interest nor an inclination to do you any harm. Perhaps the opposite.'

I frowned at her. 'Promise?'

'Promise,' the child said solemnly.

'Cross your heart and hope to die?'

She drew an *X* over her puffy jacket with one index finger. 'You don't know how much.'

Kincaid took a couple of steps up and glanced warily around

the street. 'Make up your mind, Dresden. I'm not keeping her out here for long.'

'What about him?' I asked the Archive, and nodded toward Kincaid. 'Can he be trusted?'

'Kincaid?' the girl asked, her voice whimsical. 'Can you be trusted?'

'You're paid up through April,' the man replied, his eyes still scanning the street. 'After that I might get a better offer.'

'There,' the girl said to me. 'Kincaid can be trusted until April. He's an ethical man, in his way.' She shivered and put her hands into the pockets of her puffy coat. She hunched up her shoulders and watched my face.

Generally speaking, my instincts about people (who weren't women who might potentially end up doing adult things with me) were pretty good. I trusted the Archive's promise. Besides, she was darling and looked like she was starting to get cold. 'Fine,' I said. 'Come inside.'

I stepped back and opened the door. The Archive came in and told Kincaid, 'Wait with the car. Come fetch me in ten minutes.'

Kincaid frowned at her, and then me. 'You sure?'

'Quite.' The Archive stepped in past me, and started taking off her coat. 'Ten minutes. I want to head back before rush hour begins.'

Kincaid fixed his empty eyes on me and said, 'Be nice to the little girl, wizard. I've handled your kind before.'

'I get more threats before nine a.m. than most people get all day,' I responded, and shut the door on him. Purely for effect, I locked it too.

Me, petty? Surely not.

I lit a couple of candles in order to get a little more light into the living room and stirred up the fire, adding more wood to it as soon as the embers were glowing. While I did, the Archive took off her coat, folded it neatly over the arm of one of my lumpy comfy chairs, and sat down, back straight, hands folded in her lap. Her little black shoes waved back and forth above the floor.

I frowned at her. It's not like I don't like kids or anything, but I hadn't had much experience with them. Now I had one sitting there wanting to talk to me about a duel. How the hell did a child, no matter how large her vocabulary, manage to get appointed an emissary?

'So, uh. What's your name?'

She said, 'The Archive.'

'Yeah, I got that part. But I meant your name. What people call you.'

'The Archive,' she repeated. 'I do not have a familiar name. I am the Archive, and have always been the Archive.'

'You're not human,' I said.

'Incorrect. I am a seven-year-old human child.'

'With no name? Everybody has a name,' I said. 'I'm can't go around calling you the Archive.'

The girl tilted her head to one side, arching a pale gold eyebrow. 'Then what would you call me?'

'Ivy,' I said at once.

'Why Ivy?' she asked.

'You're the Archive, right? Arch-ive. Arch-ivy. Ivy.'

The girl pursed her lips. 'Ivy,' she said, and then nodded slowly. 'Ivy. Very well.' She regarded me for a moment and then said, 'Go ahead and ask the question, wizard. We might as well get it out of the way.'

'Who are you?' I asked. 'Why are you called the Archive?'

Ivy nodded. 'The thorough explanation is too complex to convey to you here. But in short, I am the living memory of mankind.'

'What do you mean, the living memory?'

'I am the sum of human knowledge, passed down from generation to generation, mother to daughter. Culture, science, philosophy, lore, tradition. I hold the accumulated memories of a thousand generations of mankind. I take in all that is written and spoken. I study. I learn. That is my purpose, to procure and preserve knowledge.'

'So you're saying that if it's been written down, you know it?'

'I know it. I understand it.'

I sat down slowly on the couch, and stared at her. Hell's bells. It was almost too much to comprehend. Knowledge is power, and if Ivy was telling me the truth, she knew more than anyone alive. 'How did you get this gig?'

'My mother passed it on to me,' she replied. 'As I was born, just as she received it when she was born.'

'And your mother lets a mercenary drive you around?'

'Certainly not. My mother is dead, wizard.' She frowned. 'Not dead, technically. But all that she knew and was came into me. She became an empty cup. A persistent vegetative state.' Her eyes grew a little wistful, distant. 'She's free of it. But she certainly isn't alive in the most vital sense.'

'I'm sorry,' I said.

'I wouldn't know why. I know my mother. And all before her.' She put a finger to her temple. 'It's all in here.'

'You know how to use magic?' I asked.

'I prefer calculus.'

'But you can do it.'

'Yes.'

Yikes. If the reaction of my wards was any indication, it meant that she was at least as strong as any Wizard of the White Council. Probably stronger. But if that was true . . .

'If you know that much,' I said, 'if you are that powerful, why did you hire a bodyguard to bring you here?'

'My feet don't reach the pedals.'

I felt like smacking myself on the forehead. 'Oh, right.'

Ivy nodded. 'In preparation for the duel, I will need some information. Namely, where I might contact your second and what weapon you prefer for the duel.'

'I don't have a second yet.'

Ivy arched an eyebrow. 'Then you have until sundown this evening to gain one. Otherwise the match, and your life, will be forfeit.'

'Forfeit? Uh, how would the forfeit be collected?'

The little girl stared at me for a silent moment. Then she said, 'I'll do it.'

I swallowed, a cold chill rippling over me. I believed her. I believed that she could, and I believed that she would. 'Um. Okay. Look, I haven't exactly chosen a weapon yet, either. If I—'

'Simply choose one, Mister Dresden. Will, skill, energy, or flesh.'

'Wait,' I said. 'I thought I got to pick swords or guns or something.'

Ivy shook her head. 'Read your copy of the Accords. I choose what is available, and I choose the ancient ways. You may match wills with your opponent to gauge which of you is the most determined. You may match your skill at arms against his, each of you with weaponry of your individual choosing. You may wield energy forces against each other. Or you may challenge him to unarmed combat.' She considered. 'I would advise against the last.'

'Thanks,' I muttered. 'I'll take magic. Energy.'

'You realize, of course, that he will decline in that venue and you will be forced to choose another.'

I sighed. 'Yeah. But until he does, I don't have to pick another one, right?'

'Indeed,' Ivy acknowledged.

There was a knock on the door, and I got up to open it. Kincaid nodded to me, then leaned in and said, 'Ten minutes.'

'Thank you, Kincaid,' Ivy said. She rose, drew a business card from her pocket, and passed it to me. 'Have your second call this number.'

I took the card and nodded. 'I will.'

Just then, Mister emerged from my bedroom and lazily arched his back. Then he padded over to me and rubbed his shoulder against my shin by way of greeting.

Ivy blinked and looked down at Mister, and her child's face was suddenly suffused with a pure and uncomplicated joy. She said, 'Kitty!' and immediately knelt down to pet Mister. Mister apparently liked her. He started purring louder, and walked around Ivy, rubbing up against her while she petted him and spoke to him quietly.

Hell's bells. It was adorable. She was just a kid.

A kid who knew more than any mortal alive. A kid with a

scary amount of magical power. A kid who would kill me if I didn't show up to the duel. But still a kid.

I glanced up at Kincaid, who stood frowning down at Ivy fawning all over Mister. He shook his head and muttered, 'Now, that's just creepy.'

11

Ivy seemed reluctant to leave off petting Mister, but she and Kincaid left without further conversation. I shut the door after them and leaned on it, listening with my eyes closed until they'd gone. I didn't feel as tired as I should have. Probably because I had a wealth of experience that suggested I would get a lot more worn out before I got a real chance to rest.

Mister rubbed up against my legs until I'd leaned down to pet him, after which he promptly walked over to his food bowl, ignoring me altogether. I grabbed a Coke from the icebox while he ate, absently pouring a bit onto a saucer and leaving it on the floor by Mister. By the time I'd finished it, I'd made up my mind about what I had to do next.

Make phone calls.

I called the number Vincent had left for me first. I expected to reach an answering service, but to my surprise Vincent's voice, tense and anxious, said, 'Yes?'

'It's Harry Dresden,' I said. 'I wanted to check in with you.'

'Ah, yes, just a moment,' Vincent said. I heard him say

something, caught a bit of conversation in the background, and then heard him walking and a door shut behind him. 'The police,' he said. 'I've been working with them throughout the evening.'

'Any luck?' I asked.

'God only knows,' Vincent said. 'But from my perspective, it seems the only thing accomplished is deciding which department is going to handle the investigation.'

'Homicide?' I guessed.

Vincent's tired voice became dry. 'Yes. Though the mind boggles at the chain of logic that led to it.'

'Election year. City management is politicking,' I said. 'But once you start dealing with the actual police personnel, you should be all right. There are good people in every department.'

'One hopes. Have you found anything?'

'I've got a lead. I don't know how good. The thieves might be on a small craft in the harbor. I'm heading down there presently.'

'Very well,' Vincent said.

'If the lead is good, do you want me to call CPD?'

'I'd rather you contacted me first,' Vincent said. 'I am still uncertain of how much trust to place in the local police. I cannot help but think it must have been the reason the thieves fled here – that they possessed some contact or advantage with the local authorities. I'd like as much time as possible to decide whom to trust.'

I frowned and thought about Marcone's flunkies taking a shot at me. Chicago PD had an unfair reputation for corruption, thanks in part to the widespread mob activity during Prohibition. It was inaccurate, but people were people, and people aren't immune to being bought. Marcone had attained police-only information with disturbing speed before. 'Might be smart. I'll check it out and let you know. Shouldn't be more than an hour or two.'

'Very good. Thank you, Mister Dresden. Is there anything else?'

'Yeah,' I said. 'I should have thought of this last night. Do you have any pieces of the Shroud?'

'Pieces?' Vincent asked.

'Scraps or threads. I know that many samples were analyzed back in the seventies. Do you have access to any of those pieces?'

'Very possibly. Why?'

I had to remind myself that Vincent seemed to be largely a nonbeliever in the supernatural, so I couldn't come out and say that I wanted to use thaumaturgy to track down the Shroud. 'To confirm identification when I find it. I don't want to get foxed with a decoy.'

'Of course. I'll make a call,' Vincent said. 'Get a sample FedExed here. Thank you, Mister Dresden.'

I said good-bye, hung up, and stared at the phone for a minute. Then I took a deep breath and dialed Michael's number.

Even though the sky was barely light with morning, the phone rang only once before a woman's voice said, 'Hello?'

This was my nightmare. 'Oh. Uh, hello, Charity. It's Harry Dresden.'

'Hi!' the voice said brightly. 'This isn't Charity though.'

So maybe it wasn't my nightmare. It was my nightmare's oldest daughter. 'Molly?' I asked. 'Wow, you sound all grown-up now.'

She laughed. 'Yeah, the breast fairy came to visit and everything. Did you want to talk to my mom?'

Some might find it significant that it took me a second to

realize she wasn't being literal about the faerie. Sometimes I hate my life. 'Well, um. Is your dad around?'

'So you *don't* want to talk to Mom, check,' she said. 'He's working on the addition. Let me get him.'

She set the phone down and I heard footsteps walking away. In the background, I could hear recorded children's voices singing, the rattle of plates and forks, and people talking. Then there was a rustling sound, and a thump as the handset on the other end must have fallen to the floor. Then I heard the sound of heavy, squishy breathing.

'Harry,' sighed another voice from what must have been the same room. She sounded much like Molly but less cheerful. 'No, no, honey, don't play with the phone. Give that to me, please.' The phone rattled some more, the woman said, 'Thank you, sweetie,' and then she picked up the phone and said, 'Hello? Anyone there?'

For a second I was tempted to remain silent, or possibly try to imitate a recording of the operator, but I steeled myself against that. I didn't want to let myself get rattled. I was pretty sure that Charity could smell fear, even over the phone. It could trigger an attack. 'Hello, Charity. It's Harry Dresden. I was calling to speak to Michael.'

There was a second of silence during which I couldn't help but imagine the way Michael's wife's eyes must have narrowed. 'I suppose it was inevitable,' she said. 'Naturally if there is a situation so dangerous as to require all three of the Knights, you come crawling out of whatever hole you live in.'

'Actually, this is sort of unrelated.'

'I assumed it was. Your idiocy tends to strike at the worst possible place and time.'

'Oh, come on, Charity, that's not fair.'

Growing anger made her voice clearer and sharper, if no louder. 'No? At the one time in the last year that Michael most needs to be focused on his duty, to be alert and careful, you arrive to distract him.'

Anger warred with guilt for dominance of my reaction. 'I'm trying to help.'

'He has scars from the last time you helped, Mister Dresden.'

I felt like slamming the receiver against the wall until it broke, but I restrained myself again. I couldn't stop the anger from making my words bite, though. 'You're never going to give me an inch, are you?'

'You don't deserve an inch.'

I said, 'Is that why you named your son after me?'

'That was Michael,' Charity said. 'I was still on drugs, and the paperwork was done when I woke up.'

I kept my voice calm. Mostly. 'Look, Charity. I'm real sorry you feel the way you do, but I need to talk to Michael. Is he there or not?'

The line clicked as someone else picked up another extension and Molly said, 'Sorry, Harry, but my dad isn't here. Sanya says he went out to pick up some doughnuts.'

'Molly,' Charity said, her voice hard. 'It's a school day. Don't dawdle.'

'Uh-oh,' Molly said. 'I swear, it's like she's telepathic or something.'

I could almost hear Charity grinding her teeth. 'That isn't funny, Molly. Get off the line.'

Molly sighed and said, 'Surrender, Dorothy,' before she hung up. I choked on a sudden laugh, and tried to turn it into a series of coughs for Charity's benefit.

From the tone of her voice, she hadn't been fooled. 'I'll give him a message.'

I hesitated. Maybe I should ask to wait for him to return. There wasn't any love lost between Charity and myself, and if she didn't pass word along to Michael, or if she delayed before telling him, it could mean my death. Michael and the other Knights were busy with their pursuit of the Shroud, and God only knew if I'd be able to get in touch with him again today. On the other hand, I had neither the time nor the attention to spare to sit there butting heads with Charity until Michael returned.

Charity had been unreservedly hostile to me for as long as I had known her. She loved her husband ferociously, and feared for his safety – especially when he worked with me. In my head, I knew that her antagonism wasn't wholly without basis. Michael had been busted up several times when teamed up with me. During the last such outing, a bad guy gunning for me had nearly killed Charity and her unborn child, little Harry. Now she worried about the consequences that might be visited on her other children as well.

I knew that. But it still hurt.

I had to make a decision – to trust her or not. I decided to do it. Charity might not like me, but she was no coward and no liar. She knew Michael would want her to tell him.

'Well, Mister Dresden?' Charity asked.

'Just let him know that I need to talk to him.'

'Regarding?'

For a second, I debated passing Michael my tip on the Shroud. But Michael believed that I was going to get killed if I got involved. He took protecting his friends seriously, and if he knew that I was poking around he might be inclined to knock me unconscious and lock me in a closet now and apologize later. I decided against it.

'Tell him that I need a second by sundown tonight or bad things will happen.'

'To who?' Charity asked.

'Me.'

She paused, then said, 'I'll give him your message.'

And then she hung up on me.

I hung up the phone, frowning. 'That pause wasn't significant,' I told Mister. 'It doesn't mean that she was chewing over the thought of intentionally getting me killed in order to protect her husband and children.'

Mister regarded me with that mystic-distance focus in his feline eyes. Or maybe that was the look he got when his brain waves flatlined. Either way, it was neither helpful nor reassuring.

'I'm not worried,' I said. 'Not one bit.'

Mister's tail twitched.

I shook my head, got my stuff together, and headed out to investigate the lead at the harbor.

12

When I first came to Chicago I thought of a harbor as a giant bowl of ocean with ships and boats in the foreground and the faded outline of the buildings on the far side in the background. I had always imagined political subversives dressed up as tribal natives and a huge hit in the profit margin of the East India Company.

Burnham Harbor looked like the parking lot of an oceangoing Wal-Mart. It might have been able to hold a football field or three. White wharves stretched out over the water with pleasure boats and small fishing vessels in rows within a placid oval of water. The scent of the lake was one part dead fish, one part algae-coated rock, and one part motor oil. I parked in the lot up the hill from the harbor, got out, and made sure I had my equipment with me. I wore my force ring on my right hand and my shield bracelet on my left wrist, and my blasting rod thumped against my leg where I had tied it to the inside of my leather duster. I'd added a can of self-defense spray to my arsenal, and I slipped it into my pants pocket. I would rather have had my gun, but toting it around in my pocket was a felony. The pepper spray wasn't.

I locked up the car and felt a sudden, slithering pressure on my back – my instincts' way of screaming that someone was watching me. I kept my head down, my hands in my pockets, and walked toward the harbor. I didn't rubberneck around, but I tried to get a look at everything while moving only my eyes.

I didn't see anyone, but I couldn't shake the impression that I was being observed. I doubted it was anyone from the Red Court. The morning hadn't reached full brightness yet, but it was still light enough to parboil a vampire. That didn't rule out any number of other flavors of assassin, though. And it was possible that if the thieves were here, they were keeping an eye on everyone coming and going.

All I could do was walk steadily and hope that whoever was watching me wasn't one of Marcone's thugs, a vampire groupie or a rent-a-gun aiming a rifle at my back from several hundred yards away.

I found the *Etranger* in a few minutes, moored at a slip not far from the entrance. It was a pretty little ship, a white pleasure boat roomy enough to house a comfortable cabin. The *Etranger* wasn't new, but she looked neat and well cared for. A Canadian flag hung from a little stand on the ship's afterdeck. I moved on past the ship at a steady pace and Listened as I did.

Listening is a trick I'd picked up when I was a kid. Not many people have worked out the trick of it, blocking out all other sound in order to better hear one sound in particular – such as distant voices. It isn't as much about magic, I think, as it is focus and discipline. But the magic helps.

'Unacceptable,' said a quiet, female voice in the *Etranger*'s cabin. It was marked with a gentle accent, both Spanish and British. 'The job entailed a great deal more expense than was originally estimated. I'm raising the price to reflect this, nothing more.' There was a short pause, and then the woman said, 'Would you like an invoice for your tax return then? I told you the quote was only an estimate. It happens.' Another pause, and then the woman said, 'Excellent. As scheduled, then.'

I stared out at the lake, just taking in the view, and strained to hear anything else. Evidently the conversation was over. I checked around, but there weren't any people in sight moving around the harbor on a February weekday morning. I took a breath to steady myself, and moved closer to the ship.

I caught a glimpse of motion through a window in the cabin, and heard a chirping sound. A cell phone rested on a counter beside a pad of hotel stationery. A woman appeared in the window dressed in a long gown of dark silk, and picked up the cell phone. She answered it without speaking and a moment later said, 'I'm sorry. You've the wrong number.'

I watched as she put the phone down and casually let the nightgown slide to the floor. I watched a little more. I wasn't being a peeping Tom. This was professional. I noted that she had some intriguing curves. See? Professionalism in action.

She opened a door, and a bit of steam wafted out, the sound of the water growing louder. She stepped in and closed the door again, leaving the cabin empty.

I had an opportunity. I'd seen only one woman, and not well enough to positively identify her as either Anna Valmont or Francisca Garcia, the two remaining Churchmice. I hadn't seen the Shroud hanging from a laundry line or anything. Even so,

I had the feeling I'd come to the right place. My gut told me to trust my spiritual informer.

I made my decision and stepped up a short gangplank onto the *Etranger*.

I had to move fast. The woman on the ship might not be a fan of long showers. All I needed to do was get inside, see if I could find anything that might verify the presence of the Shroud, and get out again. If I moved quickly enough, I could get in and out without anyone the wiser.

I went down the stairs to the cabin with as much stealth as I could manage. The stairs didn't creak. I had to duck my head a bit when I stepped into the cabin. I stayed close to the door and checked around, listening to the patter of the water from the shower. The room wasn't large and didn't offer a bonanza of places to hide. A double bed took up nearly a quarter of the space in the room. A tiny washing machine and dryer were stacked one on another in a corner, a basket of laundry stowed atop them. A counter and kitchenette with a couple of small refrigerators used up most of the rest.

I frowned. Two fridges? I checked them out. The first was stocked with perishables and beer. The second was a fake, and opened onto a cabinet containing a heavy metal strongbox. Bingo.

The shower kept running. I reached out to pick up the strongbox, but a thought struck me. The Churchmice may have gotten themselves into a lot of trouble, but they'd evidently been good enough to avoid Interpol for a number of years. The hiding place for the strongbox was too clumsy, too obvious. I shut the fake fridge and looked around the room. I was starting to get nervous. I couldn't have much time left to find the Shroud and get out.

Of course. I took a couple of long steps to the washer and dryer and grabbed the laundry basket. I found it under several clean, fluffy towels, an opaque plastic package a little larger than a folded shirt. I touched it with my left hand. A tingling sensation pulsed against my palm, and the hairs along my arm rose up straight.

'Damn, I'm good,' I muttered. I picked up the Shroud and turned to go.

A woman stood behind me, dressed in black fatigue pants, a heavy jacket, and battered combat boots. Her peroxide-blonde hair was cut very short, but it did nothing to detract from the appeal of her features. She was elegantly pretty and pleasant to look at.

The gun she had pointed at my nose wasn't pretty, though. It was an ugly old .38 revolver, a cheap Saturday-night special.

I was careful not to move. Even a cheap gun can kill you, and I doubted I could raise a shield in time to do me any good. She'd taken me off guard. I'd never heard her coming, never sensed her presence.

'Damn, I'm good,' the woman echoed, her accent high British, a touch of amusement in her voice. 'Put the package down.'

I held it out to her. 'Here.'

I wouldn't have tried for the gun, but if she stepped closer to me it might show that she was an amateur. She wasn't, and remained standing out of grab range. 'On the counter, if you please.'

'What if I don't?' I said.

She smiled without humor. 'In that case, I'll have a dreary day of chores dismembering the body and cleaning up the blood. I'll leave it up to you.'

I put the package on the counter. 'Far be it from me to inconvenience a lady.'

'What a dear boy you are,' she said. 'That's a very nice coat. Take it off. Slowly, if you please.'

I slipped out of the coat and let it fall to the floor. 'You tricked me onto the boat,' I said. 'That second phone call was you, telling your partner to draw me in.'

'The shocking thing is that you fell for it,' the woman said. She kept giving directions and she knew what she was doing. I leaned forward and put my hands against the wall while she patted me down. She found the pepper spray and took it, along with my wallet. She made me sit down on the floor on my hands while she took my coat and stepped back.

'A stick,' she said, looking at my blasting rod. 'How very preneolithic of you.'

Aha. A professional she might be, but she was a straight. She didn't believe in the supernatural. I wasn't sure if that was going to help or hurt. It might mean that she would be a little less eager to shoot me. People who know what a wizard can do get really nervous if they think the wizard is about to try a spell. On the other hand, it meant that I didn't have either the support of the rest of the Council or the threat of my own retribution to use as leverage. I decided it was best to act like a normal for the time being.

The blonde laid my coat on the counter and said, 'Clear.'

The door to the bathroom opened, and the woman I'd heard before came out. She now wore a knit fabric dress the color of dark wine, and a couple of combs held her hair back from her face. She wouldn't stand out in a crowd but she wasn't unattractive. 'He's not Gaston,' she said, frowning at me.

'No,' said the blonde. 'He was here for the merchandise. He was just about to leave with it.'

The dark-haired woman nodded and asked me, 'Who are you?'

'Dresden,' I said. 'I'm a private investigator, Ms Garcia.'

Francisca Garcia's features froze, and she traded a look with the gun-wielding blonde. 'How did you know my name?'

'My client told me. You and Ms Valmont could be in a lot of trouble.'

Anna Valmont kicked the wall and spat, 'Bollocks.' She glared at me, gun steady on me despite her outburst. 'Are you working with Interpol?'

'Rome.'

Anna looked at Francisca and said, 'We should scrub this sale. It's falling apart.'

'Not yet,' Francisca said.

'There's no point in waiting.'

'I'm not leaving yet,' the dark-haired woman said, her eyes hard. 'Not until he gets here.'

'He isn't coming,' Anna said. 'You know he isn't.'

'Who?' I asked.

Francisca said, 'Gaston.'

I didn't say anything. Evidently Francisca could read faces well enough that I didn't have to. She stared at me for a moment and then closed her eyes, the blood draining from her face. 'Oh. Oh, *Dio*.'

'How?' Anna said. The gun never wavered. 'How did it happen?'

'Murder,' I said quietly. 'And someone set it up to point the police at Chicago.'

'Who would have done that?'

'Some bad people after the Shroud. Killers.'

'Terrorists?'

'Not that playful,' I said. 'As long as you have the Shroud, your lives are in danger. If you come with me, I can get you to some people who will protect you.'

Francisca shook her head and blinked her eyes a couple of times. 'You mean the police.'

I meant the Knights, but I knew darn well what their stance would be on what to do with the thieves once any supernatural peril was past. 'Yeah.'

Anna swallowed and looked at her partner. Something around her eyes softened with concern, with sympathy. The two of them weren't solely partners in crime. They were friends. Anna's voice softened as she said, 'Cisca, we have to move. If this one found us, others may not be far behind.'

The dark-haired woman nodded, her eyes not focused on anything. 'Yes. I'll get ready.' She rose and stepped across the cabin to the washing machine. She drew out a pair of gym bags and put them on the counter, over the package. Then she slipped into some shoes.

Anna watched for a moment and then said to me, 'Now. We can't have you running to the police to tell them everything. I wonder what to do with you, Mister Dresden. It really does make a great deal of sense to kill you.'

'Messy, remember? You'd have that dreary day,' I pointed out.

That got a bit of a smile from her. 'Ah, yes. I'd forgotten.' She reached into her pocket and drew out a pair of steel handcuffs. They were police quality, not the naughty fun kind. She tossed them to me underhand. I caught them. 'Put one on your wrist,' she said. I did. 'There's a ring on that bulkhead. Put the other through it and lock the cuffs.'

I hesitated, watching Francisca slip into a coat, her expression still blank. I licked my lips and said, 'You don't know how much danger you two are in, Ms Valmont. You really don't. Please let me help you.'

'I think not. We're professionals, Mister Dresden. Thieves we might be, but we do have a work ethic.'

'You didn't see what they did to Gaston LaRouche,' I said. 'How bad it was.'

'When isn't death bad? The bulkhead, Mister Dresden.'

'But—'

Anna lifted the gun.

I grimaced and lifted the cuffs to a steel ring protruding from the wall beside the stairs.

As a result, I was looking up them to the ship's deck when the second Denarian in twelve hours came hurtling down the stairway straight toward me.

13

I only saw it coming out of the corner of my eye, and I barely had time to register the movement and lunge as far as I could to one side. The demon went by me in a blur of rustling, metallic whispers, carrying the scent of lake water and dried blood. Neither of the Churchmice screamed, though whether this was intention or a by-product of surprise I couldn't tell.

The demon was more or less human, generally speaking, and disturbingly female. The lines of curvy hips swept down to legs that were oddly hinged, back-jointed like a lion's. She had skin of metallic green scales, and her arms ended in four-fingered, metallic-clawed hands. Like the demon form of Ursiel, she had two sets of eyes, one luminescent green, one glowing cherry red, and a luminous sigil burned at the center of her forehead.

Her hair was long. I mean like fifteen feet long, and looked like the demented love child of Medusa and Doctor Octopus. It had seemingly been cut in one-inch strips from half a mile of sheet metal. It writhed around her like a cloud of living serpents, metallic strands thrusting into the walls and the floor of the ship, supporting her weight like a dozen additional limbs.

Anna recovered from the surprise first. She already had a gun out and ready, but she hadn't been trained in how to use it in real combat. She pointed the gun more or less at the Denarian and emptied it at her in the space of a panicked breath. Since I was a couple of feet behind the demon, I flopped to one side as best I could, stayed low, and prayed to avoid becoming collateral damage.

The demon flinched once, maybe taking a hit, before it shrieked and twisted its shoulders and neck. A dozen metallic ribbons of writhing hair lashed across the room. One of them hit the gun itself, and metal shrieked as the demon tendril slashed clean through the gun's barrel. Half a dozen more whipped toward Anna's face, but the blonde thief had reflexes fast enough to get her mostly out of the way. A tendril wrapped around Anna's ankle, jerked, and sent the woman sprawling to the floor, while another lashed across her belly like a scalpel, cutting through her jacket and sprinkling the cabin with fine drops of blood.

Francisca stared at the thing for a second, her eyes huge and surrounded by white. Then she jerked open a drawer in the tiny galley, pulled out a heavy cutting knife, and lunged at the Denarian, blade flickering. It bit into the demon's arm and drew a furious shriek that did not sound at all human from her throat. The Denarian spun, silvery blood glistening on her scaly skin, and ripped one claw in a sweeping arch. The demon's claws sliced into Francisca's forearm, drawing blood. The knife tumbled to the ground. Francisca cried out and reeled back, into one of the walls.

The Denarian, eyes burning, whipped her head in a circle, the motion boneless, unnerving. Too many tendrils for me to count lanced across the room and slammed into Francisca Garcia's belly, thrusting like knives. She let out a choking gasp, and stared down at her wounds as several more tendrils thrust through her. They made a thunking sound as they hit the wooden wall of the cabin.

The demon laughed. It was a quick, breathless, excited laugh, the kind you expect from a nervous teenage girl. Her face twisted into a feral smile, showing a mouthful of metallic-seeming teeth, and both sets of eyes glowed brightly.

Francisca whispered, 'Oh, my Gaston.' Then her head bowed, dark hair falling about her face in a veil, and her body relaxed. The demon shivered and the tendril-blades whipped out of her, the last foot or so of each soaked in scarlet. The tendrils lashed about in a sort of mad excitement, and more droplets of blood appeared everywhere. Francisca slumped down to the floor, blood beginning to soak her dress, and fell limply onto her side.

Then the Denarian's two sets of eyes turned to me, and a swarm of razor-edged tendrils of her hair came whipping toward me.

I had already begun to ready my shield, but when I saw Francisca fall a surge of fury went coursing through me, filling me from toes to teeth with scarlet rage. The shield came together before me in a quarter-dome of blazing crimson energy, and the writhing tendrils slammed against it in a dozen flashes of white light. The Denarian shrieked, jerking back, and the attacking tendrils went sailing back across the cabin with their ends scorched and blackened.

I looked around wildly for my blasting rod, but it wasn't where Anna had left it when she took it from me. The pepper spray was, though. I grabbed it and faced the Denarian in time to see her raise her clawed hand. A shimmer in the air around her fingers threw off a prismatic flash of color, and with a flash of light from the upper set of eyes, the demoness drove her fist at my shield.

She hit the shield hard, and she was incredibly strong. The blow drove me back against a wall, and when the heat-shimmer of power touched my scarlet shield, it fractured into shards of light that went flying around the cabin like the sparks from a campfire. I tried to get to one side, away from the demon's vicious strength, but she snarled and strands of hair punched into the hull on either side of me, caging me. The Denarian reached for me with her claws.

I shouted a panicked battle cry and gave her the pepper spray full in the face, right into both sets of eyes.

The demoness screamed again, twisting her face away, ruining the tendril-cage, the human eyes squeezing shut over a sudden flood of tears. The glowing demon-eyes did not even blink, and a sweep of the Denarian's arm fetched me a backhanded blow that sent me sprawling and made me see stars.

I got back to my feet, terrified at the notion of being caught helpless on the ground. The Denarian seemed able to blow off my magic with a bit of effort, and she was deadly in these confined quarters. I didn't think I could get up the stairs without her tearing me apart. Which meant I had to find another way to get the demon away.

The Denarian swiped a clawed hand at her eyes and snarled in mangled, throaty English, 'You will pay for that.'

I looked up to see that Anna had dragged herself across the floor to the fallen Francisca, and knelt over her, shielding the other woman from the Denarian with her body. Her face was white with pain, or shock, or both – but she shot me a glance and then jerked her head toward the far side of the cabin.

I followed her gaze and got her drift. As the Denarian recovered and blinked watery, murderous eyes at me, I lunged toward the far side of the room and shouted, 'Get it out of the fridge! They must not have it!'

The Denarian spat out what I took to be an oath, and I felt that lionlike foot land in the middle of my back, flattening me to the floor, claws digging into my skin. She stepped over me, past me, and her tendrils tore open the real fridge, taking the door from its hinges before slithering inside and knocking everything within to the floor. She hadn't quite finished with the first fridge before her hair had gone on to tear open the dummy fridge, and dragged out the steel strongbox.

While the Denarian did that, I looked wildly around the cabin, and spotted my blasting rod on the floor. I rolled, my back burning with pain, and grabbed the blasting rod. Calling up fire within the tiny cabin was a bad idea – but waiting around for the Denarian to murder me with her hairdo was even worse.

She stood up with the strongbox just as I began channeling energy into the blasting rod. Its carved runes began to burn with golden radiance and the tip of the rod suddenly gleamed with red light and wavered with hot-air shimmer.

The Denarian crouched, demonic limbs too long, feminine shape disturbingly attractive, red light gleaming on her metallic-green scales. Her hair writhed in a hissing mass, striking sparks as one edge rasped against another. Violent lust burned in both sets of eyes for a second, and then she turned away. Her hair tore the cabin's ceiling apart like papier-mâché, and using her hair, an arm, and one long leg, she swarmed out of the ship's cabin. I heard a splash as she hit the water, taking the strongbox with her.

'What was that?' stammered Anna Valmont, clutching Francisca's limp form to her. 'What the bloody hell was that?'

I didn't drop the blasting rod or look away from the hole in the roof, because I didn't think the Denarian was the sort to leave a lot of people alive behind her. The end of the blasting rod was wavering drunkenly. 'How is she?'

I watched the hole in the ceiling for several shaking breaths until Anna said, her voice barely audible, 'She's gone.'

A stabbing feeling went through my belly, sharp and hot. Maybe I'm some kind of Neanderthal for thinking so, but it hurt me. A minute ago, Francisca Garcia had been talking, planning, grieving, breathing. Living. She'd been killed by violence, and I couldn't stand the thought of things like that happening to a woman. It wouldn't have been any less wrong had it happened to a man, but in my gut it wasn't the same. 'Dammit,' I whispered. 'How are you? Can you walk?'

Before she could answer, the ship lurched and leaned to one side. There was a wrenching, snapping roar and the rushing sound of water. Icy cold ran over my ankles and began to rise.

'The hull's breached,' Anna said. 'We're taking on water.'

I headed for the stairway, blasting rod up, to make sure it was clear. 'Can you get out?'

Light exploded behind my eyes and I dropped to my hands and knees at the bottom of the stairway. Anna had slugged me with something. A second burst of light and pain drove my head far enough down to splash some cold water against my forehead. I dimly saw Anna's foot kick my blasting rod away from me. Then she picked up the Shroud in its package from the counter, and tore off the top sheet of the hotel memo pad. I saw that she had blood on her jacket, soaked through, and staining her fatigue pants down to the top of her left leg. She grabbed my coat, wincing, and one of the duffel bags. She put my leather duster on, covering the blood. The water had filled the cabin almost to the tops of her combat boots.

I tried to get my wits together, but something was keeping me from doing much besides focusing my eyes. I knew that I needed to leave, but I couldn't get the message from my head to my arms and legs.

Anna Valmont stepped past me and went up the stairs. She stopped about halfway up, spat out another curse, and came back down them enough to reach down and splash cold water into my face. The shock jump-started something in my body, and I coughed, my head spinning, and started to move again. I'd been too drunk to stand up a time or two, but even then I'd been more capable than I was at that moment.

The blonde thief grabbed my arm and half hauled me up a couple of stairs, her face twisted in pain. I desperately held on to that momentum, struggling up another stair even after she stopped pulling.

She kept going up the stairs and didn't look back as she said, 'I'm only doing this because I like your coat, Dresden. Don't come near me again.'

Then she padded up out of the cabin and disappeared with the Shroud.

My head had started to throb and swell, but it was clearing rapidly also. But evidently I wasn't all that bright even when fully conscious, because I staggered back down into the ship's cabin. Francisca Garcia's corpse had fallen onto its side, glassy eyes staring, mouth slightly open. One of her cheeks had been half-covered by water. There were still the tracks of tears on the other one. The water around her was a cloudy, brownish pink.

My stomach heaved and the anger that came with it nearly sent me to the floor again. Instead, I sloshed through the freezing water to the counter. I picked up the cell phone there, and the blank memo pad. I hesitated over Francisca. She didn't deserve to have her body swallowed by the lake like a discarded beer bottle.

My balance wobbled again. The water had begun to rise more quickly. It covered my shins already, and I couldn't feel my feet for the cold. I tried to lift her body, but the effort brought a surge of pain to my head and I almost threw up.

I settled the body back down, unable to even curse coherently, and made do with gently closing her eyes with one hand. It was all I could do for her. The police would find her, of course, probably within a few hours.

And if I didn't get moving, they'd find me too. I couldn't afford to spend a night in the pokey while I was interrogated, charged and awaiting bail, but what else was new. I'd get in touch with Murphy as soon as I could.

I folded my arms against the growing cold, hugging the memo pad and cell phone to my chest, and slogged out of the bloody water of the *Etranger*'s cabin and onto the deck. I had to make a short jump up to the dock. A couple of people were on the sidewalk above the little harbor, staring down, and I saw a couple of folks out on the decks of their ships, also staring.

I ducked my head, thought inconspicuous thoughts, and hurried away before my morning could get any worse.

14

I've been clouted in the head a few times in my day. The bump Anna Valmont had given me was smaller than some, but my head pounded all the way home. At least my stomach settled down before I started throwing up all over myself. I shambled in, washed down a couple of Tylenol with a can of Coke, and folded some ice into a towel. I sat down by the phone, put the ice pack against the back of my head, and called Father Vincent.

The phone rang once. 'Yes?'

'It's in town,' I said. 'The two Churchmice had it on a boat in Burnham Harbor.'

Vincent's voice gained an edge of tension. 'You have it?'

'Uh,' I said. 'Not strictly speaking, no. Something went wrong.'

'What happened?' he demanded, his voice growing more frustrated, angrier. 'Why didn't you call me?'

'A third party made a grab for it, and what do you think I'm doing right now? I had a shot to recover the thing. I took it. I missed.'

'And the Shroud was taken from the thieves?'

'Thief, singular. Chicago PD is probably recovering the body of her partner right now.'

'They turned on each other?'

'Not even. A new player killed Garcia. Valmont duped the third party into taking a decoy. Then she grabbed the real McCoy and ran.'

'And you didn't see fit to follow her?'

My head pounded steadily. 'She ran really fast.'

Vincent was silent for a moment before he said, 'So the Shroud is lost to us once more.'

'For now,' I said. 'I might have another lead.'

'You know where it has gone?'

I took in a deep breath and tried to sound patient. 'Not yet. That's why it's called a lead and not a solution. I need that sample of the Shroud.'

'To be frank, Mister Dresden, I did bring a few threads with me from the Vatican, but . . .'

'Great. Get one of them to my office and drop it off with security downstairs. They'll hold it for me until I can pick it up. I'll call you as soon as I have anything more definite.'

'But—'

I hung up on Vincent, and felt a twinge of vindictive satisfaction. '"You didn't see fit to follow her,"' I muttered to Mister, doing my best to imitate Vincent's accent. 'I gotcher didn't see fit to follow her. White-collar jerk. How about I ring your bell a few times, and then you can go say Mass or something.'

Mister gave me a look as if to say that I shouldn't say such things about paying clients. I glared at him to let him know that I was well aware of it, got up, went into my bedroom, and rummaged in my closet until I found a stick of charcoal and a clipboard. Then I lit several candles on the end table next to my big comfy chair and settled down with the memo pad I'd taken from the *Etranger*. I brushed the stick of charcoal over it as carefully as I could, and hoped that Francisca Garcia hadn't been using a felt tip.

She hadn't. Faint white letters began to appear amidst the charcoal on the paper. It read *Marriott* on the first line and *2345* on the second.

I frowned down at the pad. Marriott. One of the hotels? It could have been someone's last name, too. Or maybe some kind of French word. *No, don't make it more complicated than it has to be, Harry*. It probably meant the hotel. The number appeared to be military time for a quarter to midnight. Maybe even a room number.

I glared at the note. It didn't tell me enough. Even though I may have had the time and place, I didn't know where and when.

I looked at the cell phone I'd taken. I knew as much about cell phones as I did about gastrointestinal surgery. There were no markings on the case, not even a brand name. The phone was off, but I didn't dare turn it on. It would probably stop working. Hell, it would probably explode. I would need to ask Murphy to see what she could find out when I talked to her.

My head kept pounding and my eyes itched with weariness. I needed rest. The lack of sleep was making me sloppy. I shouldn't have chanced going onto the ship in the first place, and I should have been more careful about watching my back. I'd had a gut instinct someone was watching me, but I had been too tired, too impatient, and I'd nearly gotten myself shot, impaled, concussed, and drowned as a result.

I headed into the bedroom, set my alarm clock for a couple of hours after noon, and flopped down on my bed. It felt obscenely good.

Naturally it didn't last.

The phone rang and I gave serious thought to blasting it into orbit, where it could hang around with Asteroid Dresden. I stomped back into the living room, picked up the phone, and snarled, 'What.'

'Oh, uh,' said a somewhat nervous voice on the other end. 'This is Waldo Butters. I was calling to speak to Harry Dresden.'

I moderated my voice to a mere snarl. 'Oh. Hey.'

'I woke you up, huh?'

'Some.'

'Yeah, late nights suck. Look, there's something odd going on and I thought maybe I could ask you something.'

'Sure.'

'Sullen monosyllabism, a sure sign of sleep deprivation.'

'Eh.'

'Now descending into formless vocalization. My time is short.' Butters cleared his throat and said, 'The germs are gone.'

'Germs?' I asked.

'In the samples I took from that body. I ran all the checks again just to be sure, and better than half of them turned up negative. Nothing. Zip, zero.'

'Ungh,' I said.

'Okay, then, Caveman Og. Where germs go?'

'Sunrise,' I said. 'Poof.'

Butters's voice sounded bewildered. 'Vampire germs?'

'The tiny capes are a dead giveaway,' I said. I started pulling my train of thought into motion at last. 'Not vampire germs.

Constructs. See, at sunrise it's like the whole magical world gets reset to zero. New beginnings. Most spells don't hold together through even one sunrise. And it takes a lot to make them last through two or three.'

'Magic germs?' Butters asked. 'Are you telling me I've got magic germs?'

'Magic germs,' I confirmed. 'Someone called them up with magic.'

'Like an actual magic spell?'

'Usually you call nasty hurtful spells a curse. But by tomorrow or the next day, those other samples will probably have zeroed out too.'

'Are they still infectious?'

'Assume they are. They're good as real until the energy that holds them together falls apart.'

'Christ. You're serious. It's for real.'

'Well, yeah.'

'Is there a book or a Cliff's Notes or something on this stuff?'

I actually smiled that time. 'Just me. Anything else?'

'Not much. I swept the body for genetic remains but got nothing. The cuts on the corpse were made with either a surgical scalpel or some other kind of small, fine blade. Maybe a utility knife.'

'I've seen cuts like that before, yeah.'

'Here's the best part. The same blade evidently took off the hands and head. The cuts are cleaner than a surgeon could manage on an operating table. Three single cuts. The heat from it half cauterized parts of the wounds. So what kind of tool can cut fine, precise lines and cleave through bones too?'

'Sword?'

'Have to be one hell of a sharp sword.'

'There's a few around like that. Any luck identifying the victim?'

'None. Sorry.'

''S okay.'

'You want to know if anything changes?'

'Yeah. Or if you see anyone else come in like that guy.'

'God forbid, will do. You find anything on that tattoo?'

'Called the Eye of Thoth,' I said. 'Trying to narrow down exactly who uses it around here. Oh, give Murphy a call. Let her know about those samples.'

'Already did. She's the one who told me to keep you in the loop. I think she was heading toward sleep too. Would she want me to wake her up to talk to you?'

I talked through a yawn. 'Nah, it can wait. Thanks for the call, Butters.'

'No trouble,' he said. 'Sleep is god. Go worship.'

I grunted, hung up the phone, and didn't get to take the second step toward my bed when someone knocked at the door.

'I need one of those trapdoors,' I muttered to Mister. 'I could push a button and people would fall screaming down a wacky slide thing and land in mud somewhere.'

Mister was far too mature to dignify that with a response, so I kept a hand near my gift rack as I opened the door a crack and peeked out.

Susan tilted her head sideways and gave me a small smile. She was wearing jeans, an old tee, a heavy grey fleece jacket, and sunglasses. 'Hi,' she said.

'Hi.'

'You know, it's hard to tell through the door, but your eyes look sunken and bloodshot. Did you sleep last night?'

'What is this thing you speak of, "sleep"?'

Susan sighed and shook her head. 'Mind if I come in?'

I stepped back and opened the door wider. 'No scolding.'

Susan came in and folded her arms. 'Always so cold in here in the winter.'

I had a couple of suggestions on how to warm up, but I didn't say them out loud. Maybe I didn't want to see her response to them. I thought about what Murphy had said about setting up a talk. I got some more wood and stirred up the fireplace. 'Want me to make some tea or something?'

She shook her head. 'No.'

Susan never turned down a cup of hot tea. I tried, but I couldn't keep a hard edge out of my voice. 'Just going to dump me and run, then. Drive-by dumping.'

'Harry, that isn't fair,' Susan said. I could hear the hurt in her voice, but only barely. I raked harder at the fire, making sparks fly up, though flames were already licking the new wood. 'This isn't easy for anyone.'

My mouth kept running without checking in with my brain. My heart maybe, but not my brain. I shot her a look over my shoulder and said, 'Except for Captain Mediocrity, I guess.'

She raised both eyebrows. 'Do you mean Martin?'

'Isn't that what this is about?' A spark flipped out of the fire and landed on my hand, stinging. I yelped and pulled my hand away. I closed the heavy mesh curtain over the fire and put the poker away. 'And before you say anything, I know damn well I'm being insane. And possessive. I know that we were quits before you left town. It's been more than a year, and it's been hard on you. It's only natural for you to find someone. It's irrational and childish for me to be upset, and I don't care.'

'Harry—' she began.

'And it's not as if you haven't been thinking about it,' I continued. Somewhere I knew that I'd start choking on my foot if I kept shoving it in my mouth. 'You kissed me. You *kissed* me, Susan. I know you. You meant it.'

'This isn't—'

'I'll bet you don't kiss Snoozy Martin like that.'

Susan rolled her eyes and walked to me. She sat down on the lintel of my little fireplace while I knelt before it. She cupped my cheek in one hand. She was warm. It felt good. I was too tired to control my reaction to the simple, gentle touch, and I looked back at the fire.

'Harry,' she said. 'You're right. I don't kiss Martin like that.'

I pulled my cheek away, but she put her fingers on my chin and tugged my face back toward her. 'I don't kiss him at all. I'm not involved with Martin.'

I blinked. 'You're not?'

She drew an invisible X over her heart with her index finger.

'Oh,' I said. I felt my shoulders ease up a little.

Susan laughed. 'Was that really worrying you, Harry? That I was leaving you for another man?'

'I don't know. I guess.'

'God, you are a dolt sometimes.' She smiled at me, but I could see the sadness in it. 'It always shocked me how you could understand so many things and be such a complete idiot about so many others.'

'Practice,' I said. She looked down at me for a while, with

that same sad smile, and I understood. 'It doesn't change anything, does it?'

'Martin?'

'Yeah.'

She nodded. 'It doesn't change anything.'

I swallowed a sudden frog in my throat. 'You want it to be over.'

'I don't *want* it,' she said quickly. 'But I think it's necessary. For both of us.'

'You came back here to tell me that?'

Susan shook her head. 'I don't have my mind set. I think it wouldn't be fair to do that without talking to you about it. We both have to make this decision.'

I growled and looked back at the fire. 'Would be a lot simpler if you just gave me the Dear John speech and left.'

'Simpler,' she said. 'Easier. But not fair and not right.'

I didn't say anything.

'I've changed,' Susan said. 'Not just the vampire thing. There's a lot that's been happening in my life. A lot of things that I didn't know.'

'Like what?'

'How dangerous the world is, for one,' she said. 'I wound up in Peru, but I went all over South America, Central America. I couldn't have imagined what things are like there. Harry, the Red Court is *everywhere*. There are whole villages out in the country supporting groups of them. Like cattle bred for the lord of the manor. The vampires feed on everyone. Addict them all.' Her voice hardened. 'Even the children.'

My stomach twitched unpleasantly. 'I hadn't ever heard that.'

'Not many know.'

I mopped a hand over my face. 'God. Kids.'

'I want to help. To do something. I've found where I can help down there, Harry. A job. I'm going to take it.'

Something in my chest hurt, a literal pain. 'I thought this was our decision.'

'I'm coming to that,' she said.

I nodded. 'Okay.'

She slipped to the floor next to me and said, 'You could come with me.'

Go with her. Leave Chicago. Leave Murphy, the Alphas, Michael. Leave a horde of problems – many of them ones I'd created for myself. I thought of packing up and heading out. Maybe fighting the good fight. Being loved again, held again. God, I wanted that.

But people would get hurt. Friends. Others who might be in my kind of danger and have no one to turn to.

I looked into Susan's eyes and saw hope there for just a moment. Then understanding. She smiled, but it was somehow sadder than ever. 'Susan—' I said.

She pressed a finger to my lips and blinked back tears. 'I know.'

And then I understood. She knew because she was feeling the same way.

There are things you can't walk away from. Not if you want to live with yourself afterward.

'Now do you understand?' she asked.

I nodded, but my voice came out rough. 'Wouldn't be fair. Not to either of us,' I said. 'Not being together. Both of us hurting.'

Susan leaned her shoulder against mine and nodded. I put my arm around her.

'Maybe someday things will change,' I said.

'Maybe someday,' she agreed. 'I love you. I never stopped loving you, Harry.'

'Yeah,' I said. I choked on the end of the word, and the fire went blurry. 'I love you too. Dammit.' We sat there and warmed up in front of the fire for a couple of minutes before I said, 'When are you leaving?'

'Tomorrow,' she said.

'With Martin?'

She nodded. 'He's a co-worker. He's helping me move, watching my back. I have to put everything in order here. Pack some things from the apartment.'

'What kind of work?'

'Pretty much the same kind. Investigate and report. Only I report to a boss instead of to readers.' She sighed and said, 'I'm not supposed to tell you anything else about it.'

'Hell's bells,' I muttered. 'Will I be able to reach you?'

She nodded. 'I'll set up a drop. You can write. I'd like that.'

'Yeah. Stay in touch.'

Long minutes after that, Susan said, 'You're on a case again, aren't you?'

'Does it show?'

She leaned a little away from me, and I drew my arm back. 'I smelled it,' she said, and stood up to add wood to the fire. 'There's blood on you.'

'Yeah,' I said. 'A woman was killed about five feet away from me.'

'Vampires?' Susan asked.

I shook my head. 'Some kind of demon.'

'Are you okay?'

'Peachy.'

'That's funny, because you look like hell,' Susan said.

'I said no scolding.'

She almost smiled. 'You'd be smart to get some sleep.'

'True, but I'm not all that bright,' I said. Besides, I didn't have a prayer of falling asleep now, after talking to her.

'Ah,' she said. 'Is there anything I can do to help?'

'Don't think so.'

'You need rest.'

I waved a hand at the stationery pad. 'I will. I just have to run down a lead first.'

Susan folded her arms, facing me directly. 'So do it after you get some rest.'

'There probably isn't time.'

Susan frowned and picked up the pad. 'Marriott. The hotel?'

'Dunno. Likely.'

'What are you looking for?'

I sighed, too tired to stick to my confidentiality guns very closely. 'Stolen artifact. I think the note is probably about a site for the sale.'

'Who is the buyer?'

I shrugged.

'Lots of legwork, then.'

'Yeah.'

Susan nodded. 'Let me look into this. You get some sleep.'

'It's probably better if you don't—'

She waved a hand, cutting me off. 'I want to help. Let me do this for you.'

I opened my mouth and closed it again. I guess I could relate. I knew how much I'd wanted to help her. I couldn't. It had been tough to handle. It would have been a relief to me to have done her some good, no matter how small it was.

'All right,' I said. 'But just the phone work. Okay?'

'Okay.' She copied down the word and the number on a sheet she tore from the bottom of the memo pad and turned toward the door.

'Susan?' I said.

She paused without turning to look back at me.

'Do you want to get dinner or something? Before you go, I mean. I want to, uh, you know.'

'Say good-bye,' she said quietly.

'Yeah.'

'All right.'

She left. I sat in my apartment, in front of the fire, and breathed in the scent of her perfume. I felt cold, lonely, and tired. I felt like a hollowed-out husk. I felt as if I had failed her. Failed to protect her to begin with, failed to cure her after the vampires had changed her.

Change. Maybe that's what this was really about. Susan had changed. She'd grown. She was more relaxed than I remembered, more confident. There had always been a sense of purpose to her, but now it seemed deeper, somehow. She'd found a place for herself, somewhere where she felt she could do some good.

Maybe I should have gone with her after all.

But no. Part of the change was that she felt hungrier now, too. More quietly sensual, as if every sight and sound and touch in the room was occupying most of her attention. She'd smelled drops of blood on my clothing and it had excited her enough to make her move away from me.

Another change. She had an instinctive hunger for my blood.

And she could throw vampires twenty feet through the air. She sure as hell wouldn't have any trouble tearing my throat out in an intimate moment if her control slipped.

I washed my face mechanically, showered in my unheated shower, and went shivering to my bed. The routine hadn't helped me. It only delayed me from facing the harshest truth of my relationship with Susan.

She had left Chicago.

Probably for good.

That was going to hurt like hell in the morning.

15

I had bad dreams.

They were the usual fare. Flames devoured someone who screamed my name. A pretty girl spread her arms, eyes closed, and fell slowly backward as dozens of fine cuts opened all over her skin. The air became a fine pink spray. I turned from it, into a kiss with Susan, who drew me down and tore out my throat with her teeth.

A woman who seemed familiar but whom I did not recognize shook her head and drew her hand from left to right. The dream-scenery faded to black in the wake of her motion. She turned to me, dark eyes intent and said, 'You need to rest.'

Mickey Mouse woke me up, my alarm jangling noisily, his little hand on two and the big hand on twelve. I wanted to smack the clock for waking me up, but I reined in the impulse. I'm not against a little creative violence now and then, but you have to draw the line somewhere. I wouldn't sleep in the same room with a person who would smack Mickey Mouse.

I got up, got dressed, left a message for Murphy, another for Michael, fed Mister, and hit the road.

Michael's house did not blend in with most of the other homes in his neighborhood west of Wrigley Field. It had a white picket fence. It had elegant window dressings. It had a tidy front lawn that was always green, even in the midst of a blazing Chicago summer. It had a few shady trees, a lot of well-kept shrubberies, and if I had found a couple of deer grazing on the lawn or drinking from the birdbath, it wouldn't have surprised me.

I got out of the Beetle, holding my blasting rod loosely in my right hand. I opened the gate, and a few jingle bells hanging on a string tinkled happily. The gate swung shut on a lazy spring behind me. I knocked on the front door and waited, but no one answered. I frowned. Michael's house had never been empty before. Charity had at least a couple of kids who weren't old enough to be in school yet, including the poor little guy they'd named after me. Harry Carpenter. How cruel is that?

I frowned at the cloud-hazed sun. Weren't the older kids getting out of school shortly? Charity had some kind of maternal obsession with never allowing her kids to come home to an empty house.

Someone should have been there.

I got a sick, twisty feeling in the pit of my stomach.

I knocked again, put my ear against the door, and Listened. I could hear the slow tick of the old grandfather clock in the front room. The heater cycled on for a moment, and the vents inside whispered. There were a few sounds when a bit of breeze touched the house, the creaks of old and comfortable wood.

Nothing else.

I tried the front door. It was locked. I stepped back off the porch, and followed the narrow driveway to the back of the property.

If the front of the Carpenter home would have qualified for *Better Homes and Gardens*, the back would have been fit for a Craftsman commercial. The large tree centered on the back lawn cast lots of shade in the summer, but with the leaves gone I could see the fortresslike tree house Michael had built for his kids in it. It had finished walls, an actual window, and guardrails anywhere anyone could possibly have thought about falling. The tree house had a porch that overlooked the yard. Hell, I didn't have a porch. It's an unfair world.

A big section of the yard had been bitten off by an addit-ion connected to the back of the house. The foundation had been laid, and there were wooden beams framing what would eventually be walls. Heavy contractor's plastic had been stapled to the wooden studs to keep the wind off the addition. The separate garage was closed, and a peek in the window showed me that it was pretty well filled with lumber and other construction materials.

'No cars,' I muttered. 'Maybe they went to McDonald's. Or church. Do they have church at three in the afternoon?'

I turned around to go back to the Beetle. I'd leave Michael a note. My stomach fluttered. If I didn't get a second for the duel, it was likely to be a bad evening. Maybe I should ask Bob to be my second. Or maybe Mister. No one dares to mess with Mister.

Something rattled against the metal gutters running the length of the back of the house.

I jumped like a spooked horse and scrambled away from the house, toward the garage at the back of the yard so that I could get a look at the roof. Given that in the past day or so no less than three different parties had taken a poke at me, I felt totally justified in being on edge.

I got to the back of the yard, but couldn't see the whole roof from there, so I clambered up into the branches, then took a six-foot ladder up to the main platform of the tree house. From there, I could see that the roof was empty.

I heard brisk, somewhat heavy footsteps below me, and beyond the fence at the back of the little yard. I froze in place in the tree house, Listening.

The heavy footsteps padded up to the fence at the back of the yard, and I heard the scrape of chain link dragging against dry leaves and other late-winter detritus. I heard a muted grunt of effort and a long exhalation. Then the footsteps came to the base of the tree.

Leather scraped against a wooden step, and the tree shivered almost imperceptibly. Someone was climbing up.

I looked around me but the ladder was the only way down, unless I felt like jumping. It couldn't have been more than nine or ten feet down. Odds were I could land more or less in one piece. But if I misjudged the jump I could sprain an ankle or break a leg, which would make running away both impractical and embarrassing. Jumping would have to be a last resort.

I gathered in my will and settled my grip on my blasting rod, pointing it directly at where the ladder met the platform. The tip of the blasting rod glowed with a pinpoint of bright red energy.

Blonde hair and the top half of a girl's angelic young face appeared at the top of the ladder. There was a quiet gasp and her blue eyes widened. 'Holy crap.'

I jerked the tip of the blasting rod up and away from the girl, releasing the gathered energy. 'Molly?'

The rest of the girl's face appeared as she climbed on up the ladder. 'Wow, is that an acetylene torch or something?'

I blinked and peered more closely at Molly. 'Is that an earring in your eyebrow?'

The girl clapped her fingers over her right eyebrow.

'And your *nose*?'

Molly shot a furtive look over her shoulder at the house, and scrambled the rest of the way up to the tree house. As tall as her mother, Molly was all coltish legs and long arms. She wore a typical private-school uniform of skirt, blouse, and sweater – but it looked like she'd been attacked by a lech with razor blades where fingers should have been.

The skirt was essentially slashed to ribbons, and underneath it she wore black tights, also torn to nigh indecency. Her shirt and sweater had apparently endured the Blitz, but the bright red satin bra that peeked out from beneath looked new. She had on too much makeup. Not as bad as most kids too old to play tag but too young to drive, but it was there. She wore a ring of fine gold wire through one pale gold eyebrow, and a golden stud protruded from one side of her nose.

I worked hard not to smile. Smiling would have implied that I found her outfit amusing. She was young enough to be hurt by that kind of opinion, and I had a vague memory of being that ridiculous at one time. Let he who hath never worn parachute pants cast the first stone.

Molly clambered in and tossed a bulging backpack down on the wooden floor. 'You lurk in tree houses a lot, Mister Dresden?'

'I'm looking for your dad.'

Molly wrinkled up her nose, then started removing the stud from it. I didn't want to watch. 'I don't want to tell you how to investigate stuff, but generally speaking you won't find him in tree houses.'

'I came over, but no one answered the door when I knocked. Is that normal?'

Molly took out the eyebrow ring, dumped the backpack out onto the floorboards, and started sorting out a long skirt with a floral print, a T-shirt, and a sweater. 'It is on errands day. Mom loads up the sandcrawler with all the little snot-nosed Jawas and goes all over town.'

'Oh. Do you know when she's due back?'

'Anytime,' Molly said. She hopped into the skirt, and wriggled out of the tattered skirt and tights in that mystifyingly modest way that girls always seem to manage to acquire sometime in their teens. The shirt and pink sweater went on next, and the ripped up sweater and, to my discomfort, the bright red bra came out from under the conservative clothes and got tucked back into the backpack.

I turned my back on the girl as well as I could in the limited space. The link of handcuff Anna Valmont had slapped onto my wrist chafed and pinched. I scratched at it irritably. You'd think I'd been cuffed enough times that I should have gotten myself a key by now.

Molly took a wet-wipe from somewhere and started peeling the makeup from her face. 'Hey,' she asked a minute later. 'What's wrong?'

I grunted and waved my wrist vaguely, swinging the cuff around.

'Hey, neat,' Molly said. 'Are you on the lam? Is that why you're hiding in a tree house, so the cops won't find you?'

'No,' I said. 'It's kind of a long story.'

'Ohhhh,' Molly said wisely. 'Those are fun-time handcuffs, not bad-time handcuffs. I gotcha.'

'No!' I protested. 'And how the hell would you know about fun-time handcuffs anyway? You're like ten.'

She snorted. 'Fourteen.'

'Whatever, too young.'

'Internet,' she said sagely. 'Expanding the frontiers of adolescent knowledge.'

'God, I'm old.'

Molly clucked and dipped into the backpack again. She grabbed my wrist firmly, shook out a ring of small keys, and started trying them in the lock of the cuffs. 'So give me the juicy details,' she said. 'You can say "bleep" instead of the fun words if you want.'

I blinked. 'Where the bleep did you get a bunch of cuff keys?'

She looked up at me and narrowed her eyes. 'Think about this one. Do you *really* want to know?'

I sighed. 'No. Probably not.'

'Cool,' she said, and turned her attention back to the handcuffs. 'So stop dodging the issue. What's up with you and Susan?'

'Why do you want to know?'

'I like romance. Plus I heard Mom say that you two were a pretty hot item.'

'Your mom said that?'

Molly shrugged. 'Sorta. As much as she ever would. She used words like "fornication" and "sin" and "infantile depravity" and "moral bankruptcy." So are you?'

'Morally bankrupt?'

'A hot item with Susan.'

I shrugged and said, 'Not anymore.'

'Don't move your wrist.' Molly fiddled with one key for a moment before discarding it. 'What happened?'

'A lot,' I said. 'It's complicated.'

'Oh,' Molly said. The cuffs clicked and loosened and she beamed up at me. 'There.'

'Thanks.' I rubbed my sore wrist and put the cuffs in my coat pocket.

Molly bent over and picked up a piece of paper. She read it and said, 'Ask Michael about duel? Whiskey and tobacco?'

'It's a shopping list.'

Molly frowned. 'Oh.' She was quiet for a moment and then asked, 'So was it the vampire thing?'

I blinked at the girl again. 'Was there a PBS special or something? Is there some kind of unauthorized biography of my life?'

'I snuck downstairs so I could listen to Dad tell Mom what had happened.'

'Do you eavesdrop on every private conversation you can?'

She rolled her eyes and sat down on the edge of the platform, her shoes waving in the air. 'No one says anything interesting in a public conversation, do they? Why did you guys split up?'

I sat down next to her. 'Like I said. It was complicated.'

'Complicated how?'

I shrugged. 'Her condition gives her . . . an impulse-control problem,' I said. 'She told me that strong emotions and uh, other feelings, are dangerous for her. She could lose control and hurt someone.'

'Oh,' Molly said, and scrunched up her nose again. 'So you can't make a play for her or—'

'Bad things could happen. And then she'd be a full vampire.'

'But you both want to be together?' Molly asked.

'Yeah.'

She frowned. 'God, that's sad. You want to be with her but the sex part—'

I shuddered. 'Ewg. You are far too young to say that word.'

The girl's eyes shone. 'What word? Sex?'

I put my hands over my ears. 'Gah.'

Molly grinned and enunciated. 'But the *bleep* part would make her lose control.'

I coughed uncomfortably, lowering my hands. 'Basically. Yeah.'

'Why don't you tie her up?'

I stared at the kid for a second.

She lifted her eyebrows expectantly.

'What?' I stammered.

'It's only practical,' Molly stated firmly. 'And hey, you've already got the handcuffs. If she can't move while the two of you are bleeping, she can't drink your blood, right?'

I stood up and started climbing down the ladder. 'This conversation has become way too bleeping disturbing.'

Molly laughed at me and followed me back to the ground. She unlocked the back door with another key, presumably from the same ring, and that was when Charity's light blue minivan turned into the driveway. Molly opened the door, darted into the house, and returned without her backpack. The minivan ground to a halt and the engine died.

Charity got out of the van, frowning at me and at Molly in more or less equal proportions. She wore jeans, hiking boots, and a heavy jacket. She was a tall woman, only an inch or so under six feet, and carried herself with an assurance that conveyed a sense of ready strength. Her face had the remote beauty of a marble statue, and her long blonde hair was knotted behind her head.

Without being told, Molly went to the rolling side panel door, opened it, and reached inside, unloading children from safety seats, while Charity went to the rear of the van and opened the rear doors. 'Mister Dresden,' she said. 'Lend a hand.'

I frowned. 'Uh. I'm sort of in a hurry. I was hoping to find Michael here.'

Charity took a twenty-four-pack of Coke from the van in one arm and a couple of bulging paper grocery sacks in the other. She marched over to me and shoved them at my chest. I had to fumble to catch them, and my blasting rod clattered to the ground.

Charity waited until I had the sacks before heading for the van again. 'Put them on the table in the kitchen.'

'But—' I said.

She walked past me toward the house. 'I have ice cream melting, meat thawing, and a baby about to wake up hungry. Put them on the table, and we'll talk.'

I sighed and looked glumly at the groceries. They were heavy enough to make my arms burn a little. Which probably isn't saying much. I don't spend much time working out.

Molly appeared from the van, lowering a tiny, towheaded girl to the driveway. She was wearing a pink dress with a clashing orange sweater and bright purple shoes and a red coat. She walked up to me and said, words edged with babyish syllables, 'My name is Amanda. I'm five and a half and my daddy says I'm a princess.'

'I'm Harry, Your Highness,' I said.

She frowned and said, 'There's already a Harry. You can be

Bill.' With that, she broke into a flouncing skip and followed her mother into the house.

'Well, I'm glad that's settled,' I muttered. Molly lowered an even smaller blonde girl to the driveway. This one was dressed in blue overalls with a pink shirt and a pink coat. She held a plush dolly in one arm and a battered-looking pink blanket in the other. Upon seeing me, she retreated a couple of steps and hid around the corner of the van. She leaned out to look at me once, and then hid again.

'I've got him,' said an accented male voice.

Molly hopped out of the van, grabbed a grocery bag from the back, and said, 'Come on, Hope.' The little girl followed her big sister like a duckling while Molly went into the house, but Hope glanced back at me shyly three or four times on the way.

Shiro emerged from the van carrying a baby seat. The little old knight carried the walking stick that concealed his sword on a strap over one wide shoulder, and his scarred hands held the chair carefully. A boy, probably not yet two years old, slept in it.

'Little Harry?' I asked.

'Yes, Bill,' Shiro said. His eyes sparkled behind his glasses.

I frowned and said, 'Good-looking kid.'

'Dresden!' snapped Charity's voice from the house. 'You're holding the ice cream.'

I scowled and told Shiro, 'Guess we'd better get in.'

Shiro nodded wisely. I took the groceries into the Carpenters' big kitchen and put them on the table. For the next five minutes, Shiro and Molly helped me carry in enough groceries to feed a Mongol horde.

After all the perishables got put away, Charity fixed a bottle of formula and passed it off to Molly, who took it, the diaper bag, and the sleeping boy into another room. Charity waited until she had left, then shut the door. 'Very well,' she said, still putting groceries away. 'I haven't spoken to Michael since you called this morning. I left a message with his cell phone voice mail.'

'Where is he?' I asked.

Shiro laid his cane on the table and sat down. 'Mister Dresden, we have asked you not to get involved in this business.'

'That isn't why I'm here,' I said. 'I just need to talk to him.'

'Why are you looking for him?' Shiro asked.

'I'm dueling a vampire under the Accords. I need a second before sundown or I get disqualified. Permanently.'

Shiro frowned. 'Red Court?'

'Yeah. Some guy named Ortega.'

'Heard of him,' Shiro said. 'Some kind of war leader.'

I nodded. 'That's the rumor. That's why I'm here. I had hoped Michael would be willing to help.'

Shiro stroked a thumb over the smooth old wood of his cane. 'We received word of Denarian activity near St Louis. He and Sanya went to investigate.'

'When will they get back?'

Shiro shook his head. 'I do not know.'

I looked at the clock and bit my lip. 'Christ.'

Charity walked by with an armload of groceries and glared at me.

I lifted my hands. 'Sorry. I'm a little tense.'

Shiro studied me for a moment, and then asked, 'Would Michael help him?'

Charity's voice drifted out of the cavernous walk-in pantry. 'My husband is sometimes an idiot.'

Shiro nodded and said, 'Then I will assist you in his stead, Mister Dresden.'

'You'll what?' I asked.

'I will be your second in the duel.'

'You don't have to do that,' I said. 'I mean, I'll figure out something.'

Shiro lifted an eyebrow. 'Have the weapons been set for the duel?'

'Uh, not yet,' I said.

'Then where is the meeting with the emissary and your opponent's second?'

I fished out the card I'd gotten from the Archive. 'I don't know. I was told to have my second call this number.'

Shiro took the card and rose without another word, heading for the phone in the next room.

I put my hand on his arm and said, 'You don't need to take any chances. You don't really know me.'

'Michael does. That is enough for me.'

The old Knight's support was a relief, but I felt guilty, somehow, for accepting it. Too many people had been hurt on my behalf in the past. Michael and I had faced trouble together before, looked out for each other before. Somehow, it made it easier for me to go to him and ask for help. Accepting the same thing from a stranger, Knight of the Cross or not, grated on my conscience. Or maybe on my pride.

But what choice did I have?

I sighed and nodded. 'I just don't want to drag someone else into more trouble with me.'

Charity muttered, 'Let me think. Where have I heard that before?'

Shiro smiled at her, the expression both paternal and amused, and said, 'I'll make the call.'

I waited while Shiro made a call from the room that served as the family study and the office for Michael's contracting business. Charity stayed in the kitchen and wrestled a huge Crock-Pot onto the counter. She got out a ton of vegetables, stew meat, and a spice rack and set to chopping things up without a word to me.

I watched her quietly. She moved with the kind of precision you see only in someone who is so versed at what they are doing that they are already thinking of the steps coming twenty minutes in the future. I thought she took her knife to the carrots a little more violently than she needed to. She started preparing another meal somewhere in the middle of making the stew, this one chicken and rice and other healthy things I rarely saw in three dimensions.

I fidgeted for a bit, until I stood up, washed my hands in the sink, and started cutting vegetables.

Charity frowned at me for a moment. She didn't say anything. But she got a few more veggies out and put them down next to me, then collected what had been cut so far and pitched them into the Crock-Pot. A couple of minutes later she sighed, opened a can of Coke, and put it on the counter next to me.

'I worry about him,' she said.

I nodded, and focused on cucumbers.

'I don't even know when he'll be home tonight.'

'Good thing you have a Crock-Pot,' I said.

'I don't know what I would do without him. What the children would do. I'd feel so lost.'

What the hell. An ounce of well-intentioned but irrational reassurance didn't cost anything. I took a sip of the Coke. 'He'll be all right. He can handle himself. And he has Shiro and Sanya with him.'

'He's been hurt three times, you know.'

'Three?' I asked.

'Three. With you. Every time.'

'So it's my fault.' My turn to chop vegetables like teenagers in a slasher movie. 'I see.'

I couldn't see her face but her voice was, more than anything else, tired. 'It isn't about blame. Or whose fault it is. All that matters is that when you're around, my husband, my children's father, gets hurt.'

The knife slipped and I cut off a neat little slice of skin on my index finger. 'Ow,' I snarled. I slapped the cold water on in the sink and put my finger under it. You can't tell, with cuts like that, how bad they're going to be until you see how much you're leaking. Charity passed me a paper towel, and I examined the cut for a minute before wrapping the towel around it. It wasn't bad, though it hurt like hell. I watched my blood stain the paper towel for a minute and then I asked, 'Why didn't you get rid of me, then?'

I looked up to see Charity frowning at me. There were dark circles under her eyes that I hadn't noticed before. 'What do you mean?'

'Just now,' I said. 'When Shiro asked you if Michael would help me. You could have said no.'

'But he would have helped you in an instant. You know that.'

'Shiro didn't.'

Her expression became confused. 'I don't understand.'

'You could have lied.'

Her face registered comprehension, and some fire came back into her eyes. 'I don't like you, Mister Dresden. I certainly don't care enough for you to abandon beliefs I hold dear, to use you as an excuse to cheapen myself, or to betray what my husband stands for.' She stepped to a cabinet and got out a small, neat medical kit. Without another word, she took my hand and the paper towel and opened the kit.

'So you're taking care of me?' I asked.

'I don't expect you to understand. Whether or not I can personally stand you, it has no bearing on what choices I make. Michael is your friend. He would risk his life for you. It would break his heart if you came to grief, and I will not allow that to happen.'

She fell silent and doctored the cut with the same brisk, confident motions she'd used for cooking. I hear that they make disinfectants that don't hurt these days.

But Charity used iodine.

16

Shiro came out of the office and showed me an address written on a piece of paper. 'We meet them tonight at eight.'

'After sundown,' I noted. 'I know the place. I'll pick you up here?'

'Yes. I will need a little time to prepare.'

'Me too. Around seven.' I told them good-bye and headed for the door. Charity didn't answer me but Shiro did. I got into my car. More kids came pelting into the house as I did, two boys and a girl. The smaller of the two boys stopped to peer at my car, but Charity appeared in the door and chivied him inside. She frowned at me until I coaxed the Blue Beetle to life and pulled out.

Driving home left me with too much time to think. This duel with Ortega was something I had no way to prepare for. Ortega was a warlord of the Red Court. He'd probably fought duels before. Which meant that he'd killed people before. Hell, maybe even wizards. I'd squared off against various toughs but that had been free-for-all fighting. I had been able to find ways to cheat, by and large. In a one-on-one duel, I wasn't going to be able to fall back on cleverness, to take advantage of whatever I could find in my environment.

This was going to be a straight fight, and if Ortega was better than me, he'd kill me. Simple as that. The fear was simple, too. Simple and undeniable.

I swallowed, and my knuckles turned white. I tried to relax my fingers but they wouldn't. They were too afraid to let go of the wheel. Stupid fingers.

I got back to my apartment, pried my fingers off the steering wheel, and found my door halfway open. I ducked to one side, in case someone had a gun pointed up the narrow stairway down to my apartment door, and drew out my blasting rod.

'Harry?' called a quiet, female voice from my apartment. 'Harry, is that you?'

I lowered the blasting rod. 'Murph?'

'Get inside,' Murphy said. I looked down the stairway and saw her appear in the doorway, her face pale. 'Hurry.'

I came down the stairs warily, feeling out my wards as I did. They were intact, and I relaxed a little. I had given Murphy a personalized talisman that would let her through my defenses, and it would only have worked for her.

I slipped into my apartment. Murphy shut the door behind me and locked it. She'd started a fire in the fireplace and had one of my old kerosene lamps lit. I went to the fireplace and warmed up my hands, watching Murphy in silence. She stood with her back and shoulders rigid for a moment, before she came over to stand beside me, facing the fire. Her lips were held into a tense, neutral line. 'We should talk.'

'People keep saying that to me,' I muttered.

'You promised me you'd call me in when you had something.'

'Whoa, there, hang on. Who said I had anything?'

'There is a corpse on a pleasure ship in Burnham Harbor and several eyewitnesses who describe a tall, dark-haired man leaving the scene and getting into a multicolored Volkswagen Beetle.'

'Wait a second—'

'There's been a *murder*, Dresden. I don't care how sacred client confidentiality is to you. People are dying.'

Frustration made me clench my teeth. 'I was going to tell you about it. It's been a really busy day.'

'Too busy to talk to the police about a murder you may have witnessed?' Murphy said. 'That is considered aiding and abetting a first-degree murder in some places. Like courts of law.'

'This again,' I muttered. My fingers clenched into fists. 'I remember how this one goes. You slug me in the jaw and arrest me.'

'I damn well should.'

'Hell's bells, Murph!'

'Relax.' She sighed. 'If that was what I had in mind you'd be in the car already.'

My anger evaporated. 'Oh.' After a moment, I asked, 'Then why are you here?'

Murphy scowled. 'I'm on vacation.'

'You're what?'

Murphy's jaw twitched. Her words sounded a little odd, since she kept her teeth ground together while she talked. 'I've been taken off the case. And when I protested I was told that I could either be on vacation or collecting unemployment.'

Holy crap. The muckety-mucks at CPD had ordered Murphy off a case? But why?

Murphy answered the question I hadn't asked yet. 'Because when Butters looked at the victim from the harbor, he determined that the weapon used to kill her and the one used on that victim you saw last night were the same.'

I blinked. 'What?'

'Same weapon,' Murphy said. 'Butters seemed pretty confident about it.'

I turned that over in my head a few times, trying to shake out the kinks in the chains of logic. 'I need a beer. You?'

'Yeah.'

I went over to the pantry and grabbed a couple of brown bottles. I used an old bottle opener to take off the lids and took the drinks back to Murphy. She took her bottle in hand and eyed it suspiciously. 'It's warm.'

'It's the new recipe. Mac would kill me if he heard I served his brown cold.' I took a pull from my bottle. The ale had a rich, full flavor, a little nutty, and it left a pleasant aftertaste lingering in the mouth. Make what jokes you will about trendy microbrews, Mac knew his stuff.

Murphy made a face. 'Ugh. Too much taste.'

'Wimpy American,' I said.

Murphy almost smiled. 'Homicide got wind that there was a link between the killing in Italy, the one here by the airport, and the one this morning. So they pulled strings and hogged the whole thing.'

'How did they find out?'

'Rudolph,' Murphy spat. 'There's no way to prove anything but I'll bet you the little weasel heard me on the phone with Butters and ran straight over there to tell them.'

'Isn't there anything you can do?'

'Officially, yes. But in real life people are going to start accidentally losing reports and forms and requests if I try to file them. And when I tried to apply some pressure of my own, I got put down hard.' She took another angry drink. 'I could lose my job.'

'That both sucks and blows, Murph.'

'Tell me about it.' She frowned and looked up at my eyes briefly. 'Harry. I want you to back off on this case. For your own sake. That's why I came over here.'

I frowned. 'Wait a minute. You mean people are threatening *you* with *me*? That's a switch.'

'Don't joke about it,' Murphy said. 'Harry, you've got a history with the department, and not everyone thinks well of you.'

'You mean Rudolph.'

'Not just Rudolph. There are plenty of people who don't want to believe you're for real. Besides that, you were near the scene of and may have witnessed a felony. They could put you away.'

Obviously my life was too easy already. I swigged more beer. 'Murph, cop, crook, or creature, it doesn't matter. I don't back off because some bully doesn't like what I do.'

'I'm not a bully, Harry. I'm your friend.'

I winced. 'And you're asking me.'

She nodded. 'Pretty please. With sugar.'

'With sugar. Hell, Murph.' I took a drink and squinted at her. 'How much do you know about what's going on?'

'I had some of the files taken away before I could read them.' She glanced up at me. 'But I can read between the lines.'

'Okay,' I said. 'This might take a little explaining.'

'You aren't backing off, are you?'

'It isn't an option.'

'Stop there then,' Murphy said. 'The less you tell me, the less I can testify to.'

Testify? Hell. There should be some kind of rule about being forced to dodge several kinds of legal land mines at the same time. 'This isn't a friendly situation,' I said. 'If straight cops go into it like it's normal business, they're going to get killed. I'd be really worried even if it were SI.'

'Okay,' Murphy said. She didn't look happy. She drank her beer in a long pull and set the bottle on my mantel.

I put my hand on her shoulder. She didn't snap it off at the wrist. 'Murph. This looks bad already. I have a hunch it could get worse, fast. I have to.'

'I know,' she said. 'I wish I could help.'

'Did you get the information on that cell phone?'

'No,' she said. But as she said it, she passed me a folded piece of paper. I unfolded it with my fingers and read Murphy's printing: *Quebec Nationale, Inc, owner. No phone number. Address a P.O. box. Dead end.*

A dummy company, probably, I thought. The Churchmice could have it set up to do a lot of the buying and selling for them. Maybe dead Gaston had been from Quebec instead of France.

'Got it. Thanks, Murph.'

'I don't know what you're talking about,' Murphy said. She picked up her jacket from where she'd tossed it on my couch and shrugged into it. 'There's no APB out for you yet, Harry, but I'd be discreet if I were you.'

'Discreet. That's me.'

'I'm serious.'

'Serious, yep.'

'Dammit, Harry.' But she smiled when she said it.

'You probably don't want me to call you if I need help.'

She nodded. 'Hell, no. That would be illegal. Keep your nose clean, walk the straight and narrow.'

'Okay.'

Murphy paused and asked, 'I don't think I've seen you without that coat outside of summer. Where's your duster?'

I grimaced. 'Missing in action.'

'Oh. You talk to Susan?'

I said, 'Yeah.'

I felt Murphy's eyes on my face. She got it without being told. 'Oh,' she said again. 'Sorry, Harry.'

'Thanks.'

'See you.' She opened my door, kept her hand near her gun, and then warily padded on out.

I shut my door after her and leaned against it. Murphy was worried. She wouldn't have come to me in person if she weren't. And she'd been extra careful with the legal stuff. Were things that dicey in the CPD?

Murphy was the first head of Special Investigations not to get her rear bounced onto the street after a token week or three of unsolvable cases. Generally speaking, when the administration wanted someone off the force, they'd get promoted to running SI. Or at least working in it. Every cop there had some kind of failing that had landed them what everyone else considered to be a cruddy assignment. It had, by and large, created a strong sense of camaraderie among the SI officers, a bond only made tighter by the way they occasionally faced off with one kind of nightmarish creature or another.

SI cops had taken down several half-assed dark spellslingers, half a dozen vampires, seven or eight ravening trolls, and a demon that had manifested itself out of a mound of compost-heated garbage behind a pawnshop in Chinatown. SI could handle itself pretty well because they played careful, they worked together, and they understood that there were unnatural beings that sometimes had to be dealt with in ways not strictly in accordance with police procedure. Oh, and because they had a hired wizard to advise them about bad guys, of course. I liked to think that I had contributed too.

But I guess every bucket of fruit has something go rotten sooner or later. In SI the stinker was Detective Rudolph. Rudy was young, good-looking, clean-cut, and had slept with the wrong councilman's daughter. He had applied some industrial-strength denial to his experiences with SI despite freak encounters with monsters, magic, and human kindness. He had clung to a steadfast belief that everything was normal, and the realm of the paranormal was all make-believe.

Rudy didn't like me. Rudy didn't like Murphy. If the kid had sabotaged Murphy's investigation in order to curry favor with the folks in Homicide, maybe he was angling to get out of SI.

And maybe he'd lose a bunch of teeth the next time he walked through a quiet parking garage. I doubted Murphy would take that kind of backstabbing with good grace. I spent a moment indulging myself in a pleasant fantasy in which Murphy pounded Rudy's head against the door of her office at SI's home building until the cheap wood had a Rudolph-shaped dent in it. I enjoyed the thought way too much.

I gathered up a few things from around my apartment, including the antivenom potions Bob had helped me with. I checked on Bob while I was in the lab, and got a sleepy and incoherent response that I understood to mean that he needed more rest. I let him, went back upstairs, and called my answering service.

I had a message from Susan, a phone number. I called it, and a second later she answered. 'Harry?'

'You've become clairvoyant. If you can do a foreign accent you could get a hot line.'

'Like, sure, as if,' Susan drawled ditzily.

'California isn't foreign,' I said.

'You'd be surprised. How did things go?'

'Okay, I guess,' I said. 'I got a second.'

'Michael?' she asked.

'Shiro.'

'Who?'

'He's like Michael but shorter and older.'

'Oh, uh. Good. I did the legwork.'

I thought of some work I'd seen Susan's legs do before. But I only said, 'And?'

'And the downtown Marriott is hosting an art gala this very night, including a gallery sale and a fund-raiser auction for charity.'

I whistled. 'Wow. So lots of art and money moving around, changing hands, being shipped hither and yon.'

'Hither maybe, but I don't think UPS does yon,' Susan said. 'Seems like a good place to sell a hot article or three. And it's all sponsored by the Chicago Historical and Art Society.'

'Who?'

'A very small and very elite club for the upper crust. Gentleman Johnny Marcone is chairman of its board of directors.'

'Sounds like smuggling country all right,' I said. 'How do I get in?'

'You put up a five-thousand-dollar-per-plate donation to charity.'

'Five *thousand*,' I said. 'I don't think I've ever had that much all in one place at one time.'

'Then you might try option two.'

'Which is?'

Susan's voice took on a note of satisfaction. 'You go with a reporter from the *Midwest Arcane* on her last assignment for her editor. I talked to Trish and got two tickets that had originally been given to a reporter on the *Tribune*.'

'I'm impressed,' I said.

'It gets better. I got us formal wear. The gala begins at nine.'

'Us? Uh, Susan. I don't want to sound like an ass, but do you remember the last time you wanted to come on an investigation with me?'

'This time I'm the one with the tickets,' she said. 'Are you coming with me or not?'

I thought about it for a minute but didn't see any way around it. There wasn't time for a long argument, either. 'I'm in. I have to meet the Reds at McAnnally's at eight.'

'Meet you there with your tux. Eight-thirty?'

'Yeah. Thank you.'

'Sure,' she said quietly. 'Glad I could help.'

Silence stretched long enough to become painful for both of us. I finally broke it at the same time as Susan. 'Well, I'd better—'

'Well, I'd better let you go,' Susan said. 'I have to hurry to get all of this done.'

'All right,' I said. 'Be careful.'

'Stones and glass houses, Harry. See you this evening.'

We hung up, and I made sure I was ready to go.

Then I went to pick up my second, and work out the terms to a duel I was increasingly certain I had little chance of surviving.

17

I put on an old fleece-lined denim jacket and went by my office. The night security guy gave me a little trouble, but I eventually browbeat him into opening the safe in the office to retrieve my envelope from Father Vincent. I opened it and found a plastic case the size of a playing card, like the kind coin collectors use to frame paper money. In the exact center of the case was a single, dirty white thread about two inches long. The sample from the Shroud.

It wasn't much to work with. I could use the thread to create a channel to the rest of the Shroud, but nothing was certain. The thread had presumably been absent from the rest of the Shroud for going on thirty years. Not only that, but it had presumably been handled by various scientists or clergy, and it was possible that they had left enough of a psychic residue on the thread to cloud a seeking spell.

On top of all that, the thread was tiny. I would have to be extremely careful if I used a spell to go hunting the Shroud, or the forces in it would overload the thread in the same way that enough electrical current will overload the filament in a lightbulb. I'm not so great with delicate spell work. I've got plenty of power, but fine control of it could be a problem. By necessity, I would have to use a very gentle spell, and that would put severe limits on the range of it.

The spell would be a metal detector, rather than a radar dish, but it was a whole lot better than nothing. I hit the door.

Rather than inflicting another Charity encounter upon myself, I pulled the Beetle up to the curb in front of Michael's house and honked the horn. A moment later, Shiro appeared. The little old man had shaved the white down from his head, and where he didn't have liver spots, the skin shone. He wore some kind of loose-fitting black pants that looked a lot like the ones I'd seen Murphy wear at one of her aikido tournaments. He also wore a black shirt and a white gi jacket with a scarlet cross on either side of his chest. A belt of red silk held the jacket closed, and he wore his sword through it, still in its wooden cane-sheath. He opened the door, slipped into the Beetle, and held his sword across his lap.

I got going, and neither of us said anything for a while. My knuckles were getting white again, so I started talking. 'So you've done one of these duels before?'

'*Hai*,' he said, nodding. 'Many times.'

'Why?'

Shiro shrugged. 'Many reasons. Protect someone. Force something to leave an area in peace. Fight without involving others.'

'To the death?'

Shiro nodded. 'Many times.'

'Guess you're pretty good at it then,' I said.

Shiro smiled a little, eyes wrinkling even more. 'Always someone better.'

'You ever dueled a vampire?'

'*Hai*. Jade Court. Black Court.'

'Jade Court?' I said. 'I've never heard that there was such a thing.'

'Southeast Asia, China, Japan. Very secretive. But they respect the Accords.'

'Have you dueled any of the Denarians?'

He frowned out the window. 'Twice. But they do not honor agreements. Treachery both times.'

I thought that over for a while before I said, 'I'm going for energy. If he won't take it, we'll do will.'

Shiro glanced aside at me and nodded. 'But there is a better choice.'

'What?'

'Don't fight. Can't lose a fight you don't have.'

I felt a snort coming on but I held it back. 'I'm sort of locked into it now.'

'Both parties want to quit, duel over,' Shiro said. 'I will be talking to Ortega's second. Ortega will be there. Smart for you try to talk him out of it.'

'I don't think he'll do it.'

'Maybe. Maybe not. Not fighting always smarter.'

'Says the militant Knight of the Cross and his holy blade?'

'I hate fighting.'

I glanced at him for a second, then said, 'You don't usually hear that from someone good at it.'

Shiro smiled. 'Fighting is never good. But sometimes necessary.'

I blew out a deep breath. 'Yeah. I guess I know what you mean.'

The rest of the ride to McAnnally's was quiet. In the street-lights, my knuckles looked the same color as the rest of my hands.

McAnnally's is a tavern. Not a bar, not a pub, but an actual, Old World-style tavern. When I went in, I stepped down three steps to the hardwood floor and looked around the place. The bar has thirteen stools at it. There were thirteen columns of dark wood, each one hand-carved with swirling leaves and images of beings of tale and fantasy. Thirteen tables had been spaced out around the room in an irregular pattern, and like the columns and bar stools, they had been intentionally placed that way in order to deflect and scatter random magical energies. It cut down on the accidents from grumpy wizards and clueless kids just discovering their power. Several ceiling fans whirled lazily, and were low enough that I always felt a bit nervous about one of them whirling into my eyebrows. The place smells of wood smoke, old whiskey barrels, fresh bread, and roasting meat. I like it.

Mac stood behind the bar. I didn't know much about Mac. He was tall, medium build, bald, and somewhere between thirty and sixty. He had large and facile hands and thick wrists. All I've ever seen him wear is dark pants with a loose white shirt and an apron that somehow remained free of splatters of grease, spilled drinks, and the various other things he prepared for customers.

Mac caught my eye when I came in and nodded to my left. I looked. A sign on the wall said, ACCORDED NEUTRAL GROUND. I looked back at Mac. He drew a shotgun out from behind the bar so that I could see it and said, 'Got it?'

'No problem,' I answered.

'Good.'

The room was otherwise empty, though normally there would be a couple of dozen members of the local magical scene. Not full-fledged wizards or anything, but there were plenty of people with a dab of magical talent. Then there were a couple of different Wiccan groups, the occasional changeling, scholars of the arcane, a gang of do-gooder werewolves, members of secret societies, and who knew what else. Mac must have put out the word that a meeting was happening here. No one sane wants to be anywhere close to what could be a fight between a White Council member and a Red Court warlord. I knew I was sane because I didn't want to be there, either.

I walked over to the bar and said, 'Beer.' Mac grunted and plopped down a bottle of brown. I pushed some bills at him but he shook his head.

Shiro stood at the bar next to me, facing the opposite way. Mac put a bottle down beside him. Shiro twisted off the cap with one hand, took a modest sip, and set the bottle back down. Then he glanced at it thoughtfully, picked it up, and took a slower sip. '*Yosh*.'

Mac grunted, 'Thanks.'

Shiro said something in what I guessed was Japanese. Mac answered monosyllabically. A man of many talents and few syllables is Mac.

I killed time with a couple more sips and the door opened.

Kincaid walked in, in the same outfit I'd seen that morning, but without the baseball cap. His dark blonde hair was instead pulled back into an unruly tail. He nodded at Mac and asked, 'All set?'

'Ungh,' said Mac.

Kincaid prowled the room, looking under tables and behind columns, and checked the rest rooms and behind the counter as well. Mac said nothing, but I had the impression that he felt the precaution to be useless. Kincaid went to a corner table, nudging other tables back from it a bit, and put three chairs around it. He drew a gun out of a shoulder rig and set it on the table, then took a seat.

'Hi,' I said toward him. 'Nice to see you, too. Where's Ivy?'

'Past her bedtime,' Kincaid said without smiling. 'I'm her proxy.'

'Oh,' I said. 'She has a bedtime?'

Kincaid checked his watch. 'She believes very strongly in an early bedtime for children.'

'Heh, heh, eh-heh.' I don't fake amused chuckles well. 'So where's Ortega?'

'Saw him parking outside,' Kincaid said.

The door opened and Ortega entered. He wore a casual black blazer with matching slacks and a shirt of scarlet silk. He hadn't worn a coat despite the cold. His skin was darker than I remembered it. Maybe he'd fed recently. He carried himself with a relaxed, patient quality as he entered and surveyed the room.

He bowed slightly at the waist toward Mac, who nodded back. The vampire's eyes landed on Shiro and narrowed. Shiro said nothing and did not move. Ortega then regarded me with an unreadable expression and gave me a very slight nod. It seemed polite to nod back to him, so I did. Ortega did the same to Kincaid, who returned it with a lazy wave of one hand.

'Where is your second?' Kincaid asked.

Ortega grimaced. 'Primping.'

He hadn't finished the word before a young man slapped the

door open and stepped jauntily into the tavern. He was wearing tight, white leather pants, a black fishnet shirt, and a white leather jacket. His hair was dark and hung to his shoulders in an unruly mane. He had a male model's face, smoky grey eyes, and thick, dark eyelashes. I knew him. Thomas Raith, a White Court vampire.

'Thomas,' I said by way of greeting.

'Evening, Harry,' he answered. 'What happened to your duster?'

'There was a woman.'

'I see,' Thomas said. 'Pity. It was the only thing you owned that gave me hope that there might be a feeble flicker of style in you.'

'You should talk. That outfit you're wearing is treading dangerously close to the Elvis zone.'

'Young, sleek Elvis ain't bad,' Thomas said.

'I meant old, fat Elvis. Possibly Michael Jackson.'

The pale man put a hand to his heart. 'That hurts, Harry.'

'Yeah, I've had a rough day too.'

'Gentlemen,' Kincaid said, a note of impatience in his voice. 'Shall we begin?'

I nodded. So did Ortega. Kincaid introduced everyone and produced a document that stated he was working for the Archive. It was written in crayon. I drank some more beer. After that, Kincaid invited Shiro and Thomas to join him at the corner table. I went back to the bar, and a moment later, Ortega followed me. He sat down with a couple of empty stools between us, while Kincaid, Thomas, and Shiro spoke quietly in the background.

I finished my bottle and set it down with a thump. Mac turned around to get me another. I shook my head. 'Don't bother. I've got enough on my tab already.'

Ortega put a twenty down on the bar and said, 'I'll cover it. Another for me as well.'

I started to make a wiseass remark about how buying me a beer would surely make up for threatening my life and the lives of those I cared about, but I bit it back. Shiro had been right about fighting. You can't lose a fight you don't show up to. So I took the beer Mac brought me and said, 'Thanks, Ortega.'

He nodded, and took a sip. His eyes lit up a bit, and he took a second, slower one. 'It's good.'

Mac grunted.

'I thought you guys drank blood,' I said.

'It's all we really need,' Ortega said.

'Then why do you have anything else?'

Ortega held up the bottle. 'Life is more than mere survival. All you need is the water, after all. Why drink beer?'

'You ever tasted the water in this town?'

He almost smiled. 'Touché.'

I turned the plain brown bottle around in my fingers. 'I don't want this,' I said.

'The duel?'

I nodded.

Ortega leaned an elbow on the bar and considered me. 'Neither do I. This isn't personal. It isn't something I want.'

'So don't do it,' I said. 'We could both walk.'

'And the war would go on.'

'It's been going on for nearly two years,' I said. 'It's mostly been cat and mouse, a couple of raids, fights in back alleys. It's like the Cold War, only with fewer Republicans.'

Ortega frowned, and watched Mac cleaning the grill behind the bar. 'It can get worse, Mister Dresden. It can get a great deal worse. And if the conflict escalates, it will threaten the balance of power throughout the worlds of flesh and spirit alike. Imagine the destruction, the loss of life that could ensue.'

'So why not contribute to the peace effort? Starting with this duel. Maybe we could get some beads and some fringe and make signs that say "Make blood not war" or something.'

This time, Ortega did smile. It was a weary expression on him. 'It's too late for that,' he said. 'Your blood is all that will satisfy many of my peers.'

'I can donate,' I said. 'Let's say once every two months. You provide cookies and orange juice.'

Ortega leaned toward me, the smile fading. 'Wizard. You murdered a noble of our Court.'

I got angry. My voice gained heat. 'The only reason—'

Ortega cut me off, lifting his hand. 'I do not say that your reasons were not valid. But the fact of the matter is that you appeared in her home as a guest and representative of the Council. And you attacked and eventually killed both Bianca and those under her protection.'

'Killing me won't bring her back,' I said.

'But it will slake the thirst for vengeance that plagues many of my kinsmen. When you are no more, they will be willing to at least attempt a peaceful resolution.'

'Dammit,' I muttered, and fiddled with the bottle.

'Though . . .' Ortega murmured. His eyes became distant for a moment. 'There might be another way.'

'What other way?'

'Yield,' Ortega said. 'Yield to the duel and let me take you into custody. If you are willing to work with me, I could place you under my protection.'

'Work with you,' I said. My stomach flip-flopped. 'You mean become like you.'

'It is an alternative to death,' Ortega said, his expression earnest. 'My kinsmen may not like it, but they could not argue against it. For taking Bianca's life, you could replace it with your own.'

'As one of you.'

Ortega nodded. 'As one of us.' He was quiet for a moment, then said, 'You could bring Miss Rodriguez with you. Be together. She would not be a threat to you, were you both my vassals.' He put his beer down. 'I think you will find that we are much alike, Dresden. We're just playing for different teams.'

I rubbed at my mouth. My instinctive reaction to Ortega's offer was one of revulsion. The Red Court vampires don't look like most would think. They looked like giant, hairless bats with slick, rubbery skin. They could cover themselves with a flesh mask in order to look human, but I'd seen what was underneath the mask.

I'd been exposed to it. Thoroughly. I still had nightmares.

I opened my eyes. 'Let me ask you a question.'

'Very well.'

'Do you live in a manor?'

'Casaverde,' Ortega responded. 'It's in Honduras. There is a village nearby.'

'Uh-huh,' I said. 'So you feed on the villagers.'

'Carefully. I provide them with supplies, medical attention, other necessities.'

'Sounds reasonable,' I said.

'It's beneficial to both of us. The villagers know that.'

'Yeah, they probably do.' I finished off the bottle. 'Do you feed on children?'

Ortega frowned at me. 'What do you mean?'

I didn't bother to hide the anger in my voice. 'Do. You. Feed. On. Children.'

'It's the safest way. The more the feeding is spread among many, the less dangerous it is for all of them.'

'You're wrong. We're different.' I stood up. 'You hurt kids. We're done.'

Ortega's voice sharpened. 'Dresden. Do not lightly discard my offer.'

'The offer to make me into a blood-drinking monster in eternal slavery to you? Why would I want to do that?'

'It is the only way to keep your life,' Ortega said.

I felt the anger coalescing into rage. My upper lip curled away from my teeth, baring them in a snarl. 'I thought life is more than mere survival.'

Ortega's expression changed. It was only for a second, but in that moment I saw furious rage, arrogant pride, and violent bloodlust on his face. He regained his calm quickly, but traces of the hidden emotions thickened his accent.

'So be it. I will kill you, wizard.'

He sounded convincing. It scared me. I turned and walked to the door. 'I'll be outside,' I said to no one in particular, and stepped out into the late-February cold.

That way, I'd have an excuse to be trembling.

18

I didn't have long to wait. The door opened behind me, and Kincaid emerged. He didn't say a word to me, just got into a rented sedan and left. Ortega came next. A car swung in off the street, and he opened the passenger door. He paused and looked back at me.

'I have a measure of respect for your principles and skills, Dresden. But this situation is of your own making, and I cannot allow it to continue. I'm sorry.'

I watched him get in the car, and I didn't offer him any reply. Hell, he hadn't said a word that was untrue. Ortega had a genuine ax to grind and people – well, fellow monsters – to protect. And thus far, the Dresden-versus-vampires scoreboard read a whole bunch to zero.

If a vampire had done that to the White Council, I wonder if we would have reacted with as much reason and calm.

The taillights of Ortega's car hadn't yet gotten out of sight when Thomas emerged from the tavern and swaggered casually over to me. Thomas was a shade under six feet tall, which put him at half a head shorter than me. He was better-looking though, and despite my earlier comments about his outfit, he was one of those men who made anything look good. The fishnet shirt he wore cast patterns of shadow over the pale skin beneath it, adding to the lines of muscle on his stomach.

My stomach had muscles, but not so many that you could see them rippling. I'd have looked pathetic in a shirt like that.

'That was simple enough,' Thomas said. He drew a pair of black leather driving gloves from his jacket pocket and started tugging them on. 'Though I take it this duel isn't the only game in town at the moment.'

'Why would you say that?' I asked.

'I've had a pro hitter following me ever since I landed yesterday. The itch between my shoulder blades got annoying.'

I glanced around. 'Is he here now?'

Thomas's eyes glittered. 'No. I introduced him to my sisters.'

The White Court were the most human of the vampires and in some ways the weakest. They fed on psychic energies, on pure life force rather than on blood. Most often, they would seduce those they fed upon, drawing life from them through physical contact during the act. If a couple of Thomas's sisters had met the hired gun tailing Thomas, the assassin probably wasn't going to be a problem to anyone. Ever. My eye twitched.

'The gunman was probably Ortega's,' I said. 'He hired some goons to take out people I knew if I didn't agree to this duel.'

'That explains it, then,' Thomas said. 'Ortega really doesn't like me much. Must be the unsavory company I've kept in the past.'

'Gee, thanks. How the hell did you end up his second?'

'It's my father's idea of a joke,' Thomas said. 'Ortega asked him to be his second. Show of solidarity between the Red and White Courts. Instead, Daddy dearest found the most annoying and insulting member of the family he possibly could to stand in.'

'You,' I said.

'*C'est moi*,' Thomas confirmed with a little bow. 'One would almost think Father was trying to get me killed.'

I felt one side of my mouth tug up into a smile. 'Nice father figure. Him and Bill Cosby. How's Justine?'

Thomas grimaced. 'She's in Aruba is how she is. Which is where I was until one of pappa Raith's goons dragged me back up here.'

'What did you two decide on for the duel?'

Thomas shook his head. 'Can't tell you. Shiro is supposed to do that. I mean, technically I'm at war with you.'

I grimaced and stared after Ortega's vanished car. 'Yeah.'

Thomas was quiet for a second, then said, 'He means to kill you.'

'I know.'

'He's dangerous, Harry. Smart. My father is afraid of him.'

'I could like him,' I said. 'It's sort of refreshing to have someone trying to kill me right to my face, instead of throwing me a bunch of curveballs and shooting me in the back. It's almost nice to have a fair fight.'

'Sure. Theoretically.'

'Theoretically?'

Thomas shrugged. 'Ortega's been alive for about six hundred years. It isn't something you do by playing nice.'

'From what I've heard, the Archive will object to any monkey business.'

'It's only cheating if he gets caught.'

I frowned at him and said, 'Are you saying someone is planning to avoid getting caught?'

Thomas put his hands in his jacket pockets. 'I'm not saying anything. I wouldn't mind seeing you kick his ass, but I'm sure as hell not going to do something that would attract attention to me.'

'You intend to participate without being involved. That's clever.'

Thomas rolled his eyes. 'I won't throw a banana peel under you. But don't expect any help from me, either. I'm just making sure it's a fair fight and then I'm back at my beach house.' He drew car keys from his pocket and headed for the parking lot. 'Good luck.'

'Thomas,' I said to his back. 'Thanks for the heads-up.'

He paused.

I asked, 'Why do it?'

The vampire glanced over his shoulder at me and smiled. 'Life would be unbearably dull if we had answers to all our questions.' He walked out to a white sports car and slipped into it. A second later, loud, screaming metal music started from the car's stereo, the engine roared, and Thomas drove off.

I checked my watch. Ten more minutes until Susan arrived. Shiro emerged from McAnnally's and put on his glasses. Once he spotted me, he walked over and took the glasses off again. 'Ortega refused to cancel the duel?'

'He made me an offer I couldn't excuse,' I said.

Shiro grunted. 'Duel is wills. Tomorrow, just after sundown. Wrigley Field.'

'A stadium? Why don't we put it on pay-per-view while we're

at it.' I glowered at the street and checked my watch again. 'I'm meeting someone in a minute. I'll give you the keys to my car. I can pick it up from Michael's tomorrow.'

'No need,' Shiro said. 'Mac called me a cab.'

'Okay.' I pocketed my keys.

Shiro stood quietly for a moment, lips pursed thoughtfully, before he said, 'Ortega means to kill you.'

'Yes. Yes, he does,' I said. I managed not to grind my teeth as I said it. 'Everyone is saying that like I didn't know it already.'

'But you do not know *how*.' I frowned and looked down at Shiro. His shaved head gleamed under a nearby streetlight. 'The war is not your fault.'

'I know that,' I said, but my voice lacked conviction.

'No,' Shiro said. 'It *truly* is not your fault.'

'What do you mean?'

'The Red Court has been quietly building its resources for years,' he said. 'How else were they ready to start their attacks in Europe only days after you defeated Bianca?'

I frowned at him.

Shiro drew a cigar from inside his jacket and bit off the end. He spat it to one side. 'You were not the cause of the war. You were merely the excuse. The Reds would have attacked when they were ready.'

'No,' I said. 'That's not how it is. I mean, damn near everyone I've spoken to on the Council—'

Shiro snorted. He struck a match and puffed on the cigar a few times while he lit it. 'The Council. Arrogant. As if nothing significant could happen unless a wizard did it.'

For someone who wasn't on the White Council, Shiro seemed

to have its general attitude pretty well surrounded. 'If the Red Court wanted a war, why is Ortega trying to stop it?'

'Premature,' Shiro said. 'Needed more time to be completely prepared. The advantage of surprise is gone. He wishes to strike once and be certain it is a lethal stroke.'

I watched the little old man for a minute. 'Everyone's got advice tonight. Why are you giving it?'

'Because in some ways you are every bit as arrogant as the Council, though you do not realize it. You blame yourself for what happened to Susan. You want to blame yourself for more.'

'So what if I do?'

Shiro turned to me and faced me squarely. I avoided meeting his eyes. 'Duels are a test of fire. They are fought in the will. The heart. If you do not find your balance, Ortega will not need to kill you. You will do so for him.'

'I guess you were a psychoanalyst before you were a sword-swinging vigilante against evil.'

Shiro puffed on the cheroot. 'Either way, been alive longer than you. See more than you.'

'Like what?'

'Like this vampire warlord. How he manipulates you. He is not what he seems to be.'

'Really? I've never seen that one before,' I said. 'Someone not what they appear to be. How ever will I adjust.'

Shiro shrugged. 'He is centuries old. He is not from the same world. The world Ortega lived in was savage. Brutal. Men like him destroyed entire civilizations for gold and glory. And for hundreds of years since then, he has fought rival vampires, demons, and enemies of his kind. If he approaches you through formal, civilized channels, it is because he thinks it is the best way to kill you. Regardless of what happens in the duel, he intends to see you dead by any means necessary. Maybe before. Maybe after. But dead.'

Shiro didn't put any particular emphasis on the words. He didn't need to. They were enough to scare me without any added dramatics. I glowered at his cigar and said, 'Those things will kill you.'

The old man smiled again. 'Not tonight.'

'I'd think a good Christian boy wouldn't be puffing down the cigars.'

'Technicality,' Shiro said.

'The cigars?'

'My Christianity,' Shiro said. 'When I was a boy, I liked Elvis. Had a chance to see him in concert when we moved to California. It was a big revival meeting. There was Elvis and then a speaker and my English was not so good. He invited people backstage to meet the king. Thought he meant Elvis, so I go backstage.' He sighed. 'Found out later I had become a Baptist.'

I barked out a laugh. 'You're kidding.'

'No. But it was done, so I tried not to be too bad at being Baptist.' He rested a hand on the handle of his sword. 'Then came into this. Made the whole thing more simple. I serve.'

'Serve who?'

'Heaven. Or the divine in nature. The memory of my fathers past. My fellow man. Myself. All pieces of the same thing. Do you know the story of the blind men and the elephant?'

'Have you heard the one about the bear that walks into a bar?' I responded.

'I think that is a no,' Shiro said. 'Three blind men were shown an elephant. They touched it with their hands to determine what the creature was. The first man felt the trunk, and claimed that an elephant was like a snake. The second man touched its leg and claimed that an elephant was like a tree. The third man touched its tail, and claimed that the elephant was like a slender rope.'

I nodded. 'Oh. I get it. All of them were right. All of them were wrong. They couldn't get the whole picture.'

Shiro nodded. 'Precisely. I am just another blind man. I do not get the whole picture of what transpires in all places. I am blind and limited. I would be a fool to think myself wise. And so, not knowing what the universe means, I can only try to be responsible with the knowledge, the strength, and the time given to me. I must be true to my heart.'

'Sometimes that isn't good enough,' I said.

He tilted his head and looked up at me. 'How do you know?'

A cab swerved in from the street and rattled to a stop. Shiro stepped over to it and nodded to me. 'Will be at Michael's if you need me. Be watchful.'

I nodded at him. 'Thank you.'

Shiro said, 'Thank me after.' Then he got into the cab and left.

Mac closed up shop a minute later, and put on a dark fedora on his way out. He nodded at me on the way to his Trans Am, and said nothing. I found a shadowy spot to linger in as Mac left, and kept an eye on the street. I'd hate for someone to drive by and shoot me with a plain old gun. Embarrassing.

A long, dark limo pulled into the parking lot. A uniformed driver got out and opened the door nearest to me. A pair of long, honey-brown legs slid out of the limo on top of black stiletto heels. Susan glided out of the car, managing grace despite the shoes, which probably qualified her for superhuman status all by itself. A sleeveless sheath of shimmering black cloth clung to her, an evening gown slit high on one side. Dark gloves covered her arms to the elbow, and her hair had been done up in a pile on top of her head, held in place with a couple of gleaming black chopsticks.

My tongue dropped out of my mouth and flopped onto my shoes. Well, not literally, but if I'd been a cartoon my eyeballs would have been about six feet long.

Susan had read my face and apparently enjoyed my reaction. 'How much, good-looking?'

I looked down at my rumpled clothing. 'I think I'm a tad underdressed.'

'One tuxedo, coming up,' Susan said.

The driver opened the trunk and drew out a hanger covered with a dry-cleaning bag. When he turned around with it, I realized that the driver was Martin. All he'd done to disguise himself was don an archetypical uniform and I hadn't even recognized him until second glance. I guess sometimes it's handy to be bland.

'Is it my size?' I asked, taking the tux when Martin passed it to me.

'I had to guess,' Susan said, lowering her eyelids in a sultry expression. 'But it wasn't like I didn't know my way around.'

Martin's face might have flickered with disapproval. My heart sped up a bit. 'All right then,' I said. 'Let's get moving. I'll dress on the way.'

'Do I get to look?' Susan asked.

'It'll cost you extra,' I said. Martin opened the door for Susan and I slid in after her. I filled her in on what I'd found out about the Shroud and those after it. 'I should be able to find the thing if we get close.'

'You think there will be any more of these Denarians there?'

'Probably,' I said. 'If anything gets ugly, we'll take the best part of valor, pronto. These guys play hardball.'

Susan nodded agreement. 'Sounds like the thieves aren't exactly shy about waving guns, either.'

'And we'll have Marcone around too. Whither he goeth, there too goeth armed thugs and homicide investigations.'

Susan smiled. It was a new expression to me – a small, quiet, fierce little smile that showed her teeth. It looked natural on her. 'You're all about fun, aren't you, Harry?'

'I am the Bruce Lee of fun,' I concurred. 'Give me some space here.'

Susan slid over as far as she could to give me room to climb into the tux. I tried not to mar it too badly in the limited space. Susan glanced at me with a faint frown.

'What?' I asked her.

'You're wrinkling it.'

'This isn't as easy as I'm making it look,' I responded.

'If you weren't staring at my legs, maybe it wouldn't be such a challenge.'

'I wasn't staring,' I lied.

Susan smiled at me as the car cruised through downtown and I did my best to dress like Roger Moore. Her expression became thoughtful after a moment, and she said, 'Hey.'

'What?'

'What happened to your leather coat?'

19

The downtown Marriott was huge, brilliantly lit, and busy as an anthill. Several blue-and-whites were parked nearby, and a couple of officers were helping to direct traffic in front of the hotel. I could see maybe twenty limos on the street and pulling through the archway in front of the hotel doors, and every one of them looked bigger and nicer than ours. Valets rushed around to park the cars of guests who had driven themselves. There were a dozen men in red jackets standing around with bored expressions that some might mistake for inattention. Hotel security.

Martin pulled up to the entryway and said, 'I'll wait for you out here.' He passed a palm-sized cell phone to Susan. She slipped it into a black clutch. 'If you get into trouble, speed-dial one.'

At that point, a valet opened the door on my side, and I slipped out of the car. My rental tux felt a little awkward. The shoes were long enough for me but they were an inch and a half too wide. I shrugged my jacket into place, straightened the cummerbund, and offered a hand to Susan. She slid out of the car with a brilliant smile, and straightened my tie.

'Smile,' she said quietly. 'Everyone here is worried about image. If you walk in scowling like that we won't blend in.'

I smiled in what I thought was a camouflaging manner. Susan regarded the expression critically, nodded, and slipped her arm through mine. We walked in under the cover our smiles provided. One of the security guards stopped us inside the door, and Susan presented the tickets to him. He waved us through.

'First thing to do is find some stairs,' I said from behind my smile. 'The loading docks will be near the kitchens, and they're below us. That's where they'll be bringing in the art stuff.'

Susan held her course toward the stairs. 'Not yet,' she said. 'If we snoop around the second we get in the door someone is likely to notice. We should mingle until the auction is running. People will be distracted then.'

'If we wait, the whole thing could go down while we hobnob.'

'Maybe,' Susan said. 'But odds are that Anna Valmont and the buyer are both thinking the same thing.'

'When does the auction start?'

'Eleven.'

'Assuming the note means that the sale is at eleven forty-five, that doesn't give us much time to look around. This place is huge.'

We got onto an escalator and Susan arched an eyebrow at me. 'Do you have any better ideas?'

'Not yet,' I said. I caught a glimpse of myself in a polished brass column. I didn't look half-bad. There's a reason the tux has weathered a century virtually unchanged. You don't fix what isn't broken. Tuxedos make anyone look good, and I was a living testament to it. 'Think they will have anything to eat? I'm starving.'

'Just keep the shirt clean,' Susan muttered.

'No problem. I can wipe my fingers on the cummerbund.'

'I can't take you anywhere,' Susan said. She leaned a little against me, and it felt nice. I felt nice, generally speaking. I cleaned up pretty well, it would seem, and I had a lovely woman – no, I had *Susan* on my arm, looking lovely. It was a small silver lining compared to the troubled clouds I'd been floundering through, but it was something, and it lasted all the way up the escalator. I take the good moments wherever I can get them.

We followed the flow of formally dressed men and women up another escalator or three to a cavernous ballroom. Chandeliers hung from the ceiling and tables laden with expensive-looking snacks and ice sculptures all but overflowed onto the floor. A group of musicians played on the far side of the ballroom. They didn't seem to be stretching themselves with some relaxed and classy jazz. Couples who also weren't stretching themselves danced together on a floor the size of a basketball court.

The room wasn't crammed with people, but there were a couple of hundred there already, and more coming in behind us. Polite but insincere chatter filled the space, accompanied by equally insincere smiles and laughter. There were a number of city officials whom I recognized in the immediate area, plus a couple of professional musicians and at least one motion-picture actor.

A waiter in a white jacket offered us a tray of champagne

glasses, and I promptly appropriated a pair of them, passing the first to Susan. She lifted the glass to her mouth but didn't drink. The champagne smelled good. I took a sip, and it tasted good. I'm not a terribly impressive drinker, so I stopped after the first sip. Chugging down champagne on an empty stomach would probably prove inconvenient if it turned out I needed to do any quick thinking. Or quick leaving. Or quick anything.

Susan said hello to an older couple, and stopped for introductions. I kept my duck blind of a smile in place, and mouthed appropriately polite phrases in the right spots. My cheeks had already started hurting. We repeated that for half an hour or so, while the band played a bunch of low-key dance music. Susan knew a lot of people. She'd been a reporter in Chicago for five or six years before she'd had to leave town, but she had evidently managed to ingratiate herself to more people than I would have guessed. You go, Susan.

'Food,' I said, after a stooped older man kissed Susan's cheek and walked away. 'Feed me, Seymour.'

'It's always the brain stem with you,' she murmured. But she guided us over to the refreshment tables so that I could pick up a tiny sandwich. I didn't wolf the thing down in one bite, which was just as well, since it had a toothpick through it to hold it together. But the sandwich didn't last long.

'At least chew with your mouth closed,' Susan said.

I took a second sandwich. 'Can't help it. I got all kinds of joie de vivre, baby.'

'And smile.'

'Chew *and* smile? At the same time? Do I look like Jackie Chan?'

She had a retort but it died after a syllable. I felt her hand tighten on my arm. I briefly debated wolfing the second sandwich, just to get it out of the way, but I took the more sophisticated option instead. I put it in my jacket pocket for later, and turned to follow Susan's gaze.

I looked just in time to meet the gaze of Gentleman Johnny Marcone. He was a man of slightly above average height and unassuming build. He had handsome but unremarkable features. Central casting would have placed him as the genial next-door neighbor. He didn't have the usual boater's tan, it being February and all, but the crow's-feet at the corners of his pale green eyes remained. He looked a lot like the fictional public image he projected – that of a normal, respectable businessman, an American tale of middle class made good.

That said, Marcone scared me more than any single human being I'd ever met. I'd seen him produce a knife from his sleeve faster than a hyperstrong psychotic could swing a tire iron at him. He'd thrown another knife through a rope while spinning in circles as he hung upside down in the dark, later the same night. Marcone may have been human, but he wasn't normal. He'd taken control of Chicago's organized crime during a free-for-all gang war, and he'd run it ever since despite the efforts of both everyday and supernatural threats. He'd done it by being deadlier than anything that came after him. Of all the people in the room, Marcone was the only one I could see who wasn't wearing a fake smile. It didn't look like he was particularly troubled by the fact, either.

'Mister Dresden,' he said. 'And Miss Rodriguez, I believe. I didn't realize you were an art collector.'

'I am the foremost collector of velvet Elvii in the city of Chicago,' I said at once.

'Elvii?' Marcone inquired.

'The plural could be Elvises, I guess,' I said. 'But if I say that too often, I start muttering to myself and calling things "my precious," so I usually go with the Latin plural.'

Marcone did smile that time. It was a cool expression. Tigers with full stomachs wear smiles like Marcone's when they're watching baby deer play. 'Ah. I hope you can find something to suit your tastes tonight.'

'I'm easy,' I said. 'Any old rag will do.'

Marcone narrowed his eyes. There was a short, pointed silence while he met my gaze. He could do that. I'd gotten into a soul-gaze with him in the past. It was one of the reasons he scared me. 'In that case, I would advise you to exercise caution in your acquisitions.'

'Cautious, that's me,' I said. 'You sure you wouldn't rather make this simple?'

'In deference to your limitations, I almost would,' Marcone said. 'But I'm afraid I'm not quite sure what you're talking about.'

I felt my eyes narrow and I took a step forward. Susan's hand pressed against my arm, silently urging restraint. I lowered my voice to something between Marcone and myself. 'Tell you what. Let's start with one of your monkeys trying to punch my ticket in a parking garage. From there, we can move along to the part where I come up with a suitable reply.'

I didn't expect what happened next.

Marcone blinked.

It wasn't a huge giveaway. At a card table, only a couple of the players would have seen it. But I was right in his face, and I knew him and I saw it. My words startled Marcone, and for half a second it showed. He covered it, bringing out a businessman's smile that was a lot better than my fake smile, and clapped a hand gently to my arm. 'Don't try me in public, Dresden. You can't afford to do it. I can't afford to let you.'

A shadow fell over Marcone, and I looked up to see Hendricks hulk into view behind him. Hendricks was still huge, still redheaded, still looked vaguely like a defensive lineman a little too awkward to make it from college to pro ball. His tux was nicer than mine. I wondered if he was wearing body armor under it again.

Cujo Hendricks had a date. He had a blonde date. He had a gorgeous, leggy, blue-eyed, elegant, tall, Nordic angel of a date. She was wearing a white gown, and silver flashed at her throat, on each wrist, and on one ankle. I'd seen bikinis in issues of *Sports Illustrated* that might have felt too plain to be worn by Hendricks's date.

She spoke, and her voice was a throaty purr. 'Mister Marcone. Is there a problem?'

Marcone arched an eyebrow. 'Is there, Mister Dresden?'

I probably would have said something stupid, but Susan's nails dug into my forearm through my jacket. 'No trouble,' Susan said. 'I don't believe we've met.'

'No,' said the blonde, with a faint roll of her eyes. 'We haven't.'

'Mister Dresden, Miss Rodriguez, I believe you both know Mister Hendricks. And this is Miss Gard.'

'Ah,' I said. 'She's an employee, I take it?'

Miss Gard smiled. Professional smiles all around tonight, it would seem. 'I'm from the Monoc Foundation,' she said. 'I'm a consultant.'

'Regarding what, one wonders,' said Susan. She definitely had the sharpest smile of those present.

'Security,' Gard said, unruffled. She focused on me. 'I help make sure that thieves, spies, and poor wandering spirits don't wind up all over the lawn.'

And I got it. Whoever Miss Gard was, it seemed fairly likely that she was responsible for the wards that had torn Bob up so badly. My head of righteous fury died out, replaced by caution. Marcone had been concerned about my talents. He'd started taking steps to balance things, and Marcone wasn't one to show his hand early, which meant that he was already prepared for trouble of one kind or another with me. He was ready to fight me.

Marcone read my features and said, 'Neither one of us wants any unpleasantness, Dresden.' His eyes became flat and hard. 'If you want to talk, call my office tomorrow. In the meantime, I suggest you search for your classic renditions of Elvis elsewhere.'

'I'll take it under advisement,' I answered. Marcone shook his head and walked away to do his own mingling, which seemed to consist mainly of shaking hands, and nodding in the appropriate spots. Hendricks and the Amazonian Gard shadowed Marcone, never far away.

'What a charmer you are,' Susan murmured.

I grunted.

'Such diplomacy.'

'Me and Kissinger.' I scowled after Marcone and said, 'I don't like this.'

'Why not?'

'Because he's up to something. He set up magical defenses around his house.'

'Like he was expecting trouble,' Susan said.

'Yeah.'

'You think he's the buyer for the Shroud?'

'Would make a lot of sense,' I said. 'He's got enough contacts and money to do it. The buy is apparently going down here at his gala.' I scanned the room as I spoke. 'He doesn't do anything without planning it out to his advantage. He's probably got friends in hotel security. It would give him all kinds of freedom to meet Valmont where no one was watching.'

I spotted Marcone as he found a spot near a wall and lifted a tiny cell phone to his ear. He spoke into it, his eyes hard, and he had the look of a man who wasn't listening, only giving orders. I tried to Listen in on what he was saying, but between the band, the ballroom, and the chatter of voices I wasn't able to make anything out.

'But why?' Susan asked. 'He's got the means and the resources but what reason would he have to buy the Shroud?'

'Hell if I know.'

Susan nodded. 'He certainly isn't happy to see you here.'

'Yeah. Something unsettled him, gave him a nasty surprise. Did you see his face?'

Susan shook her head. 'What do you mean?'

'A reaction, during the conversation. I'm sure I saw it. He got caught flat-footed when I was talking to him, and he didn't like it.'

'You rattled him?'

'Maybe,' I said.

'Enough to push him into moving early?' Susan's dark eyes had also picked out Marcone, who snapped the cell phone closed and headed for one of the service doors with Gard and Hendricks behind him. Marcone paused to speak to a red-jacketed security guard and glanced in our direction.

'Looks like we'd better get moving,' I said. 'I need a minute to use the spell on this thread sample and lead us to the Shroud.'

'Why haven't you done that already?'

'Limited range,' I said. 'And the spell won't last long. We need to be close.'

'How close?' Susan asked.

'Maybe a hundred feet.'

Marcone left the room, and the security guard lifted his radio to his mouth.

'Crap,' I said.

'Relax,' Susan said, though her own voice sounded tight. 'These are the upper crust of Chicago. The security guards won't want to make a scene.'

'Right,' I said, and started for the door.

'Slowly,' Susan said, her smile in place again. 'Don't rush.'

I tried not to rush, despite the security guard closing in behind us. I saw red jackets moving in my peripheral vision as well. We kept up the slow, graceful walk of people wandering around a party, and Susan smiled enough for both of us. We got as far as the doors before another red jacket appeared in the doors in front of us, cutting us off.

I recognized the man – the gunman outside the television studio, the one who had nearly ventilated Father Vincent and me in the parking garage. His eyes widened in recognition and his hand moved toward his jacket, where a gun would be inside a shoulder holster. The body language was clear: *Come along quietly or get shot.*

I looked around us, but other than the partygoers, the dance floor, and the other security guards, nothing really seemed to present itself as an option. Then the band struck up something a little faster with a syncopated Latin beat, and several of the younger couples who hadn't been dancing previously moved out onto the floor.

'Come on,' I said, and guided Susan with me.

'What are you doing?' she asked.

'Buying some time to get across the room to those other doors,' I said. I turned to her, put one hand on her waist and took her other hand in mine, and led off onto the dance floor with an uncomplicated two-step. 'Just follow.'

I looked back to her to see her mouth open in shock. 'You told me you couldn't dance.'

'Not like in clubs and stuff,' I said. She followed me well enough to let me do a little dip and step into a restrained hustle. 'I don't do so well with rock and roll. Ballroom is something else.'

Susan laughed, her dark eyes shining, even as she watched the crowd around us for more red jackets. 'Between this and the tux, you're threatening to become classy. Where did you learn?'

I kept us moving down the dance floor, rolling Susan out to the length of our arms and then drawing her in again. 'When I first came to Chicago, I had a bunch of jobs until I hooked up with Nick Christian at Ragged Angel Investigations. One of them was as a dance partner with a senior-citizen organization.'

'You learned from little old ladies?'

'Tough to tango with someone with lumbago,' I said. 'It requires great skill.' I spun Susan again, this time bringing her back to me with her back to my chest, one hand still on her hip with the other holding her arm out. There was a subtle electricity in touching her, her waist slender and supple under my hand. Her hair smelled of cinnamon, and her dress left quite a bit of her back naked to view. It was distracting as hell, and when she glanced over her shoulder at me, her eyes were growing heated. She felt it too.

I swallowed. *Focus, Harry*. 'See those doors behind the food tables?'

Susan nodded.

I checked over my shoulder. The security guards had been slowed down by the press of the crowd, and we had beaten them to the other side of the room. 'That's where we're going. We need to ditch these guys and find Valmont before Marcone gets to her.'

'Won't security just follow us through the kitchen?'

'Not if Vanilla Martin diverts their attention before we leave the floor.'

Susan's eyes glittered and she kept dancing with me, drawing the tiny cell phone from her clutch. 'You have a devious mind.'

'Call me crazy but I'd rather not have Marcone's goons walk us out.' A little luck came our way, and the band moved to a somewhat slower number. Susan was able to stay closer to me, half concealing her cell phone. I heard the phone dialing numbers, and I tried to still my thoughts and feelings. It hadn't worked for long at the *Larry Fowler* studio, but if I could rein in my emotions, Susan should at least be able to make a call.

It worked. She spoke quietly into the phone for all of three or four seconds, then clicked it closed and put it away. 'Two minutes,' she said.

Damn. Martin was good. I could pick out a couple of security guards at the main doors. Marcone's dark-haired hitter was closer. He had trouble making his way politely through the crowd, and we had managed to gain a small lead on him as we danced.

'Do we have a signal or anything?'

'I think we wait for something distracting to happen,' Susan said.

'Like what?'

The sudden shriek of braking tires cut through the band music. There was a loud crunch, and the sound of plate glass breaking, along with shrieks from the hotel lobby below. The band stopped in confusion, and people crowded toward the exit to see what was happening.

'Like that,' Susan said. We had to swim upstream, so to speak, but it didn't look like anyone was bothering to look at us. I caught a glimpse of Marcone's hitter, heading out toward the ruckus. The ass had his gun in his hand, despite any possible field of fire he might have picked being filled with rich and influential socialites. At least he was holding the weapon low and against his leg.

The staff were just as interested in the disturbance as anyone else, and we were able to duck back into the service hallway without comment from anyone. Susan took a quick look around and said, 'Elevator?'

'Stairs if they have them. If someone shoots at us on stairs, we can scream and flail around a lot more.' I spotted a fire alarm diagram on the wall and traced my finger over it. 'Here, down the hall and left.'

Susan stepped out of her shoes while I did that. It left her a lot shorter, but her feet were silent on the utilitarian carpet. We went down the hall, found the stairs, and started down them. We went down three flights, which put us at ground level again, I guessed. I opened the door from the stairwell and took a look around. A dingy little elevator opened, and a couple of guys in the food-stained white of kitchen hands went walking down the hallway, peering ahead and chattering. I heard a siren or two wailing outside.

'I'll say this for Martin,' I muttered. 'When he distracts, he distracts.'

'He has a strong work ethic,' Susan agreed.

'Keep an eye out,' I said, and stepped back from the door. Susan's gaze flicked around the stairwell and over the hallway while I stepped back to kneel on the ground, drawing out what I would need for my seeking spell.

I pulled out a black Magic Marker and drew a smooth circle on the tiled landing, all the way around me. The marker squealed as I did, and as I closed the circle I willed it shut. A gentle barrier, something I couldn't see but could easily feel closed around me, screening out disruptive forces so that I could work my spell.

'Is that a permanent marker?' Susan asked.

'Thus do I strike a blow for anarchy whenever the mood takes me,' I muttered. 'Just a minute.' I took out the sample from Father Vincent and a windup plastic duck.

Which isn't as goofy as it sounds. Stay with me.

I touched the thread to the duck's bill, then wound the duck up. I muttered a low chant, mostly nonsense syllables, and focused on what I wanted. I set the duck down on the floor, but instead of beginning to waddle, it instead waited, completely still. I had to use a rubber band to attach the tiny thread to the duck's bill.

It was too short to tie on. I focused, brushing aside any thoughts besides those I needed for the spell, and let the gathered magic go with a whispered, 'Seek, seek, seek.'

The power poured out of me, leaving me a bit short of breath. The little yellow duck quivered and then lurched into motion, spinning about in an aimless circle. I nodded once, reached out a hand, and with an effort of will to support the gesture, I broke the circle. The screen vanished as quickly as it had arrived, and the little yellow duck quacked and marched toward the door.

I glanced up at Susan. Her dark and lovely eyes watched the duck with what could charitably be termed extreme skepticism.

I scowled at her. 'Don't say it.'

'I didn't say anything.'

'Well, don't.'

She fought down a smile. 'I won't.'

I opened the door. The duck waddled out into the hallway, quacked, and turned to the left. I stepped out, picked the duck up, and said, 'It's close. Let's move. We just check the duck at intersections.'

'Does the duck know about stairs?'

'More or less. Come on; I don't know how long the spell will last.'

I led the way. I'm not the world's mightiest athlete, but I exercise a bit, I have really long legs, and I can walk faster than some run. The duck led us down a pair of long hallways to a door with an EMPLOYEES ONLY sign on it.

I opened the door, peeked in, and reported in a whisper, 'Big laundry room.'

Footsteps sounded behind us, coming down another hallway.

Susan looked at me with wide eyes. I pushed into the room, Susan close behind me. I closed the door almost all the way, holding it from closing completely so that the lock wouldn't click and give us away.

The footsteps came closer, a couple of sets of them, and two shapes went quickly by, passing close to the cracked doorway.

'Hendricks and Gard,' I murmured to Susan.

'How do you know?' she whispered back.

'Smelled the blonde's perfume.' I counted silently to ten and opened the door, looking out. The hallway was clear. I closed the door and turned on the lights. The room was fairly large, with several commercial washing machines ranked against one wall. A bank of dryers faced them on the opposite side of the room, and in between were several long counters that held stacks and stacks of folded white sheets and towels. I put the duck on the floor, and it waddled off down the row of counters. 'This is how they had it hidden on the yacht. Concealed among laundry.'

'And those professional-thief types tend to be so predictable?' Susan asked.

I frowned and put the duck on the floor. 'Watch the door.'

The duck waddled at once over to the far side of the room, and bumped into some hanging laundry. I pulled the hanging sheets to one side, and found a large ventilation grate behind them. I knelt down, running my fingers and eyes over the edges of the grate, and found a pair of holes where screws had been. A quick tug on the grate had it off the wall, revealing a vent maybe three feet square. I stuck my head in and found a ventilation shaft running between the walls. The duck waddled in and took a determined right.

'Air duct,' I said. I twisted out of the tuxedo jacket and absently ripped off the tie from around my neck. I stepped out of the clumsy shoes and rolled up my shirtsleeves, baring my shield bracelet to view. 'Be right back.'

'Harry,' Susan began, her voice worried.

'I saw *Alien*. I'm not Tom Skerritt.' I winked at Susan, picked up the duck, and entered the air duct, moving as quietly as I could..

Evidently, it was very quiet. The duct ran straight, grates opening into utility rooms every fifteen or twenty feet. I had gone past three of the grates when I heard voices.

'This isn't according to the deal,' came Marcone's voice. It had the scratchy edges of a radio transmission to it.

Anna Valmont's smooth British accent answered it from the other side of the next grate. 'Neither was an early rendezvous. I don't like it when a buyer changes the plan.'

A radio clicked. Marcone's voice came through it, smooth and calm. 'I assure you that I have no interest in breaking faith with your organization. It isn't good business.'

'When I have confirmation of the transfer of funds, you'll get the article. Not a second before.'

'My factor in Zurich—'

'Do you think I'm an idiot? This job has already cost us more than any of us bargained for. Clear off the bloody radio and contact me when you have something worth saying or I'll destroy the bloody thing and leave.'

'Wait,' Marcone said. There was tension in his voice. 'You can't—'

'Can't I?' Valmont answered. 'Don't fuck with me, Yank. And add another million to the bill for telling me my job. I'm calling off the deal if the money isn't there in ten minutes. Out.'

I came up to the grate and found it sitting not quite squarely in its frame. Valmont must have entered the hotel and moved around through the air shafts. I peered out through the grate. Valmont had set up in a storage room of some kind. The only light in the room was a dim green shimmer that rose up from what must have been a palmtop computer. Valmont muttered something to herself beneath her breath, her eyes on the screen. She was wearing a lot of tight-fitting black clothing and a black baseball cap. She wasn't wearing my coat, dammit, but I guess I couldn't have expected to find everything wrapped up in a nice package.

I checked the duck, setting it down facing toward me. It immediately walked in a little circle and pointed toward Anna Valmont.

The thief paced the room like a restless cat, eyes on the palmtop. My eyes adjusted to the dimness over the course of a few minutes of waiting, and I saw that Valmont was pacing back and forth around a tube with a carrying strap. The tube wasn't more than five or six feet from me.

I watched Valmont pace until her expression and steps froze, eyes locking hard on the palmtop. 'Great Jupiter's balls,' she said quietly. 'He paid it.'

Now or never. I put my hands on the grate and pushed it as gently as I could. It slid soundlessly from the wall and I set it to one side. Valmont was focused entirely on her little computer. If the prospect of payment distracted Valmont for a moment more, I'd be able to slip away with the Shroud, which would be very James Bond of me. Hopefully the tuxedo would help out with that. I needed only a few seconds to creep out, nip the Shroud, and get back into the vents.

I almost died when Valmont's radio crackled again and Marcone's voice said, 'There. As agreed, plus your additional fee. Will that be sufficient?'

'Quite. You will find your merchandise in a storage closet in the basement.'

Marcone's voice gained an edge. 'Please be more specific.'

I slipped out of the vents, thinking silent thoughts. A long stretch put my fingertips on the tube's carrying strap.

'If you wish,' Valmont replied. 'The article is in a locked room, in a courier's tube. The tube itself is outfitted with an incendiary. A radio transmitter in my possession has the capacity to disarm or to trigger the device. Once I am safely on my way from the city, I will disarm the device and notify you via telephone. Until that time, I suggest you do not try to open it.'

I jerked my fingers away from the tube.

'Again you have altered our agreement,' Marcone said. He said it in a voice as smooth and cold as the inside wall of a refrigerator.

'It does seem to be a seller's market.'

'There are very few people able to speak about taking advantage of me.'

Valmont let out a quiet, bitter little laugh. 'Come, now. This is nothing more than an entirely reasonable piece of insurance,' Valmont said. 'Be a good boy and your precious cloth is in no danger. Attempt to betray me, and you'll have nothing.'

'And if the authorities find you on their own?' Marcone asked.

'You'll need a broom and a dustpan when you come for the

article. I should think you would be wise to do whatever you can to clear the path for me.' She turned the radio off.

I bit my lip, thinking furiously. Even if I took the Shroud now, Marcone would be upset when he didn't get his hands on it. If he didn't have Valmont killed, he'd at least tip off the police to her. Valmont, in turn, would destroy the Shroud. If I took it, I would have to move fast to get the Shroud away from the device. I couldn't count on simply blowing the device out with magic. It was as likely to malfunction and explode as it was to just go dead.

I would need the transmitter too, and there was only one way to get it.

I stepped up behind Valmont and pressed the bill of the plastic duck against her spine. 'Don't move,' I said. 'I'll shoot.'

She stiffened. 'Dresden?'

'Let me see your hands,' I said. She held them up, the green light of the palmtop showing columns of numbers. 'Where's the transmitter?'

'What transmitter?'

I pushed the duck against her a little harder. 'I've had a long day too, Miss Valmont. The one you just told Marcone about.'

She let out a small sound of discomfort. 'If you take it, Marcone will kill me.'

'Yeah, he takes his image seriously. You'd be smart to come with me and get protection from the authorities. Now where is the transmitter?'

Her shoulders slumped and she bowed her head forward for a moment. I felt a twinge of guilt. She had planned on being here with friends. They'd been killed. She was a young woman, alone in a strange land, and regardless of what happened, she wasn't likely to come out of this situation ahead of the game. And here I was holding a duck to her back. I felt like a bully.

'My left jacket pocket,' Valmont said, her tone quiet. I reminded myself that I was a professional and reached into her pocket to get the transmitter.

She clobbered me.

One second, I was holding the duck to her back and reaching into her pocket. The next, I was falling to the ground with a bruise shaped like one of her elbows forming on my jaw. The light from the palmtop clicked out. A small red-tinted flashlight came on, and Valmont kicked the duck out of my hand. The beam of the flashlight followed the duck for a silent second, and then she laughed.

'A duck,' she said. She dipped a hand into her pocket and came out with a small silver semiautomatic. 'I was fairly certain you wouldn't shoot, but that goes a step beyond ridiculous.'

I've got to get a concealed-carry permit. 'You won't shoot either,' I said, and started to get up. 'So you might as well put the gun d—'

She pointed the gun at my leg and pulled the trigger. Pain flashed through my leg and I let out an involuntary shout. I grabbed at my thigh as the red flashlight settled on me.

I pawed at my leg. I had a couple of smallish cuts, but I hadn't been shot. The bullet had hit the concrete floor next to me and gouged a bite out of the concrete. A flying chip or two must have cut my leg.

'Terribly sorry,' Valmont said. 'Were you saying something?'

'Nothing important,' I responded.

'Ah,' Valmont said. 'Well, it would be bad etiquette to leave a corpse here for my buyer to clean up, so it seems as though

I'll be hand-delivering to Marcone after all. We can't have you running off with what everyone is so excited over.'

'Marcone is the least of your worries,' I said.

'No, actually, he's quite prominent among them.'

'Marcone isn't going to sprout horns and claws and start tearing you apart,' I said. 'Or at least, I don't think he is. There's another group after that Shroud. Like the thing from the ship this morning.'

I couldn't see her face from the other end of the red flashlight, but her voice sounded a little shaky. 'What was it?'

'A demon.'

'A real demon?' There was a strained tone in her voice, as though she couldn't decide whether to laugh or sob. I'd heard it before. 'You expect me to believe it was a literal demon?'

'Yeah.'

'And you're some sort of angel, I suppose.'

'Hell, no,' I said. 'I'm just working for them. Sort of. Look, I know people who can protect you from those things. People who won't hurt you. They'll help.'

'I don't need help,' Valmont said. 'They're dead, they're both dead. Gaston, Francisca. My friends. Whoever these people, these *things* are, they can't hurt me any more.'

The locked door of the storeroom screamed as something tore it off its hinges and out into the hall. The hallway lights poured in through the gap in a blinding flood, and I had to shield my eyes against them for a second.

I could see dim shapes, shadows in front of the light. One was lean and crouched, with shadowy tendrils of razor-edged hair slithering around it in a writhing cloud. One was sinuous and strong-looking, like a man who had traded its legs in on the scaled body of an enormous snake. Between them stood a shape that looked human, like a man in an overcoat, his hands in his pockets – but the shadows the shape cast writhed and boiled madly, making the lights flicker and swim in a nauseating fashion.

'Cannot hurt you any more,' said the central shape in a quietly amused, male voice. 'No matter how many times I hear that one, it's always a fresh challenge.'

20

My eyes adjusted enough to make out some details. The demonic female with the Joan Jett hair, two sets of eyes, a glowing sigil, and vicious claws was the same Denarian who had attacked at the harbor that morning. The second demonic being was covered in dark grey scales flecked with bits of rust red. From shoulders to waist, he looked more or less human. From the neck up and the waist down, he looked like some kind of flattened serpent. No legs. Coils slithered out behind him, scales rasping over the floor. He too had the double pair of eyes, one set golden and serpentine, the other, inside the first, glowing faintly blue-green, matching the pulsing symbol of the same light that seemed to dance in the gleam of the scales of the snake's head.

One little, two little, three little Denarians, or so I judged the last of them. Of the three, he was the only one that looked human. He wore a tan trench coat, casually open. His clothes were tailor-fit to him and looked expensive. A slender grey tie hung loosely around his throat. He was a man of medium height and build, with short, dark hair streaked through with an off-center blaze of silver. His expression was mild, amused, and his dark eyes were half-closed and sleepy-looking. He spoke English with a faint British accent. 'Well, well. What have we here? Our bold thief and her—'

I got the impression that he would have been glad to begin one of those trademark bantering conversations all the urbane bad guys seem to be such big fans of, but before he could finish the sentence Anna Valmont turned with her little pistol and shot him three times in the chest. I saw him jerk and twist. Blood abruptly stained his shirt and coat. She'd hit the heart or an artery.

The man blinked and stared at Valmont in shock, as more red spread over his shirt. He opened his coat a bit, and looked down at the spreading scarlet. I noted that the tie he wore wasn't a tie, as such. It looked like a piece of old grey rope, and though he wore it as apparent ornamentation, it was tied in a hangman's noose.

'I do not appreciate being interrupted,' the man said in a sharp and ugly tone. 'I hadn't even gotten around to the introductions. There are proprieties to observe, young woman.'

A girl after my own heart, Anna Valmont had a quick reply. She shot him some more.

He wasn't five feet away. The blonde thief aimed for the center of mass and didn't miss him once. The man folded his arms as bullets hit him, tearing new wounds that bled freely. He rolled his eyes after the fourth shot, and made a rolling 'move this along' gesture with his left hand until Valmont's gun clicked empty, the slide open.

'Where was I,' he said.

'Proprieties,' purred the feminine demon with the wild hair. The word came out a little mangled, due to the heavy canines that dimpled her lips as she spoke. 'Proprieties, Father.'

'There seems little point,' the man said. 'Thief, you have stolen something I have an interest in. Give it to me at once and you are free to go your own way. Refuse me, and I will become annoyed with you.'

Anna Valmont's upper lip had beaded with sweat, and she looked from her empty gun to the man in the trench coat with wide, wild eyes, frozen in confusion and obvious terror.

The gunshots would bring people running. I needed to buy a little time. I leaned up, fished a hand into Valmont's jacket pocket, and drew out a small box of black plastic that looked vaguely like a remote control to a VCR. I held up the transmitter, put my thumb on it as if I knew what I was doing, and said to the man in the trench coat, 'Hey, Bogart. You and the wonder twins back off or the bedsheet gets it.'

The man lifted his eyebrows. 'Excuse me?'

I waggled the remote. 'Click. Boom. No more Shroud.'

The snakeman hissed, body twisting in restless, lithe motion, and the demon-girl parted her lips in a snarl. The man between them stared at me for a moment, his eyes flat and empty, before he said, 'You're bluffing.'

'Like the bedsheet matters to me,' I said.

The man stared at me without moving. But his shadow did. It writhed and undulated, and the motion made me feel vaguely carsick. His eyes went from me to Valmont to the courier's message tube on the floor. 'A remote detonator, I take it. You do realize you are standing next to the device?'

I realized it. I had no idea how big the incendiary was. But that was all right, since I had no idea which button to push to set it off, either. 'Yup.'

'You would kill yourself rather than surrender the Shroud?'

'Rather than letting *you* kill me.'

'Who said I would kill anyone?'

I glared at him and at the demon-girl and said, 'Francisca Garcia mentioned it.'

The man's shadow boiled but he watched me with flat, calculating eyes. 'Perhaps we can reach an arrangement.'

'Which would be?'

He drew a heavy-caliber handgun from his pocket and pointed it at Anna Valmont. 'Give me the remote and I won't kill this young woman.'

'The demon groupie headman uses a gun? You've got to be kidding me,' I said.

'Call me Nicodemus.' He glanced at the revolver. 'Trendy, I know, but one can only watch so many dismemberments before they become predictable.' He pointed the gun at the terror-stricken Valmont and said, 'Shall I count to three?'

I threw on a puppet's Transylvanian accent. 'Count as high as you vant, but you von't get one, one detonator, ah, ah, ah.'

'One,' Nicodemus said.

'Do you expect me to hand it over on reflex or something?'

'You've done such things repeatedly when there was a woman in danger, Harry Dresden. Two.'

This Nicodemus knew me. And he'd picked a pressure tactic that wasn't going to take long, however it turned out, so he knew I was stalling for time. Crap. I wasn't going to be able to bluff him. 'Hold on,' I said.

He thumbed back the hammer of the revolver and aimed at Valmont's head. 'Thr—'

So much for cleverness. 'All right,' I snapped, and I tossed the remote to him underhand. 'Here you go.'

Nicodemus lowered the gun, turning to catch the remote in his left hand. I waited until his eyes flicked from Valmont to the remote.

And then I pulled up every bit of power I could muster in that instant, hurled my right hand forward, and snarled, '*Fuego!*'

Fire rose up from the floor in a wave as wide as the doorway and rolled forward in a surge of superheated air. It expanded as it lashed out, and slammed into Nicodemus's bloodied chest. The force of it threw him back across the hallway and into the wall on the opposite side. He didn't quite go through the wall, but only because there must have been a stud lined up with his spine. The drywall crumpled in from his shoulders to his hips, and his head snapped back in a whiplash of impact. It almost seemed that his shadow was thrown back with him, slapping wetly against the wall around him like blobs of tar.

The snakeman moved with blinding speed, slithering to one side of the blast. The demon-girl shrieked, and her bladed tresses gathered together in an effort to shield her as the fire and concussion threw her back and away from the door.

The heat was unbearable, an oven-hot flash that sucked the air from my lungs. Backwash from the explosion drove me back across the floor, rolling until I hit the wall myself. I cowered and shielded my face as the scarlet flames went out, replaced with a sudden cloud of ugly black smoke. My ears rang, and I couldn't hear anything but the hammering of my own heart.

The fire spell had been something I wouldn't have done if I'd had an option. That's why I had made a blasting rod. Down-and-dirty fast magic was difficult, dangerous, and likely to run out of control. The blasting rod helped me focus that kind of magic, contain it. It helped me avoid explosions that left heat burns on my lungs.

I fumbled around in the blinding smoke, unable to breathe and unable to see. I found a feminine wrist with one hand, followed it up to a shoulder, and found Anna Valmont. I hauled on her with one hand, found the courier's tube with the other, and crawled for the ventilation duct, hauling them both behind me.

There was air in the ventilation shaft, and Valmont coughed and stirred as I dragged her into it. Enough of the storage room had caught on fire that I had light enough to see. One of Valmont's eyebrows was gone, and one side of her face was red and blistered. I screamed, 'Move!' at her as loudly as I could. Her eyes blinked with dull comprehension as I pushed her past me and toward the opening in the laundry room, and she started moving stiffly in front of me.

Valmont didn't crawl as quickly as I wanted her to, but then she wasn't the one closest to the fire and the monsters. My heart hammered in my ears and the shaft felt oppressively small. I knew that the demonic forms of the Denarians were tougher than either me or Anna Valmont. Unless I'd gotten lethally lucky, they'd recover from the blast, and it wouldn't be long before they came after us. If we couldn't shake them or get into a car, and fast, they'd catch us, plain and simple. I shoved at Valmont, growing more frantic as my imagination turned up images of whipping tendrils cutting my legs to shreds, or venomous serpent fangs sinking into my calves as scaled hands dragged me backward by my ankles.

Valmont tumbled out of the air shaft and into the laundry room. I followed her closely enough to make me think of a program I'd seen about howler monkey mating habits. My ears were starting to get their act together, and I heard the high, buzzing ring of a fire alarm in the hallway outside.

'Harry?' Susan said. She looked between Valmont and me and helped the woman to her feet. 'What's happening?'

I got to my feet and choked out, 'We need to be gone. Right now.'

Susan nodded at me, and then shoved me. Hard. I went stumbling sideways and into the wall of drying machines, slamming my shoulder and head. I looked back to see the demon-girl's hair pureeing its way out of the vents, and then the rest of the Denarian came out, scales, claws and all, rolling to all fours with dizzying grace.

Fast as the Denarian was, Susan was faster. The demon-girl came up with those rich lips split into a snarl, and Susan drove her heel right into them. She kicked hard enough that something crunched, and the demon-girl screamed in surprise and pain.

'Susan!' I shouted. 'Look—'

I was going to say 'out' but there wasn't time. Half a dozen bunches of tendrils drove at Susan like spears.

Susan dodged them. All of them. She had to fling herself across the room to the washing machines to do it, and the Denarian regained her balance and pursued. More blades drove toward Susan, but she ducked to one side, one hand ripping open the door to one of the washing machines. Susan slammed the door down on the demon-girl's hair, and without missing a beat kicked the Denarian's reverse-jointed knee in sideways.

The demon-girl shrieked in pain, struggling. I knew she was strong enough to pull free of the washing machine before long, but for the moment she was trapped. Susan reached up and tore a fold-down ironing board from where it was mounted on a nearby wall. Then she spun around and slammed it edge-on into the Denarian. Susan hit her three times, in the wounded leg, the small of the back, and the back of the neck. The Denarian shrieked at the first two blows and then collapsed into a limp heap at the third.

Susan stared down at the demon-girl for a moment, dark eyes hard and hot. The ironing board's metal frame was now bent and twisted from the force of the blows Susan had dealt with it. Susan took a deep breath and then tossed the ironing board to one side, straightened her hair with one hand, and commented, 'Bitch.'

'Wow,' I said.

'Are you all right, Harry?' Susan asked. She wasn't looking at me.

'Yeah,' I said. 'Wow.'

Susan walked over to the counter, where she'd left her clutch. She opened it, got the phone, and said, 'I'll have Martin pick us up at the exit.'

I shook myself into motion and helped draw Anna Valmont to her feet. 'What exit?'

Susan pointed wordlessly at a fire-escape diagram on the wall, still not looking at me. She spoke maybe a dozen quiet words into the phone and then folded it shut. 'He's coming. They're evacuating the hotel. We'll need to—'

I felt a surge of magical energies. The air around Susan grew darker and then coalesced into a cloud of shadows. Within a heartbeat, the cloud deepened, then solidified into a writhing tangle of snakes of all sizes and colors wrapped all around Susan. The air suddenly filled with the sound of hissing and buzzing rattles. I saw the snakes begin to strike, fangs flashing. Susan let out a scream.

I turned to the doorway and saw the snakeman Denarian standing in it. One not-quite-human hand was held out toward Susan. His serpent mouth was rolling out hissing sounds, and I could feel the thrumming tension in the air between the Denarian's outstretched hand and Susan.

Rage flooded over me, and I barely stopped myself from throwing out another blast of raw spellfire at the snakeman. With that much rage behind it, I'd probably have killed everyone in the room. Instead, I reached out to the air in the hallway beyond the Denarian and pulled it all toward him, the words, '*Ventas servitas!*' thundering off my lips.

A column of wind hit the snakeman from behind, lifted him from the floor, and flung him across the room. He slammed into the wall of washing machines, driving a foot-and-a-half-deep dent in one of them, and let out a wailing, hissing whistle of what I hoped was surprise and pain.

Susan flung herself onto the ground, rolling, tearing at snakes, flinging them away. I could see flashes of her honey-brown skin and saw the black dress tearing. Droplets of red blood appeared on the floor near her, on her skin, and on the discarded snakes, but they were hanging on. She was tearing herself apart in her panic to remove the snakes.

I closed my eyes for a second that felt a year long, and gathered together enough will to attempt to disrupt the Denarian's spell. I formed the counterspell in my head, and hoped to God that I didn't misjudge how much power I'd need to undo it. Too little and the spell might actually get stronger, like steel forged in a flame. Too much, and the counterspell could unleash the power of both spells in a random, destructive flash of energies. I focused my will on the cloak of serpents over Susan and lashed out at them with my power, letting loose the counterspell with a snarled, '*Entropus!*'

The counterspell worked. The serpents writhed and thrashed around for a second, and then imploded, vanishing, leaving behind nothing but a coating of clear, glistening slime in their place.

Susan scrambled away, still gasping, still bleeding. Her skin shone, wet and slick with the residue of the conjured serpents. Rivulets of blood laced her arms and one leg, and thick black bruises banded the skin of one arm, one leg, her throat, and one side of her face.

I stared for a second. The darkness on her skin wasn't bruising. It gained shape, as I watched, resolving itself from vague discoloration to the dark, sharp lines of a tattoo. I watched the tattoo come into being over her skin, all curves and points, Maori-style. It began on her cheek under one eye and wound down around her face, around the back of her neck, and on down over one collarbone and into the neckline of her evening gown. It emerged again winding down along her left arm and left leg, finishing at the back of her hand and over the bridge of her left foot. She hauled herself to her feet, panting and shaking, the swirling designs lending a savage aspect to her appearance. She stared at me for a moment, her eyes dark and enlarged, the irises too big to be human. They filled with tears that didn't fall, and she looked away.

The snakeman recovered enough to slither his way vertical again, looking around. He focused yellow snake eyes on Susan and let out a surprised wheeze. 'Fellowship,' he rasped, the word a hiss. 'Fellowship here.' The Denarian looked around and spotted the courier's tube still hanging by its strap from my shoulder. Its tail lashed about and the Denarian darted toward me.

I slipped to one side, keeping a table between us, and shouted, 'Susan!'

The snakeman struck the table with one arm and broke it in half. Then he came at me over the pieces – until Susan ripped a dryer out of the wall and threw it at his head.

The Denarian saw it coming and dodged at the last second, but the dryer clipped him and sent him sprawling. He hissed again, and slithered away from both of us, shooting into the air shaft and out of sight.

I panted and watched the vent for a second, but he didn't reappear. Then I hauled the still-stunned Valmont toward the door and asked Susan, 'Fellowship?'

Her lips pressed together, and she averted her too-large eyes. 'Not now.'

I ground my teeth in frustration and worry, but she was right. The smoke was getting thicker, and we had no way of knowing if tall, green, and scaly would be reappearing. I pulled Valmont along with me, made sure I still had the Shroud, and followed Susan out the door. She ran along barefoot without breaking stride, and between the pain in my lungs and the blonde thief's torpor, I could barely keep up with her.

We went up a flight of stairs and Susan opened a door on a pair of gorillas in red security blazers. They tried to stop us. Susan threw a right and a left cross, and we walked over them on our way out. I kind of felt bad for them. Getting punched out by a dame was not going to pad their goon résumés.

We left the building through a side door, and the dark limo was waiting, Martin standing beside it. I could hear sirens, people shouting, the blaring horns of fire vehicles trying to get to the hotel.

Martin took one look at Susan and stiffened. Then he hurried over to us.

'Take her,' I rasped. Martin picked up Valmont and carried her to the limo like a sleepy child. I followed him. Martin put the blonde thief in and got behind the wheel. Susan slipped in after her, and I slung the tube off my shoulder to get in behind her.

Something grabbed me from behind, wrapping around my waist like a soft, squishy rope. I slapped at the car door, but I managed only to slam it shut as I was hauled back off my feet. I landed on the ground near the fire door.

'Harry!' Susan shouted.

'Go!' I gasped. I looked at Martin, behind the wheel of the limo. I grabbed the Shroud and tried to throw it at the car, but something pinned my arm down before I could. 'Get out! Get help!'

'No!' Susan screamed, and tried for the door.

Martin was faster. I heard locks click shut on the limo. Then the engine roared, and the car screamed into the street and away.

I tried to run. Something tangled my feet and I couldn't even get off the ground. I turned to find Nicodemus standing over me, the hangman's noose the only thing he wore that wasn't soaked with blood. His shadow, his freaking *shadow* was wrapped around my waist, my legs, my hands, and it moved and wriggled like something alive. I reached for my magic, but the grasping shadow-coils grew suddenly cold, colder than ice or frosted steel, and my power crumbled to frozen powder beneath it.

One of the shadow-coils took the courier's tube from my

numbed hands, curling through the air to hand it to Nicodemus. 'Excellent,' he said. 'I have the Shroud. And I have you, Harry Dresden.'

'What do you want?' I rasped.

'Just to talk,' Nicodemus assured me. 'I want to have a polite conversation with you.'

'Blow me.'

His eyes darkened with cold anger, and he drew out the heavy revolver.

Great, Harry, I thought. *That's what you get for trying to be a hero. You get to eat a six-pack of nine-millimeter bon-bons.*

But Nicodemus didn't shoot me.

He clubbed me over the head with the butt of the gun.

Light flashed in my eyes, and I started to fall. I was out before my cheek hit the ground.

21

The cold woke me.

I came to my senses in complete darkness, under a stream of freezing water. My head hurt enough to make the wound on my leg feel pleasant by comparison. My wrists and shoulders hurt even more. My neck felt stiff, and it took me a second to realize that I was vertical, my hands bound together over my head. My feet were tied too. My muscles started jumping and twitching under the cold water and I tried to get out from under it. The ropes prevented me. The cold started cutting into me. It hurt a lot.

I tried to get loose, working my limbs methodically, testing the ropes, trying to free my hands. I couldn't tell if I was making any progress. Thanks to the cold, I couldn't even feel my wrists, and it was too dark to see.

I got more scared by the moment. If I couldn't work my hands free, I might have to risk using magic to scorch the ropes. Hell, I was cold enough that the thought of burning myself had a certain appeal. But when I started trying to reach out for the power to manage it, it slithered away from me. Then I understood. Running water. Running water grounds magical energies, and every time I tried to get something together the water washed it away.

The cold grew more intense, more painful. I couldn't escape it. I panicked, thrashing wildly, dull pain flaring in my bound limbs, and fading away into numbness under the cold. I screamed a few times, I think. I remember choking on water while I tried.

I didn't have much energy. After a few minutes, I hung panting and hurting and too tired to struggle any more, the water only getting colder, bound limbs screaming.

I hurt, but I figured the pain couldn't possibly get any worse.

A few hours went by and showed me how wrong I was.

A door opened and firelight stabbed at my eyes. I would have flinched if I had been able to move that much. A couple of large, blocky men came through the door carrying actual flaming torches. The light let me see the room. The wall beside the door was finished stone, but the walls all around me were a mishmash of fallen rubble and ancient brick, and one was made of curved concrete – some kind of piping for the city's water system, I supposed. The ceiling was all rough earth, some stone, some roots. Water poured down from somewhere, over me, and vanished down a groove worn in the floor.

They had taken me to Undertown, a network of caves, ruined buildings, tunnels, and ancient construction that underlay the city of Chicago. Undertown was dark, damp, cold, full of various creatures that shunned sunlight and human company, and might have been radioactive. The tunnels where the Manhattan Project had been housed were just the start of Undertown. The people who knew of its existence didn't come down here – not even wizards like me – unless matters were desperate.

No one knew their way around down here. And no one would be coming to find me.

'Been working out pretty hard,' I muttered to the two men, my voice a croak. 'One of you guys got a cold beer? Maybe a freeze pop?'

They didn't so much as look at me. One man took up a position on the wall to my left. The other took the wall to my right.

'I should have cleaned up, I know,' I told them. 'If I'd realized I was having company I'd have taken a shower. Mopped the floor.'

No answer. No expression on their faces. No nothing.

'Tough room,' I said.

'You'll have to forgive them,' said Nicodemus. He came through the door and into the torchlight, freshly dressed, shaved, and showered. He wore pajama pants, slippers, and a smoking jacket of Hugh Hefner vintage. The grey noose still circled his throat. 'I like to encourage discretion in my employees, and I have very high standards. Sometimes it makes them seem stand-offish.'

'You don't let your goons talk?' I asked.

He removed a pipe from his pocket, along with a small tin of Prince Albert tobacco. 'I remove their tongues.'

'I guess your human resources department isn't exactly under siege, is it,' I said.

He tamped tobacco into his pipe and smiled. 'You'd be surprised. I offer an excellent dental plan.'

'You're going to need it when the formal-wear police knock your teeth out. This is a rented tux.'

His dark eyes glittered with something ugly. 'Little Maggie's youngest. You've grown up to be a man of considerable strengths.'

I stared at him for a long second, shivering and startled into silence. My mother's name was Margaret.

And I was her youngest? As far as I knew, I had been an only child. But I knew precious little of my parents. My mother died giving birth to me. My father had suffered an aneurism when I had been about six years old. I had a picture of my father on a piece of yellowed newspaper I kept in a photo album. It showed him performing at a children's benefit dinner in a small town in Ohio. I had a Polaroid instant picture showing my father and my mother, her stomach round with pregnancy, standing in front of the Lincoln Memorial. I wore my mother's pentacle amulet around my neck. It was scarred and dented, but that's to be expected when you run around using it to kill werewolves.

They were the only concrete things I had left of my parents. I'd heard stories before, that my mother hadn't run with a very pleasant crowd. Nothing of substance, just inferences made from passing comments. I'd had a demon tell me that my parents had been murdered, and the same creature had hinted that I might have relatives. I'd shied away from the whole concept, deciding that the demon had been a dirty liar.

And given that Nicodemus and Chauncy worked for the same organization, I probably couldn't trust the Denarian either. He was probably lying. Probably.

But what if he wasn't?

Keep him talking, I decided. *Fish for information*. It wasn't like I had a lot to lose, and knowledge was power. I might find out something that would give me some kind of edge.

Nicodemus lit the pipe with a match and puffed on it a few times, watching my face with a little smile on his lips. He read me, easily. I avoided looking at his eyes.

'Harry – may I call you Harry?'

'Would it matter if I told you no?'

'It would tell me something about you,' he said. 'I'd like to get to know you, and I would rather not make this a trip to the dentist if I can avoid it.'

I glared at him, shivering under the freezing water, the bump on my head pounding, and my limbs aching beneath the ropes. 'I've got to ask – just what kind of freaking dentist do you *go* to? Ortho de Sade? Smokin' Joe Mengele, DDS?'

Nicodemus puffed on the pipe and regarded my bonds. Another expressionless man came in, this one older, thin, with thick grey hair. He pushed a room-service cart. He unfolded a small table and set it up over to one side, where the water wouldn't splash on it. Nicodemus toyed with the bowl of his pipe. 'Dresden, may I be frank with you?'

I figured the cart would open up to show an array of hardware intended to frighten me with its potential torture applications. 'If it's okay with Frank, I guess I don't mind.'

Nicodemus watched the valet set out three folding chairs and cover the table with a white cloth. 'You have faced a great many dangerous beings. But by and large, they have been idiots. I try to avoid that whenever I am able, and that is why you are bound and held under running water.'

'You're afraid of me,' I said.

'Boy, you've destroyed three rival practitioners of the Arts, a noble of the vampire Courts, and even one of the Faerie Queens. They underestimated you as well as your allies. I don't. I suppose you could think of your current position as a compliment.'

'Yeah,' I muttered, shaking freezing water out of my eyes. 'You're way too kind.'

Nicodemus smiled. The valet opened the cart and something far more diabolical than torture hardware was there. It was breakfast. The old valet started setting out food on the table. Hash browns. Some cheese. Some biscuits, bacon, sausages, pancakes, toast, fruit. And coffee, dear God. Hot coffee. The smell hit my stomach, and even frozen as it was it started crawling around on the inside of my abdomen, trying to figure out how to get away and get some food.

Nicodemus sat down, and the valet poured him some coffee. I guess pouring his own was beneath him. 'I did try to keep you out of this affair.'

'Yeah. You seem like such a sweet guy. You're the one who edited the prophecy Ulsharavas told me about?'

'You've no idea how difficult it is to waylay an angelic messenger.'

'Uh-huh,' I said. 'So why'd you do it?'

Nicodemus was not too important to add his own cream, no sugar. His spoon clinked on the cup. 'I have a fond memory or two of your mother. It cost me little to attempt it. So why not?'

'That's the second time you've mentioned her,' I said.

'Yes. I respected her. Which is quite unusual for me.'

'You respected her so much you snatched me and brought me here. I see.'

Nicodemus waved his hand. 'It worked out that way. I needed someone of a certain metaphysical mass. You interfered in my business, you were convenient, and you fit the recipe.'

Recipe? 'What recipe?'

He sipped at his coffee and closed his eyes in enjoyment. The bastard. 'I take it that this is the portion of the conversation where I reveal my plans to you?'

'What have you got to lose?'

'And apparently you expect me to tell you of any vulnerabilities I might have as well. I am wounded by the lack of professional respect this implies.'

I ground my teeth. 'Chicken.'

He picked up a piece of bacon and nibbled at it. 'It is enough for you to know that one of two things will happen.'

'Oh, yeah?' Master of repartee, that's me.

'Indeed. Either you will be freed and sit down to enjoy a nice breakfast . . .' He picked up a slightly curved and sharp-looking knife from the table. 'Or I will cut your throat as soon as I finish eating.'

He said it scary – without any melodrama to it at all. Matter-of-fact. The way most people say that they need to take out the trash. 'Ye olde "join up or die" ultimatum,' I said. 'Gee, no matter how many times I get it, that one never goes out of style.'

'Your history indicates that you are too dangerous to leave alive, I'm afraid – and I am on a schedule,' Nicodemus said.

A schedule? He was working against a time limit, then. 'I'm really inconvenient that way. Don't take it personal.'

'I don't,' he assured me. 'This isn't easy for either of us. I'd use some sort of psychological technique on you, but I haven't gotten caught up on some of the more recent developments.' He took a piece of toast and buttered it. 'Then again, I suppose not many psychologists can drive chariots, so perhaps it balances out.'

The door opened again, and a young woman came into the room. She had long, sleep-tousled dark hair, dark eyes, and a face a little too lean to be conventionally pretty. She wore a kimono of red silk belted loosely, so that gaps appeared as she moved. She evidently didn't have anything on underneath it. Like I said, Undertown is cold.

The girl yawned and stretched lazily, watching me as she did. She too spoke with an odd, vaguely British accent. 'Good morning.'

'And you, little one. Harry Dresden, I don't believe you've been introduced to my daughter, Deirdre.'

I eyed the girl, who seemed vaguely familiar. 'We haven't met.'

'Yes, we have,' Deirdre said, reaching out to pluck a strawberry from the breakfast table. She took a slow bite from it, lips sealed around the fruit. 'At the harbor.'

'Ah. Madame Medusa, I presume.'

Deirdre sighed. 'I've never heard that one before. It's so amusing. May I kill him, Father?'

'Not just yet,' Nicodemus said. 'But if it comes to that, he's mine.'

Deirdre nodded sleepily. 'Have I missed breakfast?'

Nicodemus smiled at her. 'Not at all. Give us a kiss.'

She slid onto his lap and did. With tongue. Yuck. After a moment she rose, and Nicodemus held one of the chairs out for her as she sat down. He reseated himself and said, 'There are three chairs here, Dresden. Are you sure you wouldn't like to take breakfast with us?'

I started to tell him what he could do with his third chair, but the smell of food stopped me. I suddenly felt desperately, painfully hungry. The water got colder. 'What did you have in mind?'

Nicodemus nodded to one of the goons. The man walked over to me, drawing a jewelry box out of his pocket. He opened it, offering it out to me.

I mimed a gasp. 'But this is so sudden.'

The goon glared. Nicodemus smiled. Inside the jewelry box was an ancient silver coin, like the one I'd seen in the alley behind the hospital. The tarnish on the coin was in the shape of another sigil.

'You like me. You really like me,' I said without enthusiasm. 'You want me to join up?'

'You needn't if you do not wish to,' Nicodemus said. 'I just want you to hear our side of things before you make up your mind to die needlessly. Accept the coin. Have some breakfast with us. We can talk. After that, if you don't want to have anything to do with me, you may leave.'

'You'd just let me go. Sure.'

'If you accept the coin, I doubt I'd be able to stop you.'

'So what says I wouldn't turn around and use it against you?'

'Nothing,' Nicodemus said. 'But I am a great believer in the benevolence of human nature.'

Like hell he was. 'Do you actually think you could convince me to join up with you?'

'Yes,' he said. 'I know you.'

'Do not.'

'Do too,' he replied. 'I know more about you than you do yourself.'

'Such as?'

'Such as why you chose this kind of life for yourself. To appoint yourself protector of mortal kind, and to make yourself the enemy of any who would do them harm. To live outcast from your own kind, laughed at and mocked by most mortals. Living in a hovel, barely scraping by. Spurning wealth and fame. Why do you do it?'

'I'm a disciple of the Tao of Peter Parker, obviously,' I said.

I guess Nicodemus was a DC Comics fan, because he didn't get it. 'It is all you will allow yourself, and I know why.'

'All right. Why?'

'Because you are ruled by fear. You are afraid, Dresden.'

I said, 'Of what?'

'Of what you could be if you ever let yourself stray from the right-hand path,' Nicodemus said. 'Of the power you could use. You've thought about what it might be like to bend the world to your will. The things you could have. The people. Some part of you has considered and found joy in the idea of using your abilities to take what you wish. And you are afraid of that joy. So you drive yourself toward martyrdom instead.'

I started to deny his words. But I couldn't. He was right, or at least not wholly wrong. My voice came out subdued. 'Everyone has thoughts like that sometimes.'

'No,' Nicodemus said, 'they don't. Most people never consider such actions. It never crosses their minds. The average mortal would have no sure way of taking that kind of power. But for you, it's different. You may pretend you are like them. But you are not.'

'That's not true,' I replied.

'Of course it is,' Nicodemus said. 'You might not like to admit it, but that makes it no less true. It's denial. There are a number of ways you express it in your life. You don't want to see what you are, so you have very few pictures of yourself. No mirrors, either.'

I ground my teeth. 'I'm not different in any way that matters. I'm not any better than anyone else. We all put our pants on one leg at a time.'

'Granted,' Nicodemus said. 'But a century from now, your

mortal associates will be rotting in the earth, whereas, barring amputation or radical shifts in fashion, you will still be putting your pants on one leg at a time. All these allies and friends you have made will be withered and gone, while you are just beginning to come into your full strength. You look like a mortal, Dresden. But make no mistake. You aren't one.'

'Oh, shut up.'

'You are different. You are a freak. In a city of millions, you are all but alone.'

'Which explains my dating life,' I said, but I couldn't put much zing in the words. Something in my throat felt heavy.

Nicodemus had the valet pour coffee for Deirdre, but he spooned sugar into it himself. 'You're afraid, but you don't have to be. You're above them, Dresden. There's an entire world waiting for you. Uncounted paths you could take. Allies who would stand with you over the years. Who would accept you instead of scorning you. You could discover what happened to your parents. Avenge them. Find your family. Find a place where you truly belonged.'

He'd chosen to use words that struck hard on the oldest wound in me, a child's pain that had never fully healed. It hurt to hear those words. It stirred up a senseless old hope, a yearning. It made me feel lost. Empty.

Alone.

'Harry,' Nicodemus said, his voice almost compassionate. 'I used to be much as you are now. You are trapped. You are lying to yourself. You pretend to be like any other mortal because you are too terrified to admit that you aren't.'

I didn't have an answer for that. The silver coin gleamed, still offered out to me.

Nicodemus laid one hand on the knife again. 'I'm afraid I must ask you for an immediate decision.'

Deirdre looked at the knife and then at me, eyes hot. She licked some spilled sugar off the rim of her coffee cup, and remained silent.

What if I did take the coin? If Nicodemus was on the level, I could at least live to fight another day. I had no doubts that Nicodemus would kill me, as he had Gaston LaRouche, Francisca Garcia, and that poor bastard Butters had cut into. There was nothing stopping him, and with the water still running over me, I doubted that even my death curse would be at one hundred percent.

I couldn't stop myself from imagining what it would feel like to bleed to death, there under the cold water. A hot, burning line on my throat. Dizziness and cold. Weakness fading into warmth that became perfect, endless darkness. Death.

God help me, I didn't want to die.

But I'd seen the poor bastard Ursiel had enslaved and driven mad. What he'd suffered was worse than death. And chances were that if I took the coin, the demon that came with it might coerce or corrupt me into the same thing. I'm not a saint. I'm not even particularly sterling, morally speaking. I've had dark urges before. I've been fascinated by them. Attracted to them. And more than once, I've given in to them.

It was a weakness that the demon in the ancient coin could exploit. I wasn't immune to temptation. The demon, the Fallen, would drown me in it. It's what the Fallen do.

I made my decision.

Nicodemus watched me, eyes steady, his knife hand perfectly still.

'Lead us not into temptation,' I said. 'But deliver us from evil. Isn't that how it goes?'

Deirdre licked her lips. The goon shut the box and stepped back.

'Are you certain, Dresden?' Nicodemus said in a quiet voice. 'This is your very last chance.'

I slumped weakly. There didn't seem to be much of a point to bravado anymore. I'd made the call, and that was that. 'I'm certain. Fuck off, Nick.'

Nicodemus stared at me impassively for a moment. Then he stood up with the knife and said, 'I suppose I've had enough breakfast.'

22

Nicodemus walked over to me, his expression somewhat distracted. I realized with a chill that he looked like a man planning his activities for the day. To Nicodemus, I wasn't a person anymore. I was an item on his checklist, a note in his appointment book. He would feel no differently about cutting my throat than he would about putting down a check mark.

When he got within arm's reach, I couldn't stop myself from trying to get away from him. I thrashed at the ropes, hanging on to the desperate hope that one of them might break and give me a chance to fight, to run, to live. The ropes didn't break. I didn't get loose. Nicodemus watched me until I'd exhausted myself again.

Then he took a handful of my hair and pulled my chin up and back, twisting my head to my right. I tried to stop him, but I was immobilized and exhausted.

'Be still,' he said. 'I'll make it clean.'

'Do you want the bowl, Father?' Deirdre asked.

Nicodemus's expression flickered with annoyance. His voice

came out tight and impatient. 'Where is my mind today? Porter, bring it to me.'

The grey-haired valet opened the door and left the room.

A heartbeat later there was a wheezing grunt, and Porter flew back through the doorway and landed on his back. He let out a pained croak and curled into a fetal position.

Nicodemus sighed, turning. 'Bother. What now?'

Nicodemus had looked bored when Anna Valmont emptied her gun into him. When I'd blasted a Nicodemus-shaped dent in the drywall of the hotel, he'd come through it without a ruffled hair. But when he saw the valet laying on the ground before the open door, Nicodemus's face went pale, his eyes widened, and he took a pair of quick steps to stand behind me, his knife at my throat. Even his shadow recoiled, rolling back away from the open door.

'The Jap,' Nicodemus snarled. 'Kill him.'

There was a second of startled silence, and then the goons went for their guns. The one nearest the door didn't get his weapon out of its holster. Shiro, still in the outfit he'd worn at McAnnally's, came through the opening in a flash of black and white and red, his cane in his hand. He drove the end of the cane into Goon A's neck, and the thug dropped to the ground.

Goon B got his gun out and pointed it at Shiro. The old man bobbed to his left and then smoothly rolled right. The gun went off, and sparks flew up from two of the walls as the bullet ricocheted. Shiro drew *Fidelacchius* clear of its wooden sheath as he spun closer to the goon, the movement so fast that the sword looked like a blurred sheet of shining steel. Goon B's gun went flying through the air, his shooting hand still gripping it. The man stared at the stump at the end of his arm as blood gouted from it, and Shiro spun again, one heel rising to chin level. The kick broke something in the wounded goon's jaw, and the man collapsed to the damp floor.

Shiro had taken out three men in half as many seconds, and he hadn't stopped moving. *Fidelacchius* flashed again, and the chair beneath Deirdre collapsed, spilling her onto the floor. The old man promptly stepped on her wealth of dark hair, whirled the sword, and brought its tip down to rest against the back of Deirdre's neck.

The room became almost completely silent. Shiro kept his blade to Deirdre's neck, and Nicodemus did the same to mine. The little old man didn't look like the same person I'd talked to. Not that he had physically changed, so much as that the sheer presence of him was different – his features hard as stone, weathering the years only to grow stronger. When he had moved, it had been with a dancer's grace, speed, and skill. His eyes flashed with a silent strength that had been concealed before, and his hands and forearms were corded with muscle. The sword's blade gleamed red with blood and torchlight.

Nicodemus's shadow edged a bit farther back from the old man.

I think the freezing water was blending in with my sudden surge of hope and making me a little loopy. I found myself drunkenly singing, 'Speed of lightning! Roar of thunder! Fighting all who rob or plunder! Underdog!'

'Be quiet,' Nicodemus said.

'You sure?' I asked. ''Cause I could do Mighty Mouse if you'd rather. Underdog had this whole substance-use issue anyway.' Nicodemus pressed the knife a bit harder, but my mouth was on autopilot. 'That looked fast. I mean, I'm not much of a fencer, but that old man looked amazingly quick to me. Did he look that quick to you? Bet that sword could go right through you and you wouldn't even realize it until your face fell on your feet.'

I heard Nicodemus's teeth grind.

'Harry,' Shiro said quietly. 'Please.'

I shut up, and stood there with a knife at my throat, shivering, aching, and hoping.

'The wizard is mine,' Nicodemus said. 'He's through. You know that. He chose to be a part of this.'

'Yes,' Shiro said.

'You cannot take him from me.'

Shiro glanced pointedly at the goons lying on the floor, and then at the captive he held pinned down. 'Maybe yes. Maybe no.'

'Take your chances with it and the wizard dies. You've no claim of redemption here.'

Shiro was quiet for a moment. 'Then we trade.'

Nicodemus laughed. 'My daughter for the wizard? No. I've plans for him, and his death will serve me as well now as later. Harm her, and I kill him now.'

Shiro regarded the Denarian steadily. 'I did not mean your daughter.'

I suddenly got a sick feeling in my stomach.

I almost heard Nicodemus's smile. 'Very clever, old man. You knew I'd not pass the opportunity by.'

'I know you,' Shiro said.

'Then you should know that your offer isn't enough,' Nicodemus said. 'Not by half.'

Shiro's face did not show any surprise. 'Name it.'

Nicodemus's voice dropped lower. 'Swear to me that you will

make no effort to escape. That you will summon no aid. That you will not release yourself quietly.'

'And let you keep me for years? No. But I will give you this day. Twenty-four hours. It is enough.'

I shook my head at Shiro. 'Don't do this. I knew what I was doing. Michael will need your—'

Nicodemus delivered a swift jab to my right kidney and I lost my breath. 'Be silent,' he said. He focused his attention on Shiro and inclined his head slowly. 'Twenty-four hours. Agreed.'

Shiro mirrored the gesture. 'Now. Let him go.'

'Very well,' Nicodemus said. 'As soon as you release my daughter and lay down your sword, the wizard will go free. I swear it.'

The old knight only smiled. 'I know the value of your promises. And you know the value of mine.'

I felt an eager tension in my captor. He leaned forward and said, 'Swear it.'

'I do,' Shiro said. And as he did, he placed his palm lightly along the base of his sword's blade. He lifted it to show a straight cut on his hand, already dribbling blood. 'Set him free. I will take his place as you demand.'

Nicodemus's shadow writhed and boiled on the ground at my feet, bits of it lashing hungrily toward Shiro. The Denarian let out a harsh laugh, and the knife left my neck. He made a couple of quick movements, cutting the rope holding my wrists.

Without the support of my bonds, I fell. My body screamed in pain. It hurt so much that I didn't notice him cutting my feet free until it was done. I didn't make any noise. Partly because I was too proud to let Nicodemus know how bad I felt. Partly because I didn't have enough breath to whimper anyway.

'Harry,' Shiro said. 'Get up.'

I tried. My legs and feet were numb.

Shiro's voice changed, carrying a quiet note of authority and command. 'Get up.'

I did it, barely. The wound on my leg felt hot and painful, and the muscle around it twitched and clenched involuntarily.

'Foolishness,' Nicodemus commented.

'Courage,' Shiro said. 'Harry, come over here. Get behind me.'

I managed to lurch to Shiro's side. The old man never looked away from Nicodemus. My head spun a bit and I almost lost my balance. My legs felt like dead wood from the knees down, and my back had started cramping. I ground my teeth and said, 'I don't know how far I can walk.'

'You must,' Shiro said. He knelt down by Deirdre, rested his knee on her spine, and wrapped one arm around her throat. She began to move, but the old man applied pressure, and Deirdre went still again with a whimper of discomfort. That done, Shiro gave *Fidelacchius* a flick, and the beads of blood upon it sprinkled against one wall. He sheathed the blade in a liquid movement, drew the cane-sheath from his belt, and then passed the hilt of the sword back toward me. 'Take it.'

'Uh,' I said. 'I don't have a real good record with handling these things.'

'Take it.'

'Michael and Sanya might not be too happy with me if I do.'

Shiro was quiet for a moment before he said, 'They will understand. Take it now.'

I swallowed and did. The wooden hilt of the sword felt too warm for the room, and I could sense a buzz of energy emanating from it in rippling waves. I made sure I had a good grip on it.

Shiro said quietly, 'They will come for you. Go. Second right. Ladder up.'

Nicodemus watched me as I fell back through the doorway into the dimness of the hall beyond it. I stared at Shiro for a moment. He knelt on the floor, still holding Deirdre's neck at the breaking point, his eyes on Nicodemus. From the back, I could see the wrinkled skin on the back of his neck, the age spots on his freshly shaved scalp. Nicodemus's shadow had grown to the size of a movie screen, and it covered the back wall and part of the floor, twitching and writhing slowly closer to Shiro.

I turned and headed down the tunnel as quickly as I could. Behind me, I heard Nicodemus say, 'Keep your word, Japan. Release my daughter.'

I looked back. Shiro released the girl and stood up. She flung herself away from him, and as she did Nicodemus's shadow rolled forward like an ocean wave and crashed over the old Knight. One moment, he was there. The next, the room where he stood went totally black, filled with the rasping, seething mass of Nicodemus's demon shadow.

'Kill the wizard,' Nicodemus snarled. 'Get the sword.'

Deirdre let out a wild, primal scream from somewhere inside the darkness. I heard ripping, tearing sounds. I heard popping noises that might have been bones breaking or joints being dislocated. Then I heard the steely, slithery rasp of Deirdre's hairdo, and half a dozen metallic strands whipped toward me from the darkness.

I shuffled back, and the blades fell short of me. I turned around and started hobbling away. I didn't want to leave Shiro there, but if I'd stayed, I only would have died with him. My shame dug at me like a knife.

More blades emerged from the dark, presumably while Deirdre was still transforming into her demonic aspect. It couldn't be long before she finished and came flashing down the hallway after me. If I couldn't get myself clear, I'd be done for.

So once again I ran like hell. And hated myself for doing it.

23

The shrieks died off more quickly than I would have thought, and I did my best to keep moving in a straight line. It was mostly dark. I was aware of a couple of doorways passing on my left, and I stumbled along until I found the second one on my right. I took it, and found a ladder that led up some kind of pipe or shaft, with a light shining down from about seven hundred miles above.

I got a couple of rungs off the floor when something hit me at knee level, grabbed my legs, and twisted. I fell off the ladder, the cane clattering onto the floor. I had a brief impression of a man's face, and then my attacker let out a wordless snarl and hit me hard on my left eye.

I ducked and rolled with the punch. The good news was that it didn't tear my face off or anything, which meant that the person throwing the punch was probably another mortal. The bad news was that he was built more heavily than me and probably had a lot more muscle. He piled atop me, trying to grasp my throat.

I hunched my shoulders and ducked my head as much as I could, and kept him from squeezing my head off. He threw another punch at me, but it's tough to throw a good punch when you're rolling around on the floor in the dark. He missed, and I started fighting dirty. I reached up and raked my nails across his eyes. I got one of them and he yelled, flinching away.

I managed to wriggle out from under him, giving him a hard shove that added to the momentum of the flinch. He fell, rolled, and started to rise.

I kicked him in the head with my rented formal shoes. My shoe went flying off, which I was pretty sure never happened to James Bond. The goon faltered, wobbling, so I kicked him with the other foot. He was tough. He started coming back from that one too. I bent over and slammed my fist down sledgehammer style at the back of his neck, several times. I was shouting as I did it, and the edges of my vision burned with a film of red.

The rabbit punches dropped him, and he fell limp to the ground.

'Son of a bitch.' I panted, feeling around until I found Shiro's cane. 'I didn't get my ass kicked.'

'Good day to get that lottery ticket,' Susan said. She came down the last several feet of ladder, dressed again in the black leather pants, the dark coat. She checked to make sure the goon wasn't faking it. 'Where's Shiro?'

I shook my head. 'He isn't coming.'

Susan took a breath and then nodded. 'Can you climb?'

'Think so,' I said, eyeing the ladder. I held out the cane. 'Take this for me?'

Susan reached out to take the blade. There was a flicker of

silver static and she hissed, jerking her fingers back. 'What the hell is that?'

'Magic sword.'

'Well, it sucks,' Susan said. 'Go ahead; I'll come up behind you.'

I fumbled around with the cane, slipping it as best I could through the tux's cummerbund. I started up the ladder and once again Deirdre shrieked, this time her voice wholly demonic, echoing weirdly through the stone corridors.

'Wasn't that—' Susan asked, shaking her fingers.

'Yeah. Climb,' I said. 'Climb fast.'

The action and adrenaline had done something to thaw me out, or at least it felt that way. My fingers tingled, but they were functional, and I gained speed as I climbed. 'How'd you find me?'

'Shiro,' Susan responded. 'We went to Michael's house for help. He seemed to know where to go. Like instinct.'

'I saw Michael do that once,' I said, panting. 'He told me he knew how to find where he was needed. How long is this freaking ladder?'

'Another twenty or thirty feet,' Susan said. 'Comes out in the basement of an empty building south of the Loop. Martin's waiting with the car.'

'Why did that guy talk about a Fellowship when he saw you back at the auction?' I asked. 'What Fellowship?'

'It's a long story.'

'Condense it.'

'Later.'

'But—'

I didn't get to protest any further, because I slipped and nearly fell when I reached the top of the ladder. I recovered my balance and scrambled up into a completely dark room. I looked back over my shoulder and saw Susan outlined, a dim shadow against a faint green-gold light.

'What's that light?' I asked.

'Eyes,' Susan said. Her voice was a little thready. 'Coming up. Move over.'

I did. Susan slid onto the floor as the green-gold light grew brighter, and I heard the steely rasping sound of Deirdre's hair moving below. Susan turned and drew something from her jacket pocket. There was a clinking, clicking sound. Then she whispered, 'One, one thousand, two, one thousand, three, one thousand, four, one thousand,' and dropped something down the ladder.

She turned to me, and I felt her fingers cover my eyes, pushing me away from the ladder. I got it then, and leaned away from the shaft the ladder had come up just before there was a hellishly loud noise and a flash of light, scarlet through Susan's fingertips.

My ears rang and my balance wavered. Susan helped me to my feet and started moving out through the darkness, her steps swift and certain. From the shaft, I could dimly hear the demon-girl shrieking in fury. I asked, 'Was that a grenade?'

'Just a stunner,' Susan said. 'Lots of light and noise.'

'And you had it in your pocket,' I said.

'No. Martin did. I borrowed it.'

I tripped over something faintly yielding in the darkness, a limp form. 'Whoa, what is that?'

'I don't know. Some kind of guard animal. Shiro killed it.'

My next step squished in something damp and faintly warm that soaked through my sock. 'Perfect.'

Susan slammed a door open onto nighttime Chicago, and I could see again. We left the building behind us and went down a flight of concrete steps to the sidewalk. I didn't recognize the neighborhood offhand, but it wasn't a good one. It had that wary, hard-core feel that made *The Jungle* seem like *Mary Poppins* by comparison. There was dim light in the sky – evidently dawn was not far away.

Susan looked up and down the street and cursed quietly. 'Where is he?'

I turned and looked at Susan. The dark swirls and spikes of her tattoo still stood out dark against her skin. Her face looked leaner than I remembered.

Another shrieking scream came from inside the building. 'This is a really bad time for him to be late,' I said.

'I know,' she said, flexing her fingers. 'Harry, I don't know if I can handle that demon bitch if she comes at us again.' She looked down at her own hand, where the dark tattoos swirled and curved. 'I'm almost out.'

'Out?' I asked. 'Of what?'

Her lip lifted into a quiet snarl and she swept dark eyes up and down the street. 'Control.'

'Ooooookay,' I said. 'We can't just stand here. We need to move.'

Just then, an engine growled, and a dark green rental sedan came screeching around the corner of the block. It swerved across to the wrong side of the street and came up on the curb before sliding to a stop.

Martin threw open the back door. There was a cut on his left temple and a streak of blood had dried dark on his jaw. Tattoos like Susan's, but thicker, framed one eye and the left side of his face. 'They're behind me,' he said. 'Hurry.'

He didn't have to tell either of us twice. Susan shoved me into the back of the car and piled in after me. Martin had the car moving again before she'd shut the door, and I looked back to see another sedan after us. Before we'd gone a block, a second car slid in behind the first, and the two accelerated, coming after us.

'Dammit,' Martin said, glaring at his rearview mirror. 'What did you do to these people, Dresden?'

'I turned down their recruiting officer,' I said.

Martin nodded, and snapped the car around a corner. 'I'd say they don't handle rejection well. Where's the old man?'

'Gone.'

He exhaled through his nose. 'These idiots are going to land us all in jail if this keeps up. How bad do they want you?'

'More than most.'

Martin nodded. 'Do you have a safe house?'

'My place. I've got some emergency wards I can set off. They could keep out a mail-order record club.' I bobbed my eyebrows at Susan. 'For a while, anyway.'

Martin juked the car around another corner. 'It isn't far. You can jump out. We'll draw them off.'

'He can't,' Susan objected. 'He can barely move. He's been hurt, and he could go into shock. He isn't like us, Martin.'

Martin frowned. 'What did you have in mind?'

'I'll go with him.'

He stared up at the rearview mirror for a moment, at Susan. 'It's a bad idea.'

'I know.'

'It's dangerous.'

'I *know*,' she said, voice tight. 'There's no choice, and no time to argue.'

Martin turned his eyes back to the road and said, 'Are you sure?'

'Yeah.'

'God be with you both, then. Sixty seconds.'

'Wait a minute,' I said. 'What are you both—'

Martin screeched around another corner and roared ahead at top speed. I bounced off the door on my side and flattened my cheek against the window. I recognized my neighborhood as I did. I glanced at the speedometer of the car and wished I hadn't.

Susan reached across me to open the door and said, 'We get out here.'

I stared at her and then motioned vaguely at the door.

She met my eyes and that same hard, delighted smile spread over her lips. 'Trust me. This is kid stuff.'

'Cartoons are kid stuff. Petting zoos are kid stuff. Jumping out of a car is *insane*.'

'You did it before,' she accused me. 'The lycanthropes.'

'That was different.'

'Yes. You left me in the car.' Susan crawled across my lap, which appreciated her. Especially in the tight leather pants. My eyes agreed with my lap wholeheartedly. Especially about the tight leather pants. Susan then crouched, one foot on the floorboards, one hand on the door, and offered her other hand to me. 'Come on.'

Susan had changed in the last year. Or maybe she hadn't. She had always been good at what she did. She'd just altered her focus to something other than reporting. She could take on demonic murderers in hand-to-hand combat now, rip home appliances from the wall and throw them with one hand, and use grenades in the dark. If she said she could jump out of a speeding car and keep us both from dying, I believed her. *What the hell*, I thought. It wasn't like I hadn't done this before – albeit at a fifth the speed.

But there was something deeper than that, something darker that Susan's vulpine smile had stirred inside of me. Some wild, reckless, primal piece of me had always loved the danger, the adrenaline, had always loved testing myself against the various and sundry would-be lethalities that crossed my paths. There was an ecstasy in the knife edge of the struggle, a vital energy that couldn't be found anywhere else, and part of me (a stupid, insane, but undeniably powerful part) missed it when it was gone.

That wildness rose up in me, and gave me a smile that matched Susan's.

I took her hand, and a second later we leapt from the car. I heard myself laughing like a madman as we did.

24

As we went out the door, Susan pulled me hard against her. On general policy, I approved. She got one arm around the back of my head, shielding the base of my skull and the top of my neck. We hit the ground with Susan on the bottom, bounced up a bit, rolling, and hit the ground again. The impacts were jolting, but I was on the bottom only once. The rest of the time, the impact was something I felt only through my contact with Susan.

We wound up on the tiny patch of grass two doors down from my boardinghouse, in front of some cheap converted apartments. Several seconds later, the two pursuing cars went roaring by after Martin and his rented sedan. I kept my head down until they had passed, and then looked at Susan.

I was on top. Susan panted quietly beneath me. One of her legs was bent at the knee, half holding my thigh between hers. Her dark eyes glittered, and I felt her hips twitch in the kind of motion that brought a number of evenings (and mornings, and afternoons, and late nights) to mind.

I wanted to kiss her. A lot. I held off. 'You all right?' I asked.

'You never complained,' she answered. Her voice was a little breathless. 'Nothing too bad. You? Anything hurt?'

'My ego,' I said. 'You're embarrassing me with the super-strength and whatnot.' I rose, took her hand, and drew her to her feet. 'How's a guy supposed to assert his masculinity?'

'You're a big boy. You'll think of something.'

I looked around and nodded. 'I think we'd better get off the street, pronto.'

'Is running and hiding assertively masculine?' We started for my apartment. 'The part where we don't die is.'

She nodded. 'That's practical, but I'm not sure it's masculine.'

'Shut up.'

'There you go,' Susan said.

We went only a couple of steps before I felt the spell coming. It started as a low shiver on the back of my neck, and my eyes twitched almost of their own accord up to the roof of the apartment house we were walking by. I saw a couple of bricks from one of the chimneys fall free of their mortar. I grabbed Susan's collar and sidestepped, pulling her with me. The bricks shattered into shards and red powder on the sidewalk a step from Susan's feet.

Susan tensed and looked up. 'What was that?'

'An entropy curse,' I muttered.

'A what?'

I looked around, struggling to sense where the next surge of magic might come from. 'Sort of a bad-luck spell. A really, *really* bad-luck spell. Preferred magic for getting rid of someone who annoys you.'

'Who is doing it?'

'My guess? Snakeboy. He seems to have some talent, and he could have gotten some of my blood to target me with.' I felt another gathering surge of energy to my right, and my eyes went to the power lines running overhead. 'Oh, hell. Run.'

Susan and I broke into a sprint. As we did, I heard one of the power lines snap, cables squealing. The longer end of loose cable flew toward us, trailing a cloud of blue and white sparks. It hit the ground somewhere behind us.

My clothes hadn't yet dried out from Nicodemus's guest accommodations. If it had been raining, the downed power line might have killed me. As it was, I felt a vibrating, clenching tingle wash over my legs. I almost fell, but managed to get a few more paces away from the sputtering line and regained control of my legs.

I felt another magical strike building, bringing a gust of wind with it, but before I could zero in on it Susan shouldered me to one side. I fell to the ground just as I heard a loud cracking sound. A branch as thick as my thigh slammed to the ground. I looked up to see a strip of bare white bark showing along the trunk of the old tree behind my boardinghouse.

Susan helped drag me to my feet and we ran the rest of the way to my apartment door. Even as we did, I felt another strike building, stronger than the last. I fumbled open the lock while thunder rumbled through the predawn grey, and we got inside.

I could still feel the curse growing and reaching for me. It was a strong one, and I wasn't sure that either my apartment's threshold or my standard wards would be able to keep it out. I slammed the door closed behind me, locked it. The room fell into darkness as I reached for the basket beside the door. There was a waxy lump the size of my fist in it, and I lifted it and slammed it hard against the door, across the crack between the door and the jamb. I found the wick standing out from the wax, focused on it, and drew in my will. I murmured, '*Flickum bicus*,' and released the magic, and the wick suddenly glowed with a pure white flame.

Around the room at precisely the same moment, two dozen other candles of white and butter-colored wax also lit with a gentle flicker of white fire. As they did, I felt a sudden thrum of my own magic, prepared months before, raise into a rampart around my home. The curse pulsed again, somewhere outside, and hammered against the barrier, but my protection held. The malevolent energy shattered against it.

'Boo-ya, snakeboy,' I muttered, letting out a tense breath. 'Stick that in your scaly ass and smoke it.'

'The action-hero one-liner doesn't count if you mix metaphors,' Susan said, panting.

'Looks like no Harry Dresden action figures for me,' I answered.

'Did you get him?'

'Slammed the door on his curse,' I answered. 'We should be safe for a while.'

Susan looked around her at all the lit candles, getting her breath back. I saw her expression soften, and turn a little sad. We'd eaten a lot of dinners here, by candlelight. We'd done a lot of things that way. I studied her features while she stood lost in thought. The tattoos changed her, I decided. They changed the proportions and lines of her face. They lent her features a sort of exotic remoteness, an alien beauty.

'Thirsty?' I asked. She shot me a look with a hint of frustration in it. I lifted my hands. 'Sorry. I didn't think.'

She nodded, turning a little away from me. 'I know. Sorry.'

'Coke?'

'Yeah.'

I limped to the icebox, which was going to need more ice before long. I didn't have the leftover energy to freeze the water again by magic, I grabbed two cans of Coca-Cola, opened them both, and took one to Susan. She took a long guzzle and I joined her.

'You're limping,' she said when she was done.

I looked down at my feet. 'Only one shoe. It makes me lopsided.'

'You're hurt,' she said. Her eyes were fastened on my leg. 'Bleeding.'

'It isn't too bad. I'll clean it up in a minute.'

Susan's eyes never wavered, but they got darker. Her voice grew quieter. 'Do you need help?'

I turned a bit warily so that she couldn't see the injured leg. She shivered and made an evident effort to look away. The tattoos on her face were lighter now – not fainter, but changing in colors. 'I'm sorry. Harry, I'm sorry, but I'd better go.'

'You can't,' I said.

Her voice remained very quiet, very toneless. 'You don't get it. I'll explain everything to you in a little while. I promise. But I have to leave.'

I cleared my throat. 'Um. No, you don't get it. You can't. Cannot. Literally.'

'What?'

'The defenses I put up have two sides and they don't have an off switch. We literally, physically can't leave until they go down.'

Susan looked up at me and then folded her arms, staring at her Coke can. 'Crud,' she said. 'How long?'

I shook my head. 'I built them to run for about eight hours. Sunrise is going to degrade it a little though. Maybe four hours, five at the most.'

'Five hours,' she said under her breath. 'Oh, God.'

'What's wrong?'

She waved a hand vaguely. 'I've been . . . been using some of the power. To be faster. Stronger. If I'm calm, it doesn't get stirred up. But I haven't been calm. It's built up inside of me. Water on a dam. It wants to break free, to get loose.'

I licked my lips. If Susan lost control of herself, there was no place to run. 'What can I do to help?'

She shook her head, refusing to look up at me. 'I don't know. Let me have some quiet. Try to relax.' Something cold and hungry flickered in her eyes. 'Get your leg cleaned up. I can smell it. It's . . . distracting.'

'See if you can build the fire,' I said, and slipped into my room, closing the door behind me. I went into the bathroom and closed that door too. My first-aid kit had its own spot on one of the shelves. I downed a couple of Tylenol, slipped out of the remains of my rented tux, and cleaned up the cut on my leg. It was a shallow cut, but a good four inches long, and it had bled messily. I used disinfectant soap with cold water to wash it out, then slathered it in an antibacterial gel before laying several plastic bandages over the injury, to hold it closed. It didn't hurt. Or at least I didn't pick it out from the background of aches and pains my body was telling me about.

Shivering again, I climbed into some sweats, a T-shirt, and a flannel bathrobe. I looked around in my closet, at a couple of the other things I'd made for a rainy day. I took one of the potions I'd brewed, the ones to counter the venom of the Red Court, and put it in my pocket. I missed my shield bracelet.

I opened the door to the living room and Susan was standing six inches away, her eyes black with no white to them, the designs on her skin flushed a dark maroon.

'I can still smell your blood,' she whispered. 'I think you need to find a way to hold me back, Harry. And you need to do it now.'

25

I didn't have much left in me in the way of magic. I wouldn't until I got a chance to rest and recuperate from what Nicodemus had done to me. I might have been able to manage a spell that would hold a normal person, but not a hungry vampire. And that was what Susan was. She'd gained strength in more senses than the merely physical, and that never happened without granting a certain amount of magical defense, even if in nothing but the naked will to fight. Snakeboy's serpent-cloud had been one of the nastier spells I'd seen, and it had only slowed Susan down.

If she came at me, and it looked like she might, I wouldn't be able to stop her.

My motto, after the past couple of years, was to be prepared. I had something that I knew could restrain her – assuming I could get past her and to the drawer where I kept it.

'Susan,' I said quietly. 'Susan, I need you to stay with me. Talk to me.'

'Don't want to talk,' she said. Her eyelids lowered and she

inhaled slowly. 'I don't want it to smell so good. Your blood. Your fear. But it does.'

'The Fellowship,' I said. I struggled to rein in my emotions. For her sake, I couldn't afford to feel afraid. I edged a little toward her. 'Let's sit down. You can tell me about the Fellowship.'

For a second, I thought she wouldn't give way, but she did. 'Fellowship,' she said. 'The Fellowship of Saint Giles.'

'Saint Giles,' I said. 'The patron of lepers.'

'And other outcasts. Like me. They're all like me.'

'You mean infected?'

'Infected. Half-turned. Half-human. Half-dead. There are a lot of ways to say it.'

'Uh-huh,' I said. 'So what's their deal?'

'The Fellowship tries to help people the Red Court has harmed. Work against the Red Court. Expose them whenever they can.'

'Find a cure?'

'There is no cure.'

I put my hand on her arm and guided her toward my couch. She moved with a dreamy deliberation. 'So the tattoos are what? Your membership card?'

'A binding,' she said. 'A spell cut into my skin. To help me hold the darkness inside. To warn me when it is rising.'

'What do you mean, warn you?'

She looked down at her design-covered hand, then showed it to me. The tattoos there and on her face were slowly growing brighter, and had turned a shade of medium scarlet. 'To warn me when I'm about to lose control. Red, red, red. Danger, danger, danger.'

The first night she'd arrived, when she'd been tussling with something outside, she'd stayed in the shadows for the first several moments inside, her face turned away. She'd been hiding the tattoos. 'Here,' I said quietly. 'Sit down.'

She sat on the couch and met my eyes. 'Harry,' she whispered. 'It hurts. It hurts to fight it. I'm tired of holding on. I don't know how long I can.'

I knelt down to be on eye level with her. 'Do you trust me?'

'With my heart. With my life.'

'Close your eyes,' I said.

She did.

I got up and walked slowly to the kitchen drawer. I didn't move quickly. You don't move quickly away from something that is thinking about making you food. It sets them off. Whatever had been placed inside her was growing – I could feel that, see it, hear it in her voice.

I was in danger. But it didn't matter, because so was she.

I usually keep a gun in the kitchen drawer. At the time, I had a gun and a short length of silver-and-white rope in there. I picked up the rope and walked back over to her.

'Susan,' I said quietly. 'Give me your hands.'

She opened her eyes and looked at the soft, fine rope. 'That won't hold me.'

'I made it in case an ogre I pissed off came visiting. Give me your hands.'

She was silent for a moment. Then she shrugged out of her jacket, and held her hands out, wrists up.

I tossed the rope at her and whispered, '*Manacus.*'

I'd enchanted the rope six months before, but I'd done it right. It took barely a whisper of power to set the rope into motion. It whipped into the air, silver threads flashing, and bound itself around her wrists in neat loops.

Susan reacted instantly, going completely tense. I saw her set herself and strain against the ropes. I waited, watching for a full half a minute before she started shaking and stopped trying to break them. She let out a shaking breath, her head bowed, hair fallen around her face. I started to move toward her, when she stood up, legs spread enough to brace herself firmly, and tried again, lifting her arms.

I licked my lips, watching. I didn't think she'd break the ropes, but I'd underestimated people before. Her face, her too-black eyes scared me. She strained against the ropes again, the movement drawing her shirt up, showing me her smooth brown stomach, the winding swirls and barbs of her tattoo red and stark against her skin. There were dark bruises over her ribs, and patches of skin that had been scraped raw. She hadn't come away from our tumble from Martin's car without being hurt, after all.

After a minute more, she hissed out a breath and sat down, hair a tumbled mess around her face. I could feel her eyes on me more than I could actually see them. They didn't feel like Susan's eyes anymore. The tattoos stood out against her skin, red as blood. I backed off, again deliberately, calmly, and got the first aid kit out of the bathroom.

When I came back out, she flung herself at me in blinding speed and utter silence. I'd been expecting as much, and snapped, '*Forzare!*'

The silver rope flashed with a glitter of blue light and darted toward the ceiling. Her wrists went with it and she was pulled completely from the floor. Her feet swung up, and she twisted, again in silence, fighting the bonds on her. She didn't get free, and I let her swing there until her legs had settled again, her toes barely touching the floor.

She let out a quiet sob and whispered, 'I'm sorry. Harry, I can't stop it.'

'It's okay. I've got you.' I stepped closer to examine the injuries on her midsection and winced. 'God. You got torn up.'

'I hate this. I'm so sorry.'

It hurt me to hear her voice. There was enough pain in it for both of us. 'Shhhh,' I said. 'Let me take care of you.'

She fell quiet then, though I could sense flashes of that feral hunger in her. I got a bowl of water, a cloth, and set to cleaning up the scrapes as best I could. She quivered once in a while. Once she let out a pained groan. The bruises went all the way up her back, and she had another patch of abraded skin on her neck. I put my hand on her head and pushed forward. She bowed her head and let it hang forward while I tended to the wound.

While I did, the quality of the tension changed. I could smell her hair, her skin, their scent like candle smoke and cinnamon. I became suddenly, intensely aware of the curve of her back, her hips. She leaned back a little toward me, bringing her body into contact with mine, the heat of her something that could have singed me. Her breathing changed, growing faster, heavier. She turned her head, enough to look at me over her shoulder. Her eyes burned, and her tongue flickered over her lips.

'Need you,' she whispered.

I swallowed. 'Susan. I think maybe that—'

'Don't think,' she said. Her hips brushed against the front of my sweats, and I was abruptly so hard that it hurt. 'Don't think. Touch me.'

Somewhere, I knew it wasn't the best of ideas. But I laid the fingers of one hand on the curve of her waist, wrapping them slowly to her heated skin. Soft smoothness caressed my hand.

There was a pleasure in it, a primal, possessive pleasure in touching her. I ran my palm and spread fingers over her flank, her belly, in slow and light circles. She arched at the caress, her eyes closing, and whispered, 'Yes,' over and over again. 'Yes.'

I let the washcloth fall from my other hand and reached up to touch her hair. More softness, rich texture, dark hairs gliding between my fingers. I felt a second of gathering tension in her and then she whipped her head around, teeth bared, reaching for my hand. I should have drawn my hand away. Instead, I tightened my fingers in her hair and pulled back, forcing her chin up and keeping her from reaching me.

I expected anger from her, but instead her body became pliant again, moving against me with a more willing abandon. A languid smile spread over her lips, and faded away to an openmouthed gasp as I slid my other hand up, beneath the cotton shirt, and ran my fingertips lightly over her breasts. She gasped, and at the sound all of my recent worry, fear, anger, pain – it all faded away, burned to ash by a sudden fire of raw need. To feel her under my hand again, to have the scent of her filling my head – I'd dreamed of it on too many cold and lonely nights.

It wasn't the smart thing to do. It was the only thing.

I slid both hands around her body, teasing her breasts, loving the way their tips hardened to rounded points beneath my fingers. She tried to turn on me again, but I jerked her back hard against me, my mouth pressing against the side of her throat, keeping her from turning her head. It only excited her more.

'Need,' she whispered, panting. 'Need you. Don't stop.'

I wasn't sure I could have. I couldn't get enough of the taste of her onto my lips. Impatient, I shoved her shirt up, over her breasts, to the top of her back, and spent a slow and delicious moment following the line of her spine with my lips and tongue, tasting her skin, testing its texture with my teeth. Some part of me struggled to remember to be gentle. Another part didn't give a damn. *Feel. Taste. Indulge.*

My teeth left small marks here and there on her skin, and I remember thinking that they looked intriguing beside the curling scarlet designs that swept in a spiral around her body. The dark leather of her pants blocked my mouth, a sudden ugliness beneath my lips, and I straightened with a snarl to get it out of my way.

For the record, tight leather pants don't come off easily. Berserk lust is likely not the best frame of mind for removing them. I didn't let that stop me. She gasped when I started taking them off, started squirming and wriggling, trying to help me. Mostly, it just drove me insane as she brushed against me, as I watched her move in sinuous, delicious need. Her panting gasps all had a quiet vocalization to them now, a sound that both spoke of her need and urged me on.

I got the pants down over her hips. There wasn't anything else beneath them. I shivered and paused to spend another moment savoring her with my hands, my mouth, placing delicate kisses around the scrapes, biting at unmarred skin to elicit more desperate movements, louder moans. The scent of her was driving me insane.

'Now,' she whispered, a frenzied edge to her voice. 'Now.'

But I didn't hurry. I don't know how long I stood there, kissing, touching, driving her cries into higher and more desperate pitches. All I knew was that something I'd wanted, needed, longed for had come to me again. At that moment there was nothing on earth, in heaven or hell, that meant more to me.

She looked over her shoulder at me, eyes black and burning

with hunger. She tried for my hand again, driven beyond words now. I had to control her head again, fingers knotted into her hair while my free hand got the interfering clothes out of the way. She let out mewling sounds of raw need, until I pulled her hips back against me, feeling my way, and in a rush of fire and silk felt my hardness press into her.

Her eyes flew open wide, out of focus, and she cried out, moving against me, meeting my motion with her own. I had a fleeting thought of slowing down. I didn't. Neither of us wanted that. I took her that way, my mouth on her ear, her throat, one hand in her hair, her hands stretched out over her, body straining back to meet mine.

God, she was beautiful.

She screamed and started shuddering, and it was all I could do not to explode. I fought away the inevitable for a little time more. Susan sagged down after a moment, until with my hands, with my mouth, with the thrusts of my body, I kindled the quiet moans once again to cries of need. She screamed again, the motions of her body swift, liquid, desperate, and there wasn't any way I could keep her from driving me over the brink with her.

Our cries mingled together as we intertwined. The strain of muscles and bodies and hungers overwhelmed me.

Pleasure like fire consumed us both and burned my thoughts to ash.

Time drifted by and did not touch us.

When I recovered my senses, I found myself on the floor. Susan lay on her stomach beneath me, her still-bound arms laid out above her head. Not much time had passed. Both of us were still short of breath. I shivered, and felt myself still inside her. I didn't remember releasing the spell that held the bonds up to the ceiling, but I must have done it. I moved my head to kiss her shoulder, her cheek, very softly.

Her eyes blinked slowly open, human again, though her pupils were dilated until they all but hid the dark brown of her irises. She didn't focus them. She smiled and made a soft sound, somewhere between a moan and a cat's purr. I stared at her for a moment, until I realized that the designs on her face had gone dark again, and had begun to fade away. As I watched over the next few moments, they vanished completely.

'I love you,' she whispered.

'I love you.'

'Wanted that.'

'Me too,' I said.

'Dangerous. Harry, you could have been hurt. I might have—'

I leaned down and kissed the corner of her mouth, silencing her. 'You didn't. It's okay.'

She shivered, but nodded. 'So tired.'

I felt like nothing more than dropping off to sleep, but instead I got to my feet. Susan let out a soft sound, half pleasure and half protest. I gathered her up and put her on the couch. I touched the rope, willing it to release her, and it slid away from her skin, coiling itself into neat loops in my hand. I pulled a blanket from the back of the couch and folded it over her. 'Sleep,' I said. 'Get some rest.'

'You should—'

'I will. Promise. But . . . I don't think it would be a good idea to go to sleep near you.'

Susan nodded wearily. 'You're right. I'm sorry.'

'It's okay,' I said.

'Should call Martin.'

'The phone won't call out,' I said. 'Not until the defenses go down.'

I didn't think her voice sounded particularly disappointed as she snuggled down a bit more onto my couch. 'Oh,' she said. 'We'll have to wait it out then.'

'Yeah,' I said. I stroked her hair. 'Susan—'

She touched my hand with hers, and closed her eyes. 'It's all right. I told you, I'd never be able to separate the hungers with you. It . . . it was a release. Took some of the pressure off me. I wanted it. Needed it.'

'Did I hurt you?'

She made a purring sound without opening her eyes. 'Maybe a little. I didn't mind.'

I shivered and said, 'You're okay?'

She nodded slowly. 'As I can be. Get some rest, Harry.'

'Yeah,' I said. I touched her hair again, and then shuffled into my bedroom. I didn't shut the door. I put my pillows at the foot of my bed, so that I could see the couch when I lay down. I watched her face, graced by pale candlelight, until my eyes closed.

She was so lovely.

I wished that she were with me.

26

I opened my eyes a while later, and saw Susan standing in the living room, her eyes closed. She was crouched, her hands held before her as if grasping an invisible basketball. As I watched, she moved, arms and legs gliding through gentle, circular motions. Tai chi. It was a meditative form of exercise that had originally come from martial arts. Lots of people who practiced tai chi didn't realize that the movements they followed were beautiful, slow-motion renditions of bone-breaking throws and joint locks.

I had a feeling Susan knew. She wore her T-shirt and a pair of my running shorts. She moved with the graceful simplicity of a natural talent honed by training.

A turn showed me her face, her expression set in peaceful concentration. I spent a minute watching her in silence, cataloging my own aches and pains.

She suddenly smiled, without opening her eyes, and said, 'Don't start drooling, Harry.'

'My house. I can drool as much as I want.'

'What was that rope you used?' she asked, still going through her routine. 'I've broken handcuffs before. Magic?'

Shoptalk. I had hoped for some other kind of discussion. Or maybe I'd been nervous about it. Work talk held a certain appeal for me, too. It was safe. 'Faerie make,' I said. 'Has hair from a unicorn's mane woven through it.'

'Really?'

I shrugged. 'That's what Fix said. I imagine he knows.'

'Would be handy to have around if the Denarians showed up again, don't you think?'

'Not unless they came here,' I told her. 'It's set to this place. Take it out of here and it wouldn't work.'

'Why not?'

'Because I'm not that good yet,' I said. 'It's easy to make something that works at home. Takes a lot more know-how than I have to take an enchantment on the road.' I got out of bed and got moving. The clock said that it wasn't yet ten in the morning. I hopped in and out of the shower, dressed, slapped a comb through my hair, and decided that the rakish, unshaven look was in.

By the time I got back out into the living room, Susan was dressed in the leather pants again and only four or five candles were still lit. The defensive barriers were winding down. 'What happened after Martin took off from the hotel?' I asked.

Susan slouched into a chair. 'I tried to get him to stop. He wouldn't. We fought about it and he put a gun in my face.'

I choked. 'He *what*?'

'To be fair, I wasn't being very rational.'

'Hell's bells.'

'Martin didn't want to, but I convinced him to go to Michael's place. I figured if anyone could get you out of a mess with the Denarians it would be him.'

'Seems reasonable to me,' I said. I debated between coffee and cola. The Coke won by virtue of convenience. Susan nodded at me before I could get the question out of my mouth, and I got her one too. 'What about Anna Valmont?'

'She was in shock. Charity put her to bed.'

'Did you call the police?'

Susan shook her head. 'I thought she might have known something that would help. We wouldn't be able to find out what it was if she was angry and locked away.'

'What did Michael have to say about it?'

'He wasn't there,' Susan said. 'Shiro was. Charity said that Michael and someone named Sanya hadn't come back from St Louis and hadn't called.'

I frowned and passed over the second can to her. 'That doesn't sound like him.'

'I know. They were worried.' She frowned. 'Or Charity was. I don't think Shiro was worried at all. It was almost as though he'd been expecting all of it. He was still dressed in the samurai clothes and he opened the front door before I could knock.'

'Michael's done that kind of thing before. Fringe benefit of his job, maybe.'

Susan shook her head. 'God works in mysterious ways?'

I shrugged. 'Maybe so. Did Shiro say anything?'

'He just told Martin where to turn left or right and where to park. Then he told me to give him two minutes' lead and to get ready to get you back to the car. He just . . . smiled a little, the whole time. It would have been a little spooky on anyone else. He seemed content. Maybe he just had a good poker face.'

I toyed with my can. 'Has. He has a good poker face.'

Susan arched an eyebrow. 'I don't understand.'

'I don't think he's dead. Not yet. He . . . he agreed to give himself over to the Denarians in exchange for them letting me go. The head Denarian guy, said his name was Nicodemus, made Shiro promise to not to fight back or escape for twenty-four hours.'

'That doesn't sound good.'

I shivered. 'Yeah. I figure they're archenemies. When Shiro offered himself, Nicodemus looked like a kid on Christmas morning.'

Susan sipped at her drink. 'How bad are these people?'

I thought of Nicodemus and his knife. Of the sheer helplessness I'd felt as he drew my head back, baring my throat. I thought of sliced and diced corpses. 'Bad.'

Susan regarded me quietly for a moment, while I stared at my drink.

'Harry,' she said finally. 'You going to open that or just look at it?'

I shook my head and popped the tab on the can. My wrists felt sore, and the skin around them had been pretty thoroughly abraded. Evidently Nicodemus preferred regular old ropes to special unicorn-mane custom jobs. 'Sorry. Got a lot to think about.'

'Yeah,' she said, her own voice softening. 'What's our next move?'

I checked the candles. Three to go. 'Barrier will go down in maybe twenty minutes. We'll call a cab, pick up the Beetle at McAnnally's, and head to Michael's place.'

'What if the Denarians are waiting outside for us?'

I picked up my blasting rod from the stand in the corner by the door and twirled it around in my fingers. 'They'll have to find their own cab.'

'And then?'

I picked up my staff and leaned it against the wall by the door. 'We tell Michael and Sanya what happened.'

'Assuming they're back.'

'Uh-huh.' I opened the kitchen drawer and got out my gun and its holster. 'After that, I ask the nice Denarians to let Shiro go.'

Susan nodded. 'We ask?'

I flipped open the cylinder on the gun and loaded it. 'I'll say pretty please,' I said, and snapped the cylinder shut again.

Susan's eyes flashed. 'Count me in.' She watched me while I put on a shoulder rig and slipped the gun into it. 'Harry,' she said. 'I don't want to break up the righteous-vengeance vibe, but there are a couple of questions that are really bothering me.'

'Why do the Denarians want the Shroud, and what are they going to do with it,' I said.

'Yeah.'

I got an old squall jacket out of my room and slid it on. It felt wrong. I hadn't worn anything but my old canvas duster or the newer leather one Susan had given me for the past several years. I checked the candles, and they had all gone out. I laid my hand on the wall, feeling for the defenses. There was a faint echo of them left, but nothing of substance, so I went back out into the living room and called for a cab. 'We're good to go. I think I've got an idea of what they're doing, but I can't be sure.'

She straightened my jacket collar absently. 'Very sloppy of you. Didn't you get the megalomaniacal bragfest from this Nicodemus?'

'He must have read that Evil Overlord list.'

'Sounds like someone who intends to get things done.'

He sure as hell had. 'He let a couple things slip. I think we can get ahead of him.'

She shook her head. 'Harry, when I went down there with Shiro, I didn't see much. But I heard their voices through the tunnels. There was . . .' She closed her eyes for a moment, her expression one of faint nausea. 'It's hard for me to explain. Their voices gave me a strong impression. Shiro sounded like . . . I don't know. A trumpet. Clear and strong. The other one . . . his voice stank. It was rotted. Corrupt.'

I didn't understand what would have made Susan say that. Maybe it was something that the vampires had done to her. Maybe it was something she'd learned between tai chi classes. Maybe it was just pure intuition. But I knew what she was talking about. There was a sense to Nicodemus, of something quiet and still and dangerous – of something patient and vile and malicious beyond the scope of mortal understanding. He scared the hell out of me.

'I know what you mean. Nicodemus isn't another misguided idealist, or some greedy bastard out to make money,' I said. 'He's different.'

Susan nodded. 'Evil.'

'And he plays hardball.' I wasn't sure if I was asking Susan or myself, but I said, 'You ready?'

She got her jacket on. I went to the door and she followed.

'The one bad thing about the duster,' she mused. 'I could never see your butt.'

'I never noticed.'

'If you went around noticing your own ass I'd worry about you, Harry.'

I looked over my shoulder at her, smiling. She smiled back. It didn't last long. Both of our smiles turned a little sad.

'Susan,' I said.

She put two fingertips to my lips. 'Don't.'

'Dammit, Susan. Last night—'

'Shouldn't have happened,' she said. Her voice sounded tired, but her eyes stayed steady on mine. 'It doesn't—'

'—change anything,' I finished. I sounded bitter, even to me.

She took her hand away and buttoned up the dark leather jacket.

'Right,' I said. I should have stuck to shoptalk. I opened the door and looked outside. 'Cab's here. Let's get to work.'

27

I grabbed my staff, blasting rod, and Shiro's cane, and made a note to get myself a freaking golf bag. We took the cab to McAnnally's. The Blue Beetle was still in the nearby lot, and it hadn't been stolen, vaporized, or otherwise mishandled.

'What happened to your back window?' Susan asked.

'One of Marcone's goons winged a few shots at me outside the *Larry Fowler* studio.'

Susan's mouth twitched. 'You went on *Larry Fowler* again?'

'I don't want to talk about it.'

'Uh-huh. And what about the hood?'

'Little holes are from Marcone's thug. Big dent was a chlorofiend,' I said.

'A what?'

'Plant monster.'

'Oh. Why don't you just say "plant monster"?'

'I have my pride.'

'Your poor car.'

I got out my keys, but Susan put her hand on mine, and

walked a circle around the car. She crouched down and looked beneath it a couple of times, then said, 'Okay.'

I got in. 'Thank you, double oh seven, but no one bombs a Volkswagen. They're too cute.'

Susan got in the passenger door and said, 'Cute confetti if you aren't careful, Harry.'

I grunted, revved up the car, and puttered to Michael's place.

The morning was cold and clear. Winter hadn't yet given up its grip on the Great Lakes, and where Lake Michigan went, Chicago went too. Susan got out and looked around the front lawn, frowning from behind black sunglasses. 'How does he manage to make this place so nice, run his own business, and fight demons on the side?'

'He probably watches a lot of those home-and-garden shows,' I said.

She frowned. 'The grass is green. It's February and his grass is green. Doesn't that strike you as strange?'

'Sod works in mysterious ways.'

She made a disgusted sound, and then followed me up the walk to the door.

I knocked. A moment later Father Forthill said, 'Who's there?'

'Donny and Marie,' I responded. 'Salt-N-Pepa asked us to fill in for them.'

He opened the door, smiling from behind his gold-rimmed glasses. He was the same short, stocky, balding old Forthill, but he looked strained and tired. The lines of his face had grown deeper than I remembered. 'Hello, Harry.'

'Father,' I said. 'You know Susan?'

He looked at her thoughtfully. 'By reputation,' he said. 'Come in, come in.'

We did, and as I came in, Forthill set a Louisville Slugger baseball bat down in the corner. I raised my eyebrows, traded a look with Susan, and then put my staff and Shiro's cane beside the bat. We followed Forthill into the kitchen.

'Where's Charity?' I asked.

'Taking the children to her mother's house,' Forthill said. 'She should be back soon.'

I let out a breath of relief. 'Anna Valmont?'

'Guest room. Sleeping.'

'I need to call Martin,' Susan said. 'Excuse me.' She stepped aside into the small study.

'Coffee, doughnut?' Father Forthill asked.

I sat down at the table. 'Father, you've never been closer to converting me.'

He laughed. 'The Fantastic Forthill, saving souls one Danish at a time.' He produced the nectar of the gods themselves in Dunkin Donuts paper sacks and Styrofoam cups, taking some for himself as well. 'I've always admired your ability to make jokes when faced with adversity. Matters are grave.'

'I sort of noticed,' I said through a mouthful of glazed doughnut. 'Where's Michael?'

'He and Sanya went to St Louis to investigate possible Denarian activity. They were both arrested by the local police.'

'They what? What for?'

'No charges were filed,' Forthill said. 'They were arrested, held for twenty-four hours, and released.'

'Sand trap,' I said. 'Someone wanted them out of the way.'

Forthill nodded. 'So it would seem. I spoke to them about two hours ago. They're on their way back now and should be here soon.'

'Then as soon as they get here, we have to go get Shiro back.'

Forthill frowned and nodded. 'What happened to you last night?'

I told him the short version – all about the art auction and the Denarians, but I elided over the details afterward, which were none of his chaste business. And which would have embarrassed me to tell. I'm not particularly religious, but come on, the man was a priest.

When I finished, Forthill took off his glasses and stared hard at me. He had eyes the color of robin's eggs, and they could be disturbingly intense. 'Nicodemus,' he said quietly. 'Are you *sure* that is what he called himself?'

'Yeah.'

'Without a doubt?'

'Yeah. We had a nice chat.'

Forthill folded his hands and exhaled slowly. 'Mother of God. Harry, could you describe him for me?'

I did, while the old priest listened. 'Oh, and he was always wearing a rope around his neck. Not like a ship's hawser, a thin rope, like clothesline. I thought it was a string tie at first.'

Forthill's fingers reached up to touch the crucifix at his throat. 'Tied in a noose?'

'Yeah.'

'What did you think of him?' he asked.

I looked down at my half-eaten doughnut. 'He scared the hell out of me. He's . . . bad, I guess. Wrong.'

'The word you are looking for is "evil," Harry.'

I shrugged, ate the rest of the doughnut, and didn't argue.

'Nicodemus is an ancient foe of the Knights of the Cross,' Forthill said quietly. 'Our information about him is limited. He has made it a point to find and destroy our archives every other century or so, so we cannot be sure who he is or how long he has been alive. He may even have walked the earth when the Savior was crucified.'

'Didn't look a day over five hundred,' I mumbled. 'How come some Knight hasn't gone and parted his hair for him?'

'They've tried,' Forthill said.

'He's gotten away?'

Forthill's eyes and voice stayed steady. 'He's killed them. He's killed all of them. More than a hundred Knights. More than a thousand priests, nuns, monks. Three thousand men, women, children. And those are only the ones listed in the pages recovered from the destroyed archives. Only two Knights have ever faced him and survived.'

I had a flash of insight. 'Shiro is one of them. That's why Nicodemus was willing to trade me for him.'

Forthill nodded and closed his eyes for a moment. 'Likely. Though the Denarians grow in power by inflicting pain and suffering on others. They become better able to use the strength the Fallen give them. And they gain the most from hurting those meant to counter them.'

'He's torturing Shiro,' I said.

Forthill put his hand on mine for a moment, his voice quiet, calming. 'We must have faith. We may be in time to help him.'

'I thought the whole point of the Knights was to deal-out justice,' I said. 'The Fists of God and all that. So why is it that Nicodemus can slaughter them wholesale?'

'For much the same reason any man can kill another,' Forthill said. 'He is intelligent. Cautious. Skilled. Ruthless. Like his patron fallen angel.'

I guessed at the name. 'Badassiel?'

Forthill almost smiled. 'Anduriel. He was a captain of Lucifer's, after the Fall. Anduriel leads the thirty Fallen who inhabit the coins. Nicodemus wasn't seduced into Anduriel's domination. It's a partnership. Nicodemus works with Fallen as a near-equal and of his free will. No one of the priesthood, of any of the Knightly Orders, of the Knights of the Cross, has so much as scratched him.'

'The noose,' I guessed. 'The rope. It's like the Shroud, isn't it? It has power.'

Forthill nodded. 'We think so, yes. The same rope the betrayer used in Jerusalem.'

'How many Denarians are working with him? I take it that they probably don't get along with each other.'

'You are correct, thank God. Nicodemus rarely has more than five or six other Denarians working with him, according to our information. Usually, he keeps three others nearby.'

'Snakeboy, demon-girl, and Ursiel.'

'Yes.'

'How many coins are running around the world?'

'Only nine are accounted for at this time. Ten, with Ursiel's coin.'

'So Nicodemus could theoretically have nineteen other Fallen working with him. Plus a side order of goons.'

'Goons?'

'Goons. Normal hired hands, they looked like.'

'Ah. They aren't normal,' Forthill said. 'From what we have been able to tell, they are almost a small nation unto themselves. Fanatics. Their service is hereditary, passed on from father to son, mother to daughter.'

'This gets better and better,' I said.

'Harry,' Forthill said. 'I know of no tactful way to ask this, so I will simply ask. Did he give you one of the coins?'

'He tried,' I said. 'I turned him down.'

Forthill's eyes stayed on my face for a moment before he let out a breath. 'I see. Do you remember the sigil upon it?'

I grunted in affirmation, picked up a chocolate-covered jelly, and drew the symbol in the chocolate with a forefinger.

Forthill tilted his head, frowning. 'Lasciel,' he murmured.

'Lasciel?' I said. It came out muffled, since I was licking chocolate off my finger.

'The Seducer,' Forthill murmured. He smeared his finger over the chocolate, erasing the sigil. 'Lasciel is also called the Webweaver and the Temptress,' he said, between licks. 'Though it seems odd that Nicodemus would want to free her. Typically, she does not follow Anduriel's lead.'

'A rebel angel among rebel angels?'

'Perhaps,' Forthill said. 'It is something better not discussed, for now.'

Susan stepped out of the little office, a wireless phone to her ear. 'All right,' she said to the phone, and walked past us, jerking one hand at us to tell us to follow her. Father Forthill lifted his eyebrows, and we went out to the Carpenter family's living room.

It was a fairly huge room divided into several clumps of furniture. The television was in the smallest clump, and still looked about three sizes too small. Susan marched over to it, flicked it on, and flipped through stations.

She stopped on a local station, a news report, that showed a helicopter angle of a building being consumed by a raging fire.

About a dozen yellow-and-red fire trucks circled around it, but it was obvious that they were only containing the fire. The building was lost.

'What's this?' Forthill asked.

'Dammit,' I snarled, and turned away from the television, pacing.

'It's the building Shiro took us to last night,' Susan said. 'The Denarians were in some tunnels beneath it.'

'Not anymore,' I snapped. 'They've left and covered their tracks. Hell, they've had what? Six hours? They could be a couple of states away by now.'

'Nicodemus,' Forthill said. 'It's his style.'

'We'll find them,' Susan said quietly.

'How?' I asked.

She pressed her lips together and turned away from me. She spoke quietly into the phone. I couldn't hear what she said, but it had that end-of-conversation tone to it. She turned the handset off a moment later. 'What can we do?'

'I can go to the underworld,' I said. 'Call up some answers from there. But I can't do it until the sun sets.'

Forthill said quietly, 'You mustn't do that. It's far too dangerous. None of the Knights would want—'

I slashed my hand through the air, cutting him off. 'We need information or Shiro is going to die. Not only that, but if we don't run down Nicodemus, he gets to do whatever badness he's getting ready to do with the Shroud. If I have to go to Downbelow for answers, then that's where I go.'

'What about Michael?' Susan asked. 'Couldn't he find Shiro the way Shiro found Harry?'

Forthill shook his head. 'Not necessarily. It isn't something he can control. At times, the Knights are given that kind of discernment, but they can't call it up at will.'

I checked my watch, figuring up distances. 'Michael and Sanya should be back here in what? An hour or so?'

'Barring further difficulties,' Forthill said.

'Fine. We'll see if the side of the angels wants to pitch in. If they don't, I'm calling Chauncy up as soon as the sun goes down.' I took the phone from Susan and walked out of the room.

'Where are you going?' Susan asked.

'To talk to Anna Valmont. And after that, I'm going to call my client. On the off chance I survive, I want to look like I at least tried to be professional.'

Charity kept a guest room that had slowly been engulfed in a jungle of fabric. Clear boxes full of the stuff in every imaginable color stood stacked against one wall, and a small sewing machine sat on a table, barely visible among neatly folded stacks of more. More boxes of fabric had been stacked into a rampart around a single bed, which was occupied by a lump buried underneath several quilts.

I turned on a small lamp on the sewing table and hoped that the room wouldn't burst into flame. 'Anna. Wake up.'

The lump made a mumbling sound and stirred before settling again.

I turned the phone on and let the dial tone sound in the room's silence. 'I know you're awake, Miss Valmont. And you know that I saved your ass back at the Marriott. So if you don't sit up and talk to me right now, I'm calling the cops to come pick you up.'

She didn't move. I punched in a number and let the phone start to ring.

'Bastard,' she muttered. With the British accent, it came out *bah-stuhd*. She sat up, her expression wary, holding the covers to her front. Her shoulders were bare. 'Very well. What do you want?'

'My coat, for starters,' I said. 'But since I doubt you're palming it, I'll settle for the name of your buyer.'

She stared at me for a moment before she said, 'If I tell you that, it could kill me.'

'If you don't, I'm turning you over to the police.'

She shrugged. 'Which, while unpleasant, won't kill me. Besides, you intend to turn me over in any case.'

I scowled at her. 'I saved your life. Twice.'

'I am aware of that,' she said. She stared through me for a moment before she said, 'It's so hard to believe. Even though it happened to me. It seems . . . mad. Like a dream.'

'You aren't crazy,' I said. 'Or at least, you aren't hallucinating or anything.'

She half laughed. 'I know. Cisca is dead. Gaston is dead. It happened to them. My friends.' Her voice broke, and she started blinking very quickly. 'I just wanted to finish it. So that they didn't die for nothing at all. I owed it to them.'

I sighed. 'Look, I'll make this easy for you. Was it Marcone?'

She shrugged without focusing her eyes. 'We went through an intermediary, so I can't be sure.'

'But was it Marcone?'

Valmont nodded. 'If I had to guess, I would say it was. The buyer was someone with a great deal of money and local influence.'

'Does he know that you know?'

'One doesn't mention to the buyer that you know who he is when he is taking precautions to prevent it. It's impolite.'

'If you know anything about Marcone, you know that he isn't going to pay you off and let you walk away without delivering,' I said.

She rubbed at her eyes. 'I'll offer to return it.'

'Good idea. Assuming he doesn't kill you before you finish offering.'

She glared at me for a second, angry and crying. 'What do you want from me?'

I picked up a box of tissues from behind a bunch of yellow cotton on the table and offered it to her. 'Information. I want to know everything. It's possible you've heard or seen something that might help me recover the Shroud. Help me out, and I might be able to buy you some time to leave town.'

She took the box and blotted her eyes on a tissue. 'How do I know you will deliver on that promise?'

'Earth to Larceny Spice, come in Larceny Spice. I've saved your life twice. I think you can safely assume goodwill.'

She looked down, biting her lip. 'I . . . I don't know.'

'This is a limited-time offer.'

She drew in a shaking breath. 'All right. All right, let me clean up a little. Get dressed. I'll tell you what I know.'

'Fine,' I said. 'Come on. There's a shower in the bathroom at the end of the hall. I'll get you towels and stuff.'

'Is this your house?'

'Friends'. But I've stayed here before.'

She nodded and fished around until she came up with the black shirt she'd been wearing the night before. She slipped into it and rose. She had long, pretty, and bruised legs, and as she stepped onto her right leg she let out a pained cry and fell forward. I caught her before she could hit the ground, and she leaned into me, lifting her right foot from the floor.

'Bloody hell,' she wheezed. 'I must have twisted my ankle last night.' She shot me a hard-eyed glance. 'Hands.'

I jerked my hand off something pleasantly smooth and firm. 'Sorry. Accident. Can you manage?'

She shook her head, balanced on one leg. 'I don't think so. Lend me your arm a moment.'

I helped her hobble down the hall and into the bathroom. I dug some more towels out of the linen closet, then passed them into her through a mostly closed door. She locked it behind her and started the shower.

I shook my head and went back down the hall, dialing Father Vincent's phone number. On the fifth ring, he answered, his voice sounding tired and strained. 'Vincent.'

'It's Harry Dresden,' I said. 'I know where the Shroud came into Chicago and who was buying. It got intercepted by a third party and they have it now.'

'You're certain?' Vincent demanded.

'Yeah.'

'Do you know where it is?'

'Not exactly, but I'm going to find out. I should know by this evening, maybe sooner.'

'Why will it take until this evening?' Vincent asked.

'Well, uh. It's a little hard to explain,' I said.

'Perhaps the police should handle the rest of the investigation.'

'I'd advise against it.'

'Why?'

'I have some information that indicates your mistrust may not have been misplaced.'

'Oh,' Vincent said. His voice sounded worried. 'I think we should meet and talk, Mister Dresden. I'd rather not discuss this over the phone. Two o'clock, at the room we spoke in last?'

'I can probably do that,' I said.

'Until then,' said Vincent, and hung up.

I paced back into the living room and found Susan sitting and reading the morning paper with coffee and a doughnut. One of the sliding glass doors that had previously led to the back patio was open, and on the other side was a lot of bare wood and plastic – the addition Michael was building. The rasping of a saw came through the open door.

I stepped out and found Father Forthill at work. He'd taken off his coat and collar. He had a shortsleeved black shirt underneath. He wore leather work gloves and safety glasses. He finished sawing a beam, and blew dust off the cut before rising. 'How is Father Vincent?'

'Sounds tired,' I said. 'I'm going to talk to him later, assuming we don't have something going on first.'

'I worry for him,' Forthill said. He held up the beam to the top of what would eventually be a window. 'Here, hold this for me.'

I did. Forthill started driving in a few nails, clenching several in his teeth. 'And Miss Valmont?'

'Taking a shower. She's going to cooperate with us.'

Forthill frowned, taking a nail from his lips. 'I really wouldn't have expected that from her, from the sense I had of her.'

'It's my charming personality,' I said. 'The ladies can't resist.'

'Mmmm,' Forthill said, around the nails.

'It's the only decent thing to do. And her back is against a wall, right?'

Forthill drove the nail in and frowned. He looked at me.

I looked back at him for a moment and then said, 'I'll just go check on her.'

I got about halfway across the living room before I heard a car door shut, immediately followed by a car engine. I ran to the front door and threw it open just in time to see the shattered rear window of the Blue Beetle zipping down the street and out of sight.

I fumbled at my pockets and groaned. My keys were missing. 'Son of a *bitch*,' I snarled. I punched the door frame in sheer frustration. I didn't punch it very hard. I was angry, not looking to break my own knuckles. 'The old stumble and bump and I *fell* for it.'

Susan stepped up beside me and sighed. 'Harry, you idiot. You're a good man. But an idiot where women are concerned.'

'First my coat and now my car. That's freaking gratitude for you.'

Susan nodded. 'No good deed goes unpunished.'

I stared at her. 'Are you laughing at me?'

She faced me from behind a perfectly straight face. But her voice sounded a little choked. 'No.'

'You *are*.'

Her face turned pink and she shook her head.

'Laughing at my pain.'

She turned and walked back to the living room and picked up her paper. She sat down and held it up so that I couldn't see her face. Choked sounds came out from behind the paper.

I stalked back out to the addition, growling. Forthill looked back at me, his eyebrows raised.

'Give me something to break. Or hit really hard,' I told him.

His eyes sparkled. 'You'll hurt yourself. Here, hold this for me.'

I lifted another cut board into place, while Forthill reached up to hammer it in. As he did, the sleeve of his shirt tugged up, and showed me a pair of green lines.

'Wait,' I said, and snapped my hand over to his arm. The board slipped out of my other hand and bonked me on the head on the way down. I scowled at it, wincing, but tugged the sleeve up.

Forthill had a tattoo on the inside of his right arm.

An Eye of Thoth.

'What is this?' I demanded.

Forthill looked around and tugged his sleeve back down. 'A tattoo.'

'Duh, a tattoo. I know that. What does it mean?'

'It's something I had done when I was younger,' he answered. 'An organization I belonged to.'

I tried to calm down but my voice still sounded harsh. 'What organization?'

Forthill blinked mildly at me. 'I don't understand why you are so upset, Harry—'

'*What* organization?'

He continued to look confused. 'Just several of us who took our orders together. We were barely more than boys, really. And we'd . . . well. We'd happened on to some of the stranger events of our day. And records of others. A vampire had killed two people in town, and we stopped it together. No one believed us, of course.'

'Of course,' I said. 'What about the tattoo?'

Forthill pursed his lips, thoughtful. 'I haven't thought about it in so long. Well, the next morning we went out and got the tattoos. We swore an oath to be always watchful against the forces of darkness, to help one another whenever we could.'

'Then what?'

'After the hangovers faded, we went a very good distance out of our way to make sure none of the senior clergy saw them,' Forthill responded, smiling faintly. 'We were young.'

'And then?'

'And then no other supernatural events presented themselves over the next few years and the five of us drifted apart. Until I heard from Vittorio – from Father Vincent last week, I hadn't spoken to any of them in years.'

'Wait. Vincent has a tattoo like this?'

'I suppose he could have had it removed. He might be the sort to do that.'

'What about the others in the group?'

'Passed away over the last several years,' Forthill said. He stripped off one of the work gloves and regarded his weathered hand. 'Back then, I don't think any of us thought we would ever live to be so old.'

The wheels spun in my head, and I got it. I understood what was happening, and why. On pure intuition I stalked to the front of the house, gathering up my things on the way. Father Forthill followed me. 'Harry?'

I walked past Susan, who set her paper aside and stood up to follow me. 'Harry?'

I got to the front door and jerked it open.

The engine of Michael's white pickup rattled to a halt as I did, and he and Sanya got out of the truck. They looked a little rumpled and unshaven, but fine. Michael blinked at me and asked, 'Harry? I think I just saw a woman driving your car toward the highway. What's going on?'

'Get anything you need for a fight,' I said. 'We're going.'

28

When Father Vincent answered my knock, I kicked the door into his face as hard as I could. He fell back with a grunt of surprise. I came into the room with Father Forthill's Louisville Slugger in my hands, and jabbed the broad end of the bat into Vincent's throat.

The old priest made a sick croaking sound and clutched at his neck on the way to the floor.

I didn't let it stop there. I kicked him in the ribs twice, and when he rolled over, trying to get away from me, I stomped down on the back of his neck, drew my gun, and shoved it against his skull.

'*Dio*,' Vincent whimpered, panting. '*Dio*, wait! Please, don't hurt me!'

'I don't have time to play pretend,' I said. 'Drop the act.'

'Please, Mister Dresden, I don't know what you mean.' He coughed, panting, and I saw droplets of scarlet dripping onto the carpet. I'd bloodied his nose, or maybe his lip. He turned his head a tiny bit, eyes wide with panic. 'Please, don't do anything to me. I don't know what you want, but I'm sure that we can talk about it.'

I drew back the hammer on the revolver and said, 'I'm sure that we can't.'

His face went white. 'No, wait!'

'I'm getting tired of playing pretend. Three.'

'But I don't know—' He choked, and I heard him trying not to retch. 'You have to tell me—'

'Two,' I said. 'I'm not going to elaborate about the other number.'

'You can't! You can't!'

'One,' I said, and pulled the trigger.

In the instant between the word and the deed, Vincent changed. A sheath of green scales appeared over his skin, and his legs twined together into a serpent's long and sinuous body. The eyes went last, changing to vertically slit yellow orbs while a second set of glowing green eyes opened above the first.

The trigger came down on an empty chamber. Click.

The snake twisted to bite me, but I was already getting out of the way. Michael came through the door, his unshaven face set in grim determination, *Amoracchius* blazing with its own white light. The snakeman whirled to face Michael with a hiss. Michael tried for a clean horizontal cut, but the snakeman ducked under it and went for the door in a streak of gleaming green scales.

When the snakeman went out the door, Sanya brought a four-foot length of two-by-six down on its head. The blow drove the snakeman's chin flat to the ground. It twitched a couple of times and then lay still.

'You were right,' Michael noted. He slipped the sword away into its sheath.

'Better get him back inside before some maid sees him,' I said.

Michael nodded, grabbed the snakeman's tail, and hauled him back into the hotel room.

Sanya looked in, nodded, and set the end of the length of heavy board down with a certain amount of satisfaction. I realized he'd used the thing with one arm. Good grief. I needed to get to the gym. 'Good,' the big Russian said. 'Let me put this back in the truck, and I will join you.'

A few minutes later, the snakeman woke up in the corner of the hotel room with me, Michael, and Sanya standing over him. His tongue flickered out and in a few times, and his two sets of eyes darted around the room.

'What did I miss?' it hissed. The last word came out with an extra large helping of S sounds.

'A tattoo,' I said. 'Father Vincent had a tattoo on the inside of his right arm.'

'There was no tattoo,' the snakeman insisted.

'Maybe it was covered with all the blood. You made a stupid mistake. It's understandable. Most criminals aren't all that bright, so you were working uphill from the get-go.'

The snakeman hissed, shifting its scales restlessly, a cobra-like hood flaring around its neck and shoulders.

Michael drew *Amoracchius*. Sanya did the same with *Esperacchius*. The two blades threw pure white light over the snakeman, and he subsided, flinching back from them. 'What do you want?'

'To talk,' I said. 'See, the way it works is that I ask you questions. You answer them. And as long as you do we'll all be happy.'

'And if I don't?' the snakeman hissed.

'I get a new pair of boots.'

The snake's scales and coils twined around on one another, rasping. Its eyes remained on the two Knights. 'Ask.'

'Here's what I figure happened. Somehow, your glee club heard that the Churchmice were being hired to find and take the Shroud. You thought you'd just nip it from them on their way out of town, but you missed. You caught Gaston LaRouche, but he didn't have the Shroud. So you tortured him until he told you everything.'

'And after he told us everything,' the snakeman said. 'Nicodemus was indulging his little bitch.'

'I think it's sweet to see a father and daughter doing things together. So you found out what LaRouche knew, killed him, and left his body where it would be found, pointed at where the Shroud was going. You figured you'd let the mortal authorities do the work of finding them for you, and take the Shroud when they did.'

'Drudge work. Unworthy of us.'

'You're gonna hurt my feelings, snakeboy. You found out who the Church was sending over. Then you grabbed poor Father Vincent at the airport. You took his place.'

'Any infant could reason as much,' the Denarian hissed.

I pulled up a chair and sat. 'Here's where it gets interesting. Because you decided to hire me on. Why?'

'Why do you think?'

'To keep tabs on the Knights,' I said. 'Or to distract them by making them try to keep me out of the search. Or maybe you thought I could really turn up the Shroud for you. Probably all three. No sense doing things for one reason when you can fit in a few ulterior motives for free. You even gave me a sample of the

Shroud to make it more likely I'd find it.' I leaned back in the chair. 'That's where I started seeing something wrong. I talked to Marcone about his new thug gunning for me, and he blinked.'

'I don't know what you are talking about,' the snakeman said.

'Marcone was the buyer.'

A cold laugh slithered out of the snakeman's mouth. 'A mortal. Nothing more.'

'Yeah, well, the mortal figured out that Father Vincent had been replaced, and he sent an assassin to kill you. The new guy wasn't shooting at me outside of Fowler's studio. He was after you.'

'Impossible,' the snakeman said.

'Pride goeth, legs. Marcone wasn't born yesterday.'

'I am sure you have pleased yourself with your cleverness, wizard.'

'It gets better,' I said brightly. 'See, Nicodemus didn't let much drop, other than that he was on a deadline and he needed someone savvy to the supernatural. His daughter did, though. She asked if he didn't want a silver bowl. That's a ceremonial bowl, and if I was guessing, I'd say it was meant to be used to catch lifeblood. Fuel a ritual.'

The snakeman's tail lashed around restlessly.

'I think Father Vincent was a warm-up. A test for the ritual. I think he came over here with two samples from the Shroud, and you used one of them as the focus for the plague curse that killed him. Once you knew it would work, you went after the Shroud itself.'

'You know nothing, wizard,' said the snakeman. The glowing sigil on his forehead throbbed in time with the extra set of eyes. 'You are pathetic.'

'You're hurting my feelings. Don't make me get the baseball bat,' I said. 'Nicodemus covered his tracks this morning by burning down the building you'd been in. I suppose he sent you to cover everything up nice and neat with the cops and with me. I think he's got something in mind, and I think it's tonight. So why not make this a comparatively pleasant discussion and tell me all about it.'

'Do you think that you frighten me, wizard?' said the Denarian. 'I was destroying men more powerful than you before this pathetic nation was born.'

'Where is Nicodemus and what is he doing with the Shroud? I'll give you a hint. It's got something to do with a plague curse.'

'I have served Nicodemus since—'

'Since my last dental appointment, I get it,' I said. 'But let me point something out to you. Nicodemus isn't here.' I held my palms out to either side of me, Vanna White-style. 'These two gentlemen are very much here. And very much angry.'

Sanya stared at the Denarian, the saber in his hand swishing back and forth a little. He growled. It was enough to make me want to edge away from him.

'Look,' I told him. 'We're going to find Nicodemus and push his face in. We're going to shut down whatever he's got in mind, and we're going to get Shiro back. And you're going to tell us what we need to know.'

'Or?'

Michael said, in a very quiet voice, 'I end you.'

The snakeman stared at me for a very long time. Then he started to rasp and shake. It took me a minute to realize that he was laughing at me. Snakes weren't really meant for laughter. It didn't sit well on a serpentine body.

'You cannot threaten me,' he said. 'There is nothing you can do to me.'

'I see a couple of holy swords here that make me think otherwise.'

'No,' the Denarian said. He reached up to his forehead and clawed at the sigil there, as if trying to peel off his own skin. The symbol flashed, and then faded, along with the second set of eyes. The whole of him rippled, scales abruptly melting away. For a second, the features of Father Vincent emerged from beneath the scales. Then they too faded away, replaced by a man's pinched and hardened features. He was dark of skin, maybe Moorish, and he wasn't big. Five feet and a little change, and not more than one-fifty. Average height, several centuries ago.

The man lowered his hand and let a slightly tarnished silver coin roll across the floor to Michael's feet. 'My name is Quintus Cassius, and I have long been slave to the will of the demon Saluriel.' His dark eyes glittered with malice, and his tone dripped with sarcasm. 'I beg you for mercy and the chance to mend my ways. How ever can I thank you, Sir Knight, for saving me from that torment.'

Shit. He was playing the morality card. I shot a glance at Michael.

The big man frowned at snakeboy Cassius, but didn't miss a beat in drawing out a white handkerchief embroidered with a silver cross, and folding the coin up in it. Michael and Sanya exchanged a long look, and then both of them put away their swords.

'Uh, guys. What the hell are you doing? Dangerous demon murderer here, remember?'

'Harry,' Michael said. 'We can't. Not if he's surrendered the coin and asked mercy.'

'*What?*' I demanded. 'That's *stupid*.'

'Of course it is,' Cassius said. Glee danced in his voice. 'They know that I am not sincere. They know I will turn on them at the first opportunity. That I will obtain one of the other coins and return to what I have done for centuries.'

I stood up, angry enough that the chair fell over. 'Michael, if you turn the other cheek on this bastard he'll tear it off your face. You're supposed to be the freaking Fist of God.'

'No, I'm not, Harry,' Michael said. 'The purpose of the Knights is not to destroy those who serve evil.'

'Indeed not,' Cassius said. Somehow, there was more of a hiss in his voice now than when he'd been a snake. 'They're here to save us.'

'To *save* them?' I stared at Michael. 'Is he kidding?'

Michael shook his head. 'No one else can face the Denarians, Harry. No one else can challenge the Fallen. This moment might be the only chance Cassius has to turn aside from what he has chosen. To change his path.'

'Great. I'm all for changing his path. Let's change it to a direct line to the bottom of Lake Michigan.'

Michael's expression was pained. 'The Knights are here to protect freedom. To give those who are under the oppression of dark forces the chance to win free of them. I cannot sit in judgment on this man's soul, Harry Dresden. Not for you. Not for anyone. All I can do is remain faithful to my calling. Give him the chance to see hope for his future. To show him the love and compassion any human being should show another. The rest is out of my hands.'

I watched Cassius's face while Michael spoke. His expression changed. It became harder. More brittle. And bitter. What Michael said had touched him. I didn't believe for a second that it had touched Cassius enough to change his mind. But it touched him enough to drive him toward fury.

I turned to Michael and said, 'Do you really think that thing is going to start sipping of the milk of human kindness?'

'No,' Michael said. 'But that doesn't change my purpose. He has surrendered his coin, and the influence of it. The rest is not for Sanya or me to decide. It is Cassius's choice.'

'You've seen these things,' I snarled, stalking over to face Michael. 'I've seen the corpses they've left. They would have killed me, Susan, you – hell, all of us – without blinking an eye. God only knows what they have in mind with that curse they're putting together.'

'All power has its limits, Harry.' He shook his head. 'This is the limit of mine.'

Without really thinking about it, I shoved his shoulder. 'They might already have *killed* Shiro. And you're going to let this bastard walk?'

Michael caught my arm in one hand and twisted. Michael is strong. I had to rise up onto my toes to relieve the pressure he put on my elbow, and he shoved me back from him, his eyes hard and cold and angry as hell.

'I know that,' he said in that same deadly quiet voice. 'I know they've hurt him. That they're going to kill him. Just as Shiro knew that Nicodemus would betray his promise to set you free. It's one of the things that makes us different than they are, Harry. The blood on their hands does not make it right to bloody my own. My choices are measured against my own soul. Not against the stains on theirs.' He looked at Cassius, and the Denarian flinched away from the silent flame in Michael's expression. 'It is not for me to judge his soul. No matter how much I might want to.'

'Hell's bells,' I muttered. 'No wonder Nicodemus has killed so many Knights, if you're all as idiotic as this.'

'Harry—' Michael began.

I interrupted him. 'Look at him, Michael. He isn't a victim. He's a freaking collaborator. That poor bastard Rasmussen might have been dragooned into working with the Denarians, but Cassius does it because he wants to do it.'

'There's no way for you to be sure of that, Harry,' Sanya said.

'Why are you giving him a fair chance? Which of them has *ever* turned away from their coins?'

Sanya put his dark hand on my shoulder and said, 'I did.'

I looked back at him, frowning.

'I was of their number,' Sanya said. 'I was less experienced. Foolish. Proud. I did not set out to be a monster, but that much power corrupts. Shiro faced the Fallen I had allowed in. He exposed its lies. And I made a better choice.'

'Traitor,' said Cassius, his voice cold. 'We handed you the world. Power. Glory. Everything you could have wanted.'

Sanya faced the man and said, 'What I wanted you could never give me. I had to find it for myself.' He extended a hand. 'Cassius, you can leave them just as I did. Help us, please. And let us help you.'

Cassius leaned back, as though Sanya's hand might burn him, and hissed, 'I will eat your eyes.'

'We can't leave him here,' I said. 'He'll shoot us in the back. He'll try to kill us.'

'Maybe,' Michael said quietly, and didn't move.

I wanted to be angry with Sanya and Michael. But I couldn't. I'm only human. I'd flirted with dark powers before. Made stupid deals. Bad choices. I'd been given a chance to work free of them, or I'd have been dead long ago.

I understood what Michael and Sanya were saying and doing. I understood why. I didn't like it, but I couldn't really gainsay it without making a hypocrite of myself. There but for the lack of a demon-infested coin went I.

Cassius started wheezing and laughing his dry, contemptuous laugh. 'Run along,' he said. 'Run along. I'll think over your words. Reexamine my life. Walk the straight and narrow.'

'Let's go,' Michael said quietly.

'We can't leave him,' I insisted.

'The police aren't going to have anything on him, Harry. We're not going to kill him. We're finished here. Have faith. We'll find an answer somehow.'

Cassius laughed at Michael's back as he walked out. Sanya followed him, lingering to look back over his shoulder at me.

'Fools,' Cassius murmured, rising. 'Weak fools.'

I picked up the bat again and turned to the door. 'You're wrong,' I said to Cassius.

'Weak,' Cassius repeated. 'The old man was screaming after only an hour, you know. Nicodemus started with his back. Lashed him with chains. Then Deirdre played with him.'

I gave Cassius a hard look over my shoulder.

He was sneering, lip lifted from his teeth. 'Deirdre likes to break fingers and toes. I wish I'd been able to stay longer. I only got to pull out his toenails.' His smile widened, eyes gleaming. 'The woman, the Fellowship woman. She is yours?'

I felt my lip lift away from my teeth.

Cassius's eyes gleamed. 'She bled prettily, didn't she? The next time I catch her, you won't be there to disrupt my conjuration. I'll let the snakes eat her. Bite by bite.'

I stared at him.

Cassius smiled again. 'But there is mercy for me, is there not? Forgiveness. Indeed, God is great.'

I turned away from him again and said, very quietly, 'People like you always mistake compassion for weakness. Michael and Sanya aren't weak. Fortunately for you, they're good men.'

Cassius laughed at me.

'Unfortunately for you, I'm not.'

I spun around, swinging the bat as hard as I could, and broke Cassius's right kneecap.

He screamed in shock and sudden surprise, and went down. Odd crackling sounds came from the joint.

I swung again and broke his right ankle.

Cassius screamed.

I broke his left knee for him too. And his left ankle. He was thrashing around and screaming a lot, so it took me maybe a dozen swings.

'Stop!' he managed to gasp. 'Stop, stop, stop!'

I kicked him in the mouth to shut him up, stomped his right forearm to the floor, and crushed his hand with another half dozen swings.

I pinned his left arm down the same way, and put the bat on my shoulder. 'Listen to me, you worthless piece of shit. You aren't a victim. You chose to be one of them. You've been serving dark forces your whole life. Freddie Mercury would say Beelzebub has a devil put aside for you.'

'What do you think you're doing?' He gasped. 'You can't . . . you won't . . .'

I leaned down and twisted his false priest's collar, half choking him. 'The Knights are good men. I'm not. And I won't lose a second's sleep over killing you.' I shook him with each word, hard enough to rattle his bloodied teeth. 'Where. Is. Nicodemus.'

Cassius broke, sobbing. His bladder had let go at some point, and the room smelled like urine. He choked and spat out blood and a broken tooth. 'I'll tell.' He gasped. 'Please, don't.'

I let his collar go and straightened. 'Where?'

'I don't know,' he said, cowering away from my eyes. 'He didn't tell me. Meeting him tonight. Was going to meet him tonight. Eight.'

'Meet him where?'

'Airport,' Cassius said. He started throwing up. I kept his arm pinned, so it mostly went all over himself. 'I don't know exactly where.'

'What is he doing?'

'The curse. He's going to unleash the curse. Use the Shroud. The old man's blood. He has to be moving when he completes the ritual.'

'Why?'

'Curse is a contagion. He has to spread it as far as he can. More exposure to it. Make himself stronger. A-apocalypse.'

I took my foot off of his arm and smashed the motel's phone to pieces with the bat. I found his cell phone and crushed it, too. Then I reached into my pocket and dropped a quarter on the floor near him. 'There's a pay phone on the other side of the parking lot, past a patch of broken glass. You'd better get yourself an ambulance.' I turned and walked to the door without looking back. 'If I see you again – ever – I'll kill you.'

Michael and Sanya waited for me outside the door. Sanya's face held a certain amount of satisfaction. Michael's expression was grave, worried, his eyes on mine.

'It had to be done,' I said to Michael. My voice sounded cold. 'He's alive. It's more than he deserves.'

'Perhaps,' Michael said. 'But what you did, Harry. It was wrong.'

A part of me felt sick. Another part felt satisfied. I wasn't sure which of them was bigger. 'You heard what he said about Shiro. About Susan.'

Michael's eyes darkened, and he nodded. 'It doesn't make it right.'

'No. It doesn't.' I met his eyes. 'Think God'll forgive me?'

Michael was quiet for a moment, and then his expression softened. He clasped my shoulder and said, 'God is always merciful.'

'What you did for him was actually quite generous,' Sanya said philosophically. 'Relatively speaking. He might be hurt, but he is, after all, alive. He'll have a nice, long while to reconsider his choices.'

'Uh-huh,' I said. 'I'm a giver. Did it for his own good.'

Sanya nodded gravely. 'Good intentions.'

Michael nodded. 'Who are we to judge you?' His eyes flashed, and he asked Sanya, 'Did you see the snake's face, right when Harry turned with the bat?'

Sanya smiled and started whistling as we walked through the parking lot.

We piled into the truck. 'Drop me off at my place,' I said. 'I need to pick up a couple things. Make some phone calls.'

'The duel?' Michael asked. 'Harry, are you sure you don't want me to—'

'Leave it to me,' I said. 'You've already got something on your plate. I can handle things. I'll meet you at the airport afterward and help you find Shiro.'

'If you live,' Sanya said.

'Yes. Thank you, Comrade Obvious.'

The Russian grinned. 'Was that a quarter you gave Cassius?'

'Yeah.'

'For the phone?'

'Yeah.'

Michael noted, 'Phone calls cost more than that now.'

I slouched back and allowed myself a small smile. 'Yeah. I know.'

Sanya and Michael burst out laughing. Michael pounded on the steering wheel.

I didn't join them, but I enjoyed their laughter while I could. The February sun was already sinking fast toward the horizon.

29

Back at my apartment, I called Murphy on her personal cell phone. I used simple sentences and told her everything.

'Dear God,' Murphy said. Can I summarize or what? 'They can infect the city with this curse thing?'

'Looks like,' I said.

'How can I help?'

'We've got to keep them from getting it into the air. They won't be on public transportation. Find out if any chartered planes are taking off between seven and eight-thirty. Helicopters too.'

'Hang on,' Murphy said. I heard computer keys clicking, Murphy saying something to someone, a police radio. A moment later she said, voice tense, 'There's trouble.'

'Yeah?'

'There are a pair of detectives heading out to arrest you. Looks like Homicide wants you for questioning. There's no warrant listed.'

'Crap.' I took a deep breath. 'Rudolph?'

'Brownnosing rat,' Murphy muttered. 'Harry, they're almost at your place. You've only got a few minutes.'

'Can you decoy them? Get some manpower to the airport?'

'I don't know,' Murphy said. 'I'm supposed to be a mile from this case. And it isn't as though I can announce that terrorists are about to use a biological weapon on the city.'

'Use Rudolph,' I said. 'Tell him off the record that I said the Shroud is leaving town on a chartered flight from the airport. Let him take the heat for it if they don't find anything.'

Murphy let out a harsh little laugh. 'There are times when you can be a clever man, Harry. It takes me by surprise.'

'Why, thank you.'

'What else can I do?'

I told her.

'You're kidding.'

'No. We may need the manpower, and SI is out of this one.'

'Just when I had hope for your intelligence, too.'

'You'll do it?'

'Yeah. Can't promise anything, but I'll do it. Get moving. They're less than five minutes away.'

'Gone. Thank you, Murph.'

I hung up the phone, opened my closet, and dug into a couple of old cardboard boxes I kept at the back until I found my old canvas duster. It was battered and torn in a couple of places, but it was clean. It didn't have the same reassuring weight as the leather duster, but it did more to hide my gun than my jacket. And it made me look cool. Well, maybe cooler, anyway.

I grabbed my things, locked up my place behind me, and got

into Martin's rental car. Martin wasn't in it. Susan sat behind the wheel. 'Hurry,' I said. She nodded and pulled out.

A few minutes later, no one had pulled us over. 'I take it Martin isn't helping.'

Susan shook her head. 'No. He said he had other duties that took precedence. He said that I did, too.'

'What did you say?'

'That he was a narrow-minded, hidebound, anachronistic, egotistical bastard.'

'No wonder he likes you.'

Susan smiled a little and said, 'The Fellowship is his life. He serves a cause.'

'What is it to you?' I asked.

Susan remained silent for a long time as we drove across town. 'How did it go?'

'We caught the impostor. He told us where the bad guys would be later tonight.'

'What did you do with him?'

I told her.

She looked at me for a while and then said, 'Are you all right?'

'Fine.'

'You don't look fine.'

'It's done.'

'But are you all right?'

I shrugged. 'I don't know. I'm glad you didn't see it.'

Susan asked, 'Oh? Why?'

'You're a girl. Beating up bad guys is a boy thing.'

'Chauvinist pig,' Susan said.

'Yeah. I get it from Murphy. She's a bad influence.'

We hit the first traffic sign directing us toward the stadium, and Susan asked, 'Do you really think you can win?'

'Yeah. Hell, Ortega is only the third or fourth most disturbing thing I've tangled with today.'

'But even if you do win, what does it change?'

'Me getting killed now. That way, I get to be killed later tonight instead.'

Susan laughed. There was nothing happy in it. 'You don't deserve a life like this.'

I squinted my eyes and made my voice gravelly. 'Deserve's got nothin'—'

'So help me God, if you quote Clint Eastwood at me, I'm wrapping this car around a telephone pole.'

'Do you feel lucky, punk?' I smiled and turned my left hand palm up.

I felt her hand settle lightly on mine a moment later, and she said, 'A girl's got to draw the line somewhere.'

We rode the rest of the way to the stadium in silence, holding hands.

I hadn't ever been to Wrigley when it was empty. That wasn't really the point of a stadium. You went there to be among about a bajillion people and see something happen. This time, with acres and acres of unoccupied asphalt, the stadium at its center looked huge and somehow more skeletal than when it was filled with vehicles and cheering thousands. The wind sighed through the stadium, gusting, whistling, and moaning. Twilight had fallen, and the unlit street lamps cast spidery shadows over the lots. Darkness gaped in the arches and doorways of the stadium, empty as the eyes of a skull.

'Thank God that isn't too creepy or anything,' I muttered.

'What now?' Susan asked.

Another car pulled in behind us. I recognized it from McAnnally's the night before. The car pulled up maybe fifty feet away and rolled to a stop. Ortega got out, and leaned down to say something to the driver, a man with a dark complexion and amber-tone glasses. There were two more men in the backseat, though I couldn't see much of them. I was betting they were all Red Court.

'Let's not look scared,' I said, and got out of the car.

I didn't look at Ortega, but drew out my staff with me, planted it on the ground, and stared at the stadium. The wind caught my coat, and blew it back enough to show the gun on my hip now and again. I'd traded in my sweats for dark jeans and a black silk shirt. The Mongols or somebody wore silk shirts because they would catch arrows as they entered wounds, and enable them to pull barbed arrowheads out without ripping their innards apart. I wasn't planning on getting shot with barbed arrows, but weirder things have happened.

Susan got out and walked up to stand beside me. She stared at the stadium too, and the wind blew her hair back the same way it did my coat. 'Very nice,' she murmured, hardly moving her mouth. 'That's a good look on you. Ortega's driver is about to wet his pants.'

'You say the nicest things to me.'

We just stood there for a couple of minutes, until I heard a deep, rhythmic rumbling – one of those annoyingly loud bass stereos in some moron's car. The rumbling got louder; then there was a squealing of tires taking a tight turn, and Thomas pulled into the lot in a different white sports car than I'd seen him in the night before. The music got louder as he sped across the lot and parked his car diagonally across the lines we'd unconsciously respected when we'd parked. He killed the stereo and got out, a small cloud of smoke emerging with him. It wasn't cigarette smoke.

'Paolo!' Thomas caroled. He wore tight blue jeans and a black T-shirt with a *Buffy the Vampire Slayer* logo. The laces to one of his combat boots were untied, and he carried a bottle of scotch in his hand. He pulled from it cheerfully and wove a drunken line to Ortega. Thomas offered out the bottle, his balance wobbling. 'Have a swig?'

Ortega slapped the bottle from Thomas's hand. It shattered on the ground.

'Shpoilshport,' Thomas slurred, wavering. 'Hola, Harry! Hola, Susan!' He waved at us, and all but fell down. 'I was going to offer you some too, but that plan's been blown all to hell now.'

'Maybe another time,' Susan said.

A blue light appeared in one of the tunnels from the stadium. A moment later, a vehicle somewhere between a compact car and a golf cart rolled into the parking lot, a whirling blue bubble light flashing on its roof. With the quiet hum of electric motors, it zipped over to us and stopped. Kincaid sat behind the steering wheel and nodded to the rear of the vehicle. 'In. We're set up inside.'

We walked over to the security cart. Ortega started to get on, but I held up my hand to him. 'Ladies first,' I said quietly, and gave Susan my hand as she got on. I followed her. Ortega and Thomas followed. Thomas had put on a pair of headphones and was bobbing his chin in a vague fashion that was probably supposed to be in rhythm.

Kincaid started up the cart and called over his shoulder, 'Where is the old man?'

'Gone,' I said. I jerked a thumb at Susan. 'Had to go to the bench.'

Kincaid looked from me to Susan and shrugged. 'Nice bench.'

He drove us through several passages in the stadium, somehow finding his way despite the fact that no lights were on, and I could barely see. Eventually we rolled out onto the field from one of the bullpens. The stadium was dark but for where three spotlights basted the pitcher's mound and first and third base in pools of light. Kincaid drove to the pitcher's mound, stopped, and said, 'Everyone out.'

We did. Kincaid parked the cart over home plate, then padded through the shadows to the visiting team's dugout. 'They're here,' he said quietly.

The Archive emerged from the dugout, carrying a small, carved wooden box before her. She wore a dark dress with no frills or ruffles, and a grey cape held closed with a silver brooch. She was still little, still adorable, but something in her bearing left no illusions about the difference in her apparent age and her knowledge and capability.

She walked to the pitcher's mound, not looking at anyone, her focus on the box she carried. She set it down, very carefully, and then lifted the lid from the top of the box and stepped back.

A wave of nauseating cold flooded out when she opened the box. It went past me, through me. I was the only one there to react to it. Susan put her hand on my arm, kept her eyes on Ortega and Thomas, and asked, 'Harry?'

My last meal had been a drive-through taco on the way back from the meeting with Cassius, but it was trying to leave. I kept it down and forced the sickening cold away from me with an effort of will. The sensation lessened. 'Fine,' I said. 'I'm fine.'

The Archive looked up at me, child features solemn. 'You know what is inside the box?'

'I think so. I've never actually seen it.'

'Seen what?' Thomas asked.

Instead of answering, the Archive drew a small box out of her pocket. She opened the box and delicately plucked out an insect as long as her own fingers – a brown scorpion – by its tail. She looked around to make sure she had everyone's attention. She did. Then she dropped the scorpion into the box.

There was an instant, immediate sound, somewhere between a wildcat's scream and the sizzle of bacon hitting a hot skillet. Something that looked vaguely like a cloud of ink in clear water floated up out of the box. It was about the size of a baby's head. Dozens of shadowy tendrils held the scorpion, drawing it up into the air along with the inky cloud. Dark violet flickers of flame played over the insect's shell for all of two or three seconds – and then it simply crumbled, carapace falling away in flakes and dust.

The cloudy mass rose up to a height of about five feet, before the Archive murmured a word. It stopped in place, bobbing gently, holding there.

'Damn,' Thomas said, he took the earphones out. Music with many electric guitars sounded tinnily from them. 'And this is what?'

'Mordite,' I said quietly. 'Deathstone.'

'Yes,' the Archive said.

Ortega drew in a slow breath, and nodded in understanding.

'Deathstone, huh?' Thomas said. 'It sort of looks like someone spray-painted a soap bubble. And gave it tentacles.'

'It isn't a soap bubble,' I said. 'There's a solid piece inside.

The energies it carries in it are what create that shroud effect around it.'

Thomas poked a finger at it. 'What does it do?'

I caught his wrist before he could touch it, and pushed his hand away. 'It kills. Hence the name *deathstone*, you half-wit.'

'Oh,' Thomas said, nodding with drunken sagacity. 'It looked cool when it gacked that little thing, but so what? It's a bug zapper.'

'If you disrespect this thing it's going to get you killed,' I said. 'It would kill anything living exactly the same way. Anything. It's not from our world.'

'It's extraterrestrial?' asked Susan.

'You do not understand, Miss Rodriguez,' Ortega said quietly. 'Mordite is not from this galaxy or this universe. It is not of our reality.'

I had reservations about Ortega's presence on the home-team roster, but I nodded. 'It's from Outside. It's . . . congealed antilife. A chip of this stuff makes nuclear waste look like secondhand smoke. Being near it draws the life off you bit by bit. If you touch it, it kills you. Period.'

'Precisely,' said the Archive. She stepped forward to look at both Ortega and me. 'An enchantment binds the particle in place. It is also sensitive to applied will. The duelists will face each other, the mordite between them. Will it toward your opponent. He with the greatest force of will controls the mordite. The duel will end when it has devoured one of you.'

Gulp.

The Archive continued. 'Seconds will observe from first and third bases, facing their duelist's opponent. Mister Kincaid will ensure that no undue interference is perpetrated by either second. I have instructed him to do so with extreme prejudice.'

Thomas wobbled a little and eyed the Archive. 'Eh?'

The girl faced him and said, 'He'll kill you if you interfere.'

'Oh,' Thomas said cheerfully. 'Gotcha, punkin.'

Ortega glared at Thomas and made a disgusted sound. Thomas found something else to look at and backed a prudent step away.

'I will monitor both duelists to ensure that no energies are employed on their behalf. I, too, will resolve any infractions with extreme prejudice. Do you understand?'

Ortega nodded. I said, 'Yeah.'

'Are there any questions, gentlemen?' the Archive asked.

I shook my head. Ortega did too.

'Each of you may make a brief statement,' said the Archive.

Ortega drew a band of black and silver beads from his pocket. Without making an effort, I could feel the defensive energies bound up within them. He regarded me with casual mistrust as he bound the bracelet to his left side and said, 'This can end in only one way.'

In answer, I fished one of the antivenom potions from my pocket, popped the top, and slugged it down. I burped and said, 'Excuse me.'

'You've really got class, Dresden,' Susan said.

'Class oozes out my every orifice,' I agreed. I passed her my staff and rod. 'Hold these for me.'

'Seconds, please retire to your positions,' said the Archive.

Susan put her hand on my arm, fingers clenching tight for a second. I reached up and touched her hand. She let go and backed away to third base.

Thomas offered to high-five Ortega. Ortega glared. Thomas smiled a Colgate smile and swaggered over to first base. He drew a silver flask of something from his hip pocket on the way, and took a sip.

The Archive looked back and forth between me and Ortega. She was standing on the pitcher's mound, next to the floating glob of chilling energy, so she was a shade taller than Ortega and a shade shorter than me. Her face was solemn, even grim. It didn't sit well on a child who should have been getting up for school in the morning.

'Are you both resolved to this duel?'

'I am,' Ortega said.

'Uh-huh.' I nodded.

The Archive nodded. 'Gentlemen. Present your right hands, please.'

Ortega lifted his right arm, palm faced toward me. I mirrored him. The Archive gestured, and the mordite sphere floated up until it hovered precisely halfway between Ortega and me. Tension gathered against my palm, an invisible and silent pressure. It felt vaguely like holding my hand against a recirculating outlet in a swimming pool – it was a tenuous thing, that felt like it might easily slide to one side.

If it did, I'd get to see the mordite up close and personal. My heart skittered over a couple of beats, and I took a deep breath, trying to focus and ready myself. If I was Ortega, I'd want to open up with everything I had in the first heartbeat of the contest and end it almost before it began. I took a couple of deep breaths and narrowed my focus, my thoughts, until the pressure against my hand and the deadly darkness a few feet away from it were all that existed.

'Begin,' said the Archive. She backed quickly toward home plate.

Ortega let out a shout, a battle cry, his body dipping slightly, hips twisting, shoving his hand forward like a man trying to close a vault door with one arm. His will flooded toward me, wild and strong, and the pressure of it drove me back onto my heels. The mordite sphere zipped across three of the four feet between it and me.

Ortega's will was strong. Really, really strong. I tried to divert it, to overcome it and stop the sphere. For a panicked second I had nothing. The sphere kept drifting closer to me. A foot. Ten inches. Six inches. Small tendrils of inky darkness drifted out from the cloud around the mordite, reaching out blindly toward my fingers.

I gritted my teeth, hardened my will, and stopped the thing five inches from my hand. I tried to mount up some momentum of my own, but Ortega held strong against me.

'Don't draw this out, boy,' Ortega said through clenched teeth. 'Your death will save lives. Even if you kill me, my vassals at Casaverde are sworn to hunt you down. You and everyone you know and love.'

The sphere came a bit closer. 'You said you wouldn't harm them if I agreed to the duel,' I growled.

'I lied,' Ortega said. 'I came here to kill you and end this war. Anything else is immaterial.'

'You bastard.'

'Stop fighting it, Dresden. Make it painless for yourself. If you kill me, they will be executed. By surrendering, you preserve them. Your Miss Rodriguez. The policewoman. The investigator you apprenticed under. The owner of that bar. The Knight and his family. The old man in the Ozarks. The wolf-children at the university. All of them.'

I snarled, 'Buddy, you just said the wrong thing.'

I let the anger Ortega's words had ignited flood down through my arm. A cloud of scarlet sparks erupted against the mordite sphere, and it started creeping the other way.

Ortega's face became strained, his breathing heavier. He didn't waste any effort on words now. His eyes darkened until they were entirely black and inhuman. There were ripples, here and there, under the surface of his skin – the flesh mask that contained the vaguely batlike monster those of the Red Court really were. The monstrous Ortega, the true Ortega, stirred underneath the false human shell. And he was afraid.

The sphere crept closer. Ortega renewed his efforts with another war cry. But the sphere made it to the midway point, and got closer to him.

'Fool,' Ortega said in a gasp.

'Murderer,' I said, and shoved the sphere another foot closer to him.

His jaw clenched harder, the muscles in his face bulging. 'You'll destroy us all.'

'Starting with you.' The sphere darted a little nearer.

'You are a selfish, self-righteous madman.'

'You murder and enslave children,' I said. I shoved the mordite sphere to within a foot of him. 'You threaten the people I love.' I shoved it closer still. 'How does it feel, Ortega. Being too weak to protect yourself. How does it feel to know you are about to die?'

In answer, a slow smile crept over his face. His shoulders moved a little, and I saw that one of his arms hung limply at his side, like an empty sleeve. A small bulge appeared just to one side of his stomach, like a gun being held in an overcoat pocket.

I stared at it in shock. He'd pulled his real arm out of the flesh mask. He was holding a gun on me.

'How does it feel?' Ortega asked, voice very quiet. 'Why don't you tell me?'

30

'You can't,' I said. I shot a glance toward home plate, but the Archive apparently hadn't noticed anything amiss. My will wavered, and the mordite sphere bobbed back and forth. 'They'll hear the shot. They'll kill you.'

'Quite possibly,' he agreed. 'As I said, I am prepared to accept that.'

His words chilled me, and the mordite sphere darted at my head. I caught it a couple of feet from me and held it, but just barely.

'I told you, Dresden. There's only one way this can end. I would have preferred an honorable demise for you, but any death will do.'

I stared at the hidden gun.

A dot of bright scarlet light appeared on Ortega's chest, and tracked slowly up.

My expression must have changed, because Ortega glanced down too. The bright pinpoint of the laser sight settled over his heart and became still.

Ortega's eyes widened and his expression twisted into fury.

A lot of things happened at once.

There was a hissing sound, a thump, and a big section of Ortega's chest dented in. Scarlet sprayed out behind him. An instant later, a booming sound much deeper than the crack of a rifle echoed around the stadium.

Ortega let out a screech that went off the high end of the scale. Fire erupted from the hidden gun, burning through Ortega's flesh mask and shirt to reveal the muzzle of a small-caliber revolver clenched in an inhuman black hand. The bullet Ortega had taken had half twisted him, and he missed. I thought hanging around to let him try again was a bad idea, so I threw myself to one side and gave the mordite sphere another shove.

Ortega dodged the mordite, and even wounded, he was fast. A bright red dot appeared on his thigh for half a second, and with another *hiss-thump-boom*, the unseen gunman hit him again. I heard the bones of Ortega's leg break.

Susan threw my staff and rod to me and leapt for Ortega, grabbing his free arm and twisting as if to throw him. Instead, the vampire writhed weirdly, and she wound up tearing the flesh mask from him, peeling it away like a banana skin to reveal the slime-slick, flabby-bodied creature beneath it – the true Ortega. He still held the gun though, and he turned to shoot at me again.

I screamed, '*Ventas servitas!*' at the top of my lungs, throwing my will at dirt of the pitcher's mound. It whirled up into a miniature cyclone of fine brown soil, forcing the vampire to turn its head and shield its eyes. The second shot went wild as well, and I scrambled to get my blasting rod.

The flying dirt slowed her down, but Susan still went for Ortega's gun hand. It was a mistake. Even with only one leg to support him, Ortega screeched again, twisted, and flung Susan from the pitcher's mound into the third row of seats behind first base. She hit with bone-breaking force and dropped out of sight.

Sudden screeches filled the air, and I looked up to see as many as a dozen of the Red Court, revealed in their true forms, coming into the stadium. Some climbed over the walls, some jumped in from the upper levels, and some came bursting out of private boxes in showers of exploding glass.

I spun toward Ortega, lifting my blasting rod, rammed my will through it, and shouted, '*Fuego!*' A jet of flame as thick as my arm roared at him, but one of the incoming vampires hit him at the shoulder, dragging him out of the line of fire. The newcomer was set alight though, greasy skin going up like a bonfire, and it screamed hideously as it burned.

I sensed movement behind me, and turned to find Kincaid dashing across the ground. He scooped up the Archive and raced for one of the dugouts. One of the Red Court vamps got in his way. Kincaid's arm blurred, a semiautomatic appearing in it, and without missing a step he put two shots neatly between the vampire's eyes. The vampire started to fall, and as he went by it, Kincaid pumped another half dozen shots into its belly, which erupted in a messy shower of scarlet, and left the vampire screaming and thrashing weakly on the ground.

'Harry, look out!' Thomas screamed.

I didn't look out. I figured on the worst and leapt forward. I heard a vampire hiss as it missed me, and it came rushing up behind me. I turned and unleashed another gout of fire from my blasting rod, but missed. The vampire closed on me, spraying venomous saliva into my face.

I'd been hit with vampire venom before, and the stuff worked fast, particularly in large amounts. But I'd taken the potion to block it, and all this did was make me itch. I used the time while the vampire sprayed me to prepare another blast, and unleashed the strike with the rod pressed against the vamp's flabby body. It scorched a wound in the vampire's belly the size of my fist and blew a two-foot hole in the creature's back. The vampire went into weak spasms, and I kicked it off me, rising.

Seven or eight vampires were within fifty feet of me, and coming fast. Thomas sprinted toward me, a knife gleaming in his hand, and hit one of the vamps from behind. He cut open the vampire's belly with a single slice, and the creature collapsed to the ground. 'Harry, get out!'

'No!' I shouted. 'Get Susan out of here!'

Thomas gritted his teeth, but changed course. He leapt up onto the first-base dugout and hopped neatly over the rail into the stands.

No help there, and there wasn't time to look for options. I crouched and concentrated, chanting, '*Defendre*, *defendre*,' in a steady litany. It was difficult to do without my shield bracelet to focus it, but I brought up all the defensive energy I could manage in a dome around me.

The vampires hit it, slamming against it in mindless, shrieking rage. Any one of them could have flipped my car over lengthwise with only a little effort. Their blows against the shield could have crushed concrete. Within seconds, I knew I was not going to be able to hold the defense in place for long.

Once it went down, they were going to literally tear me limb from limb. I gave the shield my all, and felt them slowly breaking it down.

Then there was a roar, and a flash of brilliant light. A jet of fire streaked over me and took one of the vampires full-on in the head. It burst into flame, screaming and waving its too-thin arms, and went down onto the field, thrashing like a half-crushed bug. My shield collapsed, overloaded, and the bracelet began burning my wrist. I crouched lower.

Another jet of fire went by, incinerating the head of another vampire. All of them stopped, crouching, shrieking in confusion.

Kincaid stood outside the dugout and dropped a smoking shotgun to the ground. He reached into a golf bag next to him, smooth and professional, and drew out another double-barreled shotgun. One of the vampires leapt at him, but Kincaid was too fast. He pulled the trigger, and the shotgun roared. A jet of flame streaked out and went through the vampire, taking this one in the neck, and continuing to the rightfield fence, where it blew a hole the size of my face in the wall. There was a sound behind him, and Kincaid spun to shoot the other barrel at a vampire bounding down through the stands above the third-base dugout. He put the shot right down the vampire's throat, literally, and the creature went up in flames. Kincaid discarded that shotgun as well, and reached for the stock of another in his golf bag.

The other vampires leapt at Kincaid when he turned his back. They got to deal with the Archive instead.

The child stepped out from behind the golf bag, the tenebrous mordite sphere floating between her hands. She released the sphere and made a single gesture.

The little cloud of darkness blurred toward the vampires an streaked into each in turn at the pace of a busy workman hammer, *bang-bang-bang*. When the mordite sphere struck then there was a flash of cold purple light, a swell of darkness, an then the sphere passed on through. It left ash and black bone raining down behind it. I could barely follow the mordite sphere path, it moved so fast. One second the vampires were all there and then they were simply gone. Black bones and grey ash littere the ground around me.

Silence fell, and the only thing I could hear was my ow ragged breathing and the roaring of my own pulse in my ears I looked around wildly, but I didn't see Ortega anywhere. Th two vampires who had been gutted writhed feebly on the groun Kincaid drew the last shotgun from the golf bag, and with tw more flaming blasts executed them both.

The mordite sphere glided gently back to rest between th Archive's tiny hands, and she stood regarding me for a long an silent moment. There was nothing in her expression. Nothin in her eyes. Nothing. I felt the beginnings of a soulgaze an pulled my face away, fast.

'Who broke the sanctity of the duel first, Kincaid?' asked th Archive.

'Couldn't tell,' Kincaid answered. He wasn't so much a breathing hard. 'But Dresden was winning.'

The Archive stood there a moment more, and then sai 'Thank you for letting me pet your kitty, Mister Dresden. An thank you for my name.'

That sounded frighteningly like a good-bye, but it was onl polite to answer, 'You're welcome, Ivy.'

The Archive nodded and said, 'Kincaid. The box, please.'

I looked up to watch Kincaid set the wooden box down on the ground. The Archive sent the mordite sphere gliding slowly down into it, and then closed the lid on the box. 'These proceedings are concluded.'

I looked around at the bones, dust, and smoldering vampire corpses. 'You think?'

The Archive regarded me with neutral eyes and said, 'Let's go. It's after my bedtime.'

'I'm hungry,' Kincaid said, shouldering his golf bag. 'We'll hit a drive-through. You can have the cookies.'

'Cookies aren't good for me,' the Archive said, but she smiled.

Kincaid said, 'Dresden, hand me that, will you?'

I looked numbly at the ground where he pointed. One of the shotguns was there. Its barrels were still smoking hot. I picked it up gingerly by the stock and passed it to Kincaid, who wrapped it with the other gun he'd used in some kind of silver-lined blanket. 'What the hell are those things?' I asked.

'Incendiary rounds,' he said. He passed my dropped staff over to me. 'Work real well on the Reds, but they're so hot they warp gun barrels. If you get unlucky, the second shot can blow back into your face, so you have to use throwaway guns.'

I nodded thanks and took my staff. 'Where can I get some?'

Kincaid grinned. 'I know a guy. I'll have him call you. See you, Dresden.'

Kincaid and the Archive started out of the stadium. A thought finally made its way through the combat adrenaline and I broke into a sprint toward the first-base dugout. Thomas had simply hopped up onto it. I managed to flop and clamber my way up, then into the stands.

Thomas was already there, on the ground with Susan. He'd

taken off her jacket and used it to elevate her feet slightly. It looked as if he'd tilted her head back a little to clear the airway. He looked up and said, 'She's unconscious, but she's alive.'

I crouched down too, and touched her throat, just to be certain. 'How bad is she hurt?'

He shook his head. 'No real way to tell.'

'We have to get her to a hospital, then,' I said, rising.

Thomas caught my arm. 'You don't want her waking up, injured and dazed, in a place packed to the roof with weakened prey.'

'Then what the hell do we do?'

'Look, if she's not dead, odds are she'll recover.' Thomas held up his hand and fished out a ballpoint pen from his pocket. He twisted it and said, 'Clear.' Then he twisted it again and put it back.

A moment later, Martin came rapidly down the aisle. He somehow made even that look boring, as if he were simply a man wanting to take his seat again before the opening pitch. It was especially impressive since he carried a huge rifle, a military sniper weapon with a telescopic sight and a laser attachment. He set the rifle aside and went over Susan for a moment, feeling here and there, before he said, 'She'll be sore.'

'You?' I asked. 'You were the gunman?'

'Obviously,' Martin said. 'Why do you think we were in Chicago to begin with?'

'Susan said she was getting her things.'

He looked up at me skeptically. 'You believed that? I would have thought you knew Susan well enough to know that material things don't hold a lot of interest for her.'

'I knew that,' I said. 'But she said . . .' I trailed off and shook my head.

Martin looked up and said, 'We knew Ortega was coming to kill you. We knew that if he succeeded, he might be able to bring the war to a peaceful conclusion, only to begin it again twenty years from now, from a much stronger position. I was sent to make sure Ortega did not kill you, and to eliminate him if I could.'

'Did you?'

Martin shook his head. 'He had planned for the contingency. Two of his vassals got to him during the fight. They pulled him out. I don't know how badly he was hurt, but it's likely he'll make it back to Casaverde.'

'You want the war to keep going. You're hoping the White Council will destroy the Red Court for you.'

Martin nodded.

'How did you find out about the duel?'

Martin didn't answer.

I narrowed my eyes and looked at Thomas.

Thomas put on an innocent expression. 'Don't look at me. I'm a drunken, chemical-besotted playboy who does nothing but cavort, sleep, and feed. And even if I had the mind to take a bit of vengeance on the Red Court, I wouldn't have the backbone to actually stand up to anyone.' He flashed me a radiant smile. 'I'm totally harmless.'

'I see,' I said. I took a deep breath, and regarded Susan's face quietly for a moment. Then I bent down, got into her pockets, and got the keys to the rental car. 'Are you leaving now, Martin?'

'Yes. I don't think our presence will be noticed here, but there's no sense in taking chances.'

'Take care of her for me,' I said.

Martin looked up at me for a second and then said, in a quiet voice, 'Everything in my power. You have my word.'

I nodded. 'Thank you.' I stood up and started for the exits, drawing the coat to cover my gun.

'Where are you going?' Thomas called.

'The airport,' I answered. 'I've got to meet some people about an old man and a bedsheet.'

31

I parked at a rental lot outside O'Hare about five minutes after seven. I got out of the car with my staff and rod in hand. There was only one old light burning on the lot, but the moon had risen huge and bright, and I had no trouble seeing Michael coming. His white truck came crunching to a halt on the gravel in front of me. I walked around to the passenger door. Sanya swung it open for me, then slid over. He was wearing blue denim and a big black cowboy hat.

'Harry,' Michael said as I got in. 'I was getting worried. You won?'

'Not exactly.'

'You lost?'

'Not exactly. I had Ortega on the ropes and he cheated. Both of us cleared the benches. I came out of it in one piece. He came out in a couple of pieces but he got away.'

'Is Susan all right?'

'She got thrown about twenty-five yards through the air and hit steel and concrete. She'll be fine.' Something tickled my nose, and I sniffed. The sharp odor of metal filled the cab of the truck. 'Michael, are you wearing the armor?'

'I am wearing the armor,' Michael said. 'And the cloak.'

'Hello, Michael. We're going to an airport. The kind with metal detectors.'

'It's all right, Harry. Things will work out.'

'Will it sound like alarms going off when they do?' I glanced at the younger Knight and said, 'Sanya isn't wearing armor.'

Sanya half turned toward me and pulled his denim jacket open, revealing a Kevlar vest beneath it. 'I am,' he said soberly. 'Fifteen layers with ceramic plating over critical areas.'

'Well, at least you don't look like a Renaissance festival,' I said. 'This thing might actually protect you, besides making a slightly less medieval fashion statement. Is this the new stuff or the old stuff?'

'New,' Sanya said. 'Will stop civilian munitions, even some military rounds.'

'But not knives or claws,' Michael murmured. 'Or arrows.'

Sanya buttoned his coat back up, frowning. 'Yours will not stop bullets.'

Michael said, 'My faith protects me.'

I exchanged a skeptical look with Sanya and said, 'Okeydokey, Michael. Do we have any idea where the bad guys are?'

'The airport,' Michael said.

I sat there silently for a second before I said, 'Needle, haystack. Where, at the airport?'

Michael shrugged, smiling, and opened his mouth to speak.

I held up my hand. 'We must have faith,' I said, doing my best to imitate Michael's voice. 'How did I guess. Did you bring *Fidelacchius*?'

'In the tool locker,' Michael said.

I nodded. 'Shiro's going to need it back.'

Michael was quiet for a moment before he said, 'Yes, of course.'

'We're going to save him.'

'I pray it is so, Harry.'

'We will,' I said. I stared out the window as Michael pulled into the airport proper. 'It's not too late.'

O'Hare is huge. We drove around in crowded parking lots and auto loading zones for nearly half an hour before Michael abruptly slowed the truck down outside the international concourse, his spine and neck straightening as if he'd heard a warning klaxon.

Sanya glanced aside at Michael and said, 'What is it?'

'Do you feel that?' Michael asked him.

'Feel what?'

'Close your eyes,' Michael said. 'Try to still your thoughts.'

I muttered, 'I sense a great disturbance in the Force.'

'You do?' Michael asked, blinking at me.

I sighed and rubbed at the bridge of my nose. Sanya closed his eyes, and a second later his expression twisted in distaste. 'Rot,' the Russian reported. 'Sour milk. Mildew. The air smells greasy.'

'There's a Pizza Hut kiosk about fifty feet away,' I pointed out, looking through the windows of the concourse. 'But maybe it's just a coincidence.'

'No,' Michael said. 'It's Nicodemus. He leaves a kind of stain everywhere he goes. Arrogance. Ambition. Disregard.'

'I only smell rotten things,' Sanya said.

'You're sensing him too,' Michael said. 'Your mind is interpreting it differently. He's here.' He started pulling forward, but a cab zipped in front of him and stopped. The cabby got out and began unloading an elderly couple's bags.

I muttered to myself and sniffed. I even reached out with my magical senses, trying to detect what Michael had. I felt nothing but the usual – patternless white noise of thousands of lives moving around us.

I opened my eyes, and found myself staring at the back of Detective Rudolph's head. He had on the usual expensive suit, and stood with a spare, well-coiffed man I recognized from the district attorney's office.

I froze for a second. Then I snatched Sanya's black Stetson and pulled it down over my head. I tugged the brim down over my eyes and slouched down as low as I could.

'What is it?' Michael asked.

'Police,' I said. I took a more careful look around. I spotted seven uniformed officers and maybe ten other men who wore suits and casual clothes but walked and stood like cops. 'I passed word to them that the Shroud might be on the way out of Chicago through here.'

'Then why are you hiding?'

'A witness reported me leaving the scene of a murder. If someone identifies me, I'm going to spend the next day or so getting questioned, and that won't help Shiro.'

Michael's brow knitted in concern. 'True. Do the police know of the Denarians?'

'Probably not. SI isn't on the case. Probably they've been told they're some kind of terrorists and to be considered dangerous.'

The cabby in front of us finally finished up, and Michael pulled away from the loading zone and toward the parking lot. 'That isn't good enough. We can't have them there.'

'As long as the police are around, it will restrict the Denarians' movements. Make them keep their heads down and play nice.'

Michael shook his head. 'Most supernatural creatures will hesitate before killing a mortal police officer. But Nicodemus won't. He has nothing but contempt for mortal authorities. If we confront him, he *will* kill anyone who attempts to stop him, as well as taking hostages to use against us.'

Sanya nodded. 'Not to mention that if this plague curse is as formidable as you say, it would be dangerous to those nearby.'

'It's worse than that,' I said.

Michael rolled the steering wheel toward a parking space. 'How so?'

'Forthill told me that the Denarians get a power boost from hurting people, right? Causing mayhem and destruction?'

'Yes,' Michael said.

'The curse is only going to last a few days, but while it does it's going to make the Black Death look like chicken pox. That's why he's here. It's one of the busiest international terminals on the planet.'

'Mother of God,' Michael swore.

Sanya whistled. 'Flights from here go directly to every major nation in the world. If the Denarians' plague is easily communicable . . .'

'I think I pretty well summed that up with the Black Death comment, Sanya.'

The Russian shrugged. 'Sorry. What do we do?'

'We call in a bomb threat. Clear out the people and shut down the planes.'

'We need to be inside immediately,' Sanya said. 'How long would it take the authorities to react?'

'It would only work if I knew who to call to get an immediate reaction.'

'Do you?' Sanya asked.

I held out my hand out to Michael. He slapped his cell phone into it. 'No,' I said. 'But I know someone who does.'

I called Murphy, trying to remain calm and hoping that the phone didn't explode against my head. When I got the connection, it was cloudy with bursts of static, but I managed to tell her what was going on.

'You're insane, Dresden,' Murphy said. 'Do you know how incredibly irresponsible – and illegal – it is to falsify a bomb threat?'

'Yeah. Less irresponsible than letting cops and civilians get in these people's way.'

Murphy was quiet for a second, and then asked, 'How dangerous are they?'

'Worse than the loup-garou,' I said.

'I'll make the call.'

'Did you get in touch with him?' I asked.

'I think so, yes. Do you need any more muscle?'

'Got plenty,' I said. 'What I'm short on is time. Please hurry.'

'Be careful, Harry.'

I hung up the phone and got out of the truck. Michael and Sanya came with me. 'Murphy's going to report a bomb threat. The cops will clear everyone out of the building. That will clear out the area for us.'

'Leaving the Denarians without anyone to infect, or take hostage,' Sanya said.

'That's the idea. After that, they'll call in the bomb squad and backup. We'll have twenty minutes, tops, to take advantage of the confusion.'

Michael unlocked the tool locker in the back of the pickup, and drew out Shiro's cane. He tied a strap to it and slung it over his shoulder. While he did, Sanya buckled *Esperacchius* to his hip, then drew a freaking assault rifle out of the tool locker.

'Kalashnikov, isn't it?' I asked. 'That's an extremely Chuck Heston look for the Knights of the Cross.'

Sanya slapped a magazine into the weapon, chambered a round, and made sure the gun's safety was on. 'I consider myself a progressive.'

'Too random for my taste,' Michael said. 'Too easy to hurt the wrong person.'

'Maybe,' Sanya said. 'But the only people inside should be the Denarians, yes?'

'And Shiro,' I said.

'I will not shoot Shiro,' Sanya assured me.

Michael buckled *Amoracchius* onto his hip. 'How much longer will it take?'

The buzzing ring of a fire alarm blared from the concourse, and the police got together. A grizzled detective in a bad suit took charge and started directing suits and uniforms around. People started hurrying out of the concourse.

'Ask and ye shall receive,' I said. 'Let's circle around. Get in through one of the service entrances.'

Sanya slipped the assault rifle into an over-the-shoulder sports bag, but kept one hand on the stock. Michael nodded to me, and I took the lead. We circled around the building until we could see some of the planes. Ground crews were rushing around in confusion, and several guys with orange flashlights were waving them at flight crews, directing the wallowing jets away from the ramps to the concourse.

We had to climb a fence and drop down a ten-foot retaining wall to get behind the concourse, but in the dark and the confusion no one noticed us. I led us through a ground-crew door and through a room that was part garage and part baggage storage. Emergency lights were on and fire alarms still jangled. I passed a section of wall covered with calendar pinup girls, pictures of trucks, and a map of the concourse.

'Whoa, stop,' I said. Sanya bumped into my back. I glowered at him, and then peered at the map.

'Here,' I said, pointing at a marked door. 'We'll come out on this stairway.'

'Midway through,' Michael noted. 'Which way do we go?'

'Split up,' Sanya suggested.

Michael and I said, 'Bad idea,' at precisely the same time.

'Think,' I muttered, mostly to myself. 'If I were an arrogant psychotic demon-collaborating terrorist out to trigger an apocalypse, where would I be?'

Sanya leaned over to look at the map and said, 'The chapel.'

'The chapel,' said Michael.

'The chapel,' I echoed. 'Down this hall, up the stairs, and to the left.'

We ran down the hall and up the stairs. I pushed open the door and heard a recorded voice telling me to be calm and proceed to the nearest exit. I checked my right before I did my left, and it saved my life.

A man in nondescript business wear stood watching the door and holding a submachine gun. When he saw me, he lifted the weapon, hesitated for a fraction of a second, and started shooting.

The slight pause was enough to let me reverse my direction.

A couple of bullets went right through the steel fire door, but I stumbled back into Sanya. The big man caught me and spun, putting his back between me and the incoming bullets. I felt him jerk and heard him grunt once, and then we hit a wall and sank down.

I knew the gunman would be coming. Right then, he was probably circling out to the far wall across from the door. Once he had a clear line of fire down the stairs, he'd move up and gun us down.

I saw his shadow in the crack under the door, and I struggled to regain my feet. Sanya was doing the same thing, and the two of us managed to do little but keep each other down. The gunman came closer, his shadow moving in the little space beneath the door's edge.

Michael stepped over me and Sanya, *Amoracchius* in hand, and shouted as he lunged forward, both hands driving the weight of the sword at the closed steel door. The sword went through the door, sinking almost to the hilt.

An erratic burst of gunfire sounded. Michael drew the sword back out of the door. Blood gleamed wet and scarlet along the length of the weapon's blade. Michael put his back against the wall of the stairwell. The gun barked a couple of times more and fell silent. After a minute, blood seeped under the door in a spreading red puddle.

Sanya and I got untangled and got up. 'You're hit.'

Michael had already moved and stood behind Sanya. He ran his hands over Sanya's back, grunted, and then held up a small, bright piece of metal, presumably the round. 'It hit a strike plate. The vest caught it.'

'Progressive.' Sanya panted, wincing.

'You're lucky the bullet had to go through a steel door before it got to you,' I muttered. I readied a shield and pressed the door slowly open.

The gunman lay on the floor. Michael's thrust had taken him just under the floating ribs, and had to have hit an artery to kill him so quickly. His gun lay in his hand, and his finger was limp on the trigger.

Sanya and Michael slipped out of the stairwell. Sanya had his rifle in hand. They stood lookout while I bent down and pried open the dead gunman's mouth. He didn't have a tongue. 'One of Nicodemus's boys,' I said quietly.

'Something is wrong,' Michael said. Blood dripped from the tip of the sword to the floor. 'I don't feel him anymore.'

'If you can feel him, can he feel you? Could he know if you were getting close to him?'

Michael shrugged. 'It seems likely.'

'He's cautious,' I said, remembering how Nicodemus had reacted when Shiro came through the door. 'He doesn't take chances. He wouldn't wait around to start a fight he wasn't sure he could win. He's running.' I stood up and headed for the chapel. 'Come on.'

Just as I got to the chapel's door, it swung open and two more men came out, both of them slapping clips into submachine guns. One of them didn't look up in time to see me, so I checked him in the forehead with a double-handed thrust of my staff, getting my whole weight behind the blow. His head snapped back and he dropped. The other gunman started to bring his weapon up, but I batted the barrel aside with a sweep of my staff, then snapped the end of it hard into his nose. Before he could recover, Sanya stepped into him and slammed the butt of the Kalashnikov against his head. He fell on top of the first guy, tongueless mouth lolled open.

I stepped over them and into the chapel.

It had been a small, modest room. There were two rows of three pews each, a pulpit, a table, and subdued lighting. There were no specific religious trappings to the place. It was simply a room set aside to accommodate the spiritual needs of worldwide travelers of every belief, creed, and faith.

Any one of them would have felt profaned by what had been done to the room.

The walls had been covered in sigils, somewhat similar to those I had seen on the Denarians so far. They were painted in blood, and still wet. The pulpit had been leaned against the back wall, and the heavy table laid along it, so that it lay at an angle to the floor. On either side of the table was a chair covered in bits of bone, a few candles. On one of the chairs was a carved silver bowl, almost entirely covered in fresh blood. The room smelled sickly sweet, and whatever was in those candles made the air thick, languid, and hazy. Maybe opium. It had probably accounted for the slowed reaction of the second two gunmen. The candles shed muted light over the table's surface.

What was left of Shiro lay on it.

He was on his back, and shirtless. Torn flesh and dark, savage bruises, some of them in the clear outline of chains, lapped around from his back. His hands and feet were grotesquely swollen. They'd been broken so badly and in so many places that they looked more like sausages than human limbs. His belly and chest had been sliced up as I'd seen before, on the real Father Vincent and on Gaston LaRouche's corpse as well.

'There's so much blood,' I whispered.

I felt Michael enter the room behind me. He made a soft, choking sound.

I stepped closer to Shiro's remains, noting clinical details. His face had been left more or less untouched. There were several items scattered around him on the floor – ritual implements. Whatever they had intended him for, they'd already done it. There were sores on his skin, fever blisters, I thought, and his throat was swollen. The damage to his skin probably hid many other such marks of pestilence.

'We're too late,' Michael said quietly. 'Have they already worked the spell?'

'Yeah,' I said. I sat down on the first pew.

'Harry?' Michael said.

'There's so much blood,' I said. 'He wasn't a very big person. You wouldn't think there could be so much blood.'

'Harry, there's nothing else we can do here.'

'I knew him, and he wasn't very big. You wouldn't think there would be enough for all the painting. The ritual.'

'We should go,' Michael said.

'And do what? The plague has already started. Odds are we have it. If we carry it out, we only spread it. Nicodemus has the Shroud and he's probably out looking for a full school bus or something. He's gone. We missed.'

'Harry,' Michael said quietly. 'We must—'

Anger and frustration suddenly burned hot and bright behind my eyes. 'If you talk to me about faith I'll kill you.'

'You don't mean that,' Michael said. 'I know you too well.'

'Shut up, Michael.'

He stepped up next to me and leaned Shiro's cane against

my knee. Then, without a word, he drew back to the wall and waited.

I picked up the cane and drew the wooden handle of the old man's sword out enough to see five or six inches of clean, gleaming metal. I slapped it shut again, stepped up to Shiro, and composed him as best I could. Then I rested the sword beside him.

When he coughed and wheezed, I almost screamed.

I wouldn't have thought that anyone could survive that much abuse. But Shiro drew in a ragged breath, and blinked open one eye. The other had been put out, and his eyelid looked sunken and strange.

'Hell's bells,' I stammered. 'Michael!'

Michael and I both rushed down beside him. It took him a moment to focus his eye on us. 'Ah, good,' he rasped. 'Was getting tired waiting for you.'

'We've got to get him to a hospital,' I said.

The old man twitched his head in a negative gesture. 'Too late. Would do no good. The noose. The Barabbus curse.'

'What is he talking about?' I asked Michael.

'The noose Nicodemus wears. So long as he bears it, he apparently cannot die. We believe the noose is the one used by Judas,' Michael said quietly.

'So what's this Barabbus curse?'

'Just as the Romans put it within the power of the Jews to choose one condemned prisoner each year to be pardoned and given life, the noose allows Nicodemus to mandate a death that cannot be avoided. Barabbus was the prisoner the Jews chose, though Pilate wanted to free the Savior. The curse is named for him.'

'And Nicodemus used it on Shiro?'

Shiro twitched his head again, and a faint smile touched his mouth. 'No, boy. On you. He was angry that you escaped him despite his treachery.'

Hell's bells. The entropy curse that had nearly killed both me, and Susan with me. I stared at Shiro for a second, and then at Michael.

Michael nodded. 'We cannot stop the curse,' he said. 'But we can take the place of its subject, if we choose to do it. That's why we wanted you to stay away, Harry. We were afraid Nicodemus would target you.'

I stared at him and then at Shiro. My vision blurred. 'It should be me lying there,' I said. 'Dammit.'

'No,' Shiro said. 'There is much you do not yet understand.' He coughed, and pain flashed over his face. 'You will. You will.' He twitched the arm nearest the sword. 'Take it. Take it, boy.'

'No,' I said. 'I'm not like you. Like any of you. I never will be.'

'Remember. God sees hearts, boy. And now I see yours. Take it. Hold it in trust until you find the one it belongs to.'

I reached out and picked up the cane. 'How do I know who to give it to?'

'You will know,' Shiro said, his voice becoming thinner. 'Trust your heart.'

Sanya entered the room and padded over to us. 'The police heard the gunfire. There's an assault team getting ready to—' He froze, staring at Shiro.

'Sanya,' Shiro said. 'This is our parting, friend. I am proud of you.'

Sanya swallowed and knelt down by the old man. He kissed Shiro's forehead. Blood stained his lips when he straightened.

'Michael,' Shiro said. 'The fight is yours now. Be wise.'

Michael laid his hand on Shiro's bald head and nodded. The big man was crying, though his face was set in a quiet smile.

'Harry,' Shiro whispered. 'Nicodemus is afraid of you. Afraid that you saw something. I don't know what.'

'He should be afraid,' I said.

'No,' the old man said. 'Don't let him unmake you. You must find him. Take the Shroud from him. So long as he touches it, the plague grows. If he loses it, it ends.'

'We don't know where he is,' I said.

'Train,' Shiro whispered. 'His backup plan. A train to St Louis.'

'How do you know?' Michael asked.

'Told his daughter. They thought I was gone.' Shiro focused on me and said, 'Stop them.'

My throat clenched. I nodded. I managed to half growl, 'Thank you.'

'You will understand,' Shiro said. 'Soon.'

Then he sighed, like a man who has just laid down a heavy burden. His eye closed.

Shiro died. There was nothing pretty about it. There was no dignity to it. He'd been brutalized and savagely murdered – and he'd allowed it to happen to him in my place.

But when he died, there was a small, contented smile on his face. Maybe the smile of someone who had run his course without wavering from it. Someone who had served something greater than himself. Who had given up his life willingly, if not gladly.

Sanya said, his voice strained, 'We cannot remain here.'

I stood up and slung the cane on its strap over my shoulder. I felt cold, and shivered. I put a hand to my forehead, and found it clammy and damp. The plague.

'Yeah,' I said, and strode out of the room and back toward the blood-spattered stairs. 'Clock's running.'

Michael and Sanya kept pace. 'Where are we going?'

'The airfield,' I said. 'He's smart. He'll figure it out. He'll be there.'

'Who?' Michael asked.

I didn't answer. I led them back down through the garage area and out onto the airfield tarmac. We hurried down along the concourse, and then out onto the open acres of asphalt that led from the concourses to the landing fields. Once we'd gotten out there, I took off my pentacle amulet and held it aloft, focusing on it in order to cause it to begin to shed a distinctive blue light.

'What are you doing?' Sanya asked.

'Signaling,' I said.

'Who?'

'Our ride.'

It took maybe forty-five seconds before the sound of a helicopter's blades whirled closer to us. The aircraft, a blue-and-white-painted commercial job, zipped down to hover over us before dropping down for a precise if hurried landing.

'Come on,' I said, and headed for the craft. The side door opened, and I climbed in with Michael and Sanya close behind me.

Gentleman Johnny Marcone, dressed in dark fatigues, nodded to me and to the two Knights. 'Good evening, gentlemen,' he said. 'Just tell me where to take you.'

'Southwest,' I said, yelling over the noise of the chopper. 'They're going to be on a commercial train heading for St Louis.'

Michael stared at Marcone in shock. 'This is the man who ordered the Shroud stolen to begin with,' he said. 'You don't think he's going to work with us?'

'Sure he will,' I said. 'If Nicodemus gets away with the Shroud and pulls off this big curse, Marcone's spent all that money for nothing.'

'Not to mention that the plague would be bad for business,' Marcone added. 'I think we can agree to help one another against this Nicodemus. We can discuss the disposition of the Shroud afterward.' He turned and thumped the pilot's shoulder a couple of times, and yelled directions. The pilot glanced back at us, and I saw Gard's profile against the flight instruments. Hendricks leaned in from the passenger seat, listening to Marcone, and nodded himself.

'Very well then,' Marcone called, leaning back into the cabin. He took a large-caliber hunting rifle down from a rack and settled into a seat, buckling up. 'Best strap in, gentlemen. Let's go recover the holy Shroud.'

I settled in and told Michael, 'Now, if only we had a bit of Wagner to send us on our way.'

I saw Gard's reflection in the chopper's front windows look up at my words. Then she flicked a couple of switches, and 'Ride of the Valkyries' started thrumming through the helicopter's cabin.

'Yee-haw,' I said as my elbows and knees started a nagging ache. 'As long as we're going, we might as well go out in style.'

32

After a few minutes, the ride got bumpy. The chopper started jouncing at random, lurching several feet in any given direction. If I hadn't been strapped in, I probably would have slammed my head against the walls or ceiling.

Marcone put on a headset and spoke into a microphone. He listened to the answer and then shouted to the rest of us, 'The ride may be a bit bumpier. The stabilizers are run by the onboard computer, which has failed.' He gave me a direct look. 'I can only speculate as to why.'

I looked around, picked up another headset, put it on, and said, 'Blow me.'

'Excuse me?' came Gard's somewhat outraged voice over the intercom.

'Not you, blondie. I was talking to Marcone.'

Marcone folded his arms in his seat, half smiling. 'It's all right, Miss Gard. Compassion dictates that we must make allowances. Mister Dresden is a diplomatically challenged individual. He should be in a shelter for the tactless.'

'I'll tell you what you can do with your shelter,' I said. 'Marcone, I need to speak to you.'

Marcone frowned at me, and then nodded. 'How much time before we reach the southbound tracks?'

'We're over the first one now,' Gard replied. 'Three minutes to catch the train.'

'Inform me when we reach it. Mister Hendricks, please switch the cabin headphones to channel two.'

Hendricks didn't say anything, and it made me wonder why he had bothered with a headset.

'There,' came Marcone's voice after a moment. 'We're speaking privately.'

'Why didn't you tell me?' I said.

'Tell you that I hadn't sent Mister Franklin for you?'

'Yeah.'

'Would you have believed me?'

'No.'

'Would you have thought I was playing some kind of game with you?'

'Yes.'

'Then why waste the time and make you more suspicious? Generally speaking, you are quite perceptive – given enough time. And I know you well enough to know that I do not wish to have you as my enemy.'

I glowered at him.

He arched an eyebrow, meeting my gaze without fear or hostility.

'Why do you want the Shroud?'

'That's none of your business.'

I scowled. 'Actually it is. Literally. Why do you want it?'

'Why do you?'

'Because the Denarians are going to kill a lot of people with it.'

Marcone shrugged. 'That's reason enough for me as well.'

'Sure it is.'

'It's simple business, Mister Dresden. I can't conduct business with a mound of corpses.'

'Why don't I believe you?'

Marcone's teeth flashed. 'Because given enough time, you are a perceptive individual.'

There was a beep in the headphones, and Gard said, 'Fifteen seconds, sir.'

'Thank you,' Marcone replied. 'Dresden, why should these people take the Shroud and this plague of theirs to St Louis?'

'It's another international airport,' I said. 'It's the central hub for TWA. And hell, as long as they're there, they could probably go for a swim in the Mississippi.'

'Why not simply stay in Chicago?'

I nodded toward Michael and Sanya. 'Them. Plus I figure they know that Murphy and SI would give them a hard time. Even the regular cops were out in force looking for them.'

He looked speculatively at Michael and Sanya. 'I assume you have a means to locate the Shroud if that is the correct train?'

'Yeah,' I said. 'And here's the deal. You drop us off, and we get the Shroud.'

'I'm going with you,' Marcone said.

'No, you aren't.'

'I can always order Miss Gard to return to O'Hare.'

'Where we'll all die of the plague, since we didn't stop the Denarians.'

'That may be. Either way, I'm going with you.'

I scowled at him, then shook my head and leaned back against the seat, shivering. 'You suck. You suck diseased moose wang, Marcone.'

Marcone smiled with just his mouth. 'How colorful.' He looked out the window and said, 'My people tell me there are only three trains leaving Chicago for St Louis this evening. Two freight trains and a passenger train.'

'They won't be on the passenger train,' I said. 'They'd have to ditch weapons and goons, and they won't.'

'Even odds that this is the one, then,' Marcone said.

The chopper descended until the trees near the tracks were swaying in the downblast. That's the nice part about the Midwest. Go twenty miles from a town hall and there's nothing but lightly settled farm country. I looked out the window and saw a long train rumbling along the tracks.

Michael sat bolt upright and nodded to me.

'This is it,' I said to Marcone. 'Now what?'

'I bought this helicopter as Coast Guard surplus. It's fitted with a rescue winch. We climb down it onto the train.'

'You're joking, right?'

'Nothing worth doing is ever easy, Dresden.' Marcone took off the headphones and shouted to Sanya and Michael. Sanya's reaction was about like mine, but Michael only nodded and got unstrapped. Marcone opened a locker and drew out several nylon harnesses. He strapped one on himself and passed out another to each of us. Then he hauled the side door of the helicopter open. Wind filled the cabin. Marcone opened a cabinet, and started drawing a length of cable from it. I looked and saw the winch inside. Marcone looped the cable through a ring outside the door then said, 'Who first?'

Michael stepped forward. 'Me.'

Marcone nodded and clipped the cable onto the harness. A minute later, Michael hopped out of the helicopter. Marcone flicked a switch near the electric winch, and cable began playing out. Marcone watched intently and then nodded. 'He's down.'

The winch reeled back in, and Sanya stepped up to the door. It took a couple of minutes, and it felt like the chopper was doing too much lurching around, but Marcone eventually nodded. 'Dresden.'

My mouth felt dry as Marcone checked my harness and clipped the cable to it. Then he shouted, 'Go!'

I didn't want to go but I sure as hell wasn't going to chicken out in front of Marcone. I clutched my staff and rod to me, made sure Shiro's cane was strapped to my back, took a deep breath, and jumped. I swung around a little on the cable, and then felt myself going down.

The downdraft from the chopper all but blinded me, but when I did look around I could see the train beneath me. We were being lowered onto a car just forward of the end of the train, a large metal container with a flat lid. The helicopter had a searchlight pointed at the train, and I could see Michael and Sanya crouching and looking up at me.

I swayed and dangled like a kid's first yo-yo. My legs got clipped by an outgrown tree branch that hit me hard enough to leave bruises. When I got close, Michael and Sanya grabbed me and brought me down in one piece.

Marcone came down, his rifle hanging on his shoulder. I

figured Hendricks was operating the winch. The Knights pulled Marcone safely in, and he detached the cable. It swung away and the chopper arched up and away, turning its searchlight out. It took a moment for my eyes to adjust to the brilliant moon, and I stayed crouched so that I could keep my balance.

'Harry,' Michael called. 'Where now?'

'Head for the engine and look for a boxcar,' I told him. 'Something it would be easy for them to hop into.'

Michael nodded. 'Sanya, rear guard.'

The big Russian held his rifle like trained military and fell back to the rear of our group, watching behind us. Michael took the lead, one hand on his sword, and moved forward with a predatory grace and purpose.

I glowered at Marcone and said, 'I'm not going anywhere with you behind me.'

Marcone smiled again, and took his gun off his shoulder. He looked like trained military, too. He fell into line behind Michael.

I pulled my old duster back until it fell behind the handle of my pistol, leaving it clear for a draw. It probably didn't look military. It probably looked more like a spaghetti Western. I moved in behind Marcone, staff in my left hand, rod in my right.

We all moved forward over the rumbling freight cars, just like every Western movie you've ever seen. If I hadn't been feverish and nauseous, it might have been fun.

Michael abruptly crouched and held a closed fist beside his ear. Marcone stopped immediately, crouching, the rifle at his shoulder. Closed fist means stop, check. I crouched too.

Michael turned around to face us, poked a couple of fingers

at his eyes, held three fingers up, and pointed at the car ahead of us. I took it to mean that he could see three bad guys up there. Michael beckoned Sanya, and the Russian slipped silently forward. Michael pointed at me and then at the back of the train. I nodded to him, and kept an eye out behind us.

I checked over my shoulder, and saw Michael and Sanya both swing down between the cars and out of sight.

When I faced the rear of the train again, I saw a nightmare running toward me over the cars.

Whatever creation process this thing had undergone, it hadn't been a kind one. Four-legged and lanky, it looked vaguely like a cat. But it didn't have fur. Its skin was leathery, wrinkled and mottled. Its head was somewhere between that of a jaguar and a wild boar. It had both tusks and fangs in its gaping, drooling mouth, and it moved with graceless speed.

I let out a strangled cry, lifting my blasting rod. I pushed power through it, yelled the word, and loosed a flashing bolt of fire at it. The bolt hit the thing in the face just as it gathered itself to leap at me. It let out an unnerving, wailing cry, then convulsed in pain as it jumped and sailed off the side of the car.

The fire blinded me for a moment, leaving a bright green dot over my vision. I heard the next one coming, but I couldn't see it. I dropped down to my stomach and yelled, 'Marcone!'

The rifle cracked three times in deliberately spaced reports. I heard the thing squeal, and then saw it as my eyes started to adjust. It lay on top of the car maybe ten feet from me, hindquarters dragging, struggling to haul itself forward with one claw.

Marcone stepped closer, lifted the hunting rifle, and coolly put another shot right between its eyes. The creature twitched, fell, and slid bonelessly over the side of the train.

Marcone peered after it. 'What was that?'

'Some kind of guard dog,' I said.

'Interesting. Demon?'

I pushed myself to my feet. 'Doubt it. Demons are usually a lot tougher.'

'Then what was it?'

'How the hell should I know? Never seen anything like it before. Where are Michael and Sanya?'

We went to look. The next car was an empty one with spaced wooden slats and an open top. It looked like something used to haul cattle. There were three men in it, unconscious or dead. Michael climbed the far wall of the cattle car and onto the next car in line.

We climbed down into the car. 'Dead?' Marcone asked.

'Napping,' Sanya said.

Marcone nodded. 'We should finish them. These men are fanatics. If they wake up, they'll attack us without hesitation, armed or not.'

I eyed him. 'We're not going to murder them in cold blood.'

'Is there a particular reason why not?'

'Shut up, Marcone.'

'They would show us no such mercy. And if they are allowed to live they will surely be used by the Denarians to cause pain and death. It's their purpose.'

'We're not killing them.'

Marcone's mouth curled into a bitter smile. 'How did I guess.' He snapped open a case on his belt and tossed two sets of handcuffs at Sanya. The Russian caught them and cuffed the downed men together, looping one of the sets around a metal strut of the car.

'There,' Marcone said. 'I suppose we'll just have to take the chance that none of them will chew off his own hand at the wrist and slip free.'

'Sanya!' Michael's voice thundered over the noise of the train, and a sudden, brilliant glare of white light leapt up from the top of the next car. Steel chimed on steel.

Sanya shoved his assault rifle at me. I caught it, and he pushed past me to start climbing out of the car. He hauled himself up with his right arm, his injured arm dangling, and heaved himself to the lip of the cattle car. He stood, drew *Esperacchius* in a blaze of more white light, and threw himself to the next car with a rumbling shout.

I let my staff drop and fumbled with the assault rifle, trying to find the safety. Marcone set his hunting rifle aside and said, 'You're going to hurt yourself.' He took the assault rifle out of my hands, checked a couple of things without needing to look at the weapon, and then slung it over his shoulder as he climbed out of the car. I muttered to myself and went up the wooden slats beside him.

The next car was another metal box. Michael's and Sanya's swords shone like the sun, and I had to shield my eyes against them. They stood side by side with their backs to me, facing the front of the train.

Nicodemus stood against them.

The lord of the Denarians wore a grey silk shirt and black pants. The Shroud had been draped over his body, like a contestant in a beauty pageant. The noose around his neck blew out toward the rear of the train in the wind. He held a sword in his hands, a Japanese katana with a worn hilt. Droplets of blood stained the very tip of the sword. He held the sword at his side, a small smile on his lips, to all appearances relaxed.

Michael checked over his shoulder, and I saw a line of blood on his cheek. 'Stay back, Harry.'

Nicodemus attacked in the moment Michael's attention was elsewhere. The Denarian's weapon blurred, and Michael barely managed to get *Amoracchius* into a parry. He was thrown off balance and to one knee for a fatal second, but Sanya roared and attacked, whipping his saber through whistling arcs, and driving Nicodemus back. The Russian drove the Denarian toward the far side of the car.

I saw the trap coming and shouted, 'Sanya, back off!'

The Russian couldn't stop his forward momentum entirely, but he pivoted and lunged to one side. As he did, steely blades erupted from within the car. The metal of the roof screamed as the blades pierced it, rising to a height of four or five feet in a line, a half breath behind Sanya. Nicodemus turned to pursue the Russian.

Michael got his feet, whipped the heavy blade of *Amoracchius* around, and slashed three times at the roof of the railcar. A triangular section three feet across fell down into the car, and the edges of the metal glowed dull orange with the heat of the parted steel. Michael dropped down through the hole and out of sight.

I lifted up my blasting rod and focused on Nicodemus. He shot a glance at me and flicked his wrist in my direction.

His shadow flashed across the top of the railcar and smashed into me. The shadow wrenched the blasting rod from my grip, dragged it through the air, and then crushed it to splinters.

Sanya let out a cry as a blade tore through the car's roof and one of his legs collapsed. He fell to one knee.

Then brilliant light flared up within the car beneath the combatants, spears of white lancing out through the holes the blades had cut into the metal. I heard Deirdre's demon form shriek in the car beneath us, and the blades harassing Sanya vanished.

Nicodemus snarled. He flung a hand toward me, and his shadow sent the splinters of my blasting rod shrieking toward my face. As they did, Nicodemus attacked Sanya, his sword flickering in the moonlight.

I got my arms up in time to deflect the splinters, but I was helpless to assist Sanya. Nicodemus knocked Sanya's saber out to one side. Sanya rolled, avoiding the stroke that would have taken his head. Doing it left Sanya's wounded arm on the ground, and Nicodemus crushed the heel of his boot down upon it.

Sanya screamed in pain.

Nicodemus raised his sword for the death blow.

Gentleman Johnny Marcone opened up with the Kalashnikov.

Marcone shot in three chattering bursts of fire. The first one tore through Nicodemus's chest and neck, just above the Shroud. The next hit on his arm and shoulder opposite the Shroud, all but tearing it off his torso. The last burst ripped apart his hip and thigh, on the hip opposite the Shroud's drape. Nicodemus's expression blackened with fury, but the bullets had torn half his body to shreds, and he toppled from the car and out of sight.

Below, there was another demonic shriek, and the sound of wrenching metal. The shrieks faded toward the front of the train, and a moment later Michael climbed up the ladder rungs on the side of the boxcar, his sword in its sheath.

I leapt forward and ran to Sanya. He was bleeding a lot from his leg. He had already taken off his belt, and I helped him wrap it around the leg in a makeshift tourniquet.

Marcone stepped up to where Nicodemus had fallen, frowned, and said, 'Dammit. He should have dropped in place. Now we'll have to go back for the Shroud.'

'No, we won't,' I said. 'You didn't kill him. You probably just pissed him off.'

Michael stepped past Marcone to help Sanya, tearing off a section off his white cloak.

'Do you think so?' Marcone asked. 'The damage seemed fairly thorough.'

'I don't think he can be killed,' I said.

'Interesting. Can he run faster than a train?'

'Probably,' I said.

Marcone said to Sanya, 'Do you have another clip?'

'Where is Deirdre?' I asked Michael.

He shook his head. 'Wounded. She tore her way through the front wall of the car into the next one. Too risky to pursue her alone in close quarters.'

I stood up and crawled back over to the cattle car. I clambered down in it to fetch my staff. After a moment of hesitation, I got Marcone's rifle, too, and started back up.

As it turned out, I was mistaken. Nicodemus could not run faster than a train.

He *flew* faster than a train.

He came sailing down out of the sky, his shadow spread like immense bat wings. His sword flashed toward Marcone. Marcone's reflexes could make a striking snake look sluggish, and he dodged and rolled out of the way of the Denarian's sword.

Nicodemus sailed to the next car on the train and landed in a crouch, facing us. A glowing sigil had appeared on his forehead, the sign itself something twisting, nauseating to look upon. His skin was marred and ugly where Marcone's shots had hit him, but it was whole, and getting better by the second. His face twisted in fury and a kind of ecstatic agony, and his shadow flooded forward, over the length of the railcar in front of him and dipping down between his car and ours.

There was a wrenching sound and our car shook. Then the sound of tearing metal, and our car started shuddering.

'He's uncoupled the cars!' I shouted. As I did, Nicodemus's car began drawing away from us, as our own slowed down, the gap between them growing.

'Go!' Sanya shouted. 'I'll be all right!'

Michael stood and threw himself over the gap without hesitation. Marcone ditched the assault rifle and sprinted toward the gap. He threw himself over it, arms windmilling, and landed, barely, on the other car's roof.

I got to the top of the car and did the same thing. I imagined missing the other car and landing on the tracks in front of the uncoupled end of the train. Even without an engine, pure momentum would be more than enough to kill me. I dropped Marcone's rifle and gathered my will in my staff. As I leapt, I thrust the staff back behind me and screamed, '*Forzare!*'

The raw force I sent out behind me shoved me forward. Actually, it shoved me too far forward. I landed closer to Nicodemus than either Michael or Marcone, but at least I didn't wind up sprawled at his feet.

Michael stepped up to stand beside me, and a second later Marcone did as well. He had an automatic pistol in either hand.

'The boy isn't very fast, is he, Michael?' said Nicodemus. 'You're an adequate opponent, I suppose. Not as experienced as you could be, but it's hard to find someone with more than thirty or forty years of practice, much less twenty centuries. Not as talented as the Japanese, but then not many are.'

'Give up the Shroud, Nicodemus,' Michael shouted. 'It is not yours to take.'

'Oh, yes, it is,' Nicodemus answered. 'You certainly will not be able to stop me. And when I've finished you and the wizard, I'll go back for the boy. Three Knights in a day, as it were.'

'He can't make bad puns,' I muttered. 'That's my shtick.'

'At least he didn't overlook you entirely,' Marcone answered. 'I feel somewhat insulted.'

'Hey!' I shouted. 'Old Nick, can I ask you a question?'

'Please do, wizard. Once we get to the fighting, there really isn't going to be much opportunity for it.'

'Why?' I said.

'Beg pardon?'

'Why?' I asked again. 'Why the hell are you doing this? I mean, I get why you stole the Shroud. You needed a big battery. But why a plague?'

'Have you read Revelations?'

'Not in a while,' I admitted. 'But I just can't buy that you really think you're touching off the Apocalypse.'

Nicodemus shook his head. 'Dresden, Dresden. The Apocalypse, as you refer to it, isn't an event. At least, it isn't any specific event. One day, I'm sure, there will be an apocalypse that really does bring on the end, but I doubt it will be this event that begins it.'

'Then why *do* this?'

Nicodemus studied me for a moment before smiling. 'Apocalypse is a frame of mind,' he said then. 'A belief. A surrender to inevitability. It is despair for the future. It is the death of hope.'

Michael said quietly, 'And in that kind of environment, there is more suffering. More pain. More desperation. More power to the underworld and their servants.'

'Exactly,' Nicodemus said. 'We have a terrorist group prepared to take credit for this plague. It will likely stir up reprisals, protests, hostilities. All sorts of things.'

'One step closer,' said Michael. 'That's how he sees it. Progress.'

'I like to think of it as simple entropy,' Nicodemus said. 'The real question, to my mind, is why do you stand against me? It is the way of the universe, Knight. Things fall apart. Your resistance to it is pointless.'

In answer, Michael drew his sword.

'Ah,' said Nicodemus. 'Eloquence.'

'Stay back,' Michael said to me. 'Don't distract me.'

'Michael—'

'I mean it.' He stepped forward to meet Nicodemus.

Nicodemus took his time, sauntering up to meet Michael. He crossed swords with him lightly, then lifted his blade in a salute. Michael did the same.

Nicodemus attacked, and *Amoracchius* flared into brilliant light. The two men met each other and traded a quick exchange of cuts and thrusts. They parted, and then clashed together again, steps carrying each past the other. Both of them emerged from it unscathed.

'Shooting him hardly seems to inconvenience him,' Marcone

said quietly to me. 'I take it that the Knight's sword can harm him?'

'Michael doesn't think so,' I said.

Marcone blinked and looked at me. 'Then why is he fighting him?'

'Because it needs to be done,' I said.

'Do you know what I think?' Marcone said.

'You think we should shoot Nicodemus in the back at the first opportunity and let Michael dismember him.'

'Yes.'

I drew my gun. 'Okay.'

Just then Demon-girl Deirdre's glowing eyes appeared several cars ahead of us and came forward at a sprint. I caught a glimpse of her before she jumped onto our car – still all supple scales and hairstyle by the Tasmanian Devil. But in addition she had a sword gripped in one hand.

'Michael!' I shouted. 'Behind you!'

Michael turned and dodged to one side, avoiding Deirdre's first attack. Her hair followed him, lashing at him, tangling around the hilt of his sword.

I acted without thinking. I stripped Shiro's cane from my back, shouted, 'Michael!' and threw the cane at him.

Michael didn't so much as turn his head. He reached out, caught the cane, and with a sweep of his arm threw the cane-sheath free of the sword so that *Fidelacchius*'s blade shone with its own light. Without pausing, he swung the second sword and struck Deirdre's tangling hair from his arm, sending her stumbling back.

Nicodemus attacked him, and Michael met him squarely, shouting, '*O Dei! Lava quod est sordium!*' *Cleanse what is unclean,*

O God. Michael managed to hold his ground against Nicodemus their blades ringing. Michael drove Nicodemus to one side and I had a shot at his back. I took it. Beside me, Marcone did the same.

The shots took Nicodemus by surprise and stole his balance Michael shouted and pressed forward on the offensive, seizing the advantage for the first time. Both shining blades dipped and circled through attack after attack, and Michael drove Nicodemus back step by step.

'Hell's bells, he's going to win,' I muttered.

But Nicodemus drew a gun from the back of his belt.

He shoved it against Michael's breastplate and pulled the trigger. Repeatedly. Light and thunder made even the rushing train sound quiet.

Michael fell and did not move.

The light of the two swords went out.

I shouted, 'No!' I raised my gun and started shooting again Marcone joined me.

We didn't do too badly considering we were standing on a moving train and all. But Nicodemus didn't seem to care. He walked toward us through the bullets, jerking and twitching occasionally. He casually kicked the two swords over the side of the train.

I ran dry on bullets, and Nicodemus took the gun from my hand with a stroke of his sword. It hit the top of the boxcar once, then bounced off and into the night. The train thundered down a long, shallow grade toward a bridge. Demon-girl Deirdre leapt over to her father's side on all fours, her face distorted in glee. Tendrils of her hair ran lovingly over Michael's unmoving form.

I drew up my unfocused shield into a regular barrier before me, and said, 'Don't even bother offering me a coin.'

'I hadn't planned on it,' Nicodemus said. 'You don't seem like a team player to me.' He looked past me and said. 'But I've heard about you, Marcone. Are you interested in a job?'

'I was just going to ask you the same thing,' Marcone said.

Nicodemus smiled and said, 'Bravo, sir. I understand. I'm obliged to kill you, but I understand.'

I traded a look with Marcone. I flicked my eyes at the upcoming bridge. He took a deep breath and nodded.

Nicodemus lifted the gun and aimed for my head. His shadow suddenly swept forward, under and around my shield, seizing my left hand. It ripped at my arm hard, pulling me off balance.

Marcone was ready. He let one of his empty guns fall and produced a knife from somewhere on his person. He flicked it at Nicodemus's face.

I went for his gun hand when he flinched. The gun went off. My senses exploded with a flash of light, and I lost the feeling in my left arm. But I trapped his gun arm between my body and my right arm and pried at his fingers.

Marcone went for him with another knife. It swept past my face, missing me. But it hit the Shroud. Marcone cut through it cleanly, seized it, and pulled it off Nicodemus entirely.

I felt the release of energy as the Shroud was removed, a wave of fever-hot magic that swept over me in a sudden, potent surge. When it was gone, my chills and my aching joints were gone with it. The curse had been broken.

'No!' Nicodemus shouted. 'Kill him!'

Deirdre leapt at Marcone. Marcone turned and jumped off

the train just as it rolled out over the river. He hit the water feet first, still clutching the Shroud, and was lost in the darkness.

I pried the gun from Nicodemus's fingers. He caught me by the hair, jerked my head back, and got his arm around my throat. He started choking me, hissing, 'It's going to take days to kill you, Dresden.'

He's afraid of you, said Shiro's voice in my mind.

In my memories, I watched Nicodemus edge away from Shiro as the old man entered the room.

The noose made him invulnerable to any lasting harm.

But in a flash of insight, I was willing to bet that the one thing the noose wouldn't protect him against was itself.

I reached back, fumbling until I felt the noose. I pulled on it as hard as I could, and then twisted it, pressing my knuckles hard into Nicodemus's throat.

Nicodemus reacted in sudden and obvious panic, releasing my throat and struggling to get away. I held on for dear life and dragged him off balance. I tried to throw him off the train, letting go of the noose at the last moment. He went over the edge but Deirdre let out a shriek and leapt forward, her tendrils writhing around one of his arms and holding him.

'Kill him,' Nicodemus choked. 'Kill him now!'

Coughing and wheezing, I picked up Michael's still form as best I could and leapt off the train.

We hit the water together. Michael sank. I wouldn't let go of him. I sank too. I tried to get us out, but I couldn't, and things started to become confusing and black.

I had almost given up trying when I felt something near me in the water. I thought it was a rope and I grabbed it. I was still holding on to Michael as whoever had thrown the rope started pulling me out.

I gasped for breath when my head broke water, and someone helped me drag Michael's body over to the shallows at the side of the river.

It was Marcone. And he hadn't thrown me a rope.

He'd hauled me out with the Shroud.

33

I woke up in the back of Michael's pickup staring up at the stars and the moon and in considerable pain. Sanya sat at the back of the truck, facing me. Michael lay still and unmoving beside me.

'He's awake,' Sanya said when he saw me moving.

Murphy's voice came from the front of the truck. 'Harry, be still, okay? We don't know how badly you've been shot.'

'Okay,' I said. 'Hi, Murph. It should have torn.'

'What?' Murphy asked.

'Shroud. It should have torn like wet tissue. That just makes sense, right?'

'Shhhhh, Harry. Be still and don't talk.'

That sounded fine to me. The next time I opened my eyes, I was in the morgue.

This, all by itself, is enough to really ruin your day.

I was lying on the examining table, and Butters, complete with his surgical gown and his tray of autopsy instruments, stood over me.

'I'm not dead!' I sputtered. 'I'm not dead!'

Murphy appeared in my field of vision, her hand on my chest. 'We know that, Harry. Easy. We've got to get the bullet out of you. We can't take you to the emergency room. They have to report any gunshot wounds.'

'I don't know,' Butters said. 'This X-ray is all screwed up. I'm not sure it's showing me where the bullet is. If I don't do this right, I could make things worse.'

'You can do it,' Murphy said. 'The technical stuff always messes up around him.'

Things spun around.

Michael stood over me at one point, his hand on my head. 'Easy, Harry. It's almost done.'

And I thought, *Great. I'm going to require an armed escort to make sure I get to hell.*

When I woke up again, I was in a small bedroom. Stacks and boxes and shelves of fabric filled the place nearly to the ceiling, and I smiled, recognizing it. The Carpenters' guest room.

On the floor next to the bed was Michael's breastplate. There were four neat holes in it where the bullets had gone through. I sat up. My shoulder screamed at me, and I found it covered in bandaging.

There was a sound by the door. A small pair of eyes peeked around the corner, and little Harry Carpenter stared at me with big blue-grey eyes.

'Hi,' I said to him.

He dutifully lifted his pudgy fingers and waved them at me.

'I'm Harry,' I said.

He frowned thoughtfully and then said, 'Hawwy.'

'Good enough, kid.'

He ran off. A minute later he came back, reaching way up

over his head to hold on to his daddy's fingers. Michael came in the room and smiled at me. He was wearing jeans, a clean white T-shirt, and bandages over one arm. The cut on his face was healing, and he looked rested and relaxed. 'Good afternoon,' he said.

I smiled tiredly at him. 'Your faith protects you, eh?'

Michael reached down and turned the breastplate around. There was a cream-colored material lining in the inside of the breastplate, with several deep dents in it. He peeled it back to show me layers and layers of bulletproof fabric backing ceramic strike plates set against the front of the breastplate. 'My faith protects me. My Kevlar helps.'

I laughed a little. 'Charity made you put it in?'

Michael picked up little Harry and put him on his shoulders. 'She did it herself. Said she wasn't going to spend all that trouble making the breastplate and then have me get killed with a gun.'

'She made the breastplate?' I asked.

Michael nodded. 'All of my armor. She used to work on motorcycles.'

My shoulder throbbed hard enough to make me miss the next sentence. 'Sorry. What did you say?'

'I said you'll need to take your medicine. Can you handle some food first?'

'I'll try.'

I had soup. It was exhausting. I took a Vicodin and slept without dreaming.

Over the next couple of days, I managed to piece together what had happened from talking to Michael and, on the second day, to Sanya.

The big Russian had come out of things all right. Marcone,

after getting me and Michael out of the water, had called Murphy and told her where to find us. She had already been on the way, and got there in only a couple of minutes.

The crew of the train, it turned out, had been killed. The three goons that had been trussed up on the train had bitten down on suicide pills and were dead when the cops found them. Murphy had taken us all to Butters instead of to the emergency room, since once my gunshot wound was reported, Rudolph and company could have made my life hell.

'I must be out of my mind,' Murphy told me when she visited. 'I swear, Dresden, if this comes back to bite me in the ass, I'm taking it out on your hide.'

'We're fighting the good fight, Murph,' I said.

She rolled her eyes at me, but said, 'I saw the body at the airport concourse, Harry. Did you know him?'

I looked out the window, at Michael's three youngest playing in the yard, watched over by a tolerant Molly. 'He was a friend. It could have been me instead.'

Murphy shivered. 'I'm sorry, Harry. The people who did it. Did they get away from you?'

I looked at her and said, 'I got away from them. I don't think I did much more than annoy them.'

'What happens when they come back?'

'I don't know,' I said.

'Wrong,' Murphy said. 'The answer to that question is that you don't know exactly but that you will certainly call Murphy from the get-go. You get less busted up when I'm around.'

'That's true.' I covered her hand with mine and said, 'Thanks, Murph.'

'You're gonna make me puke, Dresden,' she said. 'Oh, so you know. Rudolph is out of SI. The assistant DA he was working for liked his toadying style.'

'Rudolph the Brownnosed Reindeer,' I said.

Murphy grinned. 'At least he's not my problem anymore. Internal Affairs has to worry now.'

'Rudolph in Internal Affairs. That can't be good.'

'One monster at a time.'

On the fourth day, Charity inspected my wound and told Michael that I could leave. She never actually spoke to me, which I considered an improvement over most visits. That afternoon, Michael and Sanya came in. Michael was carrying Shiro's battered old cane.

'We got the swords back,' Michael said. 'This is for you.'

'You'll have a better idea what to do with that than me,' I told him.

'Shiro wanted you to have it,' Michael said. 'Oh, and you got some mail.'

'I what?'

Michael offered me an envelope and the cane as a unit. I took them both, and frowned at the envelope. The lettering was in black calligraphy, and flowed beautifully across the envelope.

'To Harry Dresden. And it's your address, Michael. Postmarked two weeks ago.'

Michael shrugged.

I opened the envelope and found two pages inside. One was a copy of a medical report. The other was ornately handwritten, like the envelope. It read:

Dear Mr Dresden,

By the time you read this letter, I will be dead. I have not been given the details, but I know a few things that will happen over the next few days. I write you now to say what I might not have the chance to in the flesh.

Your path is often a dark one. You do not always have the luxury that we do as Knights of the Cross. We struggle against powers of darkness. We live in black and white, while you must face a world of greys. It is never easy to know the path in such a place.

Trust your heart. You are a decent man. God lives in such hearts.

Enclosed is a medical report. My family is aware of it, though I have not shared it with Michael or Sanya. It is my hope that it will give you a measure of comfort in the face of my choice. Do not waste tears on me. I love my work. We all must die. There is no better way to do so than in the pursuit of something you love.

Walk in mercy and truth,

Shiro

I read over the medical report, blinking at several tears.

'What is it?' Sanya asked.

'It's from Shiro,' I said. 'He was dying.'

Michael frowned at me.

I held up the medical report. 'Cancer. Terminal. He knew it when he came here.'

Michael took it and let out a long breath. 'Now I understand.'

'I don't.'

Michael passed the report to Sanya and smiled. 'Shiro must

have known that we would need you to stop the Denarians. It' why he traded himself for your freedom. And why he accepte the curse in your place.'

'Why?'

Michael shrugged. 'You were the one we needed. You had al of the information. You were the one who realized Cassius wa masquerading as Father Vincent. You had contacts within th local authorities to give you access to more information, to hel us when we needed the concourse emptied. You were the on who could call in Marcone for his help.'

'I'm not sure that says anything good about me,' I said, glow ering.

'It says that you were the right man in the right place and a the right time,' Michael said. 'What of the Shroud? Does Marcon have it?'

'I think so.'

'How should we handle it?'

'We don't. I do.'

Michael regarded me for a moment, then said, 'All right.' H stood up and then said, 'Oh. The dry cleaners called. They sai they're going to charge you a late fee if you don't swing by an pick up your laundry today. I'm running out for groceries. I ca take you.'

'I don't have anything that goes to a dry cleaners,' I muttered But I went with Michael.

The dry cleaners had my leather duster. It had been cleane up and covered with a protective treatment. In the pockets wer the keys to the Blue Beetle, along with a bill to a parking garage On the back of the bill, written in flowing letters, were the word *thank you*.

So I guess Anna Valmont wasn't all that horrible a person after all.

But then, I've always been a sucker for a pretty face.

When I got back to my house, I found a postcard with a picture of Rio and no return address with my mail. There was a number on the back. I called the number, and after a few rings, Susan asked, 'Harry?'

'Harry,' I said.

'Are you all right?'

'Shot,' I said. 'It'll heal.'

'Did you beat Nicodemus?'

'I got away from him,' I said. 'We stopped the plague. But he killed Shiro.'

'Oh,' she said quietly. 'I'm sorry.'

'I got my coat back. And my car. Not a total loss.' I started opening mail as I spoke.

Susan asked, 'What about the Shroud?'

'Jury's not out yet. Marcone got involved.'

'What happened?' she said.

'He saved my life,' I said. 'Michael's too. He didn't have to do it.'

'Wow.'

'Yeah. Sometimes it feels like the older I get, the more confused everything is.'

Susan coughed. 'Harry. I'm sorry I wasn't around. By the time I was conscious, we were already over Central America.'

'It's okay,' I said.

'I didn't know what Martin had in mind,' she said. 'Honestly. I wanted to talk to you and to Trish and pick up a few of my things. I thought Martin was only coming along to help. I didn't know that he had come here to kill Ortega. He used me to cover his movements.'

'It's okay.'

'It isn't okay. And I'm sorry.'

I opened an envelope, read it, and blurted, 'Oh, you're *kidding* me.'

'What?'

'I just opened a letter. It's from Larry Fowler's lawyer. The jerk is *suing* me for trashing his car and his studio.'

'He can't prove that,' Susan said. 'Can he?'

'Whether or not he can, this is going to cost me a fortune in legal fees. Smarmy, mealymouthed jerk.'

'Then I hate to add more bad news. Ortega is back in Casaverde, recovering. He's called in all his strongest knights and let it be widely known that he's coming to kill you personally.'

'I'll cross that bridge when I come to it. Did you see the subtle humor there? Vampires, cross? God, I'm funny.'

Susan said something in Spanish, not into the phone, and sighed. 'Damn. I have to go.'

'Saving nuns and orphans?' I asked.

'Leaping tall buildings in a single bound. I should probably put on some underwear.'

That brought a smile to my face. 'You joke around a lot more than you used to,' I said. 'I like it.'

I could picture the sad smile on her face as she spoke. 'I'm dealing with a lot of scary things,' she said. 'I think you have to react to them. And you either laugh at them or you go insane. Or you become like Martin. Shut off from everything and everyone. Trying not to feel.'

'So you joke,' I said.

'I learned it from you.'

'I should open a school.'

'Maybe so,' she said. 'I love you, Harry. I wish things were different.'

My throat got tight. 'Me too.'

'I'll get you a drop address. If you ever need my help, get in touch.'

'Only if I need your help?' I asked.

She exhaled slowly and said, 'Yeah.'

I tried to say, 'Okay,' but my throat was too tight to speak.

'Good-bye, Harry,' Susan said.

I whispered, 'Good-bye.'

And that was the end of that.

I woke up to a ringing telephone the next day. 'Hoss,' Ebenezar said. 'You should watch the news today.' He hung up on me.

I went down to a nearby diner for breakfast, and asked the waitress to turn on the news. She did.

'. . . extraordinary event reminiscent of the science-fiction horror stories around the turn of the millennium, what appeared to be an asteroid fell from space and impacted just outside the village of Casaverde in Honduras.' The screen flickered to an aerial shot of an enormous, smoking hole in the ground, and a half-mile-wide circle of trees that had been blasted flat. Just past the circle of destruction stood a poor-looking village. 'However, information coming in from agencies around the world indicates that the so-called meteor was in actuality a deactivated Soviet communications satellite which decayed in orbit and fell to earth. No estimates of the number of deaths or injuries in this tragic freak accident have yet reached authorities, but it seems unlikely that anyone in the manor house could possibly have survived the impact.'

I sat slowly back, pursing my lips. I decided that maybe wasn't sorry Asteroid Dresden turned out to be an old Sovie satellite after all. And I made a mental note to myself never t get on Ebenezar's bad side.

The next day I tracked down Marcone. It wasn't easy. I ha to call in a couple of favors in the spirit world to get a beacon-spell going on him, and he knew all the tricks for losing a tail I had to borrow Michael's truck so that I could have a prayer o following him inconspicuously. The Beetle may be way sexy, bu subtle it ain't.

He changed cars twice and somehow called into effect th magical equivalent of a destructive electromagnetic pulse tha scrambled my beacon-spell. Only quick thinking and som inspired thaumaturgy combined with my investigative skills le me stay with him.

He drove right on into the evening, to a private hospital i Wisconsin. It was a long-term-care and therapeutic facility. H pulled in, dressed in casual clothes and wearing a baseball cap which alone generated enough cognitive dissonance to mak me start drooling. He pulled a backpack out of the car an went inside. I gave him a little bit of a lead and then follow him with my beacon. I stayed outside, peering in windows a lit hallways, keeping pace and watching.

Marcone stopped at a room and went inside. I stood at th window, keeping track of him. The paper tag on the door fron the hall read DOE, JANE in big, permanent marker letters tha were faded with age. There was a single bed in the room, an there was a girl on it.

She wasn't old. I'd place her in her late teens or early twenies. She was so thin it was hard to tell. She wasn't on life support, ut her bedcovers were flawlessly unwrinkled. Combined with ier emaciated appearance, I was guessing she was in a coma, vhoever she was.

Marcone drew up a chair beside the bed. He pulled out a eddy bear and slipped it into the crook of the girl's arm. He got ut a book. Then he started reading to her, out loud. He sat here reading to her for an hour, before he slipped a bookmark nto place and put the book back into the backpack.

Then he reached into the pack and pulled out the Shroud. Ie peeled down the outermost blanket on her bed, and careully laid the Shroud over the girl, folding its ends in a bit to eep it from spilling out. Then he covered it up with the blanket nd sat down in the chair again, his head bowed. I hadn't ever ictured John Marcone praying. But I saw him forming the word *lease*, over and over.

He waited for another hour. Then, his face sunken and tired, ie rose and kissed the girl on the head. He put the teddy bear ack into the backpack, got up, and left the room.

I went to his car and sat down on the hood.

Marcone stopped in his tracks and stared at me when he saw ne. I just sat there. He padded warily over to his car and said, oice quiet, 'How did you find me?'

'Wasn't easy,' I said.

'Is anyone else with you?'

'No.'

I saw the wheels spinning in his head. I saw him panic a little. saw him consider killing me. I saw him force himself to slow lown and decide against any rash action. He nodded once, and aid, 'What do you want?'

'The Shroud.'

'No,' he said. There was a hint of frustration to his voice. 'I just got it here.'

'I saw,' I said. 'Who is the girl?'

His eyes went flat, and he said nothing.

'Okay, Marcone,' I said. 'You can give me the Shroud or you can explain it to the police when they come out here to search this place.'

'You can't,' he said, his voice quiet. 'You can't do that to her. She'd be in danger.'

My eyes widened. 'She's yours?'

'I'll kill you,' he said in that same soft voice. 'If you so much as breathe in her direction, I'll kill you, Dresden. Myself.'

I believed him.

'What's wrong with her?' I asked.

'Persistent vegetative state,' he said. 'Coma.'

'You wanted it to heal her,' I said quietly. 'That's why you had it stolen.'

'Yes.'

'I don't think it works like that,' I said. 'It isn't as simple as plugging in a light.'

'But it might work,' he said.

I shrugged. 'Maybe.'

'I'll take it,' he said. 'It's all I have.'

I looked back toward the window and was quiet for a minute. I made up my mind and said, 'Three days.'

He frowned. 'What?'

'Three days,' I said. 'Three's a magic number. And supposedly that's how long Christ was wrapped in it. In three days, three sunrises, you should know whether it's going to help or not.'

'And then?'

'Then the Shroud is returned in a plain brown wrapper to Father Forthill at Saint Mary of the Angels,' I said. 'No note. No nothing. Just returned.'

'And if I don't, you'll expose her.'

I shook my head and stood up. 'No. I won't do that. I'll take it up with you.'

He stared at me for a long moment before his expression softened. 'All right.'

I left him there.

When I'd first met Marcone, he'd tricked me into a soul-gaze. Though I hadn't known the specifics, I knew then that he had a secret – one that gave him the incredible amount of will and inner strength needed to run one of the nation's largest criminal empires. He had something that drove him to be remorseless, practical, deadly.

Now I knew what that secret was.

Marcone was still a black hat. The pain and suffering of the criminal state he ruled accounted for an untold amount of human misery. Maybe he'd been doing it for a noble reason. I could understand that. But it didn't change anything. Marcone's good intentions could have paved a new lane on the road to hell.

But dammit, I couldn't hate him anymore. I couldn't hate him because I wasn't sure that I wouldn't have made the same choice in his place.

Hate was simpler, but the world ain't a simple place. It would have been easier to hate Marcone.

I just couldn't do it.

*

A few days later, Michael threw a cookout as a farewell celebration for Sanya, who was heading back to Europe now that the Shroud had been returned to Father Forthill. I was invited, so I showed up and ate about a hundred and fifty grilled hamburgers. When I was done with them, I went into the house, but stopped to glance into the sitting room by the front door.

Sanya sat in a recliner, his expression puzzled, blinking at the phone. 'Again,' he said.

Molly sat cross-legged on the couch near him with a phone book in her lap and my shopping list she'd picked up in the tree house laid flat over one half of it. Her expression was serious, but her eyes were sparkling as she drew a red line through another entry in the phone book. 'How strange,' she said, and read off another number.

Sanya started dialing. 'Hello?' he said a moment later. 'Hello, sir. Could you please tell me if you have Prince Albert in a can—' He blinked again, mystified, and reported to Molly, 'They hung up *again*.'

'*Weird*,' Molly said, and winked at me.

I left before I started choking on the laugh I had to hold back, and went out into the front yard. Little Harry was there by himself, playing in the grass in sight of his sister, inside.

'Heya, kid,' I said. 'You shouldn't be out here all by yourself. People will accuse you of being a reclusive madman. Next thing you know, you'll be wandering around saying, "Woahse-bud."'

I heard a clinking sound. Something shining landed in the grass by little Harry, and he immediately pushed himself to his feet, wobbled, then headed for it.

I panicked abruptly and lunged out ahead of him, slapping my hand down over a polished silver coin before the child could squat down to pick it up. I felt a prickling jolt shoot up my arm, and had the sudden, intangible impression that someone nearby was waking up from a nap and stretching.

I looked up to see a car on the street, driver-side window rolled down.

Nicodemus sat at the wheel, relaxed and smiling. 'Be seeing you, Dresden.'

He drove away. I took my shaking hand from the coin.

Lasciel's blackened sigil lay before my eyes. I heard a door open, and on pure instinct palmed the coin and slipped it in my pocket. I looked back to find Sanya frowning and looking up and down the street. His nostrils flared a few times, and he paced over to stand near me. He sniffed a few more times and then peered down at the baby. 'Aha,' he rumbled. 'Someone is stinky.' He swooped the kid up in his arms, making him squeal and laugh. 'You mind if I steal your playmate for a minute, Harry?'

'Go ahead,' I said. 'I need to get going anyway.'

Sanya nodded and grinned at me, offering his hand. I shook it. 'It has been a pleasure to work with you,' Sanya said. 'Perhaps we will see each other again.'

The coin felt cool and heavy in my pocket. 'Yeah. Maybe so.'

I left the cookout without saying good-bye, and headed home. I heard something the whole time, something whispering almost inaudibly. I drowned it out with loud and off-key singing, and got to work.

Ten hours later, I put down the excavating pick and glowered at the two-foot hole I had chipped in my lab's concrete floor. The whispering in my head had segued into 'Sympathy for the Devil' by the Stones.

'*Harry*,' whispered a gentle voice.

I dropped the coin into the hole. I slipped a steel ring about three inches across around it. I muttered to myself and willed energy into the ring. The whispering abruptly cut off.

I dumped two buckets of cement into the hole and smoothed it until it was level with the rest of my floor. After that, I hurried out of the lab and shut the door behind me.

Mister came over to demand attention. I settled on the couch, and he jumped up to sprawl on his back over my legs. I petted him and stared at Shiro's cane, resting in the corner.

'He said that I must live in a world of greys. To trust my heart.' I rubbed Mister's favorite spot, behind his right ear, and he purred in approval. Mister, at least for the moment, agreed that my heart was in the right place. But it's possible he wasn't being objective.

After a while, I picked up Shiro's cane and stared down at the smooth old wood. *Fidelacchius*'s power whispered against my fingertips. There was a single Japanese character carved into the sheath. When I asked Bob, he told me that it read, simply, *Faith*.

It isn't good to hold on too hard to the past. You can't spend your whole life looking back. Not even when you can't see what lies ahead. All you can do is keep on keeping on, and try to believe that tomorrow will be what it should be – even if it isn't what you expected.

I took Susan's picture down. I put the postcards in a brown envelope. I picked up the jewel box that held the dinky engagement ring I'd offered her, and that she'd turned down. Then I put them all away in my closet.

I laid the old man's cane on my fireplace mantel.

Maybe some things just aren't meant to go together. Things like oil and water. Orange juice and toothpaste.

Me and Susan.

But tomorrow was another day.

extras

www.orbitbooks.net

about the author

A martial arts enthusiast whose resumé includes a long list of skills rendered obsolete at least two hundred years ago, **Jim Butcher** turned to writing as a career because anything else probably would have driven him insane. He lives in Independence, Missouri, with his wife, his son, and a ferocious guard dog. You can visit Jim's website at www.jim-butcher.com

Find out more about Jim Butcher and other Orbit authors by registering for the free monthly newsletter at www.orbitbooks.net

if you enjoyed
DEATH MASKS

look out for

BLOOD RITES

a Dresden Files novel

also by

Jim Butcher

1

The building was on fire, and it wasn't my fault.

My boots slipped and slid on the tile floor as I sprinted around a corner and toward the exit doors to the abandoned school building on the southwest edge of Chicagoland. Distant streetlights provided the only light in the dusty hall, and left huge swaths of blackness crouching in the old classroom doors.

I carried an elaborately carved wooden box about the size of a laundry basket in my arms, and its weight made my shoulders burn with effort. I'd been shot in both of them at one time or another, and the muscle burn quickly started changing into deep, aching stabs. The damned box was heavy, not even considering its contents.

Inside the box, a bunch of flop-eared grey-and-black puppies whimpered and whined, jostled back and forth as I ran. One of the puppies, his ear already notched where some kind of doggie misadventure had marked him, was either braver or more stupid than his littermates. He scrambled around until he got his paws onto the lip of the box, and set up a painfully high-pitched barking full of squeaky snarls, big dark eyes focused behind me.

I ran faster, my knee-length black leather duster swishing against my legs. I heard a rustling, hissing sound and juked left as best I could. A ball of some kind of noxious-smelling substance that looked like tar went zipping past me, engulfed in yellow-white flame. It hit the floor several yards beyond me, and promptly exploded into a little puddle of hungry fire.

I tried to avoid it, but my boots had evidently been made for walking, not sprinting on dusty tile. They slid out from under me and I fell. I controlled it as much as I could, and wound up sliding on my rear, my back to the fire. It got hot for a second, but the wards I'd woven over my duster kept it from burning me.

Another flaming glob crackled toward me, and I barely turned in time. The substance, whatever the hell it was, clung like napalm to what it hit and burned with a supernatural ferocity that had already burned a dozen metal lockers to slag in the dim halls behind me.

The goop hit my left shoulder blade and slid off the protective spells on my mantled coat, spattering the wall beside me. I flinched nonetheless, lost my balance, and fumbled the box. Fat little puppies tumbled onto the floor with a chorus of whimpers and cries for help.

I checked behind me.

The guardian demons looked like demented purple chimpanzees, except for the raven-black wings sprouting from their shoulders. There were three of them that had escaped my carefully crafted paralysis spell, and they were hot on my tail, bounding down the halls in long leaps assisted by their black feathered wings.

As I watched, one of them reached down between its crooked legs and . . . Well, not to put too fine a point on it, but it gathered up the kind of ammunition primates in zoos traditionally rely upon. The monkey-demon hurled it with a chittering scream, and it combusted in midair. I had to duck before the noxious ball of incendiary goop smacked into my nose.

I grabbed puppies and scooped them into the box, then started running. The demon-monkeys burst into fresh howls.

Squeaky barks behind me made me look back. The little notch-eared puppy had planted his clumsy paws solidly on the floor, and was barking defiantly at the oncoming demon-chimps.

'Dammit,' I cursed, and reversed course. The lead monkey swooped down at the puppy. I made like a ballplayer, slid in feet-first, and planted the heel of my boot squarely on the end of the demon's nose. I'm not heavily built, but I'm most of a head taller than six feet, and no one ever thought I was a lightweight. I kicked the demon hard enough to make it screech and veer off. It slammed into a metal locker, and left an inches-deep dent.

'Stupid little fuzzbucket,' I muttered, and recovered the puppy. 'This is why I have a cat.' The puppy kept up its tirade of ferocious, squeaking snarls. I pitched him into the box without ceremony, ducked two more flaming blobs, and started coughing on the smoke already filling the building as I resumed my retreat. Light was growing back where I'd come from, as the demons' flaming missiles chewed into the old walls and floor, spreading with a malicious glee.

I ran for the front doors of the old building, slamming the opening bar with my hip and barely slowing down.

A sudden weight hit my back and something pulled viciously at my hair. The chimp-demon started biting at my neck and ear.

It hurt. I tried to spin and throw it off me, but it had a good hold. The effort, though, showed me a second demon heading for my face, and I had to duck to avoid a collision.

I let go of the box and reached for the demon on my back. It howled and bit my hand. Snarling and angry, I turned around and threw my back at the nearest wall. The monkey-demon evidently knew that tactic. It flipped off of my shoulders at the last second, and I slammed the base of my skull hard against a row of metal lockers.

A burst of stars blinded me for a second, and by the time my vision cleared, I saw two of the demons diving toward the box of puppies. They both hurled searing blobs at the wooden box, splattering it with flame.

There was an old fire extinguisher on the wall, and I grabbed it. My monkey attacker came swooping back at me. I rammed the end of the extinguisher into its nose, knocking it down, then reversed my grip on the extinguisher and sprayed a cloud of dusty white chemical at the carved box. I got the fire put out, but for good measure I unloaded the thing into the other two demons' faces, creating a thick cloud of dust.

I grabbed the box and hauled it out the door, and then slammed the school doors shut behind me.

There were a couple of thumps from the other side of the doors, and then silence.

Panting, I looked down at the box of whimpering puppies. A bunch of wet black noses and eyes looked back up at me from under a white dusting of extinguishing chemical.

'Hell's bells,' I panted at them. 'You guys are lucky Brother Wang wants you back so much. If he hadn't paid half up front, I'd be the one in the box and you'd be carrying me.'

A bunch of little tail's wagged hopefully.

'Stupid dogs,' I growled. I hauled the box into my arms again and started schlepping it toward the old school's parking lot.

I was about halfway there when something ripped the steel doors of the school inward, against the swing of their hinges. A low, loud bellow erupted from inside the building, and then a Kong-size version of the chimp-demons came stomping out of the doorway.

It was purple. It had wings. And it looked really pissed off. At least eight feet tall, it had to weigh four or five times what I did. As I stared at it, two little monkey-demons flew directly at demon Kong – and were simply absorbed by the bigger demon's bulk upon impact. Kong gained another eighty pounds or so and got a bit bulkier. Not so much monkey Kong, then, as Monkey Voltron. The original crowd of guardian demons must have escaped my spell with that combining maneuver, pooling all of their energy into a single vessel and using the greater strength provided by density to power through my binding.

Kongtron spread wings as wide as a small airplane's and leapt at me with a completely unfair amount of grace. Being a professional investigator, as well as a professional wizard, I'd seen slobbering beasties before. Over the course of many encounters and many years, I have successfully developed a standard operating procedure for dealing with big, nasty monsters.

Run away. Me and Monty Python.

The parking lot and the Blue Beetle, my beat-up old Volkswagen, were only thirty or forty yards off, and I can really move when I'm feeling motivated.

Kong bellowed. It motivated me.

There was the sound of a small explosion, then a blaze of

red light brighter than the nearby street lamps. Another fireball hit the ground a few feet wide of me and detonated like a Civil War cannonball, gouging out a coffin-sized crater in the pavement. The enormous demon roared and shot past me on black vulture wings, banking to come around for another pass.

'Thomas!' I screamed. 'Start the car!'

The passenger door opened, and an unwholesomely good-looking young man with dark hair, tight jeans, and a leather jacket worn over a bare chest poked his head out and peered at me over the rims of round green-glassed spectacles. Then he looked up and behind me. His jaw dropped open.

'Start the freaking car!' I screamed.

Thomas nodded and dove back into the Beetle. It coughed and wheezed and shuddered to life. The surviving headlight flicked on, and Thomas gunned the engine and headed for the street.

For a second I thought he was going to leave me, but he slowed down enough that I caught up with him. Thomas leaned across the car and pushed the passenger door open. I grunted with effort and threw myself into the car. I almost lost the box, but managed to get it just before the notch-eared puppy pulled himself up to the rim, evidently determined to go back and do battle.

'What the hell is that?' Thomas screamed. His black hair, shoulder length, curling and glossy, whipped around his face as the car gathered speed and drew the cool autumn wind through the open windows. His grey eyes were wide with apprehension. 'What is that, Harry?'

'Just drive!' I shouted. I stuffed the box of whimpering puppies into the backseat, grabbed my blasting rod, and climbed out the open window so that I was sitting on the door, chest to the car's roof. I twisted to bring the blasting rod in my right hand to bear on the demon. I drew in my will, my magic, and the end of the blasting rod began to glow with a cherry-red light.

I was about to loose a strike against the demon when it swooped down with another fireball in its hand and flung it at the car.

'Look out!' I screamed.

Thomas must have seen it coming in the mirror. The Beetle swerved wildly, and the fireball hit the asphalt, bursting into a roar of flame and concussion that broke windows on both sides of the street. Thomas dodged a car parked on the curb by roaring up onto the sidewalk, bounced gracelessly, and nearly went out of control. The bounce threw me from my perch on the closed door. I was wondering what the odds were against finding a soft place to land when I felt Thomas grab my ankle. He held on to me and drew me back into the car with a strength that would have been shocking to anyone who didn't know that he wasn't human.

He braced me with his hold on my leg, and as the huge demon dove down again, I pointed my blasting rod at it and snarled, '*Fuego!*'

A lance of white-hot fire streaked from the tip of my blasting rod into the late-night air, illuminating the street like a flash of lightning. Bouncing along on the car like that, I expected to miss. But I beat the odds and the burst of flame took Kongtron right in the belly. It screamed and faltered, plummeting to earth. Thomas swerved back out onto the street.

The demon started to get up. 'Stop the car!' I screamed.

Thomas mashed down the brakes and I nearly got reduced

to sidewalk pizza again. I hung on as hard as I could, but by the time I had my balance, the demon had hauled itself to its feet.

I growled in frustration, readied another blast, and aimed carefully.

'What are you doing?' Thomas shouted. 'You lamed him; let's run!'

'No,' I snapped back. 'If we leave it here, it's going to take things out on whoever it can find.'

'But it won't be *us*!'

I tuned Thomas out and readied another strike, pouring my will into the blasting rod until wisps of smoke began emerging from the length of its surface.

Then I let Kong have it right between its black beady eyes. The fire hit it like a wrecking ball, right on the chin. The demon's head exploded into a cloud of luminous purple vapor and sparkles of scarlet light, which I have to admit looked really neat.

Demons who come into the mortal world don't have bodies as such. They create them, like a suit of clothes, and as long as the demon's awareness inhabits the construct-body, it's as good as real. Having its head blown up was too much damage for even the demon's life energy to support. The body flopped around on the ground for a few seconds, and then the Kong-demon's earthly form stopped moving and dissolved into a lumpy looking mass of translucent gelatin – ectoplasm, matter from the Nevernever.

A surge of relief made me feel a little dizzy, and I slid bonelessly back into the Beetle.

'Allow me to reiterate,' Thomas panted a minute later. 'What. The hell. Was *that*.'

I settled down onto the seat, breathing hard. I buckled up,

and checked that the puppies and their box were both intact. They were, and I closed my eyes with a sigh. 'Shen,' I said. 'Chinese spirit creatures. Demons. Shapeshifters.'

'Christ, Dresden! You almost got me killed!'

'Don't be a baby. You're fine.'

Thomas frowned at me. 'You at least could have told me!'

'I *did* tell you,' I said. 'I told you at Mac's that I'd give you a ride home, but that I had to run an errand first.'

Thomas scowled. 'An *errand* is getting a tank of gas or picking up a carton of milk or something. It is *not* getting chased by flying purple pyromaniac gorillas hurling incendiary poo.'

'Next time take the El.'

He glared at me. 'Where are we going?'

'O'Hare.'

'Why?'

I waved vaguely at the backseat. 'Returning stolen property to my client. He wants to get it back to Tibet, pronto.'

'Anything else you're neglecting to tell me? Ninja wombats or something?'

'I wanted you to see how it feels,' I said.

'What's that supposed to mean?'

'Come on, Thomas. You never go to Mac's place to hang out and chum around. You're wealthy, you've got connections, and you're a freaking vampire. You didn't need me to give you a ride home. You could have taken a cab, called for a limo, or talked some woman into taking you.'

Thomas's scowl faded away, replaced by a careful, expressionless mask. 'Oh? Then why am I here?'

I shrugged. 'Doesn't look like you showed up to bushwhack me. I guess you're here to talk.'

'Razor intellect. You should be a private investigator or something.'

'You going to sit there insulting me, or are you going to talk?'

'Yeah,' Thomas said. 'I need a favor.'

I snorted. 'What favor? You do remember that technically we're at war, right? Wizards versus vampires? Ring any bells?'

'If you like, you can pretend that I'm employing subversive tactics as part of a fiendishly elaborate ruse meant to manipulate you,' Thomas said.

'Good,' I said. ''Cause if I went to all the trouble of starting a war and you didn't want to participate it would hurt my feelings.'

He grinned. 'I bet you're wondering whose side I'm on.'

'No.' I snorted. 'You're on Thomas's side.'

The grin widened. Thomas has the kind of whiter-than-white boyish grin that makes women's panties spontaneously evaporate. 'Granted. But I've done you some favors over the past couple of years.'

I frowned. He had, though I didn't know why. 'Yeah. So?'

'So now it's my turn,' he said. 'I've helped you. Now I need payback.'

'Ah. What do you want me to do?'

'I want you to take a case for an acquaintance of mine. He needs your help.'

'I don't really have time,' I said. 'I have to make a living.'

Thomas flicked a piece of monkey flambé off the back of his hand and out the window. 'You call this living?'

'Jobs are a part of life. Maybe you've heard of the concept. It's called work? See, what happens is that you suffer through doing annoying and humiliating things until you get paid not enough money. Like those Japanese game shows, only without all the glory.'

'Plebe. I'm not asking you to go pro bono. He'll pay your fee.'

'Bah,' I muttered. 'What's he need help with?'

Thomas frowned. 'He thinks someone is trying to kill him. I think he's right.'

'Why?'

'There have been a couple of suspicious deaths around him.'

'Like?'

'Two days ago he sent his driver, girl named Stacy Willis, out to the car with his golf clubs so he could get in a few holes before lunch. Willis opened the trunk and got stung to death by about twenty thousand bees who had somehow swarmed into the limo in the time it took her to walk up to the door and back.'

I nodded. 'Ugh. Can't argue there. Gruesomely suspicious.'

'The next morning his personal assistant, a young woman named Sheila Barks, was hit by a runaway car. Killed instantly.'

I pursed my lips. 'That doesn't sound so odd.'

'She was waterskiing at the time.'

I blinked. 'How the hell did *that* happen?'

'Bridge over the reservoir was the way I heard it. Car jumped the rail, landed right on her.'

'Ugh,' I said. 'Any idea who is behind it?'

'None. Think it's an entropy curse?' Thomas asked.

'If so, it's a sloppy one. But strong as hell. Those are some pretty melodramatic deaths.' I checked on the puppies. They had fallen together into one dusty lump and were sleeping. The notch-eared pup lay on top of the pile. He opened his eyes and gave me a sleepy little growl of warning. Then he went back to sleep.

Thomas glanced back at the box. 'Cute little furballs. What's their story?'

'Guardian dogs for some monastery in the Himalayas. Someone snatched them and came here. A couple of monks hired me to get them back.'

'What, they don't have dog pounds in Tibet?'

I shrugged. 'They believe these dogs have a foo heritage.'

'Is that like epilepsy or something?'

I snorted and put my hand palm-down out the window, waggling it back and forth to make an airfoil in the wind of the Beetle's passage. 'The monks think their great-grandcestor was a divine spirit-animal. Celestial guardian spirit. Foo dog. They believe it makes the bloodline special.'

'Is it?'

'How the hell should I know, man? I'm just the repo guy.'

'Some wizard you are.'

'It's a big universe,' I said. 'No one can know it all.'

Thomas fell quiet for a while, and the road whispered by. 'Uh, do you mind if I ask what happened to your car?'

I looked around at the Beetle's interior. It wasn't Volkswagen-standard anymore. The seat covers were gone. So was the padding underneath. So was the interior carpet, and big chunks of the dashboard that had been made out of wood. There was a little vinyl left, and some of the plastic, and anything made out of metal, but everything else had been stripped completely away.

I'd done some makeshift repairs with several one-by-sixes, some hanger wire, some cheap padding from the camping section at Wal-Mart, and a lot of duct tape. It gave the car a real post-modern look: By which I meant that it looked like something fashioned from the wreckage after a major nuclear exchange.

On the other hand, the Beetle's interior was very, very clean. My glasses are half-full, dammit.

'Mold demons,' I said.

'Mold demons ate your car?'

'Sort of. They were called out of the decay in the car's interior, and used anything organic they could find to make bodies for themselves.'

'You called them?'

'Oh, hell, no. They were a present from the guest villain a few months ago.'

'I hadn't heard there was any action this summer.'

'I have a life, man. And my life isn't all about feuding demigods and nations at war and solving a mystery before it kills me.'

Thomas lifted an eyebrow. 'It's also about mold demons and flaming monkey poo?'

'What can I say? I put the "ick" in "magic."'

'I see. Hey, Harry, can I ask you something?'

'I guess.'

'Did you really save the world? I mean, like the last two years in a row?'

I shrugged. 'Sort of.'

'Word is you capped a faerie princess and headed off a war between Winter and Summer,' Thomas said.

'Mostly I was saving my own ass. Just happened that the world was in the same spot.'

'There's an image that will give me nightmares,' Thomas said. 'What about those demon Hell guys last year?'

I shook my head. 'They'd have let loose a nasty plague, but it wouldn't have lasted very long. They were hoping it would escalate into a nice apocalypse. They knew there wasn't much chance of it, but they were doing it anyway.'

'Like the Lotto,' Thomas said.

'Yeah, I guess. The genocide Lotto.'

'And you stopped them.'

'I helped do it and lived to walk away. But there was an unhappy ending.'

'What?'

'I didn't get paid. For either case. I make more money from flaming demon monkey crap. That's just wrong.'

Thomas laughed a little and shook his head. 'I don't get it.'

'Don't get what?'

'Why you do it.'

'Do what?'

He slouched down in the driver's seat. 'The Lone Ranger impersonation. You get pounded to scrap every time you turn around and you barely get by on the gumshoe work. You live in that dank little cave of an apartment. Alone. You've got no woman, no friends, and you drive this piece of crap. Your life is kind of pathetic.'

'Is that what you think?' I asked.

'Call them like I see them.'

I laughed. 'Why do you think I do it?'

He shrugged. 'All I can figure is that either you're nursing a deep and sadistic self-hatred or else you're insane. I gave you the benefit of the doubt and left monumental stupidity off the list.'

I kept on smiling. 'Thomas, you don't really know me. Not at all.'

'I think I do. I've seen you under pressure.'

I shrugged. 'Yeah, but you see me, what? Maybe a day or two each year? Usually when something's been warming up to kill me by beating the tar out of me.'

'So?'

'So that doesn't cover what my life is like the other three hundred and sixty-three days,' I said. 'You don't know everything about me. My life isn't completely about magical mayhem and creative pyromania in Chicago.'

'Oh, that's right. I heard you went to exotic Oklahoma a few months back. Something about a tornado and the National Severe Storms Lab.'

'I was doing the new Summer Lady a favor, running down a rogue storm sylph. Got to go all over the place in those tornado-chaser geekmobiles. You should have seen the look on the driver's face when he realized that the tornado was chasing *us*.'

'It's a nice story, Harry, but what's the point?' Thomas asked.

'My point is that there's a lot of my life you haven't seen. I have friends.'

'Monster hunters, werewolves, and a talking skull.'

I shook my head. 'More than that. I like my apartment. Hell, for that matter I like my car.'

'You *like* this piece of . . . junk?'

'She may not look like much, but she's got it where it counts, kid.'

Thomas slouched down in his seat, his expression skeptical. 'Now you've forced me to reconsider the monumentally stupid explanation.'

I shrugged. 'Me and the Blue Beetle kick ass. In a four-cylinder kind of way, but it still gets kicked.'

Thomas's face lost all expression. 'What about Susan?'

When I get angry, I'd like to be able to pull off a great stone face like that, but I don't do it so well. 'What about her?'

'You cared about her. You got her involved in your life. She got torn up because of you. She got attention from all kinds of nasties and she nearly died.' He kept staring ahead. 'How do you live with that?'

I started to get angry, but I had a rare flash of insight and my ire evaporated before it could fully condense. I studied Thomas's profile at a stoplight and saw him working hard to look distant, like nothing was touching him. Which would mean that something *was* touching him. He was thinking of someone important to him. I had a pretty good idea who it was.

'How's Justine?' I asked.

His features grew colder. 'It isn't important.'

'Okay. But how is Justine?'

'I'm a vampire, Harry.' The words were cold and distant, but not steady. 'She's my girlfri—' His voice stumbled on the word, and he tried to cover it with a low cough. 'She's my lover. She's food. That's how she is.'

'Ah,' I said. 'I like her, you know. Ever since she blackmailed me into helping you at Bianca's masquerade. That took guts.'

'Yeah,' he said. 'She's got that.'

'How long have you been seeing her now?'

'Four years,' Thomas said. 'Almost five.'

'Anyone else?'

'No.'

'Burger King,' I said.

Thomas blinked at me. 'What?'

'Burger King,' I said. 'I like to eat at Burger King. But even

I could afford to do it, I wouldn't eat my meals there every ay for almost five years.'

'What's your point?' Thomas asked.

'My point is that it's pretty clear that Justine isn't just food › you, Thomas.'

He turned his head and stared at me for a moment, his expres-on empty and his eyes inhumanly blank. 'She is. She has to be.'

'Why don't I believe you?' I said.

Thomas stared at me, his eyes growing even colder. 'Drop ıe subject. Right now.'

I decided not to push. He was working hard not to give ıything away, so I knew he was full of crap. But if he didn't 'ant to discuss it, I couldn't force him.

Hell, for that matter, I didn't want to. Thomas was an nnoying wiseass who tended to make everyone he met want to ill him, and when I have that much in common with someone, can't help but like him a little. It wouldn't hurt to give him ›me space.

On the other hand, it was easy for me to forget what he was, nd I couldn't afford that. Thomas was a vampire of the White Court. They didn't drink blood. They fed on emotions, on feel-ıgs, drawing the life energy from their prey through them. The 'ay I understood it, it was usually during sex, and rumor had it ıat their kind could seduce a saint. I'd seen Thomas start to ›ed once, and whatever it was that made him not quite human ad completely taken control of him. It left him a cold, beau-ful, marble-white being of naked hunger. It was an acutely ncomfortable memory.

The Whites weren't as physically formidable or aggressively rganized as the Red Court, and they didn't have the raw, terrifying power of the Black Court, but they didn't have a the usual vampire weaknesses, either. Sunlight wasn't a proble for Thomas, and from what I'd seen, crosses and other hol articles didn't bother him either. But just because they weren as inhuman as the other Courts didn't make the Whites le dangerous. In fact, the way I saw it, it made them more of threat in some ways. I know how to handle it when some slim covered horror from the pits of Hell jumps up in my face. Bu it would be easy to let down my guard for someone near human.

Speaking of which, I told myself, I was agreeing to help hi and taking a job, just as though Thomas were any other clien It probably wasn't the smartest thing I'd ever done. It had th potential to lead to lethally unhealthy decisions.

He fell silent again. Now that I wasn't running and screamin and such, the car started to get uncomfortably cold. I rolled u the window, shutting out the early-autumn air.

'So,' he said. 'Will you help me out?'

I sighed. 'I shouldn't even be in the same car with you. I'v got enough problems with the White Council.'

'Gee, your own people don't like you. Cry me a river.'

'Bite me,' I said. 'What's his name?'

'Arturo Genosa. He's a motion-picture producer, starting u his own company.'

'Is he at all clued in?'

'Sort of. He's a normal, but he's real superstitious.'

'Why did you want him to come to me?'

'He needs your help, Harry. If he doesn't get it, I don't thin he's going to live through the week.'

I frowned at Thomas. 'Entropy curses are a nasty busine

ven when they're precise, much less when they're that sloppy. d be risking my ass trying to deflect them.'

'I've done as much for you.'

I thought about it for a moment. Then I said, 'Yeah. You ave.'

'And I didn't ask for any money for it, either.'

'All right,' I said. 'I'll talk to him. No guarantees. But if I do ıke the case, you're going to pay me to do it, on top of what ıis Arturo guy shells out.'

'This is how you return favors, is it.'

I shrugged. 'So get out of the car.'

He shook his head. 'Fine. You'll get double.'

'No,' I said. 'Not money.'

He arched an eyebrow and glanced at me over the rims of is green fashion spectacles.

'I want to know why,' I said. 'I want to know why you've een helping me. If I take the case, you come clean with me.'

'You wouldn't believe me if I did.'

'That's the deal. Take it or leave it.'

Thomas frowned, and we drove for several minutes in silence.)kay,' he said then. 'Deal.'

'Done,' I responded. 'Shake on it.'

We did. His fingers felt very cold.